THE MARAUDERS

Sam Ryker was the most powerful cattleman in Texas, a land-hungry bastard who hid behind his wealth and his vicious army of gunmen. But Ryker's gang made their last mistake when they gunned down John Tree in an attempt to take over Cimarron City. The Indian was a friend of Sundance's, and the halfbreed wouldn't rest until the only land Ryker owned was a six-foot plot.

DAY OF THE HALFBREEDS

Trouble was brewing in Canada. Led by a madman, the tribes were forming a renegade army determined to destroy whites on both sides of the border. It was up to Sundance to join the rebels and destroy them from within. But to save his country, Sundance would have to betray his own blood brothers.

SUNDANCE

THE MARAUDERS

DAY OF THE HALFBREEDS

PETER McCURTIN

LEISURE BOOKS NEW YORK CITY

A LEISURE BOOK®

May 1999

Published by

Dorchester Publishing Co., Inc.
276 Fifth Avenue
New York, NY 10001

ISBN 0-8439-4521-4

THE MARAUDERS

Chapter 1

Sundance was crossing the street to the hotel where two white men threw the old Indian out the front door onto the boardwalk. A third man tripped him and he went down in the dust. The three men laughed and one of them said in a slow Texas voice, "Look at that damn Injun. If you was to ask me I'd say he's drunk. What say we help him sober up?"

The man who did the talking was big and rangy and wore a .45 Colt in a tied-down holster. He looked like he knew how to use it. The other men were a few years younger, in their twenties, and they might have been brothers. Bunching their fists they started to crowd the old man.

"That's enough," Sundance said. "Let him be."

The big man narrowed his cold pale eyes. "If you're smart you'll keep out of this, halfbreed. This Injun here is going to take a beating."

"No," Sundance said, "he's not."

Men had come out of the hotel and stood watching. This was Oklahoma, Indian Territory, but even here the tall halfbreed with yellow hair and copper skin drew curious stares. He wore buckskins and moccasins and along with a throwing hatchet and a razor sharp Bowie he carried a long barreled Colt .44. It was hot and dusty and quiet in the long main street.

The old Indian had picked up his high crowned hat and was rubbing it with the sleeve of his rusty black coat. "Go about your business," Sundance told him. "They won't bother you."

7

Sundance hoped the three Texans would let it drop, but he knew they wouldn't. They had the look and smell of trouble. He had met their kind before, in all the wild towns between Montana and the Mexican border.

"Maybe you don't know who we are," the big man said. "I'm Ned Clingman and these two boys are Joe and Petey Sims. We're good Texas men that don't take any horseshit from an Injun, whole or half or whatever in hell you are. Now step aside before I drop you in your tracks."

For a moment the only sound was some man clearing his throat with a nervous cough.

"You can try it," Sundance said quietly, watching the big man's almost colorless eyes. Then Clingman's hand streaked for his gun, and it came out with the cylinder already turning. Sundance's Colt cleared leather a split second faster and a bullet ripped through Clingman's heart. He was still falling when Sundance swung the gun and shattered Joe Sims' gun arm. The other Texan threw his gun away from him and raised his hands above his shoulders.

"You son of a bitch!" Joe Sims yelled, grabbing at his smashed forearm. He almost made a try for the gun he had dropped, but the sound of the hammer going back stopped him.

"Let it lay or I'll blow your head off," Sundance warned. "Get in my way again and I'll kill you for sure."

Joe Sims' face was twisted with pain. "You think this is over, you lousy halfbreed. You think you can throw down on three of Sam Ryker's men and get away with it. God damn you, we'll burn this miserable town if we have a mind to."

"Go on now," Sundance said, "before I change my mind." He prodded the cartridges from their guns and threw them down the street. Then after they left he turned to the old Indian who was standing by. "You got any law in this town?"

"We had a sheriff but somebody shot him in the back last night. They killed the sheriff before him, too. Ryker's men say they'll kill any lawman that tries to stop them from shooting up the town. Do you mind telling me who you are?"

"Jim Sundance."

"I have heard of you," the Indian said. "My name is John Tree. They gave us American names at the mission school. I am a Cherokee, as are so many farmers in this part of the Territory. This town used to be a quiet place before the Texas herds started to come here. Ryker's men are the worst, half wild, crazy with whiskey. Ryker doesn't even try to control them."

"I know what Ryker is like," Sundance said. "If it's the same man, I do. A very big man with white hair, always carries a pair of matched Colts with ivory handles."

"That's the man," John Tree said. "His men used to terrorize the Kansas towns before they organized vigilantes to fight him. So now he brings his heards to the Territory. He is hated and feared by everyone, and the only law he respects are those two guns. It won't be so good for you when he hears about Clingman."

"That's something I'll have to think about," Sundance said. "But right now I'm going to get something to eat."

"Do you mind if I come with you? I would like to talk."

"The answer is 'no' to taking the sheriff's job," Sundance said. "I'm just passing through the Territory. But if you want to talk I'll listen."

In the hotel dining room, Sundance ordered a steak and a pot of coffee The girl who took the order was a full blooded Cherokee, but like John Tree she was dressed in town clothes, and after she left she watched Sundance from the door of the kitchen.

"I am on the town council," John Tree said. "The town is now more than half white, but we manage to get along. We didn't want whites coming into the Territory, but they came anyway. For the Indians, Oklahoma isn't such a bad place. Much of the land belongs to us, and now there is talk of oil in the gorund. We have schools and newspapers."

Sundance poured coffee for both of them. "What you need in Cimarron City is some law and I don't mean some farmer with a badge on his shirt. They'll kill him just for the hell of it. Get yourself a real towntamer, maybe a couple of them. Just make sure you don't hire men that will be just as bad as Ryker. Once they come in it's hard to get them out."

"You wouldn't take the job, Sundance?" The Indian's eyes were hopeful.

"No," Sundance said. "I'm no lawman and it's not my town. You can find a good man if you pay enough. The Earps are dead or out of the business, but you should be able to find somebody to stand up to Ryker. If you don't, he'll get worse. You know he burned most of a town in Kansas?"

"That's what we're afraid of here. He's crazy enough to do it."

"He may do it anyway. Where is he now?"

"About ten miles south of town. Five thousand head of cattle. He's fattening them up before he sells them. His riders—most of them—are as wild as he is. You saw how they were today. They heard I was talking about a new sheriff and didn't like it. I might be dead now if you hadn't come along."

Sundance signaled the Indian girl to bring another pot of coffee. "I still don't want the job," he said. "I've got other work to do in Texas. Get some good law and let Ryker know that he's got to control his men. Tell him he's barred from the town if he doesn't."

John Tree said, "A lot of people in Cimarron City wouldn't like that. The gamblers and whores and saloonkeepers don't care what happens as long as the Texas cowboys keep on spending money. They may shoot up the town, but all their money stays here when they leave."

"The town can't have it every way," Sundance said. "All towns have crib girls and gamblers and whiskey sellers, but don't let them run wild. Not usually. I'm sorry I can't help you. Besides, how do you know the town would want a halfbreed as a lawman?"

John Tree smiled. "They wouldn't want you in Texas or most places, but it's different here. This is still Indian Territory and the whites know it. If you wanted the job you could have it."

Sundance finished his coffee and stood up. "All I want is to get a night's sleep and start for Texas in the morning. You might do worse than leaving town for a while. The Sims brothers won't forget you after what happened to day."

John Tree said, "I'm an old man, where would I go?"

"Then watch yourself."

After John Tree left, Sundance paid for a room and went up to it. It was small and dusty and the mirror over the wash stand was cracked, but the bed was clean. On the wall was a sun-faded print of the White House. Sundance poured water from the jug into the wash basin. There was a film of dust on the surface of the water.

Before he lay down on the bed he checked the loads in his gun. If the Sims brothers came back and brought their friends he wanted to ready for them. He could

11

always get out while there was still time, but he'd be damned if he'd run. Anyway, it was getting dark now; morning was only hours away, and he planned to be gone before first light. In a few days he'd be in Texas, and Cimarron City would just have to take care of its own troubles.

He slept for a while, then turned down the lamp when he heard footsteps on the stairs. It sounded like five or six men. Sundance reached over and unlocked the door when somebody knocked cautiously. John Tree came in first followed by five other men. Two were Cherokees, men in their forties; the others were white. Sundance turned up the lamp. "You're wasting your time," he said to John Tree.

"Just hear us out," John Tree said, after introducing the men with him. "These gentlemen all run businesses here in town. They want to go on running them, so whatever money it takes..."

Sundance opened the window to let in some air, and just then a rifle cracked from the far side of the street. John Tree made a choking sound as the bullet drilled him through the neck. Blood bubbled from the corners of his mouth and his fingers clawed at the air. Sundance blew out the lamp and crouched by the windows as the other men threw themselves flat. The rifle cracked again, breaking the upper half of the window. Sundance fired at the third flash coming from the balcony of a saloon across the street. A man cried out before he toppled into the street and lay still. There was no more firing.

Sundance lit a sulphurhead watch and light flooded the room. John Tree was already dead, a pool of blood spreading out from his head. "Dear God! Dear God!" one of the white men kept saying. Down in the street a crowd had gathered to look at the dead man. The two Cherokees looked at Sundance with questions in their eyes.

"All right," Sundance said. "This changes things. I'll take the job."

They went downstairs, and found the dead man was Petey Sims. A Winchester lay a few feet away. Sundance's single shot from the long-barreled Colt had struck him just above the left eye. There was no sign of his brother. One of the white men, a merchant named Blaney, asked, "You think he was trying to kill you or John Tree?"

"Makes no difference. I'll do the job you want done or die trying. But first we have to talk it all out. Where do I find the jail?"

"Down the street," Blaney said, nervous sweat glistening on his face. "What do you plan to do?"

"First we talk. If you don't like what I say, then I'll just ride out and Ryker can have his sport with your town. You live here so you decide."

Blaney said, "You think Ryker will come in tonight?"

"I don't know what Ryker will do."

One of the Indians said, "Maybe we better get out some rifles. Nobody's going to burn my store without a fight."

Blaney wiped his face and said hurriedly, "No! No! We just hired Sundance to take care of Ryker. We're just businessmen."

"You haven't hired me yet," Sundance said as they went into the sheriff's office and jail. Inside, it was dirty and smelled of stale whiskey. Sundance closed the shutters and lit the lamp There was a half eaten plate of beans on the desk, and a smudged glass with a trickle of whiskey in it. A sheaf of yellowing posters was stuck on

13

a spike and a cast iron stove was spattered with grease. The whole place stank of fear and whiskey. Sundance sat down behind the desk.

Blaney was still sweating and he tugged anxiously at his collar, now soaked through. "Ryker probably knows your reputation, Sundance. So maybe he'll leave us alone. You already killed two of his men and crippled another. You think he'll let us be?"

"Not a chance," Sundance said. "A man like Ryker would rather get killed than back off. He's built up a reputation as a crazy, dangerous man. He put together one of the biggest outfits in Texas by killing everybody who stood in his way."

"Christ!" Blaney said, looking as if he wanted to run.

The taller of the two Cherokees was named Tom Cade. He was the one who talked about fighting back. "What did you want to talk about, Sundance?"

"If I take the job I have to make the rules," Sundance answered. "That goes from start to finish. Ryker's men have been hurrawing the town, and some night if they get enough whiskey in them they could burn it. Makes no difference if they mean to do it. Your town will be gone. They killed the last two sheriffs and wounded other men. I have to make it clear to them that I'll kill the next man I see shooting off a gun or otherwise wrecking the town. That's how it has to be because anything else won't work. I've seen what some of these Texas trailherders did to railhead towns in Kansas. All they understand is force. They can come to town all they want, but they have to behave."

"They won't like that," Blaney said.

"They're not supposed to like it," Sundance answered. "If it takes some dead cowboys to quiet this town, then so be it. It won't be easy to do, but it has been done. Masterson and Hickok and the Earps did it in

Kansas. Dallas Studenmeyer did it in El Paso. Now tell me what you think."

Blaney looked doubtful. "You don't have to turn the town into a graveyard, Sundance. I know Ryker runs a mean bunch of men, but some of the other herders aren't so bad. A lot of them are just wild young cowboys. You know that."

"I know that when you're dead you're dead. You've got women and children in this town. Would it make any difference if a woman or child got shot by one of Ryker's gun bullies or just a wild young cowboy?"

"Sundance is right," Tom Cade said.

"I know he's right, right in a way. All I'm saying is we don't want to scare off the Texans. We need the money they bring in."

Sundance was getting sick of Blaney. Like most storekeepers he put money before everything. "Look," he said, "they can still have their whiskey and their whores. Nothing wrong with either that I can see. But the shooting has to stop. Now why don't you talk it over while I look over the town."

As he walked from one end of the main street to the other, Sundance wondered how many men would have to die before he brought some kind of law to Cimarron City. Ryker would fight him, he knew, just as he knew that he would have to kill men whose names he might never know. There was a good chance of being killed himself, but that didn't matter so much because one place was as good as another to die. They wanted to hire him to do their killing, but they were already afraid of him. People who lived in towns were like that. They wanted to live in peace, but were hardly ever willing to die for it. Maybe he could count on a few of them—not many.

He walked to the livery stable and looked at his great

horse, Eagle. The big stallion whinnied when Sundance came in from the street. "Let's hope we make it to Texas," he said. Then he walked to the jail. On the way he passed the town's four saloons, but everything was quiet.

The five men looked up when he opened the door. Blaney was saying, "If we're paying this man's wages, don't we have something to say about the way he does his job?"

Sundance closed the door and said, "What's it going to be?"

Tom Cade spoke up. "Do what has to be done, Sundance. I can't see there's any other way. You'll find the sheriff's badge in the top drawer of the desk."

Sundance got out the gold star and pinned it on. He was now the law in Cimarron City.

Chapter 2

During the night Sundance cleaned up the jail as best he could. The dead sheriff had been a drunk all right, and there were empty bottles everywhere they could be hidden. By first light, most of the whiskey stink was gone. He blew out the light and unbarred the shutters on the windows facing the street. The street was empty in the gray light of dawn.

He cleaned the sheriff's shotgun, a 10-gauge with cut-down barrels. There was some pitting on the inside of the barrel, but that didn't matter so much with a shotgun. He loaded it with fat shells of Double-0 buckshot and stuffed extra ammunition in his pockets. Then, with the shotgun beside him, he stretched out in the cell and slept for two hours. Someone knocking on the door woke him about eight o'clock. He picked up the 10-gauge and opened the peephole in the thick, iron banded door. It was the young Indian girl from the hotel; she was carrying a napkin covered tray and smiling uncertainly.

"I brought you some breakfast," she said, coming in and setting down the tray on the desk. The coffee smelled strong and fresh.

"I would have come to the hotel later," Sundance said. "You didn't have to do this."

The girl tilted her chin defiantly; she was very pretty with sloe-dark eyes and long black hair pulled behind her head and held there with combs. "I know I didn't have to do it," she said. "I wanted to do it."

Sundance sat down and poured coffee. "What do they call you?" he asked.

"I know what they call you," she said. "You are the famous Jim Sundance."

"Well, I'm certainly Jim Sundance."

"My name is Sarah. It's not the name I first had, but I like it better." Again there was a defiant lift of her chin. "I think a person should be free to choose any name they like."

"Can't argue with that," Sundance said, cutting a slice of sugar-cured ham. "Are you always as outspoken as this?" He figured she couldn't be more than sixteen or seventeen; there was amusement in his eyes when he looked at her. In many ways she resembled his Cheyenne mother, dead now for so many years.

"I say what is in my mind," the girl said. "I never lie. Why should I?"

"Why indeed?" Sundance agreed. "You make good coffee, Sarah."

"Of course I do. Are you going to kill this man called Ryker? Everybody says you are. I am a Christian, but I think he deserves to be killed."

"That's not a very Christian thing to say, but you're probably right."

"Are you a Christian?"

Sundance smiled. "No. Can't say that I am. You sure ask a lot of questions for a little girl. And for so early in the morning."

Her eyes flashed with momentary anger. "I am not such a little girl. And how else will you learn things if you don't ask questions. You have been everywhere so you don't need to ask questions. I have never been anywhere but this town. It's all I know, and I would like to leave here someday."

"To do what?"

"I don't know yet, but I can read and write. I read books. What books do you read?"

"Only the Bible."

"But you are not a Christian."

"I just read it as book. It belonged to my father. All his life he carried it and read it."

"He was a white man?"

"An Englishman who did some things his family didn't like when he was very young. They sent him to America and made him promise never to return. After he married my mother he lived the rest of his life with the Cheyenne."

"Where are your mother and father now?"

"Dead. Murdered by renegades. I caught up with them."

"I would like to be your friend," the girl said suddenly. "I will pray that you won't be killed because I want to go with you when you leave this town. It would be good for you to have me with you."

"Now wait a minute," Sundance said, still smiling. "You're hardly grown yet."

"I'm grown enough. Sixteen is not young for an Indian girl. I would make a good wife for you."

"But what about your folks?"

"My mother and father are dead too. I have worked at the hotel since I was twelve. The owner, Mr. Banner, protects me from men who would bother me, but I don't like the way he looks at me sometimes. I know I will have to leave sometime."

Sundance spoke patiently, wanting her to understand that there was no place in his life for a woman. When he felt the need of a woman he found one, but that's all there was to it. Nothing else made any sense, considering the way he lived. Any day death could claim him; he had long accepted the fact that he would never get to be an old man. That was the best way to live: to get out before you got old and sick.

"You can't come with me," he said. "Anyway, you don't know a thing about me. Just a lot of talk, not half of it true. I go places and do things you can't imagine. I may not even be alive a few days from now. Ryker's going to be a hard man to tangle with. Listen to me, girl, there's no future with me. Find a decent young man and marry him and have children."

"Then you don't like me?"

"I like you fine, but that has nothing to do with it. It wouldn't work."

The girl began to gather up the dishes. "I better go back, but I'll tell you something before I go. I'm going to make you like me, then you'll see how wrong you were. The moment you walked into the hotel I decided I was going to be your woman."

Sundance smiled at her and she went out angrily, banging the door as she went. He wondered what other surprises Cimarron City would have for him: inside of twenty-four hours he had been made sheriff and received a proposal of marriage. But he had to admit that he liked the girl; and once again he was reminded of his mother.

He left the jail with the shotgun crooked under his arm and made the morning rounds. It was still quiet, with merchants sweeping out their stores and the first farmers coming to town in their wagons. Blaney was standing in front of his store talking to a farmer in a canvas coat. He looked at the scattergun and frowned, but didn't say anything but "Morning."

Sundance nodded and walked on followed by stares from both sides of the street. The sun was up full and the street shimmered in waves of heat. On the surface the town looked like any quiet town, but he knew the bloody violence that could explode without warning.

Some years before he had seen Sam Ryker and his boys go to work on Fort Griffin, Texas. They had been down to Mexico to sell a big horse herd to the Mexican Army. On their way back north they decided to celebrate in Fort Griffin, then one of the wildest towns in the West. Ryker, well likkered up, thought he'd show them how tough he was by comparison. A rival cow outfit thought they would side with the town against Ryker. Ryker's wild bunch won hands down, and a lot of dead or crippled cowpunchers lay in the street before he took his men back home. Sundance recalled Ryker as a great hulking bear of a man with snow white hair and a voice like a mad bull. Even for a Texan he bragged and swaggered more than any man had need to. He had grown up poor in the Panhandle but, by Christ, he swore he'd never be poor again. He was king of the mountain and he'd pistol whip or kill any man who said otherwise. Ryker was loyal only to his ranch and his men; the rest of the world was just there to be beaten to its knees. He looked after his men, and even if some of them hated him because he was too free with his fists, they stayed on for the top wages he paid. Before he bullied his way into the ranching business he did about everything: working on the railroad, prospecting for gold, policing riverboats on the Mississippi. They said he had even sailed on clipper ships in the China trade. Now he was rich, but he hadn't mellowed; if anything he was worse, probably because he was getting along in years, and didn't like the feeling. A lot of his men were just working cowhands, all handy with a gun; but he also kept plenty of genuine hard cases on his payroll. Few men ever rustled a cow belonging to Sam Ryker and lived to brag about it. He hung them high and left them there to rot at the end of a rope. Everything had gone his way so far.

So far, Sundance thought.

The town was still quiet at noon when he went to the hotel. Sarah's face brightened with a quick smile when he came in. "Don't you ever eat anything but steak?" she asked when he turned down the corned beef hash and the lamb stew.

"Not when I can help it," he said, settling back in his chair to scan a week-old newspaper from McAllester. It was lightly spotted with grease and somebody had ripped out a page; the biggest news in it concerned the depredations of Joe Buck and his gang of halfbreed Negro-Indians in the western part of the Territory. Five men were eating at other tables, and everytime Sundance looked he found them staring at him before their eyes darted back to their plates.

When Sarah brought the steak and a pot of coffee, she leaned over the table and whispered, "Have you thought about what we talked about this morning?"

Sundance said, "You talked about it, I didn't. Now don't you have some work you have to be doing? Mr. Banner, if that's what his name is, won't like all this palaver."

Sarah glanced at a burly man in a striped shirt with paper collar and cuffs. He kept fussing around, but his popping eyes kept coming back to Sundance and the girl. "Oh, he doesn't mind," she said. "Don't you know you're good for his business. People will be coming from all over to get a look at you. See that man over there with his hat on the table? The one with the big mustache?"

"I see him. What about him?"

"You don't know who he is?"

"Who is he?"

"That's Mr. Ned Buntline, the famous author. They say he's written over three hundred dime novels. He was asking about you this morning. He was passing through town, but decided to stay over and meet you. He's written books about all the famous gunfighters and outlaws."

"Ned Buntline is the biggest liar in the country."

"I told him I was a good friend of yours."

"You're not such a bad liar yourself. Be a good girl and let me eat my steak."

"Oh, all right, Mr. Sundance, if that's what you want." Sarah walked away quickly with a saucy swing of her hips. Just then Ned Buntline dabbed at his thick mustache with a napkin and stood up. A moment later he was sitting down at Sundance's table without asking if he could. Sundance regarded him with cold eyes. Buntline was a braggart and a liar and a womanizer who drank at least a quart of whiskey a day. A strong smell of whiskey came from him now, and when he smiled he showed a big set of cigar-yellowed teeth.

"I hope you don't mind the intrusion," Buntline said as pleasantly as he could. It wasn't easy for him. He looked like a treacherous dog about to bite. "My name is Ned Buntline. You've probably heard of me."

"Everybody has."

"I'm flattered, sir."

"Don't be. What do you want?"

Buntline ignored Sundance's curt manner; he was a man with a very thick skin. "What I want is to write your life story. Fascinating, sir, simply fascinating. Readers are just waiting to hear of your marvelous exploits in all parts of our Great American West. Your dedicated struggle on behalf of the noble Red Man. Your friendship with General George Crook, a great soldier and a fine gentleman. Are you interested at all, Mr. Sundance? There would be some money in it for you. Not a lot at first naturally. Later, however."

"Not interested," Sundance said.

Buntline, not at all put off, took out a leather-covered cigar case. Sundance waved away the cigar that was offered to him. All the other men there were staring openly at them. Buntline lit the cigar with exaggerated care after rolling the end around in his mouth. He blew a jet of smoke at the ceiling and made himself more comfortable.

"You know I've been hearing about you for years, Mr. Sundance. Everywhere I go I hear stories about you, and yet have never had the pleasure of meeting you, and now here we are. Tell me, how do you intend to deal with Mr. Ryker? A famous man in his own way, I might say. Good pioneer stock, and so on. Do you think it will come to a showdown between you?"

"Buntline, I don't want to talk to you, now or later," Sundance said, as he fished in his pocket for a dollar. "Any man who makes Jesse James out to be a hero lies in his teeth. Jesse was a crazy killer who should have been killed in his cradle. Now I'd be obliged if you'd take yourself away from this table."

Buntline showed his yellow teeth in a vicious smile. "There's no need to take that tone with me, sir. I have dined with Presidents and the owners of railroads."

"Then go dine with them now. You're killing my appetite."

"You won't have much appetite when Ryker gets through with you, Mr. Sundance. I offer you a sound business proposition in good faith, and you treat me like a carpetbagger..."

Buntline was interrupted by a fat man with a white apron who came bustling in from the street. "They're wrecking my saloon," he said, breathing wheezily. "Two young cowboys—not from Ryker's outfit—are breaking up my place. You're the sheriff. You have to..."

Sundance threw a dollar on the table and went out with Buntline hurrying behind him on stumpy legs. Down the street a chair came through a window and broke in the street. The breaking window was followed by a wild yell. Sundance quickened his long-legged stride, spinning the chamber of the Colt; he had stuck the sawed-off inside his weapons belt.

"You better stay back," he told Buntline, who was trying to keep up with him. "There could be shooting in a minute."

Buntline said, "It's a free country. I can go where I please."

Sundance reached the saloon, Dyer's Palace, and eased his way to the door. The saloon was empty except for two cowboys staggering from one wall to the other. Both were very young, maybe less than twenty, and their guns were still holstered. As Sundance walked in with the shotgun steady in both hands, one of the cowboys threw a bottle through the mirror behind the bar. They both turned, unsteady and bleary-eyed, when they heard the creak of the door. Buntline was watching from the boardwalk.

They were very drunk; about ready to fall down and sleep it off. The one with the fawn colored Stetson pointed at the shotgun, rock steady in Sundance's hands. "What in hell is that for? We're just having ourself a fine ol' time. No need for that God damn thing." He lurched against the bar and had to hold on to keep from falling.

"Henry here, is drunk," the second cowboy said, winking at Sundance. "Can't hold his likker, that's his trouble. Now me, I can hold it fine. You ain't going to give us a bad time, are you, Sheriff? We wouldn't like it if you did that. Tried to do that, I mean."

The shotgun was already cocked, and they were

close enough so he could kill them with one blast. Both barrels were so short that the big lead slugs would fan out and tear them to shreds. He didn't want to do it—these two fools didn't look anything like Ryker's bravos—but he wasn't taking any chances. He raised the shotgun so that now they were looking right down the ugly twin barrels.

"Drop your gunbelts," he ordered. "Just let them slide, then we'll talk about paying for the damage. After that you can leave town—and don't ever come back. Make a move for your guns and I'll cut you down. That's my rule."

"Like hell we will," the one in the Stetson mumbled. "You and your stinking scattergun! Why don't you give us a fighting chance?"

"I won't stand here talking all day," Sundance said. "Gunplay will get you killed. I won't go back on the rule. One more time I'll tell you. Then you'll never see Texas again." It would be a hell of a thing to shotgun two drunken boys, but he was ready to do it.

"Time's about up," he said, edging closer.

"What do you want to do, Henry?" the first one asked without taking his eyes away from the muzzle of the sawed-off. "You want to take on the halfbreed lawman?"

"Ah, the hell with the halfbreed! I guess we could take him."

Now Sundance was about close enough; one more fast move and he'd be all over them. It was time to finish it without killing, if he could. Henry was still mumbling something when Sundance stepped in and hit him in the jaw with the butt of the shotgun. He went down like a stone and Sundance hit the other man. Then he ripped the guns from their holsters and put them on the bar. He was prodding out the shells with the injector when

Buntline pushed open the swinging doors and came in. He looked at the two cowboys heaped up together on the floor; his smile was still wolfish. "Bravo, Mr. Sundance," he said. "It took a lot of nerve to face down two men who could barely stand up. Yes, sir, a great display of courage."

Sundance was going through their pockets, taking all the money they had left. Their faces were swelling fast, but he hadn't hit them any harder than he had to. Gathering up the money, he put it on the bar. Then he went behind the bar and found a pitcher of water and dumped it on the two men, who were starting to groan.

"Why the hell don't you get out of here, Buntline?" he said.

Buntline stayed where he was. "I wouldn't think of it, Mr. Sundance. I want to see how a real lawman works. It isn't every day I have the privilege of . . ."

Sundance spun around with a hard look in his eyes, and Buntline backed off a little, frightened by the sudden savagery he was faced with. "Scat!" Sundance rasped. "I've taken all I'm going to take from you. Get out *now*!"

"You won't be any hero when I get through with you," Buntline sneered, going out in a hurry.

"Up on your feet," Sundance ordered the cowboys. "Take your guns, leave the money. And like I said—don't ever come back to this town. Drunk or sober, don't ever come. When you get back to your outfit, spread the word that things have changed. Now move!"

Avoiding his eyes, they scooped their empty guns off the bar, and staggered out. He didn't think they'd be back, but if they did, they wouldn't get another chance. It wouldn't be so easy to deal with Ryker. It wouldn't be easy at all.

Chapter 3

Later the same day, Sundance was sitting at his desk in the jail when Blaney banged open the door. Before he got halfway in, Sundance had the Colt drawn and cocked. "That was a damn fool thing to do," he said.

Blaney looked at the Colt with frightened eye. "He's coming! Sam Ryker is riding into town. He'll be here in a minute."

Sundance holstered the gun and told the scared merchant to get a grip on himself. "How many men does he have with him?"

"That's the crazy thing. He's coming in by himself. What are you going to do? If you gun him down they'll burn the town for sure." Blaney dropped into a chair and mopped at his face.

Sundance said calmly, "What happens depends on Ryker. If he wants to talk I'll talk. Beyond that I don't know. You want to stay and hear what he has to say, if anything."

Blaney twitched with fright. "Hell no! I don't want anything to do with that man. You talk to him—that's your job."

Sundance nodded. "So it is. Just don't get in the way."

Blaney went out at a run and Sundance waited on the boardwalk in front of the jail. A few minutes later he saw Sam Ryker's great bulk coming in from the south road. He rode a chestnut Morgan horse, but somehow the big animal looked as small as a cow pony. The last one off the street was a small boy; his mother rushed out of a store and snatched him up, howling. Doors banged shut, and then there was no sound except the clip-clop of Ryker's horse. Ryker rode at a deliberate pace, looking neither right nor left. Sundance waited.

Ryker halted his mount in front of the jail, and his booming voice cut through the silence of the street. His Stetson was tilted back and his hair was bone-white in the glaring sun. His black frock coat was pinned back behind the ivory handles of his matched Colts.

"My name is Sam Ryker," he said, "You'd be Sundance. I hear you've been shooting up some of my boys. You want to talk about that? I don't like losing my boys when I take them so far from home."

"Light down," Sundance answered. "I'm ready to talk if you are."

"Smart fella," Ryker said, and swung down from the saddle. He was no longer a young man, but he did it easily. He was a bear of a man; not fat though; muscle was packed on his hard, big-boned frame. "We can talk in the jail," he said. "That suit you?"

Sundance inclined his head slightly. "Suits me all right. A talk can't hurt."

They went into the jail and when Ryker sat down the chair creaked under his weight. "This place looks cleaner than it used to be."

Sundance didn't say anything.

Ryker was completely at ease, a man used to giving orders and having them obeyed. "You killed my man, Clingman. You must be pretty good to do that. The Sims boys were never as good as Ned Clingman." Ryker leaned forward. "Why'd you have to kill him?"

"You don't know?"

"I heard something about an old Injun. I'm told the boys were just having a little fun. Nothing serious. There was no danger to his life."

29

"If you hit an old man hard enough it can kill him," Sundance said.

"It can kill any man if you hit him hard enough. This old Injun a particular friend of yours?"

"Just an old man."

"Still and all, you took a big chance. A few years back you might have been no match for Ned Clingman. What the hell, I'm not that mad about old Ned. He took on a man he didn't know. That's plain dumb. You planning to stay long in Cimarron City? I have to stay because my cows lost a lot of good beef on the trail from Texas. Got to get some meat back on their bones. But I didn't come here to talk about the cattle business."

"I figured you didn't."

Ryker gave a booming laugh. "You know I kind of like you, Sundance. You're a dangerous man, and I like dangerous men. They take chances, they know they're alive. I'm a dangerous man myself, always have been. In my nature, I guess."

"There's no cause for what's been going on here," Sundance. "You're a big man and this is just a little town trying to make its way. Why don't you leave it in peace. It wouldn't cost you a thing."

Ryker laughed again. That's true," he said. "Only I don't much like these miserable towns that are trying to get along. My boys spend a lot of money—all their money—in this town. The people look down on them like they're savages. Oh sure, they take their money and sell them watered whiskey and poxy whores. But when the money is gone they're glad to see the last of them."

"Towns are like that. That's how it works," Sundance said. "This town is no different."

Ryker said with sudden anger, "The hell with this town! This town and all the others. When I was a youngster—my folks dead—I had to work in towns like this. Sweeping out stores, swamping saloons, burying trash. I was a stableboy too. I worked for my meals, such as they were, and the stingy bastards threw me two bits now and then. So don't you tell me about little towns trying to make their way in the world. I'm no townsman, neither are you. What do you care what happens to them?"

Sundance looked at the other man. "I don't see where your hard times as a boy explains all this."

"That's because you don't know what it was like. I was just a country fool who didn't know the ropes yet. But I did in time, by Christ I did. So now I do what I like, go where I like."

"Not here, Ryker."

"So you say, Sundance. My point is, I don't especially want any trouble with you. I don't mind it, but I could pass on it just the same."

"Then why don't you?"

"Well, that's sort of what I came to talk about," Ryker said. "Let me tell you a few things, Sundance. I can't let you oppose me and get away with it. If I did that pretty soon people would get the wrong idea. It wouldn't be the same for me and my boys. The way I see it, we're the last free men in this country. We mean to stay that way. When us Texas men first started to drive our cows north we had guerrillas left over from the war trying to get money out of us by scattering our herds, then offering to round them up again. We had bushwhackers trying to raid our stock and make up herds of their own. Then we had the Injuns charging, trying to charge us for the grass our cows grazed, claiming the grass was theirs because the prairie was theirs. Lately we have the son of a bitching farmers fencing the free range with their murdering barbed wire. It was downright foolish of every last one of them to try what they did. Nothing for it but to teach them all a lesson, which is what we did. A lot of our people died in the doing of it."

Sundance kept the anger out of his voice; he had agreed to hear this man out. "I know what you're saying, Ryker, but you got your cows through in spite of all, are still getting them through. What more do you want?"

Ryker's voice didn't get any louder, just harder, more determined. "I'll tell you what I want. All these men—renegades, rustlers, Injuns, whatever—are still around, and they ain't about to go away. Why would they when the smell of money is still heavy in the air? No, sir, they're still out there somewheres, hanging back and waiting to see what happens. The minute they think us fellas are getting soft they'll be back in force like the skulkers they are, hitting at us from all sides because that's their way. So instead of getting softer, we have to get tougher. They understand that and nothing else. I say 'we' but I'm talking for myself, something I always do. Us Texas men are supplying a good part of this country with good beef. Nobody but a Texan can say something like that. If it wasn't for us, the folks back east'd be eating beans and bread three times a day."

"You don't sell yourself short, do you, Ryker?" Sundance said.

"No cause to," Ryker said. "Don't have to sell myself a-tall. They need us, you betcha. Why'd you think they been building all these railroads if it wasn't to ship Texas beef east and all over. It sure ain't to ship sweet potatoes. While we're doing a man's work these farmers and storekeepers and whiskey sellers are grubbing in the dirt for a few measly dollars. I tell you, my friend, there's no way I can have any respect for that trash. We put the fear of God into them, and we're going to keep on doing it."

"The strong against the weak, is that it?" Sundance asked.

Ryker ignored the tone of the question. "It's never been any other way. A fact of human nature, is what it is. You think, ain't it too bad about these pore Injuns out here in the Territory! Nothing but horseshit! Don't you know that even while Andy Jackson was driving them out here from the East they brung along their nigger slaves. I'm no kind of educated man, but I know that to be a fact of history. Yes, sir, the pore put-upon Cherokees had their coons just like the white folks in the South, and it's nohow their intention to work that hard when they got to the Promised Land. And let me tell you something else. The Creeks were already here in the Territory when the Seminoles were kicked out of Florida. You think maybe the good ole Creeks welcomed them with open arms, as brothers fallen on hard times. Like hell they did—they made slaves of them, is what they did."

Sundance said, "Thanks for the history lesson, Ryker, but that has nothing to do with now."

"You think so, Sundance. I'd say it has everything to do with it. You asked me a question and I gave you an answer. The strong man always wins and that's only right. It's the natural way of things. No way I can back down. Tell you the truth—might as well—it ain't all for business reasons. I like to see the shaky bastards shake when they hear a big Texas herd, my herd 'specially, is on its way to town. They get scared and greedy at the same time, which is the way of these people. They're counting their profits and shitting in their britches all at once. I get a laugh out of that, no matter how many times I see it."

Sundance said, "You want nobody to be free but you, is that it?" Sundance asked, "You want to have your way, no matter what?"

"That I do. I'd be a Godblasted hypocrite if I said no.

33

To my mind there's free and there's free. You know what I'm talking about because I know a few things about you, and I don't see you settling down and slopping hogs and planting corn and eating box lunches at church suppers. You wander this country, one end to the other, doing just as you please. I ask you this, where's your wife and brats? To be free you have to be strong. Take old Charlie Goodnight, just a few thousand cows short of being as big as John Chisholm or King. Old Charlie doesn't approve of drinking spirits so one day he laid down the law for everybody whether they worked for him or not—no more drinking south of the Red River. Drinking was all right north of the Big Red 'cause Ole Charlie didn't run any cows there. Charlie enforced his rule any way he had to, though I never heard mention that God come down and gave him the authority. South of the Red Charlie didn't need it. He had the men and the money and the guns to make it stick."

"And you like that?"

"Sure I do. You ever been with a trailherd?"

"Not lately," Sundance answered, knowing that when all the talk was finished it would still come to bullets. But he let Ryker go on because you got the measure of the man by how he talked and what he believed in.

"Nothing on this globe like a trail herd," Ryker said. "It's like an army on the move. Nothing can stand in its way, and live. Got everything it needs but nothing extra, no clutter and mess. That's how an army is. I got me a nice place down in Texas, a whole bunch of Mexicans to run the big house, but it suits me best when I'm out on the trail with the herd, and I don't ask any man to do what I won't do myself. I eat the same grub and sleep on the ground like the rest of the men. On the trail there's nothing but the smell of cows—and that's a good smell. You make camp in a place, then you move on. Nothing holds you back, nothing keeps you from moving on, nothing stops you from living free like a man ought to. A rough, good life! Rough men working together."

Sundance decided that Sam Ryker, mad or not, wasn't altogether the man he had thought him to be, from the stories he had heard. The stories were truth; he had no doubt of that, and yet there had to be more to the man than that. It made no difference, in the end. Ryker had to be stopped because all he ever saw was one side of anything, and that side was always his. The great John Chisholm was like that, and so were all the others.

"You probably think I hate Injuns, don't you?" Ryker said. "No such thing. I killed more'n my share, but I never could work up a hate for them, not even for the God damned Comanches, and the Lord knows they gave me enough trouble over the years. It was their land first, Texas land, and me and others took it away from them. They fought like sons of bitches to hold on to what was theirs. I respect a man, white or red or any color, that does that. Even while I was killing them I had respect for the sand they had. That's all that counts with a man: sand, guts, call it what you want. You know what I'm talking about. It's not the wild Injun I hate but these tame Injuns like you got here in the Territory. Same goes for the white men I had to kill, had to hang. I admire a man who tries to take away what's mine. I have what he wants and he tries to grab it and I have to kill him for it. How the hell you think I got my start?" Ryker raised his big hands and closed them into fists. "That's how. I took and I kept on taking. You understand what I'm saying?"

Sundance nodded. "I hear you," he said. "You've

35

been saying a lot. Now let me talk. What you just said changes nothing. Not a thing. You're talking in the past, living in the past. I took a job here, and I mean to do it. Nobody's asking you to change all your ways, but you've got to change some of them. This town is here and means to stay. Nobody ever said your men can't come to town and have a good time."

Ryker wasn't smiling now; all the Texas bluster was gone. "Thanks for the invitation," he said. "I don't need it, least all from you. I tried to explain my side of it, but you don't listen."

"I listen," Sundance went on, "and all I hear is you saying how you've got to keep people scared. No more, not here."

"Damn it, you do think you can stand up to me."

"I'll stand up to you."

Ryker had a foxy look that didn't go with his big, open face. "Maybe you're thinking you ought to have a try at killing me here and now. That would be one hell of a mistake, my friend. I don't know as you could take me in a fair fight. Even if you could this town would be worse off than it is. My boys would kill everything that moved, then burn the town and level it so you'd never know there ever was a town."

Sundance looked at him. "You're not so brave, Ryker. You were counting on that when you rode in. You knew I'd have that figured, and you're right."

"I usually am," Ryker said. "A man'd be a fool not to watch his back. But I'll tell you something maybe you don't know. I didn't tell my boys to raze the town if I got backshot here. No such orders were issued when I left camp today. No need. That's the kind of a man I am. 'Course if you think you can take me, we can forget the God damned piddling town and have a go at it by ourselves. I could be wrong about the boys. With me gone—I got no family, not even a will—they'd have that big herd to fight over. You want to have a go at it? It could be a way out of your present troubles. I'm game, if you are."

"Sure I am," Sundance said, and meant it, "provided you get your ramrod in here and tell him it's just between you and me. Nobody else is to mix in, no matter what happens. If you get killed, he lets the town alone, now and later. If I get killed—same thing. You could do that, give your word, make the ramrod give his. We don't have to face off here in town, if you figure somebody with a grudge and a rifle might take a shot at your back. We can face off out on the prairie, with nobody around but the gophers. That's one way of doing it."

For the first time, Sundance saw a flicker of uneasiness in the big man's eyes. Whatever he thought he saw was gone now. Maybe he hadn't seen it at all. All men were full of twists and turns. A man could be brave one minute, yellow the next, and maybe a lonely death out on the prairie scared Ryker more than dying itself. In the end, it was hard to figure any man.

Ryker said, "The ramrod would give his word. I can't be sure about the men. They might give it too, then change their minds when the whiskey started to flow. I guess we'll have to let it pass for now."

Sundance nodded. "I guess we will. You'll be going now, so I'll say one last thing so you'll know where we stand."

"I think I do."

"Let me finish. This is no brag, just fact. I'm not one to run off at the mouth, like some people we know"—Ryker smiled and looked at the backs of his hairy hands—"and I guess you know that by now. So I'll say this. Like you, I don't give a damn about the law,

37

badge or no badge, because where there ought to be law there isn't, and where there is it's mostly weak or crooked. I make my own brand of law, and that's what I'm going to do here. You make any more trouble, and I won't fight you fair. You won't find me standing in the middle of the street, polishing my badge and waiting to be shot down. I'll come at you every which way. Take my word for it, I know how it's done because I've been doing it for a long time. This town has a lot to lose. So do you. Think about that on your way back to camp. If you can burn and kill, so can I."

Ryker had a big mean grin on his face. "You sure talk funny for a lawman."

"I figured you'd understand me," Sundance said.

"Sure I do," Ryker said, still grinning, "and you're going to be sorry for every word you said. And you can take my word for that. It's going to be kind of interesting what happens after this."

"Not so interesting. I could do without it."

Ryker's laugh boomed out in the quiet of the jail. "Come on now! Where's your fighting spirit?"

"I've got enough."

"Don't doubt that you do, and you're going to need all you got, and more, when the time comes."

"When the time comes," Sundance said quietly.

"It'll come," Ryker said.

Chapter 4

Blaney came in as soon as Ryker climbed on his horse and rode out of town. Tom Cade and several other men were with him. As usual, Blaney did most of the talking. "Well, what did Ryker have to say?" he wanted to know.

"About what I expected him to say," Sundance answered. "He says his men are going to carry on like they've been doing. He thinks they are."

"That's bad," Blaney said, mopping at his sweaty face. "Then what did you say?"

"I told him what I told you," Sundance said. "No more, no less. From now on it's up to him."

Blaney said, "Maybe you didn't talk to him the right way. What I mean is you just can't threaten a man like Sam Ryker. What I mean is . . ."

Suddenly there was an edge in Sundance's voice. "I know what you mean, Blaney. You want to have it both ways, but there's no way that can be arranged. If you want a quiet town, there's only one way to get it. I thought I made that clear."

"Nobody's backing out on you," Tom Cade said.

"Now listen, Tom," Blaney said. "Who said anything about backing out? I'm just saying maybe there's some other way of handling Ryker."

Sundance tapped the star pinned to his shirt. "You can have this back any time you want it. But as long as I'm wearing it I'll do the job my own way. That's how it has to be. Nobody interferes. Ryker won't listen to talk

39

so there's only one way to deal with him. So you better make up your minds here and now."

"I thought we already decided," Tom Cade cut in. "What's left to talk about?"

"Tom's right," one of the other men said. "We'll still be talking when Ryker puts a torch to the town."

"All right! All right!" Blaney said. "I'd just like to get some idea what Sundance plans to do."

"When I decide I'll let you know," Sundance said. "Maybe I will."

"That's a hell of a thing to say," Blaney said. "And another thing, what was that trouble you had with Mr. Buntline at the hotel? Maybe you don't know it, but Ned Buntline is a very important man. People all over the country read his books. A man like that could put this town on the map."

"Mr. Blaney," Sundance said patiently, "I could get awful tired of you without trying too hard. Now if you don't mind I have things I'd like to do."

After they left, Sundance made the rounds of the town, then he saddled Eagle and rode out of town on the road going south. Sarah waved to him from the hotel porch. South of town was good range land, flat and unbroken except for a line of low hills far in the distance. Two hours later he spotted the dust of Ryker's herd in a long wide valley that cut into the hills, The bawling of thousands of cattle filled the hot still air, and the ground trembled under their hoofs. Sundance rode out wide and came back in from the far end of the valley. A creek ran through the valley and it was lined with cottonwoods on both sides. Sundance dismounted and left the big stallion in the shade of the trees before he went forward on foot. Soon he was close enough to see the riders guarding the herd as well as the chuck wagon and a scatter of tents. He counted twenty men that he could see before he eased back the way he had come. There was no sign of Ryker.

When he got back to town he went to the hotel and ate a steak. "You've been gone half the day," Sarah said. "There was talk that you had changed your mind and left town for good. I think there are some people who wouldn't be sorry to see you go. I'd like to see you go, but I'd like to go with you."

"Don't start that again," Sundance said.

"You don't owe this town anything."

"I never thought I did."

"You could get killed, and for what? These people here could stop Ryker, but they don't have the nerve. Sundance, where were you going when you arrived in this town?"

"Texas."

"I've never been to Texas. I've never been anywhere. I think I'd like to go to Texas."

"Not with me you're not. Anyway, Texas looks just like Oklahoma."

"What did you say to Ryker? Mr. Blaney said you threatened him. Is that true?"

"Depends on how you look at it. That Blaney sure gets around, doesn't he."

"Mr. Blaney doesn't like you. I can tell. Men like you make men like Mr. Blaney nervous."

Sundance smiled. "Too bad that won't work with Ryker. Now if you're all through with the questions I'll be getting back to the jail."

Sarah looked indignant. "You know you're not a very easy man to talk to."

"You talk enough for both of us," Sundance said.

"If you let me go to Texas with you I wouldn't talk so much. All you have to do is say yes and we could be halfway to Texas by tomorrow. Listen to me. You think

41

I'd try to change you, get you to settle down, but I wouldn't do that. Honest, I wouldn't."

"I'm glad to hear that."

Sarah's temper flared up again. "Will you stop making fun of me? You ought to be glad I'm making you the offer. I could marry any man I wanted to in this town, but I don't want to. I want to be as free as you are. I wouldn't care how we lived."

Sundance got up from the table. "I thank you for the offer, and maybe I'm a fool to turn it down, but it wouldn't be any good. Be a good girl and don't keep this up."

"Oh, go to blazes!" Sarah said. She went into the kitchen and banged the door.

Later that day, Sundance was in the jail when a tall man came into town in a buckboard. He climbed down stiffly and hitched the buckboard in front of the hotel. It had been a good many years since Sundance had seen Clem Bogardus, and he looked a lot older and was using a cane. He carried a worn leather grip into the hotel, then came out again and walked down to Dyer's Palace Saloon. He was sitting with a bottle and glass in front of him when Sundance came in.

"Hello, Sundance," Bogardus said, showing no surprise. "Since when did you take up the law business?"

"Just lately, Clem. What brings you to the Territory?" Sundance sat down, but shook his head when Bogardus pushed the bottle across the table.

"Looking for work is what I'm doing."

"The last I heard you were town marshal in Benton."

"And did a good job too, but then the town grew up and got too respectable for the likes of me. They got a regular police force there now. Having me around kept reminding the good citizens of what a hellhole Benton used to be like before I cleaned it up. So here I am at fifty and out of a job."

"You'll find something," Sundance said, thinking back to the days when Clem Bogardus was one of the most feared town marshals in the West. A good lawman in some ways, he was also a ruthless killer. He killed men when he didn't have to, just to be on the safe side, he claimed. With his three brothers, Dixon, Willy and Luther, he had killed enough men to fill a fair sized cemetery.

"I guess you heard Luther got killed," Bogardus said.

"No, I didn't," Sundance said.

"Poor old Luther. Got it in the back just like Hickok. In a poker game it was. Some young pup that couldn't stand to lose walked up behind him and blew half his head away. It took me and the boys nearly a month to catch up with him. We hung him from a railroad trestle. Didn't do us any good in Benton. The son of a bitch's mother was the sister of the mayor, something like that. So like I said, I'm looking for work. Law jobs are getting scarcer all the time."

"There's nothing for you here, Clem," Sundance said, waiting to see how the other man would take it.

"I'm right sorry to hear that, Sundance. I heard tell they were looking for a man right here in Cimarron City. A man to put the lid on the town, so to speak. I came all the way from West Texas. These days I do my traveling in a buckboard. Can't sit a horse that well since I took a bullet in the hip. I was hoping to settle in here in town."

"Sorry, Clem. The job's taken."

"That's a disappointment, Sundance. I like the look of this town. A man could do all right for himself with the gambling and the girls. I had some fine business interests in Benton before the town got religion. These

43

Texas drovers may be wild, but me and the boys could handle them, I'd say. They'd mend their ways after a few hard facts were explained to them. Nothing like three sawed-offs to make a man see the error of his ways."

Sundance said, "There's only room for one sheriff, Clem, and I'm it. There are plenty of other towns."

"Well, sure there are, Sundance, but I've been on the move so long I'm beginning to think I ought to settle down. I've never been one for saving, but now it's time to put away a few dollars for my old age. Dixon and Willy agree with me. We want to find ourself a home, so to speak. We'd give them law and order, if that's what they're looking for." Bogardus's eyes narrowed dangerously. "By Christ, we would. It would cost them more than usual, but that's only fair. Anyhow, what do you want this job for? You're no lawman, and you know it. On the other hand law dogging is all me and the boys have ever done. Come to think of it, it's all we know how to do. So I'd be mightily obliged if you thought about turning in that badge of yours. It wouldn't mean much to you, now would it?"

"Can't do it, Clem. I gave my word to these people."

"My word would be just as good, Sundance. They'd have a nice quiet town."

"What you mean is a nice scared town. No offense, Clem, but I know how you and the boys work. You'd end up running things, and there's nothing they could do about it."

"Somebody has to run things," Bogardus said with a faint smile. "Might as well be us. These Texans just about run it now."

"They used to run it, " Sundance said.

Bogardus sipped his whiskey. "You think you can stop them all by yourself? Even for you that's a big bite to swallow."

"I mean to give it a try just the same."

"Still and all, you're just one man. I'd say you'd be a lot smarter to turn that star over to me. That's good advice, Sundance, and I mean it sincerely."

Sundance said, "Why don't you say what's on your mind, Clem?"

"Might as well," Bogardus said. "I've come a long way to get this job, and I mean to have it. It goes against the grain to say this, but I need that star you're wearing. I don't know that we were ever any kind of friends, but I'm asking you for this favor. You can move on and make your way like you've always done."

"I have to say no, Clem."

"That could be a mistake."

"Meaning what?"

"Meaning what I just said. You don't want trouble with me and the boys."

"You think they'll be trouble?"

"It could come to that. You know I don't walk away from things."

Sundance said, "Maybe you should do it just this once. Another thing, I don't know that I'd let you take the sheriff's job even if I was ready to give it up. I know what you and your brothers did in Benton. I wouldn't want the same thing to happen here."

Bogardus poured another drink and looked carefully at Sundance. "I don't take that as friendly, but we'll let it pass for now. I'm no preacher and don't pretend to be. I mean to run this fat little town and you'd best stay out of my way."

"You'll have to get the job the hard way, Clem."

"Oh, that can be done. I've done things just as hard in my time. You know me so you know I'm speaking the truth. Dixon and Willy will be here in a day or two, then we'll see what happens."

Sundance said quietly, "You wouldn't want to try it

45

by yourself, would you, Clem? We can face off right now, if you have a mind to. Who knows, you might get lucky."

"I make my own luck. Always give yourself the best odds you can find. Three against one sounds like good odds to me. Course there's no cause for all this. Ride out and forget you ever saw this town. That would be the sensible thing to do."

Sundance smiled. "You know you're threatening an officer of the law, Clem. I could lock you up for that."

"You could try, Sundance, but you won't. I know you too well. Anyhow, I haven't done anything. Not so far. I'm just having a quiet drink, waiting for my brothers to show up. You don't know Dixon and Willy, do you?"

"I know about them."

Bogardus said, "Dixon's all right, but Willy's a bad one. Mean as a snake when he lets go of his temper. We're all pretty mean when we don't get our way. I guess it's the way we're built."

"I'll try to remember that," Sundance said.

"Try hard," Bogardus said. "You sure you won't have a drink. This is pretty fair sippin' whiskey. You sure you don't have anything to say before I go on over to the hotel and get some sleep? That trip from Texas like to rattled my teeth loose."

The two men walked out to the street. Sundance said, "You've been free with the advice, Clem. Now let me give you some. There's nothing to stop you from staying in town, so I'll tell you this so you can tell Dixon and Willy when they get here. Go up against me and I'll gun you down. I'm the law and you're not."

"Well, that's plain enough," Bogardus said.

Sundance said, "As plain as I can make it."

Leaning on his cane, Bogardus looked up and down the main street. It was late afternoon now, and the town was bustling with farm wagons. "A right lively little town," Bogardus said. "Yes, sir, I know I'm going to like it here."

Chapter 5

Late that night Sundance was passing the hotel when Tom Cade came hurrying out with an angry look on his face. "You better come inside," he said. "The town council is talking to that man Bogardus about giving him the sheriff's job. Blaney is in favor of it. I don't know about the others."

In the dining room, several tables had been pushed together to make one long one. Blaney and the other members of the council sat behind it. As head of the council, the fat storekeeper sat in the center. He was rapping the table with a gavel when Sundance came in. Bogardus sat at a separate table with Ned Buntline.

"All right, gentlemen, let's get on with it," Blaney said without looking at Sundance. "Mr. Bogardus has been proposed as permanent sheriff of Cimarron City. His credentials are impressive. His most recent job was town marshal of Benton, Texas. He was there for ten years before he retired. Where else did you say, Mr. Bogardus?"

Bogardus said, "Before that I was marshal of Kilbride, Texas. And before that I was marshal of Scofield, New Mexico. Altogether I have been a lawman for twenty-seven years. Mr. Buntline here knows who I am."

"Indeed I do, sir," Buntline said.

"What's he got to do with it?" Sundance asked.

"Mr. Buntline is here at the invitation of the council," Blaney answered, trying not to look at Sundance. "Please continue, Mr. Buntline."

Buntline glared at Sundance before he went on. "I have known Mr.—I should say Marshal—Bogardus for many years. I first made his acquaintance when I was writing a book on William Bonney, otherwise known as Billy the Kid. He is a fine, dedicated lawman feared by lawbreakers throughout the West. I have no hesitation in recommending him for the job of permanent sheriff of your town. I might add that I know very little of Mr. Sundance save that he has a notorious reputation as a gunfighter and adventurer."

"Is that true, Sundance?" Tom Cade asked.

"I've been called worse," Sundance said.

"Answer the question," Blaney prompted.

"I'm no killer, if that's what you mean," Sundance said angrily.

Blaney said, "I think we're wasting time. I'm in favor giving Mr. Bogardus the appointment. This town needs a man who knows his job, and in my opinion Mr. Bogardus is such a man. We will now take a vote."

Sundance looked at Tom Cade. "What about you? You promised to back me on this."

"I still do," Cade said, turning to the other members of the council. "First we begged this man to take the job. Now some of you are trying to get rid of him. I say give him a chance to show what he can do."

"You're out of order, Tom," Blaney interrupted. "I say we put it to a vote. For myself, I urge everybody to vote for Mr. Bogardus."

There were ten men on the council, and seven of them voted to appoint Bogardus. Blaney looked directly at Sundance for the first time. "That's it," he said, smiling with self satisfaction. "Mr. Bogardus is our new sheriff. You will hand over your badge, Mr. Sundance."

Sundance shook his head. "Like hell I will. I'll hand it

over when I'm good and ready. I'm not turning this town over to Bogardus. If he gets in here you'll never get him out. Bogardus and his brothers will loot this town and there won't be a damned thing you can do about it. Hire yourself a real sheriff and I'll quit that same day. Until then I'm the law."

Blaney's face got very red. "This is crazy," he said. "We just voted you out. That means you're out. You can't stay on if we don't want you. Mr. Bogardus, you're the sheriff now. Order this man to hand over his badge. Arrest him if he doesn't."

Now all the council members were looking at Bogardus. "You want to arrest me, Clem?" Sundance asked. "You're wearing a gun, so you're welcome to try."

Buntline said, "Call his bluff, Sheriff. Show him what a real lawman looks like."

"You think I'm bluffing, Clem?" Sundance asked. "Go on, show them what a real lawman looks like. If you get lucky you'll be on your way to owning a town."

"A day or two won't make any difference," Bogardus said. Sundance could tell Bogardus wasn't scared, just careful. "We'll wait till my brothers get here. Then we'll do it nice and legal. That's how it's going to be from now on, everything legal."

Sundance smiled to show his contempt. "Spoken like a real lawman."

A spark of anger flickered for a moment in Bogardus's eyes. Then it was gone just as quickly. "Don't push it too hard, Sundance," he warned.

"Only as far as I have to, Clem. And now I'm going to make my rounds."

Tom Cade walked out with Sundance. Cade said, "These two brothers that are coming, what do you know about them?"

"Nothing good. They're killers just like Clem. They get away with it because they walk around behind a badge. They use the badge to settle private scores, or they kill to keep people scared."

"What'll you do when they get here? Legally, Bogardus is sheriff. You can't take on all three of them."

"Not much else I can do. I can't let them take over the town. You people made me sheriff so I'm going to see that you get a fair deal, in spite of Blaney and the others. They'll gut your town like a hog, if they get the chance."

Cade said, "They'll call it murder if you kill any of them. You could hang. You sure as hell walked into something when you came to this town. I feel kind of rotten about the whole thing. Maybe this town doesn't deserve a decent sheriff."

"Some of the people here-are all right," Sundance said.

"I'll still back you."

"Just stay out of it. No sense getting killed. Clem Bogardus would shoot you like a dog."

"You didn't make any friends here tonight," Cade said. "The council didn't like the way you faced them down. It makes them look bad, not being able to get rid of their own sheriff." Cade laughed. "I'm going to remember the look on Blaney's face for a long time. That fat fool doesn't have the brains of a frog. The rest of them go along with Blaney because he talks longer and louder than any man, in town."

"He'll have plenty to talk about if the Bogardus boys take over," Sundance said before he went back to the jail.

Sundance knew he would have to kill the Bogardus brothers. He sat up thinking about it. There was no way

51

out of it; it had to be done. It was just a matter of when. They were tough and mean; nothing would scare them off, especially when there was a whole town for the taking. All their lives they had killed and looted in the name of the law, and nothing would change them now, and if he killed one he would have to kill all three. If he didn't the survivors would dog his trail until he killed them or was killed himself. Clem was the fastest gun of the three; at least he had built the biggest reputation, and it was well deserved. Clem was the smartest of the brothers, and they followed blindly wherever he led. Their favorite weapon was the sawed-off shotgun, and they used it with ruthless efficiency. There was no way to meet them head-on, and hope to live; the shotguns would see to that. So he had to figure out how he was going to do it, how he was going to stay alive. But no plan was foolproof; besides, he was going up against men who had survived dozens of shoot-outs. They knew his reputation so they would be making plans of their own. What he had to do now was watch himself every minute of the day and night, for though he still wore the sheriff's badge he had put himself on the other side of the law. He was keeping the badge at the point of a gun, so if they killed him it would be all legal and proper. He had turned the town against him, and Blaney would hurry it along, so now he was completely on his own. But that was all right: he had been on his own as long as he could remember.

In the morning, Sundance went to the hotel for breakfast. Bogardus and Buntline were eating together at a table by the window. As Sundance came in Buntline was uncorking a flat brown whiskey bottle. He poured whiskey in his coffee and put the bottle in the side pocket of his coat. When he saw Sundance he moved his chair so he wouldn't have to look at him. Bogardus stared at Sundance for a moment, then went on talking to Buntline.

Sarah came out of the kitchen. "You're not so popular today, *Mister* Sundance. You're out of a job so why don't we go to Texas?"

Sundance smiled. "I'm not out yet."

"Blaney was in earlier," Sarah said. "He's mad because you made a fool of him."

"Blaney was a fool the day he was born."

"That makes no difference. He's the richest man in town. He swears he's going to get you out. Why wait around? We can leave right today. It's different now. Before you thought you had to stay because you gave your word. That's all changed. Don't be such a fool. We'll go to Texas and make a good life."

"No. Now be a good girl, go fetch me a steak."

"Oh, you're such a fool. I don't know what to do with you."

"Don't do a thing with me. Just get the steak."

While he was talking to the girl, Sundance saw Banner, the hotelkeeper, watching them from the kitchen. When she went back inside, Banner closed the door and Sundance could hear them arguing. In a while she came out looking furious. Sundance asked her what was wrong.

"Mr. Banner doesn't think I should be talking to you. He doesn't think I should talk to you at all. He'd tell you to get out, but he's afraid of you. They all are."

"I thought Banner said I was good for business, being so famous and all."

"Don't make a joke out of it. It isn't funny. You've got the whole town against you. I don't trust a lot of people in this town. They're scared of you, so that makes them

53

mad. Sneaky mad. Anyway, Banner hates you because I like you. I told him so."

"Look," Sundance said, sipping his coffee, "if I'm getting you in trouble with Banner I can find another place to eat. I can cook in the jail if I have to."

Now she was angry at him instead of the hotelkeeper. "That's the dumbest idea I ever heard in my life. If Banner doesn't like it he can go to blazes. I'll talk to anybody I like. You cook for yourself, don't make me laugh. You probably couldn't fry an egg."

Sundance said, "Oh, I don't know about that. I make a pretty good antelope stew."

"God Almighty!" Sarah said. "Of all the men in the world I had to pick you. Don't you dare start cooking in the jail or I'll come right over there and throw it out."

Banner called Sarah back into the kitchen and she stayed there. Sundance finished his breakfast and was about to leave when Clem Bogardus came over to his table. "Looks like you're popular with the ladies."

"Sure," Sundance answered.

"A mighty pretty girl," Bogardus said. "You know I was thinking just this morning how bad it must be to be dead. All the good things gone, wiped out like a click of your fingers. No more pretty girls, no more good grub. You're down in a hole with the worms eating on you. Me, I'd hate to be dead."

"No need to be, not right away."

Bogardus smiled. "I was thinking more of you than me."

"That was thoughtful of you, Clem."

"No, I mean it," Bogardus went on. "I thought to myself, that Jim Sundance doesn't have to die so soon. No, sir, not by a long shot. All Jim Sundance has to do is change his mind and go on living his life." Bogardus took out his silver watch. "I guess Dixon and Willy should be along some time this afternoon. The boys will want to meet up with you."

Sundance went back to the jail and took the shotgun from the rack on the wall. He hadn't been fooled by the way Bogardus looked at his watch and commented on the time he expected his brothers to arrive. They would probably get to town a lot earlier. They had no idea what was going on, so first there would be a talk with Clem. Then they might wait a day, or even more, but he didn't think so. Clem would want to move fast, to show the town what he was made of, so it figured that he would make his play before the day was over.

It got to be early afternoon, and there was still no sign of Dixon and Willy. Then, just as it was getting dark he saw them coming into town. They were big rangy men like Clem, but were younger, and they carried their scatterguns in leather boots. Both carried long-barreled pistols belted high. Sundance watched them from the window of the jail as they climbed down in front of the hotel. Clem was sitting in a rocker, waiting for them. They spoke a few words on the porch, then went into the hotel. Sundance stayed in the jail because this was one night when he wasn't going to make his rounds. He lit the lamp and turned the wick down to a glimmer. He shuttered the windows and checked the lock on the iron-banded door. There was nothing to do but wait; sooner or later they'd be along.

Nothing happened during the hours he waited, sitting with the shotgun across his knees. Piano music came from the closest saloon, but that was about the only sound he heard. It was about eleven o'clock when he heard somebody coming to the door. Then Sarah called out, "Open up, Sundance, it's me."

Sundance unlocked the door and let her in. "You better not stay," he said. "Bogardus and his brothers will

55

be coming here. 1 don't know when. Go back to the hotel."

"Listen! Listen! I know they're coming after you. I heard them talking up in the older brother's room. I knew about the trouble you had with him, so I went up and listened. They're going to push a hay wagon up to the door of the jail and burn you out. If you get out alive they'll be waiting with guns. One of the brothers asked why he wanted to burn his own jail and the one called Clem said, 'Hell, we'll build ourself a brand new jail.' They all laughed at that. It looks like they don't care what they do. What're you going to do?"

"First, get you out of here. Go on back to the hotel and don't do any more listening. They'll kill you if they catch you doing it. Go on now. I have to get ready."

"I'm frightened but I don't want to go."

"Out!" Sundance said, taking her firmly by the shoulders and pushing her out the door. "I'll be all right."

"Please don't get killed," she said.

"Go on now," Sundance ordered.

After she left, Sundance took the Winchester and the shotgun and went to the other side of the street after locking the door of the jail. There was an alley between a general store and a harness maker, and Sundance went halfway to the end of it. He could see the jail from where he was. First, they would run in all the way while keeping away from the windows. They would soak the load of hay in coal oil before setting it off. It would be in full blaze before they ran it up flush with the jail door. Well, it wasn't such a bad plan, Sundance decided. If he didn't roast to death in the fire they would be waiting to blow him to bits when he came out of there blinded by smoke. A cold night wind blew through the alley stirring pieces of torn newspaper. There was no moon, but he wouldn't need a moon once the wagon started to burn. He would have surprise on his side, but he'd have to do it quickly. If he could get them close enough together, it was just possible that he might be able to kill them with a single blast. He didn't think he would because the Bogardus boys knew their dirty job too well. They had been in too many gunfights to know not to stay bunched up. Maybe he could get two of them together; it wouldn't be so easy if he couldn't get two at one time.

The town had gone to bed; the saloons were closed and nearly every light had gone out. Another thirty minutes passed before he heard them; first the creak of the wagon, then the low mutter of their voices. His pockets were stuffed with shells for the shotgun, but he knew the fight wouldn't last very long. He had to end it before they came at him from three directions.

From the middle of the alley, he could make out their shapes in the darkness. They pushed the wagon closer to the jail, then stopped where it couldn't be seen by anyone inside. Sundance had cocked the twin hammers of the shotgun. All it needed was the pressure of his finger to send metal death flaming through the darkness. He raised the shotgun and waited, then a wood match flared and the wagon went up with a whomping. Clem yelled and they all pushed together. Then they let go of the wagon while they were still out of sight of the jail windows. The wagon bumped against the door and stopped, burning fiercely. The door caught fire and then the roof of the jail. They had their backs turned to him when he fired the first barrel. Dixon and Willy were close but not close enough to kill both of them at the same time. Dixon died instantly as the blast tore through his spine. A scatter of pellets took Willy in the back of the head, but he was still alive when

57

he went down screaming. Clem whirled and brought up the shotgun as Sundance's finger squeezed the trigger a second time. Clem died as quickly as Dixon, but Willy was still yelling. Sundance drew his Colt and shot him in the head.

The roof of the jail was starting to collapse. The flames roared up into the night sky, throwing long shadows into the street. Lights began to go on all over town. Sundance saw Sarah running toward him from the hotel. Windows were pushed up and frightened voices echoed up and down the street. Blaney, the store keeper, ran out of his house half-dressed.

Tom Cade was the first man to get to where the bodies lay. "My God!" he said in a hushed voice. "You killed all of them."

"Nothing else I could do," Sundance said. "They fired the jail thinking I was inside. They meant to kill me with fire or with bullets. Looks like you'll be needing another jail. This one is done for. Better get these men buried. I'm going to get some sleep."

Blaney was scared enough to be reckless. "You murdered these men, Sundance."

"No," Sundance said, "not murdered."

"You're going to be sorry for this," Blaney warned. "One of those men was a sheriff of this town."

"Well, he doesn't look like much of anything right now," Sundance said.

Chapter 6

They buried the Bogardus brothers at noon the next
day. From the door of the livery stable, Sundance
watched the hearse, one coffin inside, two strapped to
the roof, creak its way to the cemetery on a hill outside
town. Blaney and the town council had turned out; a
safe act of defiance, he guessed. Tom Cade was the
only member of the council who wasn't there. Buntline
came out of the hotel, looking drunk, and joined the
men walking behind the hearse. The neck of a pint
bottle stuck out of the pocket of his coat. As he passed
the stable, he took off his hat in mock gallantry, and
smiled his vicious smile. Sundance didn't do anything.
None of the other men looked at Sundance. It looked
like the New York scribbler was having a good time.
The killing of the Bogardus boys would be good for at
least one dime novel. Buntline would write it in his usual
blood and thunder style; it would make him that much
richer. Sundance smiled briefly. He would be the villain
of the piece, the back-shooting, sneaky halfbreed. Well,
it had been a busy week: he had killed five men, and the
showdown with Ryker was yet to come.

He had set up headquarters in a storeroom in the
livery stable. The stableman didn't argue about it. At
sometime he had lived there, but now he bunked
elsewhere. There was a cot, a chair, a table, and not
much else. It suited Sundance better than the jail. He
had been in too many jails, on the wrong side of the
bars, ever to be comfortable in one, even as the keeper.
He liked the good smell of hay and horses, and except

for a few people, he had always liked animals better than humans.

Sarah came down from the hotel with a tray, balancing it expertly on the palm of one hand. She looked very young and pretty in the sunlight. Banner, the hotel keeper, came out on the porch and looked after her, then went back inside when he saw Sundance.

"You didn't come for your breakfast," she said. "What a terrible place to live."

Sundance showed her where to set down the food. "I don't mind it," he said. He pulled up an empty nail keg to the table and let her have the only chair. There were two plates under the napkin which covered the tray. One of them had his usual thick steak on it, a cut of beef just barely cooked.

"What in hell are you eating?" he asked.

"Vegetables, just vegetables," she said. "I read in the paper that there are people back in Boston who don't eat anything else. They call themselves vegetarians. They claim meat is bad for you. I thought I would try it."

"These Boston people don't know what they're missing," Sundance said, cutting into his steak.

"They call people who eat meat 'corpse eaters.' Well, it makes sense, doesn't it?"

"Not to me. Forget about the vegetables. You know you shouldn't be here. I'm about as popular in this town as Ryker. Maybe less."

"I'm worried so I talked about vegetables. If you don't like the town, why don't you leave and take me with you?"

"I'll be glad to leave," Sundance said, "but not yet. I gave my word."

"Take it back. They don't want it anymore," Sarah said angrily. "You should have heard Blaney and that

60

man Buntline talking at breakfast this morning. Buntline was saying you ought to be hanged from the highest tree in the Territory."

The steak was just right, and there was plenty of it. "That sounds like Buntline. Why couldn't it be a low tree?"

"I don't think that's funny. Now you have Ryker *and* the town to deal with. Buntline's been calling you a murderer, saying you ought to be arrested and tried for killing those men."

"But who's going to arrest me?"

"There are Federal marshals in the Territory."

"Then why don't these marshals do something about Ryker?"

"I'm trying to talk sense, and you keep asking questions. You know Buntline has influence."

"Sure," said Sundance. "He dines with presidents and important railroad men."

"Oh damn you, Sundance! This town is going to be your grave. I don't want to walk behind your hearse."

"I doubt if they'd go to that much expense. I'm here and here I stay."

"But why?"

"I'm not going to keep talking about it, so I'll say this. An old man got killed maybe because of me. Probably that was why he got killed. Anyway, that's why I took the job. First I was warned off by Ryker, then Bogardus. I don't take to that. Now I'm being bad-mouthed by Blaney and Buntline. I don't take to that either. I'm like the doctor who makes you take your medicine, no matter how rotten it tastes."

"Oh spare me!" Sarah said, poking around in her plate of greens without too much interest.

Sundance said, "You know, this is as bad as being married."

Sarah looked up quickly. "You mean you've been married?"

"Not a chance."

"No wonder you haven't."

Sundance poured the first cup of coffee. "You want some?" he said, "or is that against the law in Boston?"

"You're going to get killed," Sarah said. "Shot or hanged. Anyway—dead."

Sundance said, "Well, I won't let them hang me."

"What's the difference?"

"There's a difference."

"Buntline's been saying somebody younger and faster than Clem Bogardus could handle you," Sarah said. A worried frown creased her smooth forehead. "He was saying that to Blaney this morning. They didn't talk while I was bringing in their breakfast, but you know how loud Buntline talks. I listened from the kitchen. He mentioned some man in El Paso. A Dallas...something. The last name was a long one. I didn't get it. I'm sorry."

"Don't be. He was talking about Dallas Studenmeyer."

"It sounded like that."

"It was Studenmeyer all right."

"You know him?"

"Somewhat. I used to. A few years back Studenmeyer was city marshal in El Paso. German. A German family from East Texas. Studenmeyer saved his bullets for killing white men. That was his boast. He killed Mexicans with a club. He always said he wouldn't dirty his gun by killing a greaser with it. Now I hear he runs a saloon and gambling hall. I doubt if he'd come all the way to Oklahoma. Got too much money now. Buntline was just talking."

Sarah looked anxiously at Sundance. "Studenmeyer wasn't the only name Buntline mentioned."

"Buntline knows all the badmen in the West," Sundance said. "He ought to, the old windbag. He's made a fortune telling lies about them."

"Then he's got enough money to send for the best... or the worst."

Sundance had thought about that. Buntline was known to be a skinflint, but he would come up with the money that would make him more money. It was said, though the truth of it was never known, that Buntline money was behind the killing of Jesse James by Bob Ford. The New York scribbler would do anything to make a dirty dollar; anything that would help to sell his ten-cent books. He had written a book about how Ford killed Jesse; later he wrote another book when one of Jesse's Missouri cousins named O'Kelley shotgunned Ford to death in front of his saloon in Crede, Colorado.

"That's possible," Sundance said. "I wouldn't put it past him."

"Then get out now before it happens!"

"No way I could do that. If he comes I'll be waiting for him."

Sarah said, "It wouldn't have to be someone famous. It could be somebody right here in town. It could happen any night you're making the rounds of the town. Not even at night. Anytime. A man, a boy with a rifle. From an alley, from a window, from a roof. Not a brave man, not even a good shot. Someone who wanted to be famous so Ned Buntline could write about him."

Sarah stared at the wall, though there was nothing on it but some old harness. "Have you thought about that, Sundance?"

He nodded. It could happen like that. That was how Johnny Ringo got it. Johnny was fast, maybe the fastest of them all, no matter what the legends said. Johnny wasn't as well known as Hardin, Hickok or the others. He had never been a showman, didn't dress up fancy or get his name in the papers very much. He never had much to say, never made much money from his outlawing and general badness. He was just about the fastest gunfighter who ever lived. In Waco, Texas, he killed five men with five shots, and came out of the fight without a scratch. Then, a year and a half later, some town kid with a cheap .32 and shaky hands shot him in the back.

Sundance pushed his plate away. "That was a good steak," he said.

"Then you won't listen?" Sarah said impatiently.

"I'm listening," Sundance said. "You can't run away from your death."

"That's not true."

"I think it is. Anyway, that's how I live. Maybe that's not how they live their lives in Boston, but it works well enough out here."

"What do you know about Boston?"

Sundance liked this gentle young Indian girl very much, in spite of all her notions, or maybe because of them. "Oh I don't know," he said. "I was in Boston once."

"You were in Boston?"

"With my old friend George Crook."

"The general?"

"That's the one. Three Stars went there to make a speech to some society, and wanted me to go along. A bunch of ladies there have a society to help the redskins. That means you and me."

"You're only half redskin," Sarah said, smiling at last.

"I like that half," Sundance said, smiling back at her. "I like the other half too."

Sundance didn't mean more than he said but Sarah frowned angrily. "Maybe you'd like a white girl better than me. You and your yellow hair and blue eyes!"

"I'll black my hair if it makes you feel better. What I can do about the eyes I don't know."

"Why do you call a great man like General Crook 'Three Stars'?" Sarah asked, breaking away from the talk of white women. "You have no respect for anybody."

Sundance said, "The general is a three star general last I heard. That's what the Indians call him, and so do I. For Three Stars I have more respect than for any man."

"What about women?"

"You mean for you? That's what you're asking."

"That's what I'm asking."

"A lot," Sundance said. "Maybe it's time you went back to the hotel. Your boss Banner looked after you when you came down here, and he didn't look pleased."

Sarah was almost prim. "I thank you for the respect, kind sir—but do you like me?"

Sundance said, "Don't get back on that track. All right, I like you. Like you a lot. Will that hold you for now?"

"For now," Sarah said, using her new prim manner "Later you'll like me a lot more."

"We'll see," Sundance said.

"Of course we will," Sarah said, gathering up the dishes and putting them on the tray. She looked around the dusty stable storeroom and sniffed. "You must be a savage to live in a place like this."

Sundance said, "That's what they called me in Boston."

"And so you are. I'm going to clean this place up."

"No," said Sundance. "I like the dust the way it is. Be a good girl now. Don't come back. It can't do you any good. You'll have to live in this town long after I'm gone."

"You won't be gone without me," Sarah said, defiant as ever. "Just now you said you liked me, liked me a lot. A few days ago you wouldn't even say that much."

"Next you'll have me proposing."

"I never said anything about getting married. The missionary school didn't change me that much."

While they were still talking, an old Indian who worked as an odd job man at the hotel knocked fearfully on the side of the stable door. Sarah stared at the two old leather grips he was carrying. "Mr. Banner say to bring you these," he said haltingly. "He say you like it down here, then you stay here. That is what he tell me to say. I am sorry."

The old Indian set down the two grips in the open doorway and went away. Sarah carried them into the storeroom. "Are you going to kick me out too, or can I stay? You keep telling me to go. This time I'll do it if you say so."

Sundance looked at her. "Where would you go?"

"You don't have to worry about that. Just tell me what you want me to do."

"What about a rooming house? I have some money. You're welcome to it."

The girl's dark eyes snapped with anger. "To blazes with you and your money." She picked up the grips. "I'll go, you damn fool!"

In his time, Sundance had fought and beaten men twice his size, but this frail girl had worn him down. "Stay," he said. "Damn you—stay! Just don't be sorry later."

Her face was very happy. "No matter what happens I won't be sorry. Even if we don't stay together, you'll remember me. I'll make you remember me."

Sundance smiled. "I doubt that anybody could forget you. But you know there will be danger. Even if

Buntline is just bluffing about hiring a gunman, there's always Ryker. I don't know why he's holding back. But he'll get here and it won't be good when he does. If I get killed and Ryker's men take you..."

He didn't finish the rest of it. There was no need. Sarah had lived long enough to know what a bunch of drunken cowboys could do to a woman.

"I'll take my chances with you," Sarah answered. "You've told me everything there is to tell, and I understand what you're saying. Please don't say it again, Sundance. If we only have a little time together, I would like it to be as happy as we can make it."

"All right," Sundance said. "That's how we'll do it."

Chapter 7

When Sundance came back from making his rounds Sarah had swept out the storeroom and was scraping rust off the old cook stove against the back wall. Her face was smudged and her hair had come undone as she worked vigorously on the stove with a wet rag covered with sand. Sundance thought she looked very pretty. She had unpacked the few dresses she had and hung them on a nail on the wall.

"At least this is better than that hotel," she said over her shoulder. "I never want to go in that place again. We can sleep in the hayloft. What do you think of that?"

Sundance sat down at the table and watched her. He didn't offer to help. "The hayloft is fine. Don't work so hard on that stove. We won't be here that long."

They wouldn't. It would be over in a day or two, maybe a lot less. Ryker would come and men would die. That was as certain as the next day's sunrise. If they managed to come out of it alive, then he would have to think about the girl. It was all wrong, he knew, but just the same they were together now. She was cleaning a dirty old stove and he was watching her, and for the moment anyway it didn't seem so wrong.

The stableman, one of the Indian-Negro halfbreeds that were common in the Territory, came in and Sundance gave him money to get the things Sarah needed to set up house. He was a fairly old man with a glum look on his face that never went away. It didn't change when he saw the girl.

"Get some good steaks," Sundance told him, peeling

off money and handing it to him. "Keep a dollar for yourself."

"I know how to buy meat, mister," the stableman said, putting the money in his faded canvas pants, "and I don't need your dollar. I'm doing this for nothin' and not just because you're wearing a gun."

Sundance looked at him with interest. "What do they call you?" he asked.

"They call me Micah. I don't care what they call me long as they pay what they owe me."

"You keep to yourself, don't you?"

"That's what I do. The town hasn't much use for me, me for the town, for you neither. For nobody," he added. "I got nothin' agin you and the girl. Stay here long as you want."

After he went out again, Sarah laughed. "Micah's a peculiar man, but he's all right. He won't turn on you like the rest. Tom Cade won't either. The white people in town don't think Micah shows enough respect. They're right, he doesn't and won't. But he knows horses like nobody around."

"I like him better than Blaney," Sundance said.

Micah came back with a coffee pot, a fry pan, and the other supplies. He set them down carefully and counted out the exact change. "They's stove wood out back in the lean-to. It's good and seasoned," he said. "In the stores they tried to pump me about what you was doing up here."

"You mean Blaney?"

"Him and others. Blaney ain't the only weasel in this town."

"And what did you say, Micah?" Sarah asked, smiling at the old man's sorrowful face.

Micah's face was a color hard to describe; the skin was a reddish black, and only his nose was completely Negro. "What did I tell them?" he repeated. "I told them to mind their business. Blaney 'specially didn't like that. Blaney and the good people"—Micah put a sneer into the words—"don't hold with my drinkin'. And speakin' of which I feel like a snort right about now."

The old halfbreed dug into a barrel and produced a bottle. It was almost full. "Good moon, make it myself, out at my place. The slop they sell here in the saloons ain't fit to wash floors." He held out the bottle to Sundance. "You want a jolt?"

Sundance didn't want it, but he knew it was as close as the old man could come to friendship. He took a fair-sized swallow, wiped off the bottle with his sleeve and gave it back. "That's good moon all right," he said. It was the worst whiskey he ever tasted, and the strongest. It went down like fire and kept on burning after it got there.

Sarah wiped her stove blackened hands on a rag. "What about me?" she asked, holding out one of the tin cups Micah had brought from the store.

Micah's face took on an even gloomier look. "You sure you want to drink this stuff, girl? You'll burn the supper for sure, you drink from this bottle."

Sarah said she'd be all right. She filled about a quarter of the cup. "I feel good today," she said. "And a drink is going to make me feel better than that." She drank it down and her eyes watered with the effect. She sat down on the barrel with a silly look on her face.

Micah said after he took a long, gurgling swallow, "They's good spring water in that bucket over there. Don't use it myself, but the horses like it."

Sarah giggled. "Why would I want to drink water?"

70

she said. "When I drink whiskey, I drink whiskey, when I drink water, I drink water."

"It's gettin' to her all right," Micah said to Sundance. "You want another? This ain't the only bottle on the premises."

Sundance said no. "Can't handle it, never could. A few more drinks of that and I'd start to howl."

Sarah said to Micah, "We could always tie him up."

"Leave him be," Micah said. "The man know his own mind. Me, I could never handle it neither and I got the scars on my old hide to prove it. Many a time I did me some cuttin', and got cut, when the moon was in me. Now I'm too old to be wild, so I just sit back and drink in peace. Me and the moon has had our times."

Sarah reached for the bottle again. "You know, that was the first drink of whiskey I ever had in my life. No wonder people drink it. It makes you feel so good."

"Amen to that!" Micah said, passing her the bottle.

"This time a very small drink," Sundance warned, taking the bottle away from her.

Sarah made a face. "We're not married yet, you know."

"That's all for you," Sundance said, pouring a trickle of whiskey into the cup. "I don't want to have to carry you up to that hayloft."

Another giggle came from Sarah as she knocked back the moonshine. "You oughtn't talk like that in front of Micah. It isn't decent."

"Don't mind me," Micah said, taking another deep draught of the vile tasting liquor. "Used to have a woman myself, but she kept dumping out my moon, so I had to get rid of her. Had a lot of women in my day. All them had that same fault. Couldn't let them get away with such foolishness. Then one day I say to myself, what in hell do you need women for? You got your moon, ain't that enough for you? Damn right, Micah, I say to myself."

"Were you ever married legal?" Sarah asked, as if the question had great importance for her.

"Once I was," Micah said, "by a real preacher. They was this woman that was mostly white and she had notions like that. So I grind my teeth and go through the ceremony. I didn't mind the married part of it if she hadn't started pouring out my moon."

Sarah said, "What happened to her?"

Micah looked thoughtful. "Can't be sure, girl. Never did see her again." He took another big drink, and now the bottle was nearly empty. "She was a right good lookin' woman. Big as a house. Couldn't cook worth a damn though cookin' was never my main interest. Now and then I throw a big steak on the fire and have a go at that."

Sarah asked, "You want to have supper with us. Looks like you bought enough meat for five or six people."

Sarah looked over at Sundance. "Sure," he said, "stay and eat with us. Be glad to have you."

The old man's face was suddenly shy, and he stared down at the floor between his feet. "You mean you're asking me to supper? If you mean what you say, and ain't just talkin', I'd be honored to share the table with you. All right then, you got yourself a deal. I'll go out back and dig out the stove wood and kindling." Micah looked from Sundance to the girl. "I'm obliged. Been a long time since I et with a fellow human."

Micah got up unsteadily. "Yes, sir, a long time."

"You start supper. I'm going to take a look around," Sundance said, picking up the shotgun. It was a Greener, the best ever made, and Clem Bogardus had killed a lot of men with it. The two other sawed-offs

72

taken from the dead brothers stood against the wall in a corner.

"If I'm not here and somebody—anybody—bothers you ..." He pointed to the shotguns. "They're loaded," he said. "All you do is ear back the hammers, point and pull the triggers."

"I don't think I could do it, Sundance."

"Do what I tell you. Use the shotgun if you have to."

"All right," Sarah said, but she shuddered.

Micah came with the wood. "I couldn't but hear what you was saying just now. Ain't nobody goin' to bother you woman with me around." Micah was more than half drunk, but he meant what he was saying. "You can depend on that like nothing else in you life."

"I'll do that," Sundance said quietly.

As he made the rounds of the town, he could feel the sharp edge of tension in the air. He could feel them watching him from doors and windows. They were afraid of him now, and hated him for it. They had shifted their fear of Ryker to hatred for him. It wasn't dark yet, and Blaney and Buntline and another man were sitting in rockers on the hotel porch. Buntline had a tall glass in one hand, a fat cigar in the other, and he looked about as drunk as usual. He raised his glass when Sundance passed with the shotgun crooked under his arm.

In the saloons it was quiet. Dyer, who owned the Palace Saloon, was standing in front of it. He had been friendly enough after Sundance had given him the money he had taken from the two drunken cowhands. Now his eyes were blank and as hostile as they dared to be. The tinkle of a mechanical came from inside the saloon, but there wasn't the usual noise and bustle of a lot of men drinking and gambling.

"How's business?" Sundance asked, not giving a damn how it was.

"Rotten. Couldn't be worse," Dyer snapped. He turned abruptly and went through the swinging doors.

Sundance smiled a brief sour smile. Another enemy. He met Tom Cade before he reached the end of the street. Cade looked worried but he fell in step with him.

"It's bad," Cade said, "and it can only get worse. I don't know what to think anymore. They're scared of you, Sundance. Blaney says you're doing what you accused Bogardus of trying to do. Take over the town and hold it at the point of that shotgun."

Eyes followed them as they walked down the middle of the dusty street. "You don't see me running whores and poker games, do you?" Sundance said.

Cade said, "Blaney swears you're just biding your time. That you'll make your move when you're ready."

Sundance hefted the shotgun. "I'd like to stuff both barrels down Blaney's throat." Cade looked frightened. "But I won't."

"The saloon keepers hate you the most," Cade said. "Even the local ranchers and farmers have stopped coming in, or if they do come in for a few beers they get out fast. I'm in the lumber business so it makes no difference to me. Well, maybe it does make a difference to me. Most of these people are my friends."

"Sounds like you're wavering, Cade."

"No . . . no, I'm not wavering, just trying to figure out what's the right thing to do."

"What do you think that might be?"

"I swear I don't know."

"Then I'll tell you. What I'm doing is the right thing. If you want to side with Blaney and the others, it's all right with me. No hard feelings. But it won't change a thing."

"Blaney still thinks he can talk to Ryker," Cade went on.

"You mean use Ryker to get rid of me?"

"Maybe that's what he figures. He doesn't tell me a thing since I voted against him. But I'm pretty sure what he's thinking. You killed two of Ryker's men and talked tough to him. That means Ryker wants to get you more than he wants to wreck the town. Now the town has turned against you, so that puts the town on the same side as Ryker. I figure Blaney sees that as a good sign."

They had stopped outside Cade's lumber yard. There was a pungent smell of freshly cut timber in the air. Cade took out a bunch of keys and jangled them nervously.

"That's how I figure it," he said.

Sundance said, "Could be your're right, but if that's what Blaney thinks, he's wrong. Bad as he is, Ryker hates gutless men, and Blaney has less guts than any man I ever met. Ryker would kill me quick as a wink if he got the chance, then he'd turn on the town like the crazy man he is. Most likely, Blaney would be the first to be dragged at the end of a rope."

"It's a hell of a thing," Cade said.

Sundance walked on. There was no one on the hotel porch now. Cade was right: it was a hell of a thing, and maybe Sarah was right. All he had to do was throw the sheriff's star in the dust and leave Cimarron City behind. Then let Ryker have his rough sport with the gutless town. It didn't deserve any better. There were enough men in town to burn out with rifles and shotguns and blow Ryker's bullies out of their saddles the next time they ran wild. The people of Northfield, Minnesota, had done just that to the James gang when they rode in to rob the bank. But maybe people in Minnesota had more nerve. It was hard to tell what people would do. And though his thoughts were savage, Sundance knew that he couldn't back down. He was a professional fighting man, and he had given his word to rid the town of Sam Ryker. What was even more important, he had given his word to himself. It wasn't so much a matter of pride. That wasn't altogether true. Some of it was pride. The quiet pride of a man who always does what he says he's going to do. If he backed out of this fight, talk of how he ran would dog him for the rest of his life. Men who had always trusted his word would no longer be sure about him, and when you lived by the gun that made all the difference. He no longer cared much about the town. He had to be honest about that. What he was doing he was doing for himself. In the end, it was that simple.

He walked to the other end of town, and by then it was getting dark. In a deep gully years of trash from the town was piled up. It smoked night and day, and the stink of it was carried on the wind. Rats scurried through the mounds of rusted cans, broken bottles, broken furniture, and greasy bones. An old piano that looked as if somebody had worked on it with an ax lay on its side.

Sundance turned away in disgust. Towns! The people who lived in them would always be something of a mystery to him. They huddled together out of fear, or maybe it was something else he didn't understand. They couldn't even take the time to bury their filth. And yet all you had to do was ride out a few miles on the prairie, and it was as if towns didn't exist. You could camp beside a clear flowing creek when night came, and listen to it running over rocks in the darkness before you went to sleep. If he lived through this, that's the first thing he would do when he left Cimarron City. Find a sheltered place with good grass and water for Eagle, and breathe clean air while the coffee cooked.

It was dark at the end of the street where the livery

stable was, and before he even got close to the door, he heard the sharp click-click of shotgun hammers being eared back. He smiled. Old Micah was as good as his word.

"Say who you are," the halfbreed called out in a calm voice. "Or get ready for Kingdom Come."

Sundance said his name.

Micah didn't lower the sawed-off until Sundance was standing in the light of a coal oil lantern. "Just being careful," he said. "Anybody can say another man's name."

"Supper's just about ready," Sarah said, turning from the glowing stove.

Once again, Sundance thought about making night camp beside a clear running creek. Yes, he thought, right or wrong, I guess I'll take her along.

While he'd been gone, she had washed the dirt off her face and hands and had changed into a soft gingham dress with red roses on a blue background. Her hair was combed back, and it shone in the light of the lantern. Her face was happy, and she smiled at him. She had scrubbed the table top with the sandy rag, and it was still wet. Looking at her, Sundance wondered what lay in store for them, then pushed the thought from his mind. This was the here and now, and it was all they might ever have. But that was all right. He guessed it was. It was all they had, and it would have to do. A day, or a month, or a year, what was the difference? No difference, not if you looked at it the right way. That was how he had always seen it, without thinking. The violence of his life had forced this upon him; he had accepted it willingly. It was . . .

Sarah broke in on his thoughts. "What did you say?" she asked.

"I said stop staring at me and eat your supper."

Chapter 8

Micah had washed his face and slicked down his lank grey hair with water. The smell of strong yellow soap came from him. His big hands were battered and scarred from years of rough work, but he cut his meat delicately, and was all the time offering to pass Sarah this and that. Salt, pepper, coffee, anything he could think of that was on the table.

Finally, Sarah said, "Stop fussing, Micah, and eat your supper. You're making me nervous."

Micah looked hurt. "Not my intention to do that. You cook a fine steak, girl, and I thank you for it. I am truly sorry I said you'd burn the blamed things."

Micah turned to Sundance. "She ain't had a drop since you went out."

Sarah laughed. "You'd think I was a drunkard!"

Sundance wondered what George Crook would say if he could see them together in the dull yellow light of the coal oil lantern. He thought he knew. Three Stars would give out his big booming laugh that always sounded if it came from way down in his boots. He knew Three Stars, a man among men, would be glad to draw up a chair and dig into a thick steak, and afterward the fragrant smell from his beloved Havana cigars would mingle with the smell of horses and hay. Sundance knew Crook would like both of them, and the fact that one was an orphan waitress and the other was a drunken old stablekeeper wouldn't make a damned bit of difference. Nothing made any difference to George Crook, if he liked you: you could be a buffalo hunter, a barkeep, a saloon girl. That was the measure of the man.

Micah drank whiskey with his steak. A second bottle was on the table, and it was half gone. Now he was drinking from a cup. He finished another drink and said, "I been thinkin' about you, Sundance, and I decided you ain't such a bad fella. You and your woman has treated me decent, and no cause for that I can see. People never treated me decent and I treated them back the same way. Nobody ever give me nothin' and I wouldn't of took it if they had. The way I see it, and I see more things than people give me credit for, you're in a peck of trouble. Turn me down if you like, but I'll say it plain. You want some help?"

"Any I can get," Sundance answered.

"Then you got it," Micah said. "I'm getting old now, but I can still shoot off a gun. Better than most, I'd say. In the old days I run with some pretty tough boys. I like the way you stood up to this Ryker and the slack bellies that run this fleabit little town. So I'll be right behind you when the shootin' starts. Let me keep that shotgun and I'll put it to the best use when the time comes. I'll give it back when it's all over."

Sundance said, "Keep it, Micah—and thanks."

"No thanks needed. Only one thing"—Micah stared at his plate—"you wouldn't want to make me some kind of deputy, would you?"

"Sure," Sundance said.

Micah looked up in surprise. "You mean that's all there is to it. You say 'sure' and that makes me a deputy? I thought there was more to it than that."

Sundance sensed the old man's disappointment. "Of course, there's the swearing in. Raise your right hand."

Micah's mournful face brightened. "That's more like it," he said.

Sundance didn't know all the words, but what he said was close enough. Micah repeated what he said.

It was about as legal as holding up a train, but Micah didn't seem to mind. Sundance had taken a few deputy badges and he gave one to the old man. Micah pinned it on with obvious pride. "By God," he said, "I'm a deputy." He polished the badge with his shirt sleeve.

"I thank you for the fine supper, girl," he said to Sarah, "but now I'm going to go out front and stand guard. No tellin' what them sneaks are up to."

"You've got a funny army, Sundance," Sarah said when Micah went out.

"I think it's a fine army," he said.

"What do you think about us?"

"It's going to be all right. I thought about it and that's what I decided."

"I pushed myself on you. You have no regrets?"

"Regret is a waste of time. Some people enjoy it, not me. We'll do the best we can, now and later."

Later, lying together in the sweet smelling hayloft, he caressed her smooth young body. "This time, with you, was the first time," Sarah said. "Did you like me?"

"You were fine," Sundance answered.

"There won't ever be anyone else."

"No need to say anything."

"I know there isn't. I just wanted you to know how I feel. I promise never to be a bother to you. There will be times when you have to go away, to places where I can't go. I'll wait for you. These separations will make it even better for us."

"I have good friends who have a ranch in South Texas. Their name is Tolliver and they'd be glad to have you. You could stay with them, the times I have to go away. You understand I have to go on with my work. I wouldn't be any good if I didn't."

Sarah turned in the half darkness of the loft. He could see the shine of her hair. "You don't have to explain. I will take you the way you are, any way you are, and I will never compalin or try to change you. And if you ever get tired of me..."

"Hush now!" Sundance said.

"No, let me say it," Sarah said. "If you get tired of me, I'll remember what we had. It's best to be honest about everything."

"It'll be all right."

"Oh, I know it will. I'm just so happy." Sarah hesitated. "Have you known many women? I'm sorry I said that."

"I don't mind. Not so many women. I don't get to stay long in one place."

"Were they nice women?"

"Not all of them. A few."

Sarah reached out and touched the many scars that criss-crossed his lean body. "You have been wounded so many times. I could kill the men who injured you."

"Most of them you won't have to. Let's not be talking about killing, our first night together."

"I don't want to hear any more about your women," Sarah said. "Don't ever mention them again, please. Do you think I'm crazy?"

"Sure. It's the kind of craziness I like. I won't try to change you either."

"For a man who has done so much fighting, you are gentle, Sundance."

"Don't let it get around."

"Tell me about your mother. What was she like?"

"A lot like you. Proud, honest. My father was a wanderer, and she went where he went. He worked at many trades to support us. My mother never complained. All she wanted was to be with him. My father

81

never knew anything about making money, or how to hold onto it when he had it. It didn't matter. We were a good family. Then one day it was gone, wiped out. I have been on the move ever since."

"Do you still miss them?"

"No," Sundance said. "I think of them every day of my life, but I don't miss them. We had our time, and then it was over. It was good that they died together. One would have been lost without the other."

"You think they would have liked me?" Sarah asked shyly.

"They would have liked you fine."

Sarah started to say something, then her voice trailed off into sleep. Sundance covered her with a blanket and got dressed. It was time to take over the watch from Micah.

"Nothin' to tell you," the old halfbreed said when Sundance relieved. "Ain't no reason to leave your woman. My age you don't sleep much anyhow."

"No matter. I'm up now. I'll just take a tour of the town, then you turn in."

"I'll stay till hell cools down," Micah said. "When do you figure this Ryker will come?"

"Anytime. Could even be tonight."

"We have to take him from both sides. You blast Ryker and I'll get the men close to him. We have four scatterguns. That gives us four double blasts one after the other. Four doubles or eight singles ought to slow the sons of bitches down. These Texicans may think they is hell on wheels, but I don't know that many men willin' to face up to four sawed-offs."

Sundance said, "There's no telling we're going to come out of this."

Micah spat in the dust. "You don't say. Makes no difference to me if I do or not. To die with a man you like ain't such a bad way to go. I'd say it's a damn sight better than dying out there at my place. Maybe lying in my own dung, not even able to get up to drink a dipper of moon. There's not a man in this town'd come out to see how I was, not that I'd want any one of these sheep to come bleating out to my place. So don't concern yourself with what happens to me. I'll be proud to stand with you when the time comes."

"And I'll be proud to have you."

The night passed quietly. Micah snored in one of the empty stalls while Sundance stood guard, but he was up again before first light. During the last hours of darkness, Sundance thought about Sam Ryker. He could feel the threat of the big man camped there in the valley with his herd. They were like two locomotives coming at each other on a single track. There was no stopping what had to happen. Ryker had plenty of men, but he couldn't bring all of them into town and leave the huge herd unguarded. He had well over fifty thousand tied up in that herd and madman though he was he wouldn't leave it where it could be run off and scattered. Sundance figured how many men he and the old man would have to face. At least fifteen, maybe more. The four shotguns would make some difference.

Micah helped himself to whiskey, then corked the bottle and put it in the barrel. He picked up the water bucket and dumped some water over his head. He shivered in the early morning cold.

"Course we could always ambush them," he said. "Lay out there on the edge of town, pick a good place and let fly when they ride through. Have our re-loads ready so we can fire and load as fast as we please. We could kill eight or ten of those Texicans. The rest of them'd take the hint. Be fools if they didn't. Anyhow, that's my thinkin' on the subject."

"We could do it that way," Sundance agreed. "It would probably work. We can't, just the same." He smiled at the bloodthirsty old man. "But thanks for thinking of it."

"You'll have to kill them sooner or later," Micah said. "They'll be just as dead."

"Let them start it," Sundance said. "Then we'll kill them if we have to. We'll let go with the shotguns and keep on shooting till they're dead or we are. I'm not going to take any prisoners. I'd have to let them go and they'd only come back."

Micah said, "Now, sir, that's the kind of talk I likes to hear. Never did like Texicans much."

"Don't argue with me. You stay out of sight when they come. I won't tell you again," Sundance told Sarah. "With Micah's help I think I can handle them."

Sarah's dark eyes glowed with anger. "You mean you don't want my help?"

"That's right, I don't want it. I don't want you getting hurt. I don't mind you arguing with me about everything else. This is different. If you say no, you can take your things and get out."

Sarah banged down her coffee cup. "Oh, why don't you go to blazes! I'll do what I please."

Sundance pointed. "Then there's the door and out you go."

"For God's sake, you make me sick."

"You heard what I said. What's it going to be?"

"All right, I'm not deaf and I'm not dumb." Sarah got up from the table and threw wood into the stove. She was as mad as Sundance had seen her and that, he decided, was pretty mad.

Old Micah was cutting into his steak and potatoes.

"Sundance is right, girl," he said. "I'd hate to see a purty girl all shot up. Would hate to have it on my conscience."

Sarah turned away from the stove after slamming down the lid. "You too!" she snapped.

"It's the truth," Micah said.

She was still furious. "Why don't you shut up and have a drink? That'll keep you quiet for a spell."

The old man wasn't offended. "Don't mind if I do. Fact is, that's the best idea I heard this past twenty minutes." He reached for his jug of corn. "Always did prefer drinkin' to eatin'. More nourishment in the bottle than in the fry pan."

Sundance grinned at Micah, then at the girl. "At least you can cook," he said.

Sarah wasn't ready to make up. Not just yet. "How would you know? I wouldn't be surprised if you ate dog in your time."

"And it was good. The Cheyenne cook it just right. Of course, any old hound won't do. Got to get a young one. You ever eat dog, Micah?"

"Hell yes. I et just anything you can make. Horse, mule, bear, rattler. Most folks don't cotton to snake meat. Sort of tastes like chicken."

Sarah began to gather up the dishes; a pan of water was heating on the stove, and she rattled the tin plates into it. "This is a disgusting conversation," she said.

Sundance said, "You're the one that brought up the dog, not me."

"He's got you there, girl," Micah remarked.

"Nobody's got me," Sarah snapped, and then she smiled. "You got me, Sundance?"

Sundance didn't answer. He heard them coming. Micah heard them too. Both men grabbed their shotguns. "I'll take the far side of the street," Micah said.

Sundance nodded. "Stay put," he told Sarah.

Sundance and Micah had taken their positions by the time Ryker and his men rode down the street at an easy canter. Ryker was in the lead. Sundance expected them to come in a blaze of gunfire, but instead Ryker reined in and waved to Sundance standing by the stable door with the shotgun dangling from one hand. Micah was out of sight on the far side of the street.

"What can I do for you?" Sundance asked Ryker. Ryker's pet hard cases were crowed in close to their boss.

"It's mighty nice of you to ask," Ryker said. "What you can do for me is get out of this town. This is going to be the last time I ask you that. Next time it'll be different."

Sundance wondered why Ryker was being so talky. There was something going on. Suddenly behind him a shotgun expolded twice. He didn't turn around. At the same time some of Ryker's hard cases reached for their guns. Sundance fired one barrel and blew a man out of the saddle. Micah fired a blast from the far side of the street and killed another. The other hard cases had their hands hovering over their guns.

"No, boys, no!" Ryker shouted as he looked straight into the mouth of the shotgun in Sundance's hands. His jaw dropped as Sarah came to the stable door with a shotgun held very steady.

"Two men came in the back way. I killed them," she said. Sundance knew she was shaking inside, but her voice was as steady as her hands.

"Didn't work, did it?" Sundance said to Ryker. "Want to try again. We still got two loads left."

"Four," Sarah said. "I reloaded." Her gun was pointing at Ryker.

"Four loads ought to take care of you. I'm not talking

86

about anybody else but you, Ryker." Sundance moved the shotgun from Ryker's belly to his face. "What about it?"

Ryker wheeled his horse and led his men out of town. •

Chapter 9

Micah cackled and helped himself to a drink of moonshine. "We sure as hell showed them Texas men. God damn if we didn't. First off I thought we was in for a real shoot-out. That was until your lady downed them two rats in the back of the stable. If she hadn't done for them we be in it for sure. Ryker was holdin' his fire till his boys got a chance to sneak up on us from the rear. He backed down quick enough when them two blasts went off one after t'other. That was nice work, young lady."

Sarah shook her head when Micah offered to pass her the whiskey bottle. "I don't want to drink, and I don't want to talk about men."

Micah drank instead. "No cause to feel bad about it. They'd have gunned down the lot of us. That includes you."

Sundance was checking his guns. Now he looked up. "Let her alone, Micah. She said she didn't want to talk about it."

"Sure," Micah said. "I just don't want your woman feeling low."

Sarah looked over at Sundance. "What else could I do?"

"Not a thing."

Sarah said, "I heard the back door creak, then there they were with guns in their hands. If I'd been a man they would have shot me down. But they held back when they saw it was a woman. I did what you told me, Sundance. I didn't aim the shotgun. I just brought it up and fired it. And then they were dead. I saw a man killed once in the hotel, but he was just shot. But those men...."

"Maybe you better have the drink," Sundance said. "It would make you feel better."

Again, she shook her head. "It wouldn't. I'm just glad we're all still alive. I'm going to go up in the loft and lie down."

After she had climbed the ladder, Micah said quietly, "Now there's a girl with grit."

"She is. Now Ryker will be looking to kill her as badly as he wants to kill us. I wish I could get her out of this town."

"You know she won't go."

"You could pack her out before they come back. Tie her if you have to."

"You sure they'll be back?"

"They'll be back. Ryker's that kind of man. Between us we killed four of his men and he came within a hair of dying himself. A sane man would let it drop."

"Then we should've shot it out."

"Ryker had too many men. More than I figured. We wouldn't have lasted in that storm of lead. I'm going to ride out and keep a watch on the south road. Ryker's probably halfway back to the herd by now. To round up more men. They may not come back tonight, but I think they will. Ryker's boiling mad so he won't want to wait to finish it. You stay here with Sarah."

Micah corked the bottle. "I'd go but I don't move so fast any more. I guess you better watch the road. I'll watch over your woman with my life."

Sundance nodded and picked up his rifle. "I won't fire any shots, give any signal," he said. "I'll just come back. We'll be set for them when they get here."

Micah said, "It's as good as we can do."

Sundance saddled Eagle and rode out through town

on the south road. Everybody in town was staying off the street, and very few lights were showing in any of the houses. All the saloons were closed; Cimarron City was like a ghost town with people still living in it. It was dark, with only a sliver of moon in the sky. The wind had some of the heat of the day left in it, but soon it would be cool.

He rode cautiously, keeping a watch for any bushwhackers Ryker might have stationed along the road. There was nothing, so he kept going until he was about three miles from town where the road went up and over a hill. From the top of the hill he could see a long way south. When they came, if they came, he could turn and be back in town before they even got close to it.

Nothing moved out on the prairie—then he heard it, the rattle of gunfire coming faintly on the wind. If the wind had been blowing from the south he might not have heard it at all. But this was a north wind. Rightaway he knew what it was, and his scalp tightened with rage and fear, and for a moment there was a fierce hatred for himself. He got hold of it quickly and pushed it out of his mind. Ryker had outsmarted him, hadn't gone back to the herd at all. He had started out on the south road, then circled the town and come back in from the north. And maybe he hadn't brought them all in from the north. Some could have come in from two other sides, sneaking through the darkened alleys of the scared town, with nobody to face up to them but a young girl and an old man.

He touched the big stallion's flanks with his heels, urging the animal to greater speed. Eagle responded immediately and the road flew away behind his steel-shod hoofs. Gunfire still came down the wind, but before he had covered two miles it began to die away.

He topped a low ridge and now he could see that something was burning far away in town. Flames licked up into the night sky. It didn't look like all the town was burning, just a small part of the far end of it, where Micah's livery was. Again, he felt the tug of real fear, but not for himself. Ryker would die for this. No matter what happened, Ryker would die for this!

At any other time he would have ridden in with caution. Caution, not fear. But he rode in boldly because there still might be a chance to save her if he got there in time. Now, instead of being quiet, the main street swarmed with people with frightened, questioning faces. So Ryker was gone: the townspeople would never crawl out of their ratholes if he had still been there.

He rode into the crowd, scattering them. He didn't care if he trampled some of them underfoot. Blaney ran into his store when he saw them. Ned Buntline was standing on the hotel porch looking up the street at the burning stable. If the New York scribbler had waved Sundance might have shot him dead. The crowd parted to let him through and he rode on down to the stable. A murmur of scared voices followed him, then in the light of the still burning stable he saw old Micah's body dangling from the hay-hoist. The old halfbreed had been shot up badly, then hoisted at the end of a rope. They must have been in a hurry because they hadn't hoisted him very high; the shotgun lay on the ground only a foot below his feet.

Sundance reached up and cut the rope with his knife, and the old man's body crumpled into a heap. He looked like a pile of old clothes. Tom Cade came running from past the stable. He was wearing nothing but pants and undershirt. His voice was out of control. Three dead men were lying in front of the livery stable.

"The girl's at my house," he said. "You better come quickly. She's been shot . . . and. . . ."

Sundance reached down and grabbed him by the sirrt. "Did they rape her?"

Cade said, "Some of them did. Come on—she's dying. Go on—I'll look after Micah."

Sundance's mouth twisted in contempt. "Like you always did."

Down the street lights were blazing in Cade's house. Men were on the porch and Sundance sent one of them sprawling when he got in his way. In the parlor, Sarah lay on a sofa with pillows behind her head. A doctor, an old man, was bending over her. Mrs. Cade and her daughter looked on with anxious eyes. The doctor looked up when Sundance came in, still carrying the rifle.

"What about it?" Sundance asked quietly. Sarah's eyes were closed and her breathing was quick and shallow. Blood from the wounds in her chest had soaked through the blanket that covered her. Her face was bruised and bloody and her long black hair was tangled about her shoulders.

The doctor shook his head. "I gave her something for the pain. That's all I can do."

Sundance gestured with the rifle barrel. "Then get out. All of you get out. Close the door."

Sarah opened her eyes when she heard his voice. Her eyelids fluttered and for a moment she was having trouble seeing him. She smiled and tried to reach out her hand. Sundance pulled a chair close to the sofa and took her hand, and for the first time since the death of his mother and father he felt a great sadness. In a few minutes Sarah would be gone, and all they had talked about doing would never be done. Her life was ebbing away; there was nothing anyone could do.

Smiling up at him, she said in a whisper, "It's all right, Jim. It doesn't even hurt now. I was afraid but now I'm not. What we had didn't last very long, did it?"

"How long doesn't matter. We had it for a while."

"You did get to love me?"

"Yes," Sundance said. "It wasn't hard." There was no use saying he was sorry. Sorry that he hadn't taken her away from this godforsaken little town. He had told her that you couldn't run away from your death. Anyway, it didn't matter how true or false that was. Not now.

She was going fast and her voice began to weaken. Then suddenly her frail body stiffened as if the pain had returned. Her voice rambled. "They came at us out of the dark. Micah shot some of them before they killed him. They shot me before I could get to the gun. Then they. . . . And after they shot me they. . . . And when they finished they shot me again. . . ."

Sarah's hand tightened on Sundance's. She shuddered and died.

Sundance stood up and opened the door. Mrs. Cade and her daughter were waiting outside with frightened faces. The daughter, a girl of about Sarah's age, was more frightened than the mother. Tom Cade was there too, pouring a drink.

"She's dead," Sundance said. "You can see to her if you want to. If you don't I'll do it."

"Of course we'll do it," Mrs. Cade said, whispering to her daughter. "It wasn't the women of the town that caused this thing."

"Somebody caused it," Sundance said.

Cade poured himself another big drink and looked at Sundance. "I guess you think we're pretty gutless."

Sundance glanced around the neat little house: the framed pictures, the factory-made lace curtains on the windows, the heavy furniture gleaming with polishing oil. Once Tom Cade had been an Indian. Now what was he—a red-white man? In the other room, behind the closed door, Sarah lay dead. Sarah, the sassy, the brave, and the loving.

"You're gutless all right," Sundance said. "Not you especially, Cade. You were better than the rest of them."

Cade held up the bottle. "You want a drink?"

"The hell with the drink! Tell me what happened. I know what happened, but tell me what you know. Where were you when it happened?"

"In bed," Cade said. "Safe in bed."

"Don't get to feeling sorry for yourself, Cade. I don't give a damn what you feel. Just get on with it."

Cade wasn't used to drinking and he smiled foolishly, then wiped the smile off his face. "I was half awake, half asleep. You know how it is when you're worried but still tired and want to sleep. No, I guess you don't. There wasn't a sound and then the yelling and the shooting started. I heard a shotgun going off, more than one, I guess, and after that a lot of other shooting. The shooting didn't last that long. Then I heard a woman screaming."

Sundance refused to think about the screaming; later he would think about it when he caught up with Ryker and his men.

"I ran to the window." Cade said, "and there was a building burning. I knew it was the stable burning. The flames lit up this whole end of the street. There was no more shooting. I didn't know where you were. I thought you were dead with the others. First thing I thought: now they're going to burn the town like there was always talk of. But they didn't, and while I was still looking out the window, Ryker went riding up and down the street, yelling in that bull voice for everybody to come out. In that same crazy bull voice he swore he'd burn the town if we didn't come out when he told us to."

"Then what?"

Cade said, "Blaney was one of the first ones out. I saw him running up the street waving his hands. Others came out. I could see everything plain in the light from the flames. I went down and Ryker was running his big horse back and forth, all his bullies trying to keep up with him. Up the street I saw the shape of a man hanging from the hay-hoist. First, I thought they'd gone for you and hung you up, but when the fire burned up brighter, I saw it wasn't."

Sundance asked what next.

Cade said, "Blaney was trying to explain something I couldn't hear to Ryker. Ryker cursed him and kicked him in the chest. Blaney went down but got up again, still running off at the mouth, I guess trying to plead with Ryker not to burn his property. Not ours—just his. I got close enough to hear what Ryker was saying. He was saying—where were you? His boys hadn't turned you up in their quick search. Blaney was saying he didn't know where you were, and didn't care, because the town didn't want you around anymore than Ryker did. Ryker didn't believe Blaney, pulled a pistol and cocked it and aimed it right at his face. Blaney started yelling and sweating, saying on his mother's grave he didn't know. Then Ryker started laughing, drinking now and them from a bottle one of his men handed him, and said he thought a yellowbelly like Blaney didn't know, or he'd tell. More of Ryker's men rode up from different parts of town and said they couldn't flush you. Maybe I'm wrong but it looked like Ryker got a scared look on his face."

Sundance said, "It'll get worse as time goes on."

"It's true," Cade said. "Ryker looked scared to me,

knowing you were still out there somewhere and alive. Coming after him for what he'd done to Sarah."

Sundance's pale eyes were deadly. "Don't mention her name, Cade. What else about Ryker?"

Cade put more whiskey in his glass. "I think Ryker, drunk or crazy or not, suddenly knew what he'd done to you, and knew all over again who you were, and what you'd—could do to him—and wanted to get away from Cimarron and wanted to get away from here as fast as he could. I think he would have burned the town, if you'd been dead. I'd say he'll never come back here, or anywhere near here. Least we have you to thank for that."

"Don't be thankful, Cade. Be glad I won't burn this town myself."

"You'd do that?"

"If I drank your whiskey, I would. I won't. Ryker won't ever bother you again. I'll see to that."

"What're you going to do to Blaney?"

"Not a thing."

"To Buntline?"

"The same."

Cade had been drinking too much whiskey. He stared at the wet, whiskey-ringed table instead of at Sundance. He said, "I'm sorry, Sundance. I should have stood with you in this."

"You'd just be dead too. We can't all be brave, Cade. No offense, but we can't. The brave ones are usually dead."

Cade said, "When will you be starting after Ryker?"

"Tomorrow. You say Ryker went out the north road, the way he came in?"

Tom Cade said yes.

"Well, that was how he came in, but that was just a blind. Ryker's going back to Texas. That's where his money and his power is. You heard that he sold the herd."

There was surprise in Cade's dark eyes. "No, I didn't. I guess he must have, if he did this."

"I figured that too. Down in Texas even the Rangers don't bother Ryker much. The Rangers are great at running down two-bit bandits, but they don't bring down the rich men much. Politics."

Cade said, "Then you won't have much of a chance to get at him there."

"It's a ways to Texas," Sundance answered, "and he's not there yet. Won't even be there the day after tomorrow. Wouldn't make any difference where he was, where he went. I'd find him. Mexico. Guatemala. South America."

"You say you'll be staying till tomorrow," Cade said. "That means you'll be staying. . . ."

"For the funerals."

"My God," said Tom Cade, "the things that people do to each other."

Sundance stood up. Enough had been said. But he said one more thing: "And do them back, Cade."

The look that Tom Cade gave Sundance was awkward. "Where are you going to stay tonight, Sundance?"

"Doesn't matter."

"We'd be glad to have you stay here. She'll—I won't say her name—will be buried from this house. I want to do that."

Well, thought Sundance, everybody couldn't be brave, but they could be decent and kind. Tom Cade wasn't brave, but he was decent, and he didn't want to think of Sarah lying under the tin-roof of the undertaker's shop.

He relented a little. "You can say her name, Cade.

She said you were pretty decent to her."

Cade ignored that. "It might be a comfort to be under the same roof on your last night with her."

"Well, yes, it would," Sundance said.

Cade said Sundance could bunk in his son's room; the boy was away at the new agricultural college in Tulsa.

Sundance carried his rifle upstairs after he put Eagle in the stable at the back of the house. The big stallion looked at him with dark liquid eyes, knowing that something was very wrong. Man and animal had been together for a long time.

Upstairs in the boy's room, he lay on the bed without even taking off his boots. In a while, Cade's wife knocked timidly on the door and asked if he wanted something to eat. Sundance said no—nothing. There was a feeling of nothingness inside his head, and he hadn't felt that way since the death of his parents. This was one time when he couldn't force himself to sleep. He lay awake for hours, staring at the ceiling, with the lamp turned low. His own spirit was burning low.

Hours later, he heard them bringing in the coffin. Hushed voices were downstairs in the hall. The door of the parlor, where Sarah lay, opened and closed. Then it opened again and Mrs. Cade came upstairs. Sundance got up off the bed. He knew what she was going to say. Did he want to take a last look at his woman before they screwed down the lid?

They had washed the blood off her face, combed her hair, put her in a fresh white dress. Her expression was mild; she might have been asleep. He stood looking at her for a long time. Then he turned to Mrs. Cade, who was standing outside the door. "You can do it now."

Then he waited for morning to come.

Chapter 10

Sundance buried Sarah and Micah the next day. He rode out to old Micah's place behind the hearse, then told the undertaker to get away from there. The coffins, hastily made, lay side by side in the sun yellowed grass while he dug the graves. They had been his only friends in Cimarron City, and it was only fitting that they should be together in death. What he would do with the rest of his life he wasn't sure. He guessed he would go on with his work, as he had always done. The only sound in the bright sunshine was the little creek that ran close to the weathered house. There were trees along the creek, and the grass was still green under the trees.

He didn't feel much of anything. All he knew was that Sam Ryker had to die; the hatred he had for the man had become cold determination. There was no hurry because Ryker was already a dead man, and nothing he might say or do could buy him back his life. He could scream and beg and say he was sorry when the time came; nothing would change. Of that Sundance was sure as he was sure of nothing else.

When the graves were finished he used a white hot poker to burn their names into two slabs of wood. Just their names—SARAH and MICAH—and nothing else. He had never known their last names; it didn't matter: they had been his friends. Now it was done, and he stood by the creek looking at the twin mounds of freshly turned earth. He didn't read over them. "I won't forget you," was all he said. He thought of the first day Sarah had come to the jail with the tray of food, of the things she said. He remembered her quick temper, and of how her face softened a moment later. There was so much to remember: they had packed a lifetime into a few days. She had wanted to make something of her life, and a bunch of savages had taken it away from her. It was time to go.

He rode south without going through Cimarron City. There was nothing left there for him, no one he ever wanted to see again. Then he remembered that he was still wearing the sheriff's star and he threw it in the dust. It didn't mean anything, not now. He had no way of knowing how long it would take to find Ryker. He'd be heading back to Texas, back to his fine house. He had a good start, but that made no difference.

When Sundance got to the top of the hill that led down to Micah's place he turned for one last look. It was hot, quiet, peaceful along the banks of the little creek. One last look, then he forced the grief from his mind. From now on he would track Ryker with the cold skill of the professional hunter. He would tackle the job ahead with patience and cunning. That was how he would do it; to rush in with hot blood would only get him killed. He wasn't afraid to die, but he wanted to live long enough to send Ryker to his grave. What happened after that wasn't important.

Two hours later he could see the narrow valley where Ryker had fattened up his huge herd. The herd was still there. He rode closer, watching for an ambush. He dismounted when he was about half a mile south of the valley and went forward on foot, leaving Eagle in the shade of a cluster of cottonwoods. The tents he had seen before were gone, and instead of Ryker's bunch there were other men guarding the herd. He wasn't even close before two men with rifles stepped out from behind a big rock. The rifles were both cocked.

"Stand easy," one of the riflemen ordered. He was

lean and lanky and he didn't sound Texas. More like Kansas. "What you doing sneaking around Mr. McCoy's herd of cows?"

The other man went behind Sundance and took his rifle and belt gun. "The man asked you a question," he said. "If we wasn't peaceable folk you'd be dead by now."

He sounded Kansas too.

"I'm looking for Sam Ryker," Sundance said. There was nothing to be lost by telling the truth. "He killed my woman and a friend of mine last night. I'm going to kill him when I find him."

The lanky man said, "Then you'd be this Jim Sundance. We know about the killing. One of the boys just got back from town with supplies. God damned shame. Ryker's a son of a bitch sure enough and more power to you when you catch up with him. You could be Sundance. It ain't up to us to let you go. You're going to have to talk to Mr. McCoy."

"The big cattle buyer from up in Kansas?"

"Kansas and Chicago—the real McCoy. Nobody bigger. That's him down by the creek soaking his feet." The lanky man pointed with the rifle.

They held their guns on Sundance as they walked him down to meet a heavy-set middle aged man in a dark town suit and a derby hat. The legs of his trousers were rolled up and his feet were in the water. This was the legendary Joseph McCoy, the Chicago beef buyer who was responsible for half the boom-towns in Kansas. He had pushed the railroad through to towns like Abilene that were just wide places in the road before he came along. He was a tough, hard man but nobody ever said he wasn't honest.

"What have you got there, Nathan?" he asked without taking his feet out of the water.

Nathan was the lanky man. "Caught him sneaking up

on the herd," he said. "Claims to be looking for Sam Ryker. I guess he's this Jim Sundance. Says he's going to kill Ryker."

"Somebody ought to kill him," McCoy said. "That was a bad thing he did in Cimarron." Without getting up, McCoy reached out his hand and Sundance shook it.

"Sit down a minute," McCoy said. "Ryker's long gone from here. I got here yesterday and we dickered a long time about the price of his beef. We couldn't fix on a fair price, then he took most of his bunch and rode into town. Said he wouldn't get back to making a deal till he cleared up some pressing business. Then last night he came back in a mighty big hurry, his horse all sweated, and took my offer without a word. Well, sir, that surprised the hell out of me because I had no idea what the bastard had done. I wouldn't have bought a God damned cow at any price if I'd known. You have to believe that, Mr. Sundance."

Sundance said he did. "When did he leave?"

"Soon as I gave him the money. Didn't even wait till first light. Just took his bunch and started out in the dark. Wasn't my business to ask why the hurry. I was glad to see the last of that man. I knew there was something eating on him though. It was like he'd lost his nerve. I'm awful sorry about your woman, Mr. Sundance. Anything I can do to help you on your way. Supplies, money, a fresh horse? You'll be taking on a rotten bunch of men."

Sundance stood up. McCoy got up too. "I don't need anything, Mr. McCoy," Sundance said. "But I thank you anyway. You're pretty sure he's headed for Texas?"

"I would say yes to that. He rules the roost in his part of the state. Figures he'll be safe, I guess. Looking at you, I'd say he's dead wrong. You had anything to eat today?"

Sundance hadn't thought about it. "Not since yesterday."

McCoy pulled on his socks and boots. "Have to eat, Mr. Sundance. You'll stay and have a bite with me." He waved the two guards away.

Later they ate two big steaks dished up by an old Chinaman with a flat hat and a pigtail. Sundance didn't realize how hungry he was until he smelled the meat cooking on a grill over a bed of coals. McCoy said, "Never do I butcher a cow I just bought. Meat's too tough if you don't let it season a while. Always carry my own supply of steak. Ah, what the hell am I saying? You don't want to talk about beef."

"That's all right, Mr. McCoy," Sundance said. He liked McCoy.

"Watch out for Ryker all the time," McCoy said. "I know the man and know what I'm talking about. A few years back he used to take his cows up to Kansas till they drove him out. Too bad they didn't hang him instead. This whole country would be better off with him six feet under. Just now I said watch out for him. He's crazy in the head, but that doesn't say he isn't smart. He'll do what you won't expect him to do. Rat smart is what he is and he'll round on you like a God damned rat. My advice is wear him down, run him ragged, isolate him from that bunch of gunnies he has working for him."

"That's what I plan to do, Mr. McCoy. I guess I'll be going now. I thank you for the meal."

Sundance whistled and Eagle came at a gallop from the shade of the trees. The big stallion whinnied with pleasure at the sight of his master.

"No wonder you didn't want another horse," McCoy said, holding out his hand again.

Sundance mounted up.

"Will you do something for me, Mr. Sundance?" Joseph McCoy asked.

103

"If I can."

"Give him one for me."

Sundance nodded. He liked McCoy all right. Just talking to the man had made him feel better. The whole world wasn't made up of Blaneys and Ned Buntlines— or Rykers. There were a few decent people—not many—but some. He turned the stallion and rode back to the road.

Ryker had a good start on him, a lot longer than he had figured, but he had gone without sleep to get away in a hurry. He would have to sleep sooner or later. No man could go more than two or three days without sleep. After that, if he tried it, he wouldn't be any good. Years back when Sundance was hunting the men who had killed his mother and father he had gone without sleep for four days and nights, but at the end of that time he was seeing things that didn't exist and hearing voiced that weren't there. And when he finally slept it was bad sleep filled with nameless fears. He hoped it would be like that for Ryker: never knowing when retribution would come out of the dark.

Sundance guessed that Ryker would post men on his back trail. These would be the meanest men he had, the best paid of the bunch, and there would be a bonus if they could come along later and bring his head in a sack to prove that the job had been done.

He rode on without hurry for the rest of the day. At times when he saw places up ahead where an ambusher might lie in wait he took his horse off the road and circled far out. But still there was nothing, and so he rode on until it was dark and then he made camp far off the road, in a sandy hollow. There was water and grass for Eagle. He made a small fire, one that could be kicked into darkness with a bootful of sand. He wasn't hungry. There was dried meat in his saddlebag, but instead he filled a small pipe with the Mexican weed *potaguaya* and smoked it with his back resting against a flat rock.

And while he smoked, sucking the sweetish smoke deep into his lungs, he thought of so many things, but mostly of Sarah. Now and then he smiled when he thought of her. The marijuana didn't dull his mind; if anything, it sharpened it. Regret had left him. In a way regret was guilt, and he no longer felt guilty about anything. Sarah was gone and maybe she was better off. He forced himself to admit that finally and at last there would have been no future for them. They had talked about it so much that they were ready to believe it.

It made no difference now.

Sundance stifled the fire with sand and wrapped himself in his blanket.

In the morning, well before first light, he was on his way again after a breakfast of cold water and dried meat. In the half light the prairie stretched out as if the wet, waving sea of grass had no boundaries. Up ahead, about fifty miles away, he knew there was a sprawl of low hills, and past there it would be Texas. After that it was hundreds of miles to where Ryker had his big spread in Deaf Smith County. But it could end long before that. It could end anywhere.

Long before the sun was full up, the grass was dry and it was hot, and all he could tell from the road was that a lot of men were riding south at one time. When the sun was noon-high he watered Eagle and ate some meat. The only man he met on the long stretch of road was an old Indian in a wagon. The old man said a large party of men had passed that way, heading south, early the day before. They had stopped to fill their canteens at the well on his farm. Yes, there was a big man with white hair. He was their leader, he gave the orders. He had thrown down a silver dollar to pay for the water. He had been angry when the old Indian said there was no whiskey in the house, but he let him keep the dollar.

"Then they rode on. Very fast," the old Indian said. "The man with the white hair had a loud voice."

Sundance thanked the old man and rode on. At noon he let Eagle drink while he boiled up a pot of coffee near an old cattle tank. He heated beans without taking them out of the can. He was traveling light. So was Ryker: he had left the chuck wagon back in the valley.

Eating the bubbling soldier beans and drinking bitter black coffee, Sundance began to figure it out. So far he hadn't done much of that. He was all right now; the numb feeling in his head had gone; his killer instinct was as strong as ever. He knew he would go on living; there would be no suicidal attacks against too-heavy odds. Anyway, the odds would get better as he went along: he would kill some of Ryker's men, others would desert. Those would be the riders who just worked for a living. They would duck out when they got the chance, men with no others names than Slim or Bandy or Zack, and hope never to hear the name Sundance again. He wasn't even sure what all of them looked like, so there was no hope of ever catching up with all of them. The gunslingers would stay, maybe five or six, in all. They had done the killing and the raping. To them the murder and rape of an Indian girl would have less importance than smoking a cigarette.

Most likely, they would make their first try at him in the hills. The country where he was now was flat except for a few dips and swells. Not much cover anywhere. Ryker wouldn't stay around. He'd leave some of his

106

gunmen behind and keep on going. Ryker was tough, but he'd be getting tired by now. Sure, he could grab a few hours sleep here and there. But he'd be sleeping with one eye open, and sleep like that could wear out a man faster than staying awake.

One advantage to Sundance was how Ryker looked: his massive body and bone-white hair. All his life he had used his great size and bull's voice to set him apart from other men. Now they would mark him like a signpost. People who saw Ryker never forgot him, so all Sundancce had to do was keep on asking questions.

Sundance finished the beans and buried the empty can; only the white man left his trash to clutter up the land. It was hot and the range of hills shimmered about thirty miles ahead. He mounted up and rode on through the day. The sun was beginning to make its westward slide by the time he reached the foothills.

He made cold camp in a dry wash. After making a mound of dead wood and rocks, he covered it with his blanket and sat motionless behind a boulder about thirty yards. It was dark now, not a sound except for some small animal scratching in the brush. He threw a rock, and whatever it was scurried away. There were no sounds after that. He sat for hours, alert and still. He had trained himself never to be impatient, never to be restless. When it was well after midnight he went to sleep where he was. Now and then he woke up and listened for sounds. Nothing.

Next morning he didn't start out until the light was good. The feeling of impending danger prickled along his spine. It would come soon; his instinct rather than his brain told him that men were waiting to kill him. He didn't question the feeling, for it was seldom wrong. How many men? When Ryker came into town the first time he had about twenty-five men. He had lost four.

When he came back for the attack he lost three more. That put his number at less than twenty, and some of those twenty might have already ducked out on him. He had six real hard cases. These men were his personal bodyguard, and he wouldn't want to throw them all into one fight, so likely as not he would split them. That meant Sundance had to face three men, maybe four. All this was guessing; instinct didn't tell you anything about numbers.

They would pick the best place they could find. That wasn't what he would have done because a good place for an ambush isn't hard to spot, if you know what to look for. They would set up a crossfire, two men on opposite sides of the road, one back a bit from the other so they wouldn't get hit by their own bullets; another man probably dead ahead. A fourth man, if there was one, could be anywhere.

He rode away from the road, climbing a long slope and going over it. The other side of the slope was covered with sliding shale. He got down and led Eagle to the bottom. He climbed another long slope looking for an opening in the thick thorn bush that grew along the crest. It took a while to find it, but fifteen minutes later he was at the bottom of an old dry waterbed that snaked into the hills.

In most places the dry river wasn't more than a mile from the road. It couldn't be seen from the road, not even from a high place, because of the line of ridges in between. Here and there, it was grown over with brush, and he had to fight his way through. After he had gone about two miles he had to climb over a rockslide. Past there the dead river grew narrow and shallow and soon it began to be choked with brush. It was time to see what there was to see.

He led Eagle up through a wide split in the

riverbank. Then there a long climb to the top of a ridge. Two more ridges lay between him and the road. It took a long time to get to the safe slope of the last ridge. The last ridge was higher than the others. If there was anything to be seen there was a good chance of seeing it from there. Leaving Eagle out of sight, he inched his way to the crest of the ridge. His eyes ran along the road as it twisted its way into the hills.

He saw the horses before the men. The three horses were tied behind a big jumble of rocks, out of sight to anybody coming down from Oklahoma. At first he didn't see anything else, but now his eyes were fixed on another scatter of rocks about a hundred yards ahead of the horses. That's where they had to be. The road was narrow at that point, just the spot a bushwhacker would choose. They knew their business all right, and maybe they knew it too well.

· He waited. Then he saw a movement in the rocks on the near side of the road. A man took off his hat and wiped the sweat off his face. For Sundance that was all it took: he had a fix on one of them. He stayed where he was until he figured where the others were. Then he saw the second man, high in a crack in the rocks facing down the road. The last man didn't show himself.

First thing was to run off the horses. Nothing rattled a man more than to find himself afoot in strange country. Sundance ran along the safe side of the ridge until he was directly above the horses. Even if the man on the high ground turned around he wouldn't be able to see him.

Sundance ran lightly down the slope, hardly making a sound in moccasined feet. The horses whinnied nervously when he came close, and he spoke to them soothingly until they quieted down. Then, using all his strength, he uprooted the bush to which they were

Chapter 11

Sundance was halfway up the slope by the time the horses galloped past the first ambusher high in the rocks. "God damn horses are getting away!" he heard him yell. Boots scraped on rock as he dropped down from his perch, cursing and yelling. Sundance couldn't see any of them yet, but he knew the other two bushwhackers were coming out of their holes. Quickly he climbed up in the crack in the rocks where the first shooter had been. This was the best place to shoot from. If he could get them together on the narrow road there was no way he could miss.

There they were, running after the horses. Sundance sighted the rifle on one man but didn't fire. He would get them coming back. The horses hadn't run far, no more than two hundred yards from the ambush point. The bush slowed them down and now they stood sweating and nervous. Approaching them cautiously, fearful that they would spook again, the three men unhitched the reins and began to lead them back. Sundance let them come, keeping out of sight as they got closer. He recognized two of them as hard cases; the third man he didn't know. In a minute or two Ryker was going to lose three top guns. The plan had worked fine.

It was time for the three gunslingers to die. Sundance thought of Sarah as he sighted in on the first man's chest. He was a big man in a dark blue flannel shirt and a floppy hat rammed down hard on his bullet head. It had to be done fast. Sundance put the sight on the big man's heart and squeezed the trigger and while he was still falling he swung the rifle and killed the second man. The horses spooked and the last man tried to make a dive for the rocks. The bullet caught him in mid-air and he went down in a sprawl of arms and legs. Suddenly it was quiet except for the horses' hoofs drumming on the road as they galloped away.

One of the men moved and Sundance shot him again. Then, sighting carefully, he shot the others. Nothing moved after that. Sundance climbed down from the rock and looked at the three bodies. He took their guns and threw them far into the rocks. His only regret was that the three killers had died so easily. If there had been time he would have made them suffer. But they were dead, and in the end that was all that mattered.

He mounted up and stayed on the road. There might be another ambush up ahead, but he'd have to take his chances on that. If there was one, he guessed it wouldn't be soon. What he hoped was that Ryker would get confident, figuring his killers had done their work. He might even ease up, stop off in some town along the way. Ryker was the kind of man who liked his whiskey and women more than most.

Sundance didn't know this part of the country; as near as he could tell, there was a town called Longhorn just over the Texas line. It was all flat country after that. Well grassed and flat as a flapjack.

Sundance kept going, stopping now and then to scan the hills in front of him. There was nothing. It was getting on toward late afternoon when he saw the buzzards flapping their wings by the side of the road, and he knew that whatever it was wasn't dead yet. It could just be a dead horse, it could be anything.

He rode cautiously now, the rifle ready in his hand. Then he saw that it was a man, a young cowhand with blood caked all over his shirt. Sundance knew him to be one of Ryker's men. He climbed down and waved the buzzards away with his hat. They flapped away screeching but didn't go far.

There was death in the young rider's face, but he was still alive. Just barely. His eyes fluttered open when Sundance got close. His mouth jerked several times before he was able to speak. "Water," he mumbled. "I got to have water!"

Sundance knelt beside him "Where's Ryker?" he said roughly.

"Ryker shot me," the cowboy whispered. "I tried to get away from him—and he shot me! Called me a deserter—and he shot me. Please give me water!"

"How far ahead is he?" Sundance said, making no move to give his canteen.

"Maybe a day. No way to tell."

"You were there when they burned the stable?"

"I was there, but I didn't use my gun. Ryker said he'd kill any man that didn't go along. I guess I'm about dead."

Sundance felt no pity for the dying man. "You will be," he said. He stood up and shot him in the head.

Well, he thought with bitter satisfaction, it looked like Ryker was losing men left and right. The dead man didn't look like he'd been any kind of hard case, but he'd been there, and a man ought to be ready to die before he'd help kill a harmless girl.

It was getting dark now but Sundance rode on into the hills. He had to close the distance that lay between him amd Ryker. It was about midnight when he reached the highest point in the hills. Then the road began to run down into Texas. He watered Eagle and kept on going. A few hours later he saw lights far below on the flat. That would be Longhorn, and it looked like somebody was keeping late hours. It took him another hour and a half before he could make out the sprawl of the town, dark and quiet except for one building still blazing with light. The saloon.

He rode in to the edge of town, then dismounted and went through an alley until he was in back of the saloon. Two horses were hitched out in front; there was a lot of noise inside. It was dark behind the saloon, and the ground was littered with rusted cans and empty bottles. He moved one foot at a time expecting gunfire to erupt at any moment, knowing that this could be another of Ryker's tricks. But nobody shot at him, and then he was at the back door of the saloon. He tried the door; it wasn't locked.

A gun went off and a man started to laugh. Then he let out a Texas holler. "I'm the meanest son of a bitch that ever came down the pike!" he yelled. It wasn't Ryker's voice though it was loud and all Texas. The gun went off again. "And I'll gut-shoot the first man that says I ain't. I shot up more saloons than you got bottles behind that bar. I can rassle a grizzly bear, knock down a buffalo with a blow of my fist. Iffen a rattler bites me he dies. Black John Keegan is who I am. The Fort Worth Terror is what they call me, and I ain't afraid of no man alive."

Sundance knew the name. Keegan was a bully and a brawler. Mostly he was a trail boss, one of the toughest and maybe the toughest. Sundance eased open the door and stepped into the back room of the saloon. Light from the saloon came through the half-open door. Keegan was still bragging out in front.

Sundance stood in the darkness watching him. Keegan was a big man in his middle thirties. He hadn't shaved lately and his ham-like face was matted with coarse black stubble. It grew up high on his flat cheekbones and gave him the appearance of wearing a mask. He wore a dirty checked shirt and a sweat-stained sombrero. The only men in the saloon were Keegan, a scared looking bartender and a drunk snoring at a table.

Sundance stepped into the light and the bartender saw him first. His mouth hung open at the sight of the tall, yellow haired halfbreed. Keegan was still letting the world know how mean he was. Then he stopped abruptly and reached across the bar and grabbed the bartender by the shirt.

"You ain't listening to what I'm saying, you baldy headed son of a bitch. And what in hell are you gaping at?"

The bartender jerked his head toward Sundance and Keegan turned with a look of astonishment. "Well, I'll be God damned to the fires of hell. Who and what are you? You wouldn't be pointing that rifle at me, would you. I'd have to consider that unfriendly, if you was."

Sundance didn't move the rifle. "I'm looking for a man named Sam Ryker. You seen him?"

"I don't take to questions asked at the point of a gun," Keegan growled. "And what's the idea of sneaking in the back door in the dead of night?"

"Just being careful," Sundance said. "You don't work for Ryker, do you?"

Keegan had a holstered Colt, but he kept his hand away from it. He picked up a bottle off the bar with his gun hand and drank from it. "You sure ask a lot of questions for a back door sneak. It's my business who I work for. But the answer to the last question is no. I wouldn't work for that son of a bitch if he made me a partner. Now I'll tell you something else. I don't like your looks, my friend. Nobody points a gun at Black John Keegan."

With surprising speed for a man of his size, Keegan

threw the bottle at Sundance. It hit him a glancing blow on the side of the head but didn't break. Instinctively, he fired the rifle, but the shot went wild. For a moment he was stunned and before he could recover Keegan was all over him, yanking the rifle from his hands and punching him in the belly at the same time. The big man had fists like chunks of wood, knobbed and scarred by years of hard work.

Keegan hit him again, hammering him back toward the wall. Sundance shook his head, trying to clear the bright spots that danced in front of his eyes. He blocked the next punch and hit Keegan as hard as he could. The big man grunted but bored in again, blowing whiskey breath in Sundance's face. He kept growling like a bear. Sundance's head was clear now, but he was taking punishment. Keegan was taller than he was by several inches, and fifty pounds heavier, and there was no fat on his frame. Keegan used his bulk to drive Sundance back against the wall. Sundance knew that if the big brawler got him in a bear hug he could break his spine. Keegan tried for a bear hug, but Sundance broke loose and punched Keegan in the face. Keegan's face was as hard as the rest of him. He lunged in again and this time he wrapped his arms around Sundance and began to squeeze. Sundance felt the breath going out of him; in a minute he would begin to lose consciousness. The thought of dying while Ryker was still alive made him desperate.

Keegan grinned with brutal satisfaction and kept on squeezing. Then, in a wild surge of strength, Sundance smashed his forehead into the grinning face. Keegan's nose snapped and he yelled with pain. Sundance brought up his knee into Keegan's crotch, and the bear hug was broken. Now it was Sundance's turn to dish out the punishment. He bored in, using his fists like hammers. Keegan staggered. Sundance lay back and hit him with all his strength. Keegan went down like a felled tree and lay still.

"Dear sweet Christ!" the bartender said, gaping at the two big men. "You knocked down Black John Keegan! No man ever did that."

"Give me water," Sundance said, and when he got it he dumped it in the big man's face. Then he picked up the rifle and pointed it. "I was asking you a question. Stay down. You can talk where you are. You jumped me. That says you work for Ryker."

In spite of his broken nose, Keegan began to laugh. "You sure can hit hard, you know that. Who in hell are you?"

"You still say you don't work for Ryker?"

Keegan growled, "I told you and I told you. I don't work for Ryker."

"Then why did you jump me?"

"I didn't like your ways of doing things. People don't point guns at me."

"There's one pointing at you now."

Keegan grimaced with pain. "Who in hell are you, stranger? And what's all this business with Sam Ryker? Look, I'm all through jumping you. I need a God damned drink."

Sundance said, "All right, get up. I'll blast you if you try anything else."

The bartender set up another bottle and Keegan threw coins on the bar. Then he sat down heavily at a table and poured a drink, slopping whiskey all over the table. He stared at Sundance. "You mind saying who you are?"

Sundance said who he was, then told Keegan why he was after Ryker. When he finished Keegan shook his head. "The dirty murdering bastard. Jesus! To do a thing like that. I'm sorry I came at you, Sundance. If I'd of known..."

"Well, I didn't mean to break your nose. You were fixing to kill me."

"I probably wouldn't have," Keegan said. "The hell with the nose. It's been broken before. One time with a pick handle. I like what you did with your head. First time that trick's been used on me. It's a hell of a thing about your woman. About Ryker, he came through here sure enough. Looked like the devil was on his tail. I guess that's you. The son of a bitch asked me to sign on with him. Said he'd pay me double. I told him what he could do with his stinking money. It'll be a sorry day when I have to work for the likes of him. You got your work cut out for you, you know that?"

Sundance nodded. "No matter."

Keegan said, "I'd sure hate to have you after me. But you better know that Ryker is a big man down where he lives. He owns the law and just about everything else."

Sundance asked the bartender if he had any coffee, and the bald headed man went to get it.

"How much do you know about Ryker?" Keegan asked. "The more you know about a man the easier it is to kill him."

Sundance said he didn't know all that much.

Keegan said abruptly, "You know the bastard is scared of snakes, Gila monsters, things like that. I don't know how come he is, but he is. A big tough man like that. I guess everybody's afraid of something. One time in El Paso some drunk taunted him about it in a saloon in front of a crowd of men. Ryker went wild and shot the man in both legs. Crippled him for life."

Sundance was reaching for the coffee pot the barkeep brought in when Keegan yelled, "Watch out! The door!" Sundance and Keegan drew their guns at the

118

same time. A man was aiming a rifle across the double doors. He fired and Keegan took the bullet instead of Sundance. Sundance fired and hit the killer squarely in the forehead. When he got to the door there was nobody in the street but the dead man.

Keegan lay on the floor coughing out his life. The bullet had ripped through a lung. His face twisted in pain. "I was just a mite too slow," he whispered. "You get him?"

"I got him, Black John," Sundance said, thinking this is one more thing I owe Sam Ryker.

Keegan's body jerked violently, and he died.

Sundance looked down at the dead brawler. No doubt he had been a brutal man, and maybe a stupid one as well, but there had been something decent about him. The trouble with some men was that they got to believing their own legends, glorying in the stories other men told about them. And yet he had died saving the life of a man he had just done his best to kill. There was no understanding people, no matter how long you lived.

He took money from his pocket and put it on the bar. "You know if he had any family?" he asked the bartender, who wanted nothing more than to close his doors for the night. "He ever say where they might be? A wife, kids?"

The bartender shook his head. "Don't know a thing about him. Mostly what he did was brag about how tough he was, all the saloons he broke up. Got into town yesterday. Started drinking and stayed over an extra day. On his way north, he said. Montana I guess he said. Had a top-hand job waiting for him up there. I just hoped he wouldn't wreck my place before he moved on."

Sundance shoved the money across the whiskey-wet

bar. "That should be enough to buy him a decent burial."

"It's enough," the bartender said, picking up the money.

"Bury him decent," Sundance. "Get a stone made, put his name on it. Don't take his gun or boots. Do what you like with his horse."

"Anything you say, mister. I'll tell the county sheriff what happened when he gets over this way. Longhorn isn't big enough to have law of its own."

"I don't care about the sheriff," Sundance said. "Just bury Keegan right. Come out front and take a look at the man I killed. Bring a light."

The bartender didn't want to go, but the edge in Sundance's voice prodded him.

Outside, the wind whipped the flame of the lamp against the glass chimney, streaking it with black. Sundance took the lamp and held it close to the dead man's face. His rifle lay beside him. He had been no more than twenty-five but all the teeth he was missing gave his sallow face an old, mean shrunken look. His thin lips were drawn back in the grin of death. The bullet hole in his forehead looked very neat, as if it had been drilled by a bit-and-brace.

"You ever see him before?" Sundance asked. It was important to know whether the dead man had been one of Ryker's steady hands or some stray killer picked up along the way.

Still scared, the bartender nodded vigorously. "Rode in with Ryker's bunch," he said. "The other men knew him, called him Dave, something like that. I thought they were going to get drunk and break up the place, but they didn't stay that long. Ryker said they had to get moving. Keegan there told the truth about Ryker wanting him to ride along. Keegan told Ryker to dirty himself. For a minute I thought Ryker was going to draw on him, but he let it drop. I was purely glad to see them leave. Keegan was bad enough all by himself. What you want done with the Ryker man?"

"Nothing," Sundance answered. "Throw him in a hole."

He mounted up and rode into the darkness.

Chapter 12

He traveled on into the night. Ryker had used up some time, not much, in the saloon, but he still had a fair headstart. By riding all night Sundance could cut his edge somewhat. By morning Ryker couldn't be that far ahead. Beyond Longhorn it was prairie country, so Ryker wouldn't have to stay on the regular trails. He could send a few men off as a diversion, then take another direction himself. Sundance would look for a sign but couldn't read more into it than there was. He would have to count on guesswork when the time came.

Two hours before dawn he got down, unsaddled Eagle and let the big stallion drink. Then he rubbed the animal down with handfuls of grass. He chewed meat, and drank water himself. When all this was done he slept until the stars began to fade and the darkness thinned out.

Texas stretched out in front of him like a sea—an ocean—of grass. It was a land as limitless as the sea itself, and the towns scattered across its vast distances were the ports of call. Deaf Smith County was over west toward the New Mexico line. Hereford was the county seat, and that's where Ryker would head finally, though he might do some fancy dodging along the way. It was good cow country over that way, as good as any in the state. Sundance knew that Ryker's ranch began about fifteen miles outside town. It was about the biggest in that part of the country, and he kept on trying to make it bigger. He had a fine house and gave lavish parties and dinners for the politicians, buying their support for the future when he was ready to make his move into politics. They said he had his eye on the United States Senate or the Texas governor's mansion. It was long past time to cut him down to size. It would be good to kill him, something that should have been done a long time before.

Sundance knew the first fair sized town he would come to on his way west was Wichita Falls. Now and then he checked the trail and it looked like the Ryker bunch were staying together. That was good because he didn't want to ride all over the country looking for them. So far everything Ryker had thrown at him had failed, which was not to say that the next time he wouldn't succeed. Sundance wasn't one of those men who believed that he couldn't be killed. Hickok believed that and died at the hand of a nervous little backshooter. You had to figure the odds, then accept them or try something else. That was the only way you stayed alive, or hoped to.

He rode all day and they were still ahead of him so it figured that Ryker's bunch had spare horses. He knew that for sure when, just about nightfall, he came on the camp of a freighting outfit. Five tired looking horses were in a rope corral and the men gathered around a fire were shaggy bearded and mean looking. They saw him coming and straightened up. They all had rifles, all buffalo guns.

"Hello the camp!" Sundance yelled from far out.

"Come ahead!" one of the men yelled back.

They didn't point their rifles at him, but they were all ready to shoot. The five wagons were clean enough; there was still the stink of blood hides. But instead of untreated buffalo hides there were crates and barrels. A lot of the oldtime buffalo hunters had gone into the freighting business; washing down the wagons with coal oil didn't do much for the stink. Once a wagon was soaked in old buffalo blood it was impossible to get it out. The five men at the campfire smelled just as bad as the wagons.

"What might we do for you?" the boss freighter asked. A chunky man in his early forties, he might have looked all right if he took a bath and trimmed his hair and beard. He had all his teeth, an unusual thing for a buffalo hunter or whatever he was now. He wore a blanket lined canvas coat, stained and dirty. His small blue eyes were shrewd.

"I'm looking for a man named Sam Ryker," Sundance said. "Big man, white hair, riding a Morgan horse." He didn't say anything about the five horses, didn't even look at them. At the best of times these buffalo hunters were wild and dangerous. They were the scum of the West, hated by the Indians and shunned by everybody else. They took a kind of left-handed pride in being hated and despised. They asked for nothing and got nothing.

"I might have seen him," the boss freighter said. "It'll cost you a few dollars to find out."

Sundance asked, "How many dollars?"

"I'd say ten if you got that much."

Sundance hadn't stepped down because nobody invited him. He gave the shaggy man the money.

"My name is Bowdry," the shaggy man volunteered. "You want something to eat? Got a couple of tough old birds cooking in a stew. Got them in a trade for some shotgun shells. Too old to fry."

It was all right to get down now. "Sure," Sundance said. "I wouldn't mind a plate of stew."

There was no way to hurry these men. Bowdry was

the only one who talked and that didn't happen until they were downing the stew. It was all right, Sundance decided. It was stew and it was hot and he was hungry.

Bowdry jerked his head toward the rope corral. "Those are Ryker's horses, used to be. Got them real cheap. Guess your friend is in a hurry. Yep, he passed through all right. Five men with him. Now you'll be wanting to know how long ago, seeing he's such a good friend of yourn."

Bowdry had a sense of humor. "I won't charge you extra for that. I'm poor and I'm not honest, but I have my own ways, you understand."

Sundance nodded.

"Maybe twelve hours ago," Bowdry said, looking at Eagle. "You wouldn't want to trade that stallion, would you? I'll trade you the five Ryker horses for the stallion. I guess you don't."

Sundance began to scrape off his plate. "I like that horse," he said.

Bowdry laughed hoarsely. "So do I. Never fear—we ain't going to try to take him from you."

Sundance stood up, not sure they wouldn't try. "Don't get tempted. You'd be first."

Bowdry laughed again. It was a real laugh. "Don't I know it," he said. "I don't mind you, halfbreed, so I'm going to tell you something else for nothing."

"What's that?"

"Ryker paid us money to kill you. Guess he figured you'd spot the horses and know cow ponies wouldn't belong with a freighting outfit. Then you'd want to know how we got them. While you were stepping down from your horse all five of us would let fly at the same time. Five buffalo guns all going off together would play hell with you. Not a man of us would miss. We been shooting all our life. What do you think of that?"

"I know you wouldn't miss," Sundance said easily. "You still figure to do it?"

"God no!" Bowdry. "Wouldn't have told you if we did." For a moment the boss freighter was truculent. "We still could if we wanted to, and don't you forget it." He laughed. "I told you I have my ways and drygulching isn't one of them. Anyhow, I didn't like the way Ryker looked and talked. Sure I took his money. I'll take anybody's money, dirty and clean. Life's been downright miserable since the buffalo disappeared. Now what did they want to do that for? Wouldn't have made that much difference if they hadn't, I suppose. The ladies back east ain't buying as much fur robes as they was. Be seeing you now."

"Thanks for the information and the stew," Sundance said, still wary. He swung up on Eagle's back, ready to start killing. This was one time, if the shooting started, he'd be sure to die. But nothing happened and by the time he rode away they had already turned back to the fire.

Paying the buffalo men to drygulch him was the smartest trick Ryker had tried so far. Would there be others? He guessed there would though by now Ryker might be willing to believe he was dead. By all odds he should be dead. Ryker had only five men now; they were all running scared.

Traveling was easy and he kept going, a tall, relentless man on a surging horse that nobody could stop. There was a moon and it washed the prairie in cold yellow light. The wild felt good in his face. A few hours later he saw the lights of Wichita Falls in the distance. It was about nine o'clock and the big cow town was fully awake... and maybe Ryker was there.

He rode in two hours later and the town was shaking with noise and light. It even had street lamps and they were all lit. He decided to take a look around and that would take some doing in a big burg like that.

Taking the Winchester in its beaded scabbard, he started first with the saloons. He drank a few glasses of beer and nobody stared at him too hard. This town was a crossroads and all kinds of people came through. In the last place he looked, the biggest and the gaudiest, they had rooms for rent and BATHS FOR SALE 50¢. It was a three story frame building painted a bright yellow. He went into the glare and uproar. The long bar was three deep in drinkers and against a back wall a real band—cornet, fiddle and piano—was making a lot of noise. Three bartenders, all dressed alike in candy striped shirts with rosette armbands, were working like madmen setting up drinks and pulling corks out of beer bottles. A sign said the beer was ice cold. Five couples, men and saloon girls, were ripping up the floor to the music of the band. A fat pretty woman with a beauty spot on her cheek went up the steps to the bandstand and sang with the band, or did her best to. Sundance guessed the band was playing one tune and the fat woman was singing another. It didn't matter; she wouldn't have been heard anyway. The air was blue with tobacco smoke and the stink of stale beer and in spite of the fifty cent baths there was plenty of old sweat. Above the bar a huge painting of a buxom, half-naked woman simpered down at the spenders.

Two men, both very drunk, got up from a table and staggered out. Sundance sat down and looked around for a waiter. Instead a dark-skinned girl with oiled black hair came over and sat in the other chair. She was pretty and painted and might have been Mexican or Indian. It was hard to tell what she was under all the paint. A strong smell of cheap perfume came across the table.

127

She smiled at Sundance. "I haven't seen you in here before."

"That's right," Sundance said. "You the waiter?"

She laughed a fake laugh and fanned herself with a pearl-backed fan. "Do I look like a waiter?"

Sundance said, "I guess you don't. You don't have a mustache."

Her accent was faintly Spanish. "That's not a nice thing to say."

"It was a compliment."

"Oh!" She was puzzled for a moment. "Oh! You were making a joke."

"What about a drink?" Sundance asked. "Get me a bottle of that ice cold beer. You have what you like."

"Is champagne too much? I don't like to drink anything else. I don't like beer and I'm not used to whiskey."

I'll bet you aren't, Sundance thought. There was something about her that sent out a danger signal. For one thing she was nervous and smiling too hard, and that wasn't just because of her job. Maybe he was wrong. What the hell! He decided to play her along for a while and see what happened.

While he waited for her to get back he studied the rows of drinkers at the bar. Some had their backs to him; no one looked familiar; none of Ryker's men was in the faro game going on the far side of the bandstand.

Now and then one of the cowboys would go upstairs with a girl. He watched the girl with the Spanish accent get bottles and glasses from a bartender. She threaded her way daintily through the crowd, smiling all the time. After setting down the bottles she said, "The champagne is four dollars."

Sundance gave her the money and she tucked it between her small, firm breasts. Then he uncorked the champagne and poured a glass for her. It was probably ginger ale or clear cider with gas blown through it to make it fizz. Whatever it was, she made a great show of enjoying it.

"Ah, I was so thirsty!" she said, "and cold champagne is so good."

She wanted to finish the bottle in a hurry. "Beer is fine," Sundance said, drinking a little of it.

The musicians had stopped playing and were sucking on mugs of beer. But even with the band out of action for a few minutes there was still a lot of noise. Music or no music, some of the dancers were still dancing.

"My name is Marisol," the girl said as if that meant something special. She paused to look at him. She was nervous all right. "How are you called?"

"Sundance." There was nothing lost by asking about Ryker, so he did.

She smiled a quick tight smile. "Oh no, I have never seen a man like that."

There was more glass than champagne, so called, in the bottle, and after she drank three glasses it was empty. She gave him an expectant smile.

"I thought you might have seen him," Sundance said. "He'd be hard to miss."

"Then I would have seen him if he had been here. Is that not so?"

"Sure," Sundance agreed, taking another sip of beer. It wasn't as ice cold as the sign proclaimed.

She upended the bottle and let a trickle run into her glass. "Would you mind if I had more champagne?"

"Not a bit."

Marisol might have been her name. Marisol gestured toward Sundance's half empty glass. "You are not drinking your beer?" She made a face. "I don't blame you. Why don't you drink some whiskey instead? I can get you good whiskey. What Mr. Kelly drinks."

The big saloon was called Kelly's.

"No whiskey for me," Sundance said. "Go get your champagne."

She got up but tried again. "It's very good whiskey. Come on, Sundance. Drink some whiskey and we'll have a good time."

"I said I didn't want it."

Marisol pouted. "You don't have to get mad at me. I just want you to have a good time."

"I'm having a fine time and nobody's mad at you."

He watched while she got another bottle of champagne. "Ah, I feel so good," she said after she drank a glass of the doctored slop. "You are part Indian, are you not?"

Sundance said half.

"That's what I am," Marisol said. "Half. My mother was a Kiowa, my father an officer in the Mexican army."

I'll bet he was, Sundance thought. God knows what he was, but he was probably Mexican. The Indian part was probably true. She looked like a breed.

She was pretending to be a little tipsy, but the smiles were still edgy. "I like you, Sundance," she said. "Would you like to go upstairs with me? No! No! I am not one of those girls." She gestured toward the whores wheeling around the floor with the drunks. "I am a dancer here. I said what I said because I like you so much. Do you want to? Some men think I am very special."

She was up to something. No mistake about it. It wasn't the words, which were the same old tired words every saloon prostitute used on the customers. It was the nervousness, the tone of the voice.

"I'd like to," Sundance answered. "Get some more champagne and we'll go on up."

Marisol reached across the table and stroked his face, smiling hard. Her nose wrinkled prettily. "I like you so you won't mind when I tell you this. You have been traveling and you are"—she laughed affectionately—"you are sweaty and dirty. Take a bath and I will welcome you to my bed. You are not angry because of what I said?"

The sense of danger was stronger now. "Not a bit," Sundance said with a grin. "I am sweaty and dirty. Fact is I was fixing to climb in a tub."

"Oh, I am so glad you aren't mad at me, Sundance. Come on. I will show you where the bath cubicles are. My room is on the second floor. The room is Number 10. I will bring the champagne and wait for you there."

She touched his face again and Sundance knew when he was being marked for death. "Don't be long," Marisol said, still nervous but not as nervous as she had been.

She led the way to a door that opened into a long narrow hallway. Coal oil lamps burned along its length. On one side of the hallway there was nothing but the back wall of the saloon. The row of bath cubicles were housed in an addition that had been added to the building. The cubicles were narrow and the walls that separated them were just thin sheets of pine.

An old Negro with a strong whiskey breath came out of one of the cubicles. There was a big water bucket in his hand. In the bathhouse there was a powerful smell of yellow soap.

"This is a friend of mine, Abraham," Marisol said. "Take good care of him. See he gets plenty of hot water."

The Negro mumbled something. "Step this way, sir," he said to Sundance, nodding at an open door. There was a light inside.

"Don't be too long, Sundance," the girl said. "I'll be

waiting for you." She kissed him.

Sundance kept well away from the shallow tin tub while he took off his shirt to make it look good. In a few minutes the old Negro came back dragging two big steaming pails. He splashed the hot water into the tub and handed Sundance a towel and a cake of soap, a scrub brush for his feet and back. He closed the door behind him.

So that's how they were going to do it, Sundance thought with professional interest. He pulled his shirt on and leaned the Winchester against the wall. Then he threw the soap and the brush into the tub. He thought he heard the floor creak in the next cubicle. After he bunched up the towel he dipped it quietly in the water at the end of the tub until it was wet and heavy. He held it in one hand while he picked up the Winchester with the other.

The towel hit the water with a splash and the wall of the cubicle was ripped by a double shotgun blast. It made a gaping hole. Sundance screamed and started to shoot. Firing as fast as he could jack the loading lever, he walked the bullets along the wall. When the pin clicked on an empty chamber he pulled the Colt and used up three more bullets. A body fell and there was silence. Outside in the saloon the band was blaring away, but somehow it was quiet in the long hallway of the bathhouse.

With the Colt ready, Sundance kicked open the door of the cubicle. A man lay on his back with three holes in his chest. He was dead. Sundance had never seen him before.

Nobody came from the saloon to ask questions.

Chapter 13

After he reloaded the rifle and the six-gun Sundance closed the doors on the two cubicles and went out into the din of the saloon. The man playing the cornet was shaking the bottles behind the bar; the brassy instrument drowned out everything else. On the dance floor the drunks were still kicking up their heels and yelling. No one paid any heed to Sundance as he shouldered his way through the crowd and climbed the stairs to the second floor. He went down the hall on moccasined feet until he was standing outside Number 10. Inside he heard the clink of a bottle and a glass.

He turned the doorknob and the door opened with a loud squeak. Marisol gulped down the glass of whiskey when she saw him. Her eyes were wild. Her hand shook violently as she reached for the bottle on a rickety deal table beside the stained bed. Sundance let her pour and drink. She bolted the whiskey and shrank away from him.

Sundance said, "I never had a bath like that before." The Winchester was in the scabbard and the Colt was holstered.

"You killed him," she said, crouched back on the bed against the wall as far from him as she could get. It wasn't far. The room wasn't much bigger than one of the bath cubicles and the smells were different. The heavy perfume didn't quite overcome the stink of all the men who had sweated on top of her in the dirty bed.

"You killed Walker," she said, shaking all over. The whiskey wasn't helping her much.

"Who would Walker be?" Sundance wondered if he ought to kill her. How much had Ryker paid them? Not much, he guessed. Death came cheap on the frontier.

The girl said through the tears that made tracks on her painted face, "We were going to get married. Walker said we'd go away from here to a city."

"You're better off without him," Sundance said. "How much did Ryker pay you and Walker?"

"Two hundred. Ryker said there would be another two hundred if we could prove you were dead. He would have the money waiting at his ranch. That much money would have set us up."

Sundance shook his head. "You'd never have collected. Walker and Ryker, how did this get started?"

The girl rubbed her face with the back of her hand, smearing the paint worse than ever. "Ryker came in with his men, four or five, I don't know. Somebody told Walker who he was and Walker asked him for a job. Ryker said he had something that paid a lot more money if Walker had the guts to do it. Walker said he had all the guts it took. I knew he was shaking in his boots, but he wanted the money. I got to talking with them and when I heard your woman was Indian I thought you might like me. Ryker said come to think of it I did look a lot like her."

Sundance had to fight to keep from killing her. To have Sarah's name coupled with a whore's! "So you thought you would get me off guard that way. Ryker must have thought it was a good idea. I know he did. Who figured to kill me in the tub?"

"You're going to kill me anyway. I thought it up. I'm going to have a drink. Shoot me if you like."

Sundance didn't stop her, and for a girl who drank nothing but champagne she downed the whiskey like milk.

Wiping her mouth, she said, "It should have worked." At last the rotgut was getting to her. "What did you do with the money Ryker paid Walker?"

Sundance felt tired; there had been so much killing. As he looked at her he realized that there was something of Sarah. Certainly not the innocence. How old was she? Not more than a year or two older than Sarah had been. These wild cowtowns chewed up young women and spat them out. The young ones made the best money, but they didn't stay young for long. Twenty-five or thirty was old for a whore on the frontier.

"I guess the money's on Walker's body," he said. "It's still there if somebody hasn't found him by now. Better get down there. No, I'm not going to kill you. Can't say you don't deserve it though."

Before Sundance could say anything else she bounced off the bed and edged past him. He heard her running down the hall and when he reached the head of the stairs she was gone.

Late that night, sitting close to a small fire with a cup of coffee getting cold in his hand, and after thinking about it for a long time, Sundance decided to change his tactics. He was going after Ryker too hard and because of that he was putting himself in the way of danger. Ryker was no outlaw who would dodge and run for years. Once he got back to Deaf Smith County he would dig in behind his hired guns. He was the power in Deaf Smith County. There he could send for more gunmen; Sundance guessed that Ryker knew where most of them could be found, and if he couldn't hire on enough hard cases in Texas, New Mexico or Arizona, there were Mexican gunmen who would work for a dollar a day. South of the border there were out-of-work pistoleros who would kill a child for fifty cents and a fresh box of bullets.

What he had to do, Sundance decided, was to let Ryker think he was dead. That wouldn't be hard to believe: there had been enough clever traps. He had pursued Ryker day and night. Let the killer think he was done for anywhere along the long trail from Cimarron City. Give him, say, a week to start breathing easier and he would begin to loosen up, get his nerve back. There were some holes in this plan, but he thought there was more substance than there were holes.

At first Ryker would hide in his fine house, protected by his gunmen. When he first got back he would jump at his shadow, sleep poorly and maybe drink too much. Days would pass long and jumpy and then Ryker would begin to feel confident again. After all he was the biggest man in the county—and who was he to skulk and hide? By the end of the week he might start showing himself again. Come out of his rathole and start biting people again like the rabid rat he was. Then Sundance could stalk him, watch him from far off, knock him out of the saddle with a long shot. It wasn't the death he had planned for Ryker; it would do in a pinch.

Sundance cut off thick slices of salt bacon with the big Bowie and wrapped them around a stick until he was sure they wouldn't drop off into the fire. The pig meat sizzled and smelled good in the chilly night air of the plains. He wondered what his life would be like if Sarah had lived. There was no use thinking about that so he forced it from his mind. Instead, he thought of other things: how her body felt the only night they had been together and how, like the child-woman she was, she fell asleep while she was still talking. He remembered the talk of eating dog and snake and how mad she was because Micah laughed at her.

It was time to get some sleep.

Early in the morning Sundance rode on until he found a small river. He didn't know what it was called. When he got to it he rode back the way he had come. Then he took the stallion off the road and rode out wide until he found the river again. A few miles from there he found a wide shallow sandy place in the river hung over with cottonwoods. He didn't think Ryker or Ryker's men would double back on him but if they did they'd have a hell of a time finding him here.

Going over the shallow place the river ran fast and quiet and the fierce Texas sun had yellowed the grass where there was no shade. Under the trees there was shade, dark and green and cool. He unsaddled Eagle and let the big animal go down to the river to drink. After hours of darkness the water was still cold. Eagle snorted as the water got in his nose and when he had all he could drink he began to graze. Sundance looked at the stallion as he browsed along the bank of the river.

"This is not so bad, is it, boy?" he said.

Eagle whinnied.

It wasn't so bad. It was better than not-so-bad. There was clean water and shade and nobody was shooting at them for a change. A bird had flown away and now it came back. Sundance got some corn dodgers from his supplies, crumbled them in his powerful hand and threw them to the bird. Other birds, hungry but suspicious, flew in to get them.

Sundance looked at the feeding birds pecking at the hard-baked dough. He looked at Eagle grazing along the bank of the river. It was good to get away from people; the stinking white towns with their noise and their bustle and their greed. He thought of Sarah. It wasn't good to get away from everyone.

He tossed more crumbled corn dodgers to the birds and then he went down to the river with the Winchester in his hand. He found a place deeper than others and put the rifle on the riverbank where he could grab it in a hurry. The sun was inching up but the water was still cold; even had a chill to it. He stripped off and waded into the current until he was up to his chest, savoring the way the cold clean water prickled against his skin.

In the hard sunlight he looked down at the scars that criss-crossed his tall lean body. The oldest were from the time when he had been initiated into Cheyenne manhood. He hadn't been much more than a boy but he had earned the right. He had borne the terrible pain in stony silence, for to have shown any pain, any emotion, even as much as a momentary grimace or a baring of the teeth, would have disqualified him forever from becoming a warrior. Even after all the years with the Cheyenne his father, Nicholas, had walked away. But then his father was a white man after all; no one can ever hope to understand the ways of the Indian if they are not born Indian.

Women were not allowed to attend the initiation, but even while the pain was knifing through him he knew his mother was watching from afar. Young though he was, he had enemies among the Cheyenne who hated him for his white blood, and they hated his father because he had given him that white blood, and was allowed to be there. As the ropes pulled hard, tearing the pegs loose from his chest, his mother gave him strength. If he failed and cried out in pain he would disgrace his mother more than he would his father, because then his enemies would sneer and say that she had brought forth a puny halfbreed and in doing so was unworthy to remain in the Cheyenne nation.

He tugged at the ropes while the others watched in silence. No one sneered at him and no one gave him encouragement. To have done either would have meant instant banishment. Sundance knew that he was better muscled than most Indians of any tribe and that was the reason why the wooden pegs slotted into his chest would not tear loose. Once again he thought of his mother and with a great effort he tore the pegs loose from his chest.

A roar went up from his friends as he prevented himself from falling. He would not fall in front of his enemies. Under the rules of the initiation ceremony there was nothing to say that he could not fall. Most young men did. But he would not give his enemies the satisfaction of seeing him down bleeding in the dirt. With all the strength he could gather within him he remained on his feet though the hot blood coursed from his torn chest.

He knew who his enemies were and he smiled at them. They looked away in sullen fury. Later, after his wounds had been salved, there was a great feast that lasted far into the night. Two days before he had stolen two fat cows from the valley far below and now they were roasting. His father, in the white man's way, shook his hand heartily until he saw the lines in his son's face.

Sundance had risked death by going to the ranch of a Scotsman named Mulkern to steal the cows. Now, looking at the children eating hungrily, he knew it has been worth it...

There had been many other scars since them. Bullet wounds, knife wounds; he had been scarred in a fire. He had been flogged in a Mexican jail and when he broke out he came back to kill the man who did the flogging. Close to his heart there was an Apache bullet that the Army doctor said could never come out. That was when he had been serving with Three Stars in northern Sonora. He told the Army sawbones to get it out anyway. Three Stars had told him not to be such a horse's posterior. Three Stars never used stronger language than that...

Sundance ducked down under the water and scooped up a handful of fine river sand. He scoured his body with it, ducking down to get another handful when the current washed it away. He rubbed it into his shoulder-length yellow hair and washed it out again. Eagle watched him from the bank of the river while he chewed grass with strong teeth. Sundance scrubbed his body clean, then lay in a shallow place and let the water flow over him. A feeling of peace came over him. He had come through hell and out the other side. The men he had killed meant nothing to him; the others who had saved his life meant a lot, even Keegan. Now he would let the days go by without impatience. Quiet days in the sun with sleep and food prepared without hurry. He knew he had worn himself down, for even the strongest man can only push himself so far. And when the week was over he would go after Ryker like a tiger.

He climbed out of the water and lay in the sun until he was dry. White men never exposed their bodies to the sun; only their faces were sun browned. He dressed and sat in the shade of the trees working on his guns; he had given them hard use in recent days. He was more concerned with the Colt than he was with the Winchester. If you didn't beat the Winchester on a rock it would work just about forever. The Colt was different. It was a durable weapon but something could always go wrong with the cylinder stop spring, or the pawl spring, or the pawl, or even the mainspring itself. Or the notches on the hammer could go wrong.

Even so, it would still shoot. If the hammer notches broke, you could still thumb shots. If the hand or pawl, or the cylinder stop bolt or any of the springs broke, you could still turn the cylinder by hand. You could do all that but with men shooting at you while you did it, you would most likely end up dead.

The Colt was all right. He cleaned and oiled the Winchester and the Colt, and then he inspected each bullet before he reloaded. He put them away and made another pot of coffee. He drank coffee with his back against a tree.

When this was over he would head on down to the Kiowa reservation where the Indian agent was selling whiskey to the Indians with the blessing of the Indian Ring in Washington. Unless he was stopped the Kiowas would jump the reservation and wash that part of Texas in blood before they were slaughtered by the cavalry. The crooked agent's name was Jameson; Sundance knew he would have to kill him.

Sundance went to look for a prairie chicken or a rabbit. Bacon was all right but you got sick of it. He didn't want to do any shooting; he would use the straight-handled throwing hatchet. He left Eagle to graze while he walked upstream along the river. Flies buzzed in the hot silence. He was looking for a shallow muddy place where the birds came to drink and hunt for worms.

The birds heard him before they saw him, and they burst into the air in a flutter of wings. Prairie chickens

141

could fly if they had to, but their flight was slow and clumsy. Mostly they ran, darting through the long grass until they found a place to hide.

Sundance crouched in the grass behind a tree just above the muddy hole. He kept perfectly still and his breathing was soft and controlled. In a few minutes the birds began to come back. The wrens were first. They were still wary and they flew over the mud hole several times before they came down. They twittered as they drank and dug their beaks in the mud. Soon the mud hole was covered with jays and wrens. The prairie chickens, wariest of all, came last; there were only two. One was plumper than the other; that one would be his breakfast. Maybe it would.

He waited to let them get over their apprehension. The chicken would be a moving target because the instant he moved it would be off and running. He stood up and the small birds exploded into the air. The chickens started to run. Sundance threw the hatchet. It flashed from his hand like a streak of silver. The chicken squawked once as the blade dropped it in its tracks. The other chicken disappeared into the waving grass.

Sundance cleaned the hatchet blade with a handful of grass and put the weapon back in his belt. He felt the dead bird. It was young and fat. Carrying it by its legs, he started back to camp. There he plucked it before he cut off its head. Then he gutted it and buried the feathers and the guts; at the river he washed it clean.

He crumbled corn dodgers until they were powder, then he stuffed the bird and encased it in clean river mud. When the mud had firmed up in the sun, he put the chicken in a bed of coals. Slowly the mud turned to brick. It would be more than an hour before the chicken was ready to eat.

He rolled the mud oven off the fire and brushed the

ashes away with a leafy branch. God! He was hungry. He cracked the casing of mud with a rock. It split neatly in two, releasing the good smell of roast chicken.

He ate with quiet content, savoring the tender meat. Instead of coffee he drank clean river water. In his time he had eaten in fine restaurants—Sundance grinned—usually with Three Stars. This mud baked chicken was better than any of it. He buried the bones and lay with his back against a tree, and slept. Sleep was what restored a man more than anything else.

Seven quiet days passed like that; all the time he felt his strength increasing. He hunted for his food; some days he ate rabbit wrapped around with strips of salt bacon to give it flavor. He caught fish by hand in the river. Mostly it was catfish, but there was nothing better than fried cat.

He washed his clothes and slept a lot. He put Ryker out of his mind for those seven days. His mind was at ease, free of mankilling tension. He smiled when Eagle rolled in the shallows snorting with pleasure. Often at night he lay awake listening to the fast flowing water and the chirping of crickets.

There was no feeling of time; one day blended into another. He hunted, he slept, he walked along the banks of the river. The seven days were a merciful break in his violent life. The silence was what he treasured most. Always there was the great and utter silence.

On the last day he awoke with a feeling of regret. Soon he would be back in the world of men with all their cruelty and greed. He ate a good breakfast of roasted rabbit. While it was cooking he checked his weapons again. There was no need to, but he did it anyway. The sun wasn't up yet and a soft breeze rustled the branches of the overhanging trees. Eagle was down by ther river drinking water. The big horse sensed that

Chapter 14

Sundance passed through towns that were on no map but a county map. No one had seen Ryker in any of them. He ate in some of them, in places that weren't too dirty. Mostly he foraged for his food on the prairie. There was no way to keep beef from turning bad in the heat, and all he bought in a store was tomatoes and canned beans. He had more salt bacon than he wanted to eat.

It looked like he had lost Ryker's trail. That didn't matter because the trail could lead only one way, and that was west. Rested after a week by the river, he and the stallion made good time without effort. It was good to see that Eagle could take a long day and still be ready to go again in minutes. There was a long stretch of waterless country and there was nothing to drink but canteen water. It never tasted good after the first few hours in the heat. It was water and that's all you could say about it.

At a farmhouse far off the road, the sodbuster remembered having seen Ryker and his men riding across his land. "I guess that was the man," the farmer said. "Couldn't miss a man nor a horse that big."

The farmer told Sundance to stay for supper. They ate boiled pork and greens soaked in bacon grease. The coffee had more chicory than coffee in it. They were simple people, the farmer and his wife and daughter. The little girl was about eleven and she wore wire-rimmed glasses. It was good to see that there were some decent people left in the world. They said he was welcome to spend the night, but he said no. When nobody was looking he slipped a Mexican gold piece under his plate and went out to his his horse. The little girl came out to wave goodbye. Her glasses glittered in the light of the dying sun.

The farmer had proved one thing: Ryker was heading straight for home ground with no dodging this way and that. He'd be there by now even if he took it easy. Sundance knew he wouldn't. Deaf Smith County was where he ruled the roost and that's where he would go. There could be no doubt of that now.

A few miles past a place called Jimson, just a few houses and a freight station, he was stopped by a cavalry patrol commanded by a young lieutenant with red hair and a scar over his right eye. The troopers were wearing the new uniform with the suspenders of the pants in full view. The campaign hats were drab colored and wide brimmed.

Sundance reined in when the lieutenant raised his gauntleted hand. He looked Sundance over before he spoke. "We're looking for a band of renagade Comanches," he said in a Southern accent.

"This far north?" Sundance said.

"That's our information," the lieutenant said. "Not more than ten of them. They've been burning and killing, then moving on. It got too hot for them in the south so they came up here. That's our information. If they're caught they won't be sent back to a reservation. They'll hang for sure."

Sundance looked at the troopers sweating in the sun. Some of them looked green and none was in much of a fighting spirit. Only the young lieutenant was eager to do battle. It showed in the excitement in his voice when he talked about the burning and killing. A new Indian war would suit him fine. What he didn't seem to know, didn't want to know, was that the Indian fighting days were just about over. That would be hard for the lieutenant to take when the news finally got through to him. But maybe he could bother the Mormons, who didn't see eye to eye with the Government on most things.

"I haven't seen them," Sundance said.

"Just hope you don't," the lieutenant said. "But if you do see them try to get word to the nearest army post." The lieutenant was staring at Sundance's copper skin. "You're part Indian?"

"That part is Cheyenne, not Comanche."

"What's the difference?"

"To a Cheyenne a Comanche is as different as a Frenchman from an Eskimo."

Sundance watched them as they rode away. With those green troopers on his hands, the lieutenant was in for a fight if he tangled with ten renegade Comanches with a rope waiting for them. And the lieutenant might never make captain.

The next day he was stopped by another patrol, and the questions were the same. It looked like the renegades were making a lot of trouble for the army to put so many men in the field. This patrol was led by a grizzled captain old enough to have fought in the Civil War. He didn't look half as eager to fight as the lieutenant.

"You want some advice?" Sundance asked him.

"No," he snapped. Then he changed his mind. "All right, what is it? Not that I'll take it."

"Take it or leave it," Sundance said. "Look for places where there are a lot of horses. That's where they'll strike."

"They have horses, all the horses they need," the captain said irritably. "We already know that."

Sundance said, "To an Indian a horse is worth more than gold. Worth even more than a good rifle, and that's saying some."

"Don't you think they'd know we'll be watching the places with horses. Anyway, that's what they'll think so they'll steer clear."

Sundance didn't give a damn about the Comanches. "Maybe they'll figure that's what you're figuring. They're smart enough to do that."

Without a word the captain turned his horse and led his men away at a canter. Poor bastard, Sundance thought. He'd much sooner be smoking a cigar on the veranda of the officers' quarters. They didn't call the Comanches the best light cavalry in the world for nothing. That's what the Texas Rangers called them back in the '40's. And now they had guns. There was a time when the Indians were rotten shots because they didn't want to waste ammunition in practice. But the years had taught them a bitter lesson. They could shoot now.

Late the next day, with his water running low, he saw a ranch house up ahead. It was about half a mile off the road. When he got closer he saw a corral full of horses. A thick bodied man with a rifle came out of the house when he saw him coming. He raised the rifle when he saw the color of Sundance's skin, the fringed buckskin shirt, the moccasins.

"Stay where you are!" he yelled. "Stay put till I get a look at you. I mean what I say."

He advanced with the rifle at the ready. "What in hell are you?" he said at last. His hair was Prussian cut and about as long as the stubble on his wedge shaped face. A gaunt woman with a rifle in her hands looked out the door.

"I asked what are you?" the man repeated.

"I'm not a Comanche."

"How do I know that? I never even seen a Comanche. No, I guess you ain't a Comanche. You talk American as good as I do. What's your business here?"

"Just water for my canteens," Sundance said. "I'll pay for it."

The man frowned until his thick black eyebrows almost came together. "Who the hell asked you for money? That's the well over there. Take all the water you want."

Sundance took his canteens to the well. The horse rancher followed him, but the rifle was lowered. "Use that bucket to water your horse," the rancher said.

After he winched up a bucket of water for Eagle, Sundance filled the dipper and drank himself. It was good water, clear and cold. The rancher watched him while he filled the canteens. Finally, he said, "I like a man that lets his horse drink before he drinks again. You can tell a lot about a man that does that."

"I guess you like horses," Sundance said as he stoppered the canteens.

"Damn right I do. The name is Smithers. Eli Smithers. What would yours be if you care to tell me?"

"Jim Sundance," Sundance said. Then he asked Smithers about Ryker.

"Haven't seen a man like that," Smithers said, scratching the week old stubble on his face.

Looking at the horses in the corral, Sundance said, "With these Comanches on the loose you ought to have some men on guard."

Smithers cursed loudly. "What men? I run this place with the help of my son and the old woman. Let the bastards come. We'll be ready for them."

"You won't, Mr. Smithers. Two men and a woman. You won't have a chance. I still say you should hire some men."

"I thought about that," Smithers said. "Everybody in these parts is too busy looking after their own place. A yellow-leg patrol come by here. I asked the captain if he could post a few of his men till the army catches up with these Comanches. He said that was agin regulations. Anyway, he said, the Comanches wasn't likely to bother me. I don't know how he knew that. You look like a fighting man, Mr. Sundance. You wouldn't want to hire on for a spell?"

"Can't do it, Mr. Smithers. I've got pressing business."

"No need to explain. Stay a while and eat with us and don't say anything else about paying. I'd take such talk as an offense. Come on now and we'll put on our bibs."

The house was big and roomy and had a stone-flagged floor. It was cool and very clean and the floor was sprinkled with fine white sand. On a sideboard there was an old brass-clasped Bible that had been read a lot. The binding was cracked and the clasp was broken. A smell of roasting lamb came from the kitchen in back.

"Sit yourself down," Smithers said. "Can't offer you anything to drink. Don't hold with drinking or smoking though I suspect my boy does both when he goes to town. That's where he is now, fetching supplies. Don't exactly need them right now but the old woman has a sweet tooth when it comes to dried apples. Can't see it myself but you know how woman folk are."

Sundance agreed.

"I'd like you to say hello to the old woman," Smithers said. He called out, "Katie, come on in and say hello."

The old woman wasn't an old woman after all.

Sundance guessed she was a few years younger than her husband but the hard prairie life took its toll on women. She had never been pretty but she had an open pleasant face and bright blue eyes that belied her age, which was about forty. Her once light brown hair was streaked with gray and tied back in a bun. She wiped her hands on her apron and shook hands with Sundance. No Eastern woman had ever done that. Her hand was worn but strong.

"Pleased to have you, I hope you like lamb," she said.

Sundance said he liked it better than anything, which wasn't true, but he liked this straight-backed woman.

"Don't hold with beef," Smithers said. "People call me peculiar because of the views I hold. It's my belly and I'll put in what I please. This is cow country and people think a man is unpatriotic if he says a bad word against beef. Got into a row with a man one time. Told me I ought to take up herding sheep if I was so fond of them. Couldn't do anything but belt him in the jaw."

Smithers said all this with a completely serious face. "Just because a man likes lamb don't mean he wants to herd sheep. You understand what I'm saying, Mr. Sundance?"

Sundance said he understood every word of it.

"It's a pleasure talking to a man who knows what you're talking about," Smithers said. "Horses though is what I like best. You have to look after them. They get sick real easy. Mostly it's the lungs. When a horse gets pneumony there ain't much you can do. Some get over, most don't. So you see, Mr. Sundance, strong as a horse ain't exactly the right way of saying. Strong as a mule is more like it. Don't like mules much, though I like them better than cows. Mules ain't dumb, you know. I don't know any animal is smarter than a mule except it's a horse. The horse is smart in a smart-decent way. The

151

mule is crafty, first and last. If I didn't know that mules can't talk I'd say it was a mule that put around the story that mules are dumb. Cause once you get the name of being dumb you can get away with just about anything. How often have you heard it said, 'Don't mind him, he's just dumb?'"

"Lots of times," Sundance agreed.

Smithers got back on the subject of beef. He was very positive about what he liked and didn't like. "I don't even know that beef is good for a man. Don't hold with cows neither. Dirty smelly critters dumber than mules. Now horses, you take horses. Clean, intelligent beasts. Treat them right and they're as faithful as a good dog. Who in hell ever heard of a faithful cow? The only good thing about them is their milk. We don't keep a cow on the place. My neighbor, Toddy Fernald, keeps us supplied with all we want. The old woman favors a bit of beef now and then. Fernald supplies that. Me, I stick to lamb or pork. Looks like supper is about ready."

Mrs. Smithers brought in a steaming leg of lamb on a platter. Then she brought in more side dishes than Sundance had ever seen on one table at one time. While she was bringing in pitchers of water and milk, the Smithers boy came in carrying a sack of groceries.

"Who's horse is that outside?" he said. He stopped short when he saw Sundance.

"This is my son, Jared," Smithers said. "Shake hands with Mr. Sundance."

"Gosh," the boy said as they shook hands.

"That ain't polite, Jared," Smithers said. "No need to stare at a man cause he don't look like you."

The boy was about seventeen, with the open face and light brown hair of his mother. Mrs. Smithers sat down last at the table. Smithers said grace.

Smithers sliced the lamb and passed it around. Being

that she was a woman Mrs. Smithers came last. There was no insult in that, Sundance thought. Frontier people had their set ways.

Sundance said he'd take water instead of milk. The boy said he liked water too. "You'll drink milk and like it." Smithers filled his cup to the top. Then he filled his own cup and drank it down in two gulps. He filled his cup again.

The boy grinned at Sundance, then at his father. "For a man that hates cows you sure drink a lot of milk, Paw."

"Hold your tongue and eat your supper," Smithers said mildly. "You want more lamb, Mr. Sundance?"

Sundance's plate was still piled high. He said no thanks.

"We got plenty," Smithers said. "This leg ain't the only one. Katie always cooks up two in case we run short."

Jared said with a grin, "Paw eats so much lamb he'll start bleating one of these days."

"Can't get enough of it," Smithers said heartily. "You'll stay the night, Mr. Sundance?"

"Please stay," Jared said.

Mrs. Smithers said, "We'd be more than glad to have you, Mr. Sundance. We don't get many visitors. My husband isn't too popular with the ranchers, not with all his hate-cow talk."

She smiled at her husband.

"I'm just speaking the truth," Smithers said. "Course you'll stay, Mr. Sundance.

Well, Sundance thought, why not. Ryker would keep. "Thank you for the kind offer. I'll take you up on it."

When Mrs. Smithers was back in the kitchen washing the disher, Sundance said, "I'll sleep down by the horses. At least you'll have a guard for one night."

"That's no place to sleep," Smithers protested. "We got an extra room. Anyhow, Jared guards the horses half the night, me the other half. We won't have a guest standing guard for us."

Sundance shook his head. "Down by the corral will do fine. I camp out most of the time."

Smithers cursed, then looked anxiously toward the kitchen to see if his wife had heard him. "Then we'll all stand guard together. I don't sleep so good anyhow, with these Comanches on the loose."

"Look," Sundance said, "there's no saying they'll come, but if they do we have to wipe them out. If we don't the ones we don't kill will come back, and not for the horses. Even if we take some of them alive there's still a risk. We could hand them over to the military to be hanged. But Comanches have a way of breaking the stoutest jail. None of them can be left alive, do you understand? You don't want them stalking you day and night."

"My God!" Smithers said. "You mean kill even the wounded?"

"I'll do it," Sundance said. "It's the only way. But maybe they won't come at all."

"God grant they won't," Smithers said.

Mrs. Smithers came out of the kitchen. "I heard every word you said, Mr. Sundance. Well, sir, I can shoot a rifle as good as any man. Don't argue about it, Eli. This is my house too, so don't argue about it. Save your arguments for the benefits of lamb over beef."

"I'm not arguing," Smithers said. Sundance knew who was the real boss of the house.

They lay in the darkness with their rifles loaded and ready. There were no lights in the house. The horses sensed their presence and were skittish at first; gradually they calmed down. Sundance and Jared were on one side of the corral, Eli was on the other. Mrs. Smithers was crouched behind a water trough not far from the house. Sundance had told her, "If you come in, you fire first. Just one shot, then get down. They'll be firing at you first thinking you're all there is. So stay down after the first shot. We'll hit them from the rear. You can start shooting again when we start shooting."

Sundance didn't think she should be a part of this, but it wasn't his place to say it.

"I'll do what you say, Mr. Sundance," she said. "I have no mind to get shot."

It was well into the night and there wasn't a sound except for the movement of horses in the corral. Then Sundance heard them coming. None of the Smithers' heard anything. Sundance squeezed the boy's arm. Then he threw a pebble at Eli Smithers; that was the signal.

Sundance watched the renegades as they came through the darkness. Outlines at first, then solid shapes. He watched while the leader raised his hand and brought it down sharply. They kicked their horses into a gallop, screaming and yelling as they came. They swept past firing shots at the house. Mrs. Smithers fired back and killed one of them. They swept past and Sundance fired fast and killed three more. Smithers and the boy opened fire. Two more Comanches were knocked off their horses.

Still screaming, they tried to break out. Sundance killed one man, wounded another. Time to kill him later. Only three Comanches were still on their horses. A bullet hit Smithers in the side and he went down. Jared jumped to his feet before Sundance could stop him. The boy aimed and fired, aimed and fired. Another Comanche toppled from the saddle. Sundance got the last two as he swept past, still yelling.

"See to your father," Sundance said. He drew the Colt and went from one body to another, firing a single bullet into each head. Jared was helping his father to his feet. Mrs. Smithers ran to help him.

In the house Sundance cut open Smithers shirt and looked at the wound. "He'll be all right if it doesn't get infected," he told Mrs. Smithers.

"Guess we better start burying them," he told the boy. "They'll stink up the place if we don't."

Mrs. Smithers was boiling water on the stove. She turned and said, smiling, "I'm sure glad you stayed to supper, Mr. Sundance."

Chapter 15

He was far into Deaf Smith County. Another day's ride would bring him close to the Ryker place. Suddenly he knew he was being followed. The feeling came instantly and it was very strong. He turned in the saddle and scanned the country behind him. There was nothing but the brown hills and the waving grass, but he knew there was someone out there watching him. It could be a man with a long-range rifle. He touched Eagle's flanks and went away at a gallop.

He rode fast for five miles, then led Eagle into a brushy hollow and waited after he climbed up to a rock from where he could watch the road. An hour went by and nothing passed on the road except an old farm woman driving a wagon. He was close enough to see her weathered face and the clay pipe she was smoking. The wagon creaked out of sight beyond a dip in the road.

Nothing moved in the silence, yet he knew he was being tracked. He mounted up and took Eagle off the road, turning now and then to look for the glint of sun on metal, a movement—anything. Still there was nothing. The feeling of danger remained strong.

He backtracked when he was sure he couldn't be seen. He rode around a knobby hill and through a long narrow draw. The draw ran up to a high place. The bare hills ran back into the distance and there wasn't much cover. But nothing showed itself, and whoever was tracking him was good. Another man would have shrugged and decided he was wrong. Sundance knew he wasn't wrong.

Later in the day he backtracked again and saw nothing. He was wasting time; he would have to take his chances. What he had to do now was put some distance between him and the tracker. Mounted on Eagle, that would be easy to do. The big stallion responded instantly to the touch of his heels, surging forward at a powerful gallop. Sundance urged his horse to greater speed. The miles dropped behind.

After he had gone ten miles Sundance rested and watered the stallion. After a week of rest and good fodder Eagle was in perfect condition. Sundance grinned. He didn't think the tracker, whoever he was, had a mount like Eagle. If he hoped to catch up he would have to travel fast. That would mean dust. Sundance looked for dust but didn't see it.

It was getting dark now and by morning he would be in sight of Ryker's place. Maybe the tracker hoped to creep up on him while he was scouting the ranch. He knew the man who was tracking him was no ordinary bushwhacker. Ryker's hard cases had failed all along the line, so maybe he had sent for a professional killer, a marksman with a far-reaching rifle. This would be no fast draw artist, no saloon braggart but a cold, careful mankiller who took his time before he tried for a shot. It couldn't be Charlie Bassett, the range war killer, because Sundance had killed Bassett in South Texas not so long before. There were only four or five professional marksman-killers in the West. It wasn't likely to be Tom Horn; the army scout turned killer was busy killing small ranchers up in Wyoming. Morgan Jakes was about to be hanged in Fort Smith, Arkansas. That left Morse, Glidden and Bates. Or it could be somebody new, somebody he hadn't heard of yet. There was always a new batch of killers growing up.

Late that night he lay behind a grass mound on the

west side of a creek. He was far back from the creek. There was no way to cross the creek without making some noise because it was shallow and floored with rocks. Black clouds rolled across the moon and if the tracker started across the creek it would be tricky shooting at best. He lay in the grass, listening for sounds in the dark. Hours dragged by and nothing happened.

Sundance didn't need to sleep after a week of sleep and rest. His mind and his body were completely alert. He stayed where he was all through the night. There wasn't the slighest movement on the other side of the creek. It began to get light.

Sundance moved on before the light was full. The tracker could be waiting until there was enough light to shoot. Not much later he was down out of the hills and into the good grassland that ran all the way to Hereford. Beyond Hereford was Ryker's ranch.

From far out Hereford looked like a fat, prosperous town. He circled the town. A good road went out toward Ryker's place. Sundance stayed away from it.

From the top of a hill he could see the big swing gate that was the start of Ryker's land. A wooden sign was nailed to the gate. It was the biggest gate sign Sundance had ever seen. It just said RYKER, but the letters were enormous. There was no guard on the gate. A high wire fence ran away from both sides of the gate and far into the distance. It looked like Ryker had fenced in his whole property, at least the home ranch. Sundance rode along the wire for several miles.

He hated to use his throwing hatchet to cut the wire, but there was no other way through. He guessed the main house would be four or five miles from where he was. The home ranch was hilly but well grassed; there would be some cover.

He chopped at the wire where it passed over a post.

The keen, tempered blade bit into the wire and it twanged away. The blade of the hatchet was blunted, but it wasn't too badly damaged. He stuck it in his belt and led Eagle through the gap in the wire. What he didn't understand was why there was no guard on the gate. He had expected to see at least one guard. There were no fence riders either. That could mean that Ryker had regained his nerve, or was planning a trap.

Soon he heard the bawling of cows not full grown yet coming from the other side of a hill. He dismounted and crawled to the top of the hill. He could see the top of Ryker's house across the top of a long rolling hill. All he could see was the top of the house; he would have to get closer.

He rode Eagle through the mass of cows until he was on the safe side of the last hill. From there on there would be no more cover. Now the main house and the bunkhouse were less than a quarter mile away. To one side of the corrals was a huge red-painted barn. The doors of the barn were closed. No smoke came from the cookhouse chimney. At this hour of the morning the ranch should have been bustling with activity, but there was no one in sight. The whole place looked dead and silent as if everybody had just up and left.

The sun grew hot and Sundance sipped water from a canteen while he waited and watched. It didn't make sense, or maybe it did. It could be a very elaborate trap. But how could Ryker know when he'd be coming? In the meantime the ranch was going unattended. The restless bawling of the cows was proof of that. The only thing to do was wait it out.

He watched for the slightest movement and there was none. The ranch baked in the blaze of the sun. Not even a dog ran around. He watched and waited all through the day. Only once did he leave his position and that was to let Eagle drink water from his hat. In minutes he was back at his watch-point. Then suddenly he realized that he was no longer being watched. He hadn't been watched for a long time; his instincts were never wrong.

Then what was it? If the tracker had stopped tracking him it had to be something else. All through the day he had lain in an exposed place, yet there had been no attempt to kill him. And, strangely, he got no feeling of danger from the ranch. But why was it deserted, if deserted it was?

It got dark and no lights showed down below. Not even the glow of a cigarette cupped in a man's hand. He watched all through the night and when the sky turned from black to gray he decided not to wait any longer. He couldn't lie up on this hill forever waiting for something to happen. Finally, as always, a man had to take his chances. He had come too far to be careful any longer.

If they were waiting he'd be seen long before he got close to the house. They would wait until he got close enough to kill. So be it.

He saddled Eagle and rode down the last slope and onto the flat. Cows were bawling again as the sun came up. There was nothing he could hide behind now. He kept going with the Winchester cocked and ready. Cows ran away from him bawling and kicking up their heels. His eyes moved from the house to the bunkhouse to the barn. The windows of the house were closed as if nobody waited behind them. But that could be just another part of a well planned trap.

The house was dead ahead and maybe he'd be dead in minutes. He got down and left Eagle by a tree. Then he walked to the front door of Ryker's house and opened it. He braced for the bullets to bite into him. There wasn't a sound.

With the rifle steady he went through the house from

one room to another. Ryker had done well by himself. A lot of money had gone into making this house the biggest and the best. A kitchen was built onto the back of the house. A steak had been frying in a skillet on the stove. It had been left on the fire until it was burned black. A pot of coffee stood on a table. Sundance took off the lid and smelled it. The coffee in the pot looked oily and old. Days old. A slab of butter that hadn't been put back in the cooler had turned rancid.

Ryker was gone all right. But why and where? So the hunt would have to begin all over again. Sundance knew Ryker hadn't taken his men out to look for him because that wouldn't explain the deserted ranch. Even if he took every man he had he wouldn't take the cook. Food wouldn't be rotting in the kitchen; the cows wouldn't be bawling. There would be some signs of life and there were none.

There were a lot of questions and Sundance had no answers for any of them. Ryker hadn't sold the place and headed for parts unknown. The new owner would have taken possession the minute the papers were signed and the money paid. And if Ryker had sold and pulled out he would have taken his clothes and boots. But the closets in Ryker's bedroom were filled with fancy, hand-stitched boots. A small fortune in boots, some of them not worn yet. A gold watch lay on a table beside Ryker's four-poster bed. Sure as hell he would have taken that. Only one thing was sure and that was that Ryker had left in a hurry.

Sundance stopped trying to find answers. All he could do now was to pick up Ryker's trail again and keep on going. That might not be so easy now. No matter. He'd find him.

Sundance looked around at the fine house built with money made with fists and guns. How many men had been trampled under so that Ryker could live like a king? The dining room was the fanciest room in the house. There was a long polished table that must have weighed a ton. On it were silver candlesticks. Overhead was a chandelier. Glowering down from the mantelpiece was an oil portrait of Ryker dressed in a white suit. Even in a picture Ryker wanted everyone to know that here was a man with the world firmly under his boot.

The house was a monument to one man's arrogance. Sundance smiled bitterly. As soon as he burned it, it would be nothing at all. He went from room to room collecting coal oil lamps. He smashed the first one on the polished table in the dining room. The breaking glass scarred the surface of the table and oil slopped on the floor. He flung the second one at Ryker's portrait. He smashed the last two against the walls. Oil dripped down and puddled on the floor.

Sundance stood back and struck a wood match on the wall. It flared up. Then a cold voice behind him said, "Hold that thing steady, my friend."

Still holding the burning match Sundance turned slowly to face an old man with a Sharps rifle pointing straight at his chest.

"Come on in, boys," the old man said.

Chapter 16

"Blow out that match real easy now," the long haired old man with the Sharps carbine ordered. "Try to drop it lit and I'll blow you through the wall. Won't do you any good if you do drop it. We can still douse the fire before it spreads. Go on now, do what I tell you or get ready to die."

The fancy Mexican wall hangings and the polished hardwood floor of the big room stank of coal oil. Sundance looked at the burning wood match between his fingers. Then he looked at the heavy Sharps steady in the old man's spotted hands. The old man had the long hair and trimmed beard favored by oldtime Indian fighters. In all, there must have been ten guns, rifles and shotguns, pointing straight at him. The men holding the weapons looked ready to kill. Sundance blew out the match and rubbed the burnt part between his fingers and put the match in his shirt pocket.

"That's the way to do it, sonny," the old man said with a wintry smile. "You and you, take his weapons. Look for a knife in his boot. A man'd be nekkid without a knife in his boot."

Sundance held his arms out wide and high while the two men unbuckled his weapons belt and slid the thin-bladed knife from his boot. "That's better," the old man said. "Don't want this feller going wild till a few things are explained to him."

"You mean with a bullet or a rope," Sundance said, thinking: well, here's where it all ends. "Or have you something fancier in mind?"

The old man jerked his head without taking his eyes

away from Sundance. "Outside," he said. "Could never stand the smell of that stuff."

Outside, they walked Sundance into the shade of a wide spreading cottonwood. So it was going to be the rope. There was still no sign of Ryker. So far nobody had started coiling a noose. Sundance saw an even larger party of armed men over by the corrals. Maybe now was the time to make a run for it. He knew he'd be dead seconds later, but a quick bullet was better than the rope. Anything was better than the rope. Yet he waited. Something was going on that didn't fit together in his mind. They had been hiding in the barn, but they hadn't tried to kill him.

The old man's voice was still mild. "Set your self down there," he said, "and I'll hunker where I am." Under the ancient tree was a white painted bench. Though he wasn't much under seventy the old man sat down lightly on his heels, still holding the Sharps.

"Couldn't let you burn that fine house," the old man remarked. "Don't belong to me. Can't let you do it just the same."

"I know who it belongs to, old man."

The old man smiled. "I'm spry enough for my age. My trigger finger is spry as hell. Try something and you'll find out soon enough. You used to be with Crook, didn't you? I was with Crook before you. I'd be obliged if you'd stop calling me old man. The name is Jackson MacWilliams."

Crook had spoken of Jackson MacWilliams from time to time. Said he was one of the best scouts he worked with right after he was posted to the frontier for the first time. Crook said he was probably dead.

Sundance looked at MacWilliams. "What's a man like you doing on Ryker's side? It doesn't figure."

It was cool under the big tree. MacWilliams

pretended to look surprised. "That's one hell of a thing to say. Who said I was working for Ryker besides you?"

"Then what are you doing?"

"Making sure you don't burn his wife's house. She's going to be needing it to live in"—MacWilliams paused—"now that Ryker's left the country."

Sundance stood up and MacWilliams waved him back with the Sharps. "That's right," MacWilliams went on, "we finally run him off. Should have done it years back."

"Why?"

MacWilliams said, "What finally made up our minds was what he did to your woman."

"How did you find out? It's a long way back to Oklahoma."

"One of his riders, a real young feller, got drunk in town before he rode south. Said he wished he had the guts to kill Ryker for the terrible thing he did in the Territory. Something real bad was eating on that young man. Kept on drinking up the wages he'd collected and the more he drank the more he talked. The men in the saloon kept prodding him till the whole rotten story came out. He seemed like a straight man and everybody knew he wasn't lying. Knowing Sam Ryker they knew the things he did when the whiskey and craziness was on him. Well, sir, the murder of that young Injun girl was all it took to do it. Didn't matter she was an Injun—don't mind me saying the hard truth—she was still a woman. Most men, bad as they may be in other ways, don't hold with killing women. Course there were plenty other reasons. For years Ryker's been riding roughshod over this good country, grabbing land, pushing people off. Now it's his turn to be pushed off."

Sundance said, "He didn't give you a fight?"

"I think he had a mind to when we sent him the message. Ever since he got back he's been looking to hire on the worst hard cases he could find. Getting ready for you, I suppose. Had hired five or six last I heard. Well, after I heard about your woman I sort of took charge. I have a nice little spread that abuts on Ryker's so I had other reasons besides the Injun girl. So I rode around the county talking to men I know. Explained the facts to them. Time to chase him, says I. They listened when I said Ryker had sullied the fair name of Texas. Then break out your guns and let's go, says I."

"So he went. I'm glad you didn't have to kill him."

MacWilliams understood. "You'll be wanting to do that. Some of the men wanted to swing him from a tree. No, don't do that, says I. Let the bastard take nothing but his horse and get the hell out of Texas. We had the house surrounded on all sides. Must have been fifty or sixty of us, all men who knew how to use their weapons. It was a pretty sight to see them so-called hard cases come trailing out looking scared. I told them if they were still in the county by nightfall they'd dangle. Not a one has been seen since. Then we pointed Ryker toward the New Mexico line and said don't ever come back. We gave him his beltgun and rifle, some ammunition, water to last him a while. Might as well hang him if we didn't. Mrs. Ryker's away visiting her sister in Amarillo. Don't know anything about this. I'd say she won't break out in tears when she hears about it. I hear she's wanted to get away from him for years, only was too afraid of him. A nice quiet woman. Don't know why in hell she married a man like Ryker. That's why we couldn't let you burn her house."

"You figured out what I was going to do?"

"Sort of. That's what I'd do. When you strike at a

man's home you're getting close to the bone."

Sundance said, "You didn't just follow me here today? You've been tracking me a lot longer than that?"

MacWilliams had an old man's conceit. "That I have. I rode out to greet you, so to speak. I used to be pretty good at tracking a man without getting caught at it. Hell! I'm still good at it."

"I knew somebody was following me," Sundance said. "I backtracked a few times, but always there was nothing."

MacWilliams laughed. "I *know* you backtracked a few times. That's why you found nothing. One of these days you'll get to be as good as I was—still am."

Sundance knew he was better. He could have found the man who was trailing him if he wanted to take the time. He didn't say it. "You don't have to keep holding that rifle on me, MacWilliams. I don't want to burn the house. Not now."

"Don't know it would do you any good if you did. Some of the boys are going to sit right here till Mrs. Ryker gets back. I guess it's time you took out after Ryker. I'd say he'll cross into New Mexico at Clovis. You know where that is?"

"I can find it."

One of the men brought Sundance's weapons belt and he buckled it on. They gave him his Winchester. "I'm going to fill up on water," he told MacWilliams. "Hay my horse."

"Anything to help you on your way. Everything's been taken care of: your canteens washed out and filled. Your stallion has eaten and drunk his fill."

MacWilliams lowered the rifle at last and held out his hand. "Good hunting, Sundance. You mind a word of advice?"

Sundance was in the saddle. "You mean a warning?"

"Whatever," MacWilliams said amiably. "Don't come back to Deaf Smith County. Us uns over this way are getting all respectable like. Raising fine Herefords now, longhorns just about a thing of the past. Or soon will be."

"You mean like me?"

"Whatever," MacWilliams said. "Seeing you, folks would be reminded of Sam Ryker. They wouldn't like that. Neither would Mrs. Ryker. We're going to look out for her."

Sundance smiled. "Too bad I didn't have you up in Oklahoma, Mac."

MacWilliams said, "You did all right by yourself."

"No," Sundance said, "I didn't."

They watched him as he rode away.

Sundance followed Ryker's trail to the New Mexico line and crossed it at the town of Clovis, the center of ranching country. It was a bigger town than he expected it to be, with streets running off the long main street. There was a big stone town hall, sheriff's department, and jail. The name of the town was American, but some Mexican influence remained. He rode in very early in the morning and ate a big breakfast of steak and fried eggs in a saloon that opened for business before the others. The few beer drinkers in the place stared at Sundance while he dug into the big meal. Damn! He was hungry. While he ate, remembering the good food Sarah used to dish up, he didn't feel bad any more. He was close to the end; it looked as if Ryker was at last on his own. No money, no power; just a rifle, a handgun, and a horse.

Way out past Clovis the desert began and stretched away for many days ride. Out there Ryker would have nothing to hide behind but a rock or an organ cactus. There was no real hurry now.

When the bartender came to take away the plates, Sundance asked him if he'd seen a big, white-haired man on a Morgan horse. "Very big, hair white as a bone," Sundance said. "Maybe he came in here."

"Nobody of that description in this town," the bartender answered.

"Not from here, from Texas."

"Makes no difference where he's from I ain't seen him. Try the other saloons. Course he'd be a damn fool to eat or drink in them places. Here we don't water down the whiskey and the beef doesn't die of old age."

There were four other saloons in Clovis and Sundance asked about Ryker in all of them. The answer was the same. No, they hadn't seen him.

Sundance mounted up and kept on heading west. Nobody had seen Ryker, but that didn't mean a thing. Ryker could have ridden through Clovis late at night, or even circled the town. The sun was a copper ball glowing in the pitiless blue sky; soon the grassland gave out and due west was the desert. Sundance had lived much of his life in the Southwestern desert and knew how to survive there. With Ryker it would be different. He was a well-fed cattleman from well-grassed cow country. It wouldn't be so easy for him.

"Don't die on me, Ryker," Sundance murmured. Death from thirst was a terrible way to die; it would be too good for Ryker. Sundance wondered what would be a bad enough death for Ryker. He couldn't decide what it might be. If it came to using a bullet then that's what he'd use. But he hoped he could take Ryker alive. Sundance knew that the savage side of his nature, the Indian side, was taking over control of him. He let it. He hadn't felt this way since the murder of his father and mother. He had given the killers agonizing deaths, and he hadn't done anything so savage for many years. Maybe it was time to stop thinking like a white man. At least for a while. Time enough to start acting civilized again when Ryker was dead.

The country dipped down where the desert began. At first it was just rocky and dry, then the great rolling white sand dunes were in sight, the powdery sand on their crests stirred by the hot furnace wind. The glare coming off the white sand was like the glare of snow in bright sunlight. This was country fit only for sidewinders and Gila monsters. The sun beat down without mercy as if daring anybody to travel into the dead land it had killed thousands of years in the past.

The white dunes gave away to rock and sand for a few miles. At the end of this long stretch Sundance saw a canteen lying between two rocks. The stopper was pulled out and it was empty. Ryker was going crazy because only a madman threw away a canteen empty or not. There could always be a waterhole, if only a trickle of muddy water where it could be refilled.

Sundance took the empty canteen along. About three miles from where he found the canteen Ryker's coat lay on the ground. He got down and felt the armholes for sweat. They were dry, and even though sweat dried fast in the desert heat the dryness meant that Ryker was some distance ahead.

Then, after he had ridden five more miles, he spotted the dying Morgan horse lying with a broken leg in some rocks. The animal's hoof was still jammed between two small rocks. The foreleg was broken and the splintered bone stuck out through the animal's glistening brown hide. Ryker hadn't taken the time to kill the dying animal, or was afraid the shot would give him away. Sundance aimed the rifle between the horse's eyes and squeezed the trigger. There was no echo in the vast spaces of the desert.

The day was wearing on, but there was still plenty of light. It was still a few hours to dark when he caught sight of Ryker staggering across the top of a shifting dune. His huge body stood out against the stark white of the sand. He turned and looked back, then seemed to stumble and fall. Sundance rode on patiently waiting for Ryker to start shooting from the top of the dune. He didn't. Sundance slid out the Winchester and waited. When he was sure that Ryker wasn't there he rode Eagle up along the side of the dune, not going straight up as a green rider might have tried to do.

When he reached the crest he spotted Ryker running for a line of small rocks with mounds of sand blown against them by the wind. Bullets were already coming at Sundance by the time he brought the stallion to the bottom of the dune. But the range was long and Ryker was firing too fast. Sundance jumped down and waved Eagle away from him. Then he found cover behind a rock. It wasn't good cover, but it was all there was. A bullet spanged off the top of the rock. He kept his head down while Ryker kept yelling and shooting at the same time. He was wasting bullets like a fool. Now he had switched from the rifle to the handgun. Sundance counted the shots. He didn't think Ryker was keeping count. When the hammer dropped for the sixth time, Sundance jumped to his feet and ran straight at Ryker, making no attempt to zig-zag like an Apache. As he ran he could see Ryker's wildly contorted face. Then he saw him raise the handgun and put the muzzle to his head. Sundance dived over the rocks as the pin fell on an empty chamber.

Ryker tried to scramble away but Sundance caught him behind the right ear with the butt of the Winchester. He dropped as if he'd been shot. Sundance whistled for Eagle and the stallion came at a run. Digging into his warbag, Sundance found a length of rawhide and tied Ryker's wrists and ankles after stripping off his shirt. Then he turned him over and he lay on his back. He squinted in the rays of the dying sun after Sundance slapped him awake.

"Go ahead—do it!" Ryker said. "Kill me. I don't care."

"You'll care, Ryker. Why did you have to do it?"

"I don't know why I did it. I wish I could set it right."

"No way to do that. Not with money, not with anything. And you don't even have money now. Too late for everything."

"Then go ahead and shoot, you lousy breed. Your mother was a dirty poxed-up Injun squaw."

"No way to get me mad, Ryker. I'm all over being mad. You just have to pay for what you did." Sundance had been thinking all day about what he said next. "What's the one thing you're most afraid of in the world, Ryker? I don't mean dying itself. What's the way you'd hate to die."

"Go to hell," Ryker said.

"I'll tell you what you're most afraid of. Rattlers, Gila monsters. I'd say Gila monsters more than rattlers. You don't always die of a rattler bite, but nobody survives the Gila. They're so full of poison it drips from their mouths. Once they sink their teeth they don't let go unless you cut off the head. The man they bite swells up and takes hours to die. They tell me the pain is bad as can be. How'd you like to die that way, Ryker?"

Ryker's huge body was trembling and his ruddy face was white. Spittle hung like silver thread from the corner of his mouth. "Jesus! You wouldn't do that. God in heaven, you wouldn't do that. I didn't even mean to kill the girl. It just happened."

"She's dead. You should have listened to what I told you that day in the sheriff's office. There was no need for any of this. But there's no going back so you have to pay."

Ryker's eyes were bright with fear. "You're a savage!"

"No more than you. Maybe less. It's time to start looking for a Gila."

Ryker struggled to break loose but the rawhide thongs held him securely. He lay on his back gasping for breath while Sundance took the empty rifle and started poking under rocks. For all its deadliness the Gila was a retiring creature but was ferocious when provoked. It took a while before Sundance felt the muzzle of the rifle poke into something that wasn't sand. He poked again and there was a hissing spitting noise. He poked again before the ugly nightmarish reptile emerged from its nest, its tongue flicking in and out. Sundance poked it in the mouth and felt the sharp teeth close on the barrel. He twisted the barrel away and kept on backing toward Ryker. The lizard, now completely enraged, scurried after him. The hideous mouth opened and closed; the poison-filled, garishly banded body quivered with mindless fury.

Ryker raised his head and saw it coming and screamed a long, high despairing scream. Sundance moved away as the monster sprang at Ryker and sank its rows of teeth in his head. It dug in deeper and hung on, its jaws clamped tight, its beady bright eyes glazed.

Already the poison was starting to work, but it took several hours to kill him. Ryker's eyes were open and he stared up at the darkening sky in utter horror. In his nightmares he had run from this ultimate horror, and now it was happening at last.

"Let's go, boy," Sundance said to Eagle.

Book 2

SUNDANCE

DAY OF THE HALFBREEDS

One

"What do you want, halfbreed?"

The challenge was hurled at Jim Sundance by a burly Scotsman in the scarlet coat of the Royal North West Mounted Police. The policeman, wearing sergeant's stripes on his sleeve, made no attempt to hide his hostility. His pale-blue eyes were hard, his meaty face lined with bitterness. As he spoke, he touched the flapped-over holster with his thumb.

It was November 16, 1885, a bright, biting cold morning in Regina, Saskatchewan, and thousands of people had come to witness the hanging of the most loved and hated man in Canada. Louis Riel had finally come to the end of his road; Sundance had come a very long way to see him off.

"I have a pass," Sundance said, handing the paper to the Mountie.

He waited while the sergeant sent a trooper to find a superior officer. Overhead, the sky was a brilliant blue; on the prairie around the raw new frontier town, hoarfrost glittered in the sun.

The double line of militiamen and Mounties stood watching Sundance, for even in the wild North West

Territories—a land of halfbreeds—he was an unusual sight, with his flowing yellow hair and skin the color of an old penny. Tall and lean, he was dressed in buckskins and carried himself with the assurance of a professional fighting man. Hanging from his tooled leather belt were a long-barreled Colt .44, a razor-edged Bowie knife, and a straight-handled throwing hatchet.

"My name is Mackenzie," the Mountie officer said, coming back with the pass in his gloved hand. His wind-burned face was tired, showing the strain of the execution that was to take place in less than an hour. "You'll have to give up your weapons before you can go in. Everybody is on edge. I'll walk along with you in case one of the guards gets nervous."

Sundance nodded. Only eight weeks had passed since Louis Riel had led his army of halfbreeds and Indians against the government of Canada. The whole country was braced for another outbreak of violence. Soldiers from all over Canada had been drafted to the North West Territories, and men slept with guns beside their beds. The cold, clear air crackled with tension.

Mackenzie thumped on the door with his fist, giving the password when it was called for. High up on the stone tower of the jail and police barracks, two Gatling guns were mounted, ready to rake the square with lead as the hour of execution grew closer.

Inside the jail, it was colder than it was outside in the sunshine. An iron-faced door banged open and shut; nail-shod boots echoed in the hallways.

"I've heard of you, Mr. Sundance," Mackenzie said. "It's hard to think that it would come to this. If only Riel hadn't come back. Nobody would ever have bothered him in Montana. But he came back and had to be stopped."

"That's right. He had to be stopped. That won't make his people feel any better after he's dead. It won't make me feel any better."

184

"You think there will be peace now?"

"That's hard to say. Your government has the money and the guns."

"But it's their government too. We couldn't just let Riel start his own country right in the middle of Canada."

Try telling that to the halfbreeds, Sundance thought. He knew what it was like to be a halfbreed, a man caught between the races, belonging no place. Though Louis Riel, madman or patriot (depending on which side you were on), had very little Indian blood, he had fought long and hard for those he considered to be his people.

"Well, he's stopped now," Sundance said with finality, thinking of Louis Riel and John Brown and all the madmen who were ready to die for what they believed was right.

They went up a steel staircase to the third floor of the jail. On the way up, they were stopped twice by heavily armed guards.

"How is he taking it?" Sundance asked.

"You know Riel so you already know the answer," Mackenzie said. "Nothing bothers him. He writes for hours every day. I don't have the heart to tell him that nobody will ever read it. I have strict orders to destroy his papers once he's dead. In time perhaps he'll be forgotten."

Sundance said, "He won't be forgotten. It doesn't matter what you do with his papers; he won't be forgotten. Hanging him will only make it worse."

A guard stood outside the door of Riel's cell. "He's had the priest," he told Mackenzie. "Said he didn't want any breakfast, just coffee. He's still writing in that book of his."

Mackenzie spoke to Sundance. "I can only let you have fifteen minutes. If you don't want to stay that long, bang on the door. After that we'll have to get him ready. You'll be his last visitor except for..."

There was no need to complete the sentence. Riel's last

visitors would be the governor of the jail, the priest—and the hangman.

The door closed behind Sundance and the key turned in the lock. In the cold, narrow stone cell there were few furnishings except for a bunk, a small unpainted table, and a chair. Louis Riel sat at the table beneath the barred window set high in the wall. A big silver watch lay on the table beside the inkwell; the only sound was the hurried scratching of his pen.

"Is that you, Mr. Mackenzie?" Riel asked without turning his head. The pen raced on across the paper. "Surely, it isn't time yet?"

"Not yet, Louis," Sundance said quietly.

A smile spread across Riel's dark, brooding face as he stood up quickly and extended his hand. "Jim Sundance, you came all this way. I hoped you would come, but your letters were written from so far away. Do you want some coffee? It's still hot."

Sundance sat on the edge of the bunk. "I did the best I could, Louis. So did General Crook. He wrote to the President and everybody else he could think of. It didn't do any good. I'm sorry."

Riel handed Sundance a tin cup of black coffee. "No need to be sorry. I knew what I was doing all the time. I don't even blame Macdonald. He let me escape to Montana the first time. But what good would I be as a schoolteacher in Montana? Every day I was there I thought of nothing but my people, what was happening to them in the Territories. It wasn't getting better, Jim, it was getting worse. I knew I could never call myself a man if I didn't come back."

"And here you are, Louis."

Riel's English was fluent with only a trace of a French-Canadian accent. "You're taking it worse than I am. Don't you see? There are some things that can't be changed. All my life, during all my wanderings, I knew—I *knew* that this was how it had to end. But oh what a fight we gave them, Louis Riel and his *métis*! It took nearly ten-thousand of them to do it. We might even have won if they didn't have the railroad. Perhaps not won great battles, but concessions. We might have forced them to let us live in peace on the land of our fathers. You would have thought that Canada was big enough for all of us—such a vast country stretching away to the end of the world!"

"You won some things, Louis," Sundance said. "Not your own country, but many things. From now on, they'll always know they can't push people too far."

Riel nodded in agreement. "What you say is true. But what a country we could have had! Free from the stink of factories and cities! To trap and fish and hunt the buffalo."

"The buffalo is almost gone, Louis."

"We could have brought them back. That was one of the plans of my government. We could have made the Red River into a land of plenty. It could have become truly the land of free men without interference from the fatted politicians in Ottawa. There would be towns but no cities. The English and the Scotch would have been welcome there but not as speculators and and money-grubbers. The Red River settlements would have been as example to all freedom-loving peoples."

"There can still be freedom, Louis. Not exactly as you saw it, but your fight hasn't been for nothing. In your forty years you have accomplished many things."

Riel said, "If I had another forty, even another ten, I could remake this country. I have been called a madman because of what I tried to do. But if you don't burn hotly, you soon flicker out. I have seen it happen to other men with a special view of what life should be. Do you think I'm a madman, Jim?"

"I have considered the idea from time to time. I'd be a liar if I said I didn't."

Riel glanced at his watch and laughed. "That's one thing you'll never be. You told me what to expect if I went ahead with my plans. I knew you were right in many ways, but there was nothing I could do. My people needed a leader, and I was that leader. There is no boast in what I say, simply fact. If there had been a stronger leader, I would have stepped aside in his favor. People have never believed that, yet it's the truth. My people are brave, but they have lived all their lives on the prairies. Bravery isn't always enough, not when you are faced with Maxim guns and railroads and modern armies. I was the only leader who could bring their plight to the attention of the world. In the great cities—New York, London, Paris—they know who we are and what we tried to do here in the wilderness."

"They know all right," Sundance said. "There isn't an important newspaper in the world that hasn't carried the news. Right now, thousands of people are marching in Montreal and all over France."

"Good! Good!" Riel said.

Sundance said, "Will there be trouble in the Territories today? There has been talk."

"You mean more bloodshed?"

"There is talk of that, Louis. There is still time to stop it. Your people wouldn't have a chance. The militia would crush them in days. They'd drive them out onto the prairies and hunt them down to the last man. With winter coming on, no food . . . you know the rest."

"There won't be any more trouble, Jim. I could have escaped after that last battle. I stayed and let them capture me because I knew the Canadian government would be looking for a victim. Give me any name you like. I stayed so the politicians in Ottawa could take out their anger on me. You know what Macdonald said during the riots that followed my conviction for treason? 'Riel shall hang even if every dog in Quebec barks in his favor.'"

"I read that," Sundance said.

"That's how the English think of us—as dogs," Riel said. "But we bit them hard enough. You can kick a dog for just so long, then he shows his teeth."

Riel looked at this watch and smoothed back his long black hair with his fingers. His crow-black hair was the only sign of his Indian blood.

"They'll be coming in a few minutes," he said. "Don't ever blame yourself for the part you had in this."

"Maybe I should have stayed out of it."

"Nothing would have changed. You can be certain of that. Don't get discouraged because of what happened here. Continue to fight for the Indians, as you have always done. Your enemies in Washington may get you in the end, but don't ever give up. Ah yes, my friends are coming up the stairs to get me. You will walk down to the second floor with me? That's where the end comes for Louis Riel. Don't forget me, Jim."

"I would never do that, Louis."

Mackenzie came into the cell followed by the others. The hangman, a short fat man in his sixties, stood to one side while the priest offered up prayers for the dead in a loud voice.

"It's time to go," Mackenzie said.

Two

Nearly a year before, Sundance had been in Fort Riley, Kansas, when a telegram arrived from General George Crook, now commander of the Department of the Missouri, with headquarters in Chicago. There was no explanation because, between Sundance and his old friend George Crook, none was necessary. The message asked him to come to Chicago as soon as he could. Sundance was on the next available train.

The two men, halfbreed and major general in the United States Army, had been close friends for many years. They had campaigned together in the wars against Geronimo and again later on the high plains. Sundance had served under Crook as scout and hunter. Between them, there was a bond that could never be broken. When there were no wars to be fought, and when their paths happened to cross, they hunted and fished together. Crook was a no-nonsense veteran, liked by his men and respected by the Indians he had fought so long and so hard. Liquor and foul language had no place in his life, but he smoked one black cigar after another, despite the warnings of his wife and doctor. There was nothing Sundance would not have done for George Crook.

Sundance got Eagle from the box-car in which the great fighting stallion had traveled from Kansas. "Easy boy!" he said as his horse whickered nervously at the crash and roar of the city. It had been years since Sundance had been in Chicago, and he didn't like it any better now. He didn't like cities of any kind, and Chicago was one of the noisiest of them all.

It took him an hour to ride across town and find General Crook's headquarters in the newly built military reservation. It was winter. Dirty, frozen snow was on the ground and a vicious wind was blowing in from the lake. A sentry passed him through the gate and a corporal escorted him to Crook's office. He had to wait for five minutes before the general came out to greet him. A white-haired man in a gray broadcloth suit stared at Sundance as he left the room. Sundance thought he looked familiar, a face from the newspapers.

"Did you ever see such weather?" Crook said. "Lord, how I'd like to be back in Arizona. I wonder if it's true that the desert makes a man's blood thin. Come on in by the fire and get warm. I'll shout up some coffee for both of us."

A stack of logs burned in the fireplace with a cheerful crackle. "Sit down, Jim," Crook said, rubbing his large hands together. "I tell you, this new job of mine doesn't suit me at all—shuffling papers all day. You get worse saddle sores from sitting in a chair than you ever got from any saddle. I only took the job to please Mary. We're both not so young anymore, and she thought it was time we settled down to a more civilized existence. Damnation! I'd go back to sleeping in a tent any time."

Sundance smiled at the general. "You'll get the hang of it after a while."

"Absolutely not," Crook said. "I'm a fighting soldier and always was, from the first day I left the Point. Mary is fine by the way."

An orderly brought in a pot of coffee and Sundance waited while Crook poured.

Back behind his desk with a cup in one hand and a cigar in the other, Crook said, "I guess you're wondering why I sent for you, Jim. I couldn't explain in the telegram because it would take too long. Besides, too many people in and out of the army have long noses. This isn't like anything I've asked you to do before, so you're free to turn it down. I'll understand if you do."

"It isn't likely that I will, Three Stars," Sundance said, using the old Cheyenne name for General Crook. The general was known to his men as Old George; to Sundance he would always be Three Stars.

"Hear me out first," Crook said. "The whole thing is about as complicated as it can get. You know there are people in this country who would like to annex or steal Canada. Yes, sir, we have people with mighty big ideas in the U.S.A. From sea to shining sea isn't big enough for them. Now it has to be Canada, the whole Dominion. 'Manifest destiny' is the fancy name they give it. Of course, it's just another name for some plain and fancy stealing. But that's politics for you. No matter how fat a politician gets, he wants to get fatter. It's the nature of the beast."

Sundance drank his coffee. It was army coffee, which was all you could say for it.

Crook went on: "Not every politician in Washington is in favor of annexation. But lot of them are. So are their friends in business, who lick their lips every time they think of that big rich mostly empty country up there—mining, lumber, furs, millions of acres of some of the finest land in the world, all waiting to be stolen by Uncle Sam."

"What about the British," Sundance asked. "They're not known to take these things lying down."

Crook said, "I was coming to that. Some people in our

government are convinced the British will fight if it comes to a showdown. Others aren't so sure. Their argument is that Great Britain is thousands of miles away. Ever since the Civil War, this country has one of the most powerful armies in the world. Britain, they argue, isn't about to get into a major war over a wilderness like Canada."

"What do you think?"

"I honestly don't know. They're a tough people, the British, and they may see it as a matter of pride. I'd hate to see Washington shelled all over again, not to mention Boston and New York. I'm inclined to think they'll fight. That's only one man's opinion, and there are men, men I respect, who don't agree with me. Lord, I'd hate to see a war with England. But that's only part of the problem. It gets worse as it goes along. You ever hear of a man named Louis Riel?"

"The so-called halfbreed leader?"

"That's the one. How much do you know about him?"

"That he started a halfbreed rebellion in the North West Territories about fifteen years ago, was defeated, and managed to escape to Montana."

Crook said, "He didn't manage to escape. They let him escape to keep him from becoming a martyr. A lot of people wanted to see him hung, but they let him escape instead. For fifteen years he stayed in Montana, taught school, and wrote a lot of fiery speeches, and not much else was heard from him. Now he's back in the North West Territories threatening to establish a separate government dominated by halfbreeds and Indians. If the movement goes far enough, there is going to be a bloody war up there."

"I thought the Territories belonged to the Hudson Bay Company."

"Not for much longer. The company no longer has effective control over the area and is turning it over to the Canadian government. The transfer hasn't been made yet, so there is nobody in real control. That's why Riel is trying to seize control—when the situation is confused. He tried it once before, but now he has a better chance."

"Because he has outside help from this country?"

"How did you know?"

"Just a guess. Now would be the time to look for help."

"And get it," Crook said, "from the politicians and the business men. The Irish don't want to be left out either. By Irish I mean the Fenians. Any trouble that can be made for England, the Fenians are ready to take part in it. You remember the time they tried to invade Canada after the Civil War? They were beaten off by the militia and some British regulars. Now they're looking for another chance. They've been collecting money and recruiting men in New York, Boston, and even right here in Chicago. Our government isn't doing much to stop them. There's that monster of all northern politicians, the Irish vote."

Sundance said, "All the halfbreeds and Indians will suffer while the others look after their own interests."

"Riel doesn't think so. That's the information I have. Riel thinks he can handle all of them when the time comes. Look, Jim, I don't say the halfbreeds and Indians don't have just complaint. They've lived up there in the Territories for as long as man can remember. Suddenly, the Canadian government is interested in their lands, wants them to prove their titles. What do these poor people know about land titles? It's their land because they have always lived there. Now they're being trod underfoot by government surveyors. It all sounds reasonable on paper, but these people live with the hard facts of life, not scraps of paper. It's a desperate situation, and Riel is playing into the hands of men who are no friends of his people."

Sundance had been thinking of Louis Riel. That the man was a fanatic there was no doubt. But then, so were all desperate men. A halfbreed himself, he could well understand Riel's despair. Governments promised much and did nothing until desperate men broke out their guns.

"You haven't come to the worst part yet," he suggested to General Crook.

"God help me, I haven't, Jim. Riel has very little Indian blood, perhaps none, but the halfbreeds and Indians—the Crees—look up to him. They fought with him in the first rebellion and will fight harder now. Riel's plan is to call for a general uprising of all the Indian tribes on both sides of the border—all the tribes. And he thinks he can do it. If that happens, the frontier will be washed in blood. It will make all the Indian wars of the past look like skirmishes."

"Has he white support in this, Three Stars?"

"My information is that he does. It will give our government an excuse to invade Canada, to crush Riel, and scatter his forces. Once we're in, we'll want to stay to make sure of a lasting peace. The President doesn't want that to happen, but there won't be much he can do about it. There will be so much flagwaving he wouldn't even try—not and stay in office, that is. I tell you, Jim, this business scares the dickens out of me."

"How many people know about it?"

"No way to be sure. Plenty of people know about it but are afraid to take sides. They'd like to sit out the dance and perhaps make a little money when the slaughter is over. Sumner and Seward started it. They've always had their eyes on Canada. They liked to pretend it was because Canada harbored Rebels during the Civil War. Not so. They just want to steal the country."

"What about the army?"

"The high-ranking officers know about it, or have heard something. Some don't believe it because this annex Canada talk has been going on for years. It goes clear back to the Revolutionary War. Some officers would like to see another war. Nothing like a war for quick promotion. I've known too many men who have built their careers on the bones of others."

"Three Stars, what would you like me to do? What do you think I *could* do? You just drew a dismal picture."

Crook got up and walked around, angry and glum at the same time.

"I'll be blunt. You're a halfbreed and know how it feels to be treated like one. I don't say anyone has done that lately, but you were once a boy. You saw the scorn heaped on your parents. With you it isn't something learned from a book. Do you think Louis Riel knows who you are?"

"It's possible. I've been in Canada. My name has been in the newspapers, though not as often in Canada as here."

"Do you think Riel would listen to you? If you went north and explained what I have told you? I'm told those blamed Fenians, those Irishmen, are already with him. Their leader is a man named Colum Hardesty. He's thirty-eight or forty and served in the British army before landing in New York ten years ago. Hardesty has two friends, named Cunningham and Lane. It would be a shame if something happened to them."

Crook stared out the window and bit the end off another cigar. "If you know what I mean."

"I could try talking to Riel," Sundance said. "I'd have to get up there and see how everything was going. I'd probably have to offer to join up with him. I'm a halfbreed, so he wouldn't find that hard to believe."

Crook sat down again. "You know I can't help you if anything happens. They don't love you in Washington, and that's a fact. You don't even have to go if you don't want to. It's getting to the point where there isn't much any man can do. The things men will do for money! I'd like to take certain parties I know and shoot them out of hand."

"I'd be there holding your coat, Three Stars. I don't know what I can do. It may be too big for any man. But I'd

196

like to take a look. I could always kill Riel, but I'll face that when I come to it. How much do you really know about the man? I know what's in the newspapers, and that's all. You've obviously been studying up on him."

"As much as I can," the general said. "And I can't decide whether he's little crazy or big crazy. Some men are sane and crazy at the same time. Let me read you some of the notes I've made. You can't read my writing, so don't try."

"Louis Riel, born in 1844, son of Louis Riel and the daughter of the first white child born in the River Settlement. Said to be one-eighth Indian, though no proof exists of this. In 1858 sent to Sulpician College, in Montreal, to study for the priesthood. Moody, ill-tempered, wrote poetry. Left the seminary without completing his studies. On his way home to Red River worked as a clerk in a general store in St. Paul, Minnesota. Later became prominent in the *métis* (halfbreed) movement, its slogan was: 'For the first owners of the soil.' Began an association with Fenian leader W. B. O'Donoghue of Fort Garry. In 1870, now leader of the halfbreeds and Indians, Riel spoke of inviting annexation by the United States. After declaring a provisional government, Riel's forces were defeated and he was forced to flee Canada. After fifteen years in Montana, where he was a schoolteacher among other things, he recently returned to the North West Territories. During his exile, he spent two years in asylums and has been described as a religious fanatic with an often stated desire to establish his own church. Dark hair, wild staring black eyes, well educated, well spoken. Fluent in English and French. His whereabouts are not known at the present time."

General Crook put down the sheet of paper. "That's about it, Jim. He's more of a mystery than anything else. The Canadian government has tried to buy him off with the finest tracts of land in the Territories, but he just laughs at them. They offered to settle a lifetime pension, a big one, on him if he will return to his country. Money means nothing to him. Riel always says, 'I will dress no better than the poorest of my people. I will eat what they eat, and if there is not enough for me I will eat nothing.' I'm not afraid of much, my old friend, but this man frightens me. Yes, kill him if you have to. How soon can you start?"

"Today."

"You'll need money."

"I have enough money to last me. If I take too much money, they may search me and find it. If I have to use the telegraph, where do I send the messages?"

"To the Western Union general office on State Street. Send them to Edward Bellson. The manager is the only one who knows who that is. He'll get them over here as fast as a horse can run. Your best way to get to Regina—Riel is said to be close to there—in by Canadian Pacific. I hope we aren't at war with England the next time we meet."

Crook walked outside with Sundance; the wind from the lake was still bone-rattling cold. "It's colder than this where you're going," the general said. "One more thing, Jim. If you can't do any good, then let it go. More than that I can't tell you. Sometimes, these things have to take their course, and there's nothing anybody can do. Cut your losses and come on back home. I'll be waiting to hear what you have to say. Let's hope it's good news."

The two men shook hands, and the sentry passed Sundance out through the gate. Sundance had the feeling that there was a long, hard, dangerous road ahead.

Three

Sundance stabled his horse and went to get something to eat. There was blinding sunshine, a sky without a cloud, and a wind that bit through the quilted wool coat he was wearing. The big Canadian Pacific locomotive clanged through the depot at Regina, a town so new that few of its buildings had been painted. In the air was the smell of raw wood and turpentine.

Men and animals thronged the main street, filling it from one side to the other. From the saloons came the tinny rattle of mechanical pianos. A man with a flowing beard was standing on a nail barrel, telling the passersby about God. Two drunken halfbreeds were fighting about something, and it took an enormous Mountie to get them to move on.

Sundance pushed his way into a saloon called the Cromarty Place, proprietor Angus McAdams, and fought his way to the bar. A long-necked Scotsman was serving up hot whiskies with sugar and lemon in them. He gave Sundance a cautious look.

"What'll yours be?"

"One of those," Sundance said, pointing at the steaming jug. "Not too much sugar."

Some of the men at the bar turned to look at Sundance. Most of the men in the saloon were white, and he could feel them measuring him with their eyes, inspecting his array of weapons. The bartender set down the hot whiskey in front of Sundance and named a price three times higher than it should have been. Sundance paid it without question.

He relaxed as the warmth of the whiskey flowed through him. It had been an easy trip from Chicago, but he wanted to stand around and have a drink before he did anything else. He was in a strange town, a town that was clearly edgy. It looked as if people were taking sides, deciding which way to run when the shooting started. Men eyed him as much as they eyed each other.

A drunk came in from the street and got a drink at the bar. To Sundance he looked like a halfbreed, but in this country there was no way to be sure about a man. A man who looked one thing often turned out to be another.

For such a small man, the drunk had a big mouth, and he wasn't bashful about using it. Some of the men edged away from him until there was a space on both sides. He got another whiskey and drank it, then looked along the bar to where Sundance was standing.

"Hello, my friend," he said in a heavy French-Canadian accent. "I ain't see you before, have I?"

Sundance said no and turned to look in the mirror behind the bar. On his first day in town he didn't want to be bothered by a drunk. There was something not right about this man. It was just a feeling, and it became stronger when the short man sidled down the bar until he was very close.

"It's all right, mister," he said. "I'm not trying to cadge drinks. I have enough money of my own."

"Glad to hear it," Sundance said.

The man lowered his voice. "You don't have to be

careful with me. You're a 'breed just like me. We're all in this together."

By now his voice was a whisper. "Are you here to join the movement?"

"What movement?"

"In these parts, there is only one, my friend. You are either with it or against it. It's all right, you can talk to me. I know the people you have come to see. I can take you to them." He gestured toward the whites at the bar. "Pretty soon it will be all over for them. No longer will they walk around as if they owned the world. Soon it will be all changed."

"Good! That's fine."

"What did you say?"

"I said everything's fine. It's also a nice day. I just want to drink my drink."

"But you don't understand what I'm talking about. Your friends are my friends. You are not from this country, so you will need help to find your friends. There is no need to give any names. Just nod yes that you have come to join the movement."

"I still don't know what you're talking about. Now I'd be obliged if you'd let me drink my drink. I won't ask you again."

For an instant, the man's bleary eyes were clear, then he smiled stupidly and said, "No offense, my friend. I was just trying to be friendly to a stranger. I don't care. I can drink someplace else."

He went out and Sundance finished his whiskey. Turning to go, he found himself confronted by a tough-faced farmer in a bright red coat. But it wasn't trouble after all. The farmer said in a Yankee accent, "Watch yourself with that feller, whoever you are. He's a police spy."

201

Four

"My name is Jacob Sawtelle," the man said, "and I hate to see any man taken in by the likes of him. I don't know why the Mounties hire such a man. Sometimes I think I'd have done a lot better to have stayed in Vermont. But you know how restless a man can get when the countryside starts filling up. I figured why not come out here to the Territories and enjoy some peace and quiet."

"You could always go back," Sundance said. "It's not that far."

"I'm here, and here I stay. The hardest thing is not taking sides. The *métis* are fine people but fierce tempered when they feel they've been wronged. It would be good to dive down in a storm cellar and wait for this to blow over. It won't. I can't see any hope of that. Well, I'd better get to the store and get on home. The missus is as nervous as a cat these days. Watch out for that spy. I hear he gets a cash bonus for every *métis* sympathizer he turns over to the police. He goes by the name of Val Lafleche, but I'd hardly say that was his real name."

The Vermont farmer went out. Sundance watched him all the way to a hardware store down the street. Lafleche was his idea of what a sneak looked like, which didn't mean that Sawtelle wasn't a police agent too. Probably, the whole region was crawling with spies and double-crossers, the way it had been on the Kansas-Missouri border just before the war. Officially, there was no war on yet, but from what General Crook had said, it was almost unavoidable. It was the same old story of government stupidity, and now many people were going to die because of it.

Getting to Riel wasn't going to be easy. Crook said the *métis* leader had his headquarters in a town called Batoche, far up the Red River, but he moved around to the other halfbreed settlements, never staying in one place for long, always traveling with a bodyguard of one-hundred heavily armed men. All were expert frontiersmen, all deadly shots after a lifetime of hunting with little ammunition in some of the hardest country in the world.

These were the men he had to face: bitter, resentful, suspicious of all strangers, for no stranger had ever given them an honest deal. Louis Riel was their hero, and they would kill without mercy to protect him. It was no use asking questions about Riel; if the Mounties didn't throw him in jail, some of the *métis* would probably put a knife in his back. What he had to do was ride out alone and go north along the Red River. That he was a halfbreed wouldn't help as much as General Crook thought it would. After all, he was no peace-loving *métis* trapper but a professional fighting man; the *métis* would recognize that the moment they saw him.

Riel would probably know who he was, that is, if he lived long enough to be brought to the rebel headquarters. It wasn't likely any of the others would. Most were trappers and farmers; few spoke English. Sundance's plan, such as it was, was to offer his services to the *métis*. If they were working with the Fenians, they might have no hesitation in accepting him. He would just have to try it out.

He was strolling around town when something made him turn. He saw the man called Val Lafleche ducking behind a freight wagon. The movement was fast but awkward, as if Lafleche wanted to be seen. Lafleche had done nothing to attract Sundance's attention. Maybe he knew that a man like Sundance would know he was being followed. Sights and sounds had nothing to do with it. It was mostly instinct.

Sundance went into a small, crowded restaurant and sat at one of the six stools at the counter after a man picking his teeth got up and went out. After a long wait, the counter girl brought him a thick steak with hashed potatoes and coffee. In the steamed-up mirror behind the counter, he spotted Lafleche looking in the window. Then he ducked away as he had before. There was no doubt about it now. The sneak couldn't have been easier to see if he'd been beating a bass drum and foaming at the mouth.

Sundance waited for Lafleche to show his ugly face again, but he didn't. Then another man came in, as Sundance knew he would. There was nothing about him to attract attention. He was neither tall nor short, had sandy hair and a face like a thousand others, about forty years of age. He sat at a table against the wall and ordered coffee and a sandwich.

This was the real police spy, Sundance knew. How many there were in Regina he had no way of knowing. There might even be another to back this one up, but he didn't think so. The nondescript man looked as if he could handle it all by himself.

Sundance wondered if the Mounties already had some information about him. Or it could be that they simply watched every stranger who came to Regina, especially if he happened to be a heavily armed halfbreed from below the border? They said the Mounties were the best police in the world. Sundance had never thought about it. He knew he didn't want to tangle with them if he didn't have to, but he couldn't get anything done if he let them walk in his footsteps.

He paid for his meal and walked out as if going nowhere in particular. The police spy followed him outside and walked along behind him, varying the distance now and then. Sundance didn't try any fancy stopping and starting. He simply walked and let the police agent follow him. He didn't think the man would give up, even if they walked around all day, which was the last thing Sundance had in mind.

Sundance went into the Menteith Hotel and paid double for a small, clean room with a tinted picture of Queen Victoria on the wall. A few weak gasps of hot air came from a grating in the floor. The bed was narrow and hard; Sundance stretched out on it and waited for it to get dark.

Four hours later, the darkness of the northern winter came down rapidly, blurring the raw outlines of the town. He went to the door and listened for sounds in the hall. A door banged and somebody went downstairs in heavy boots. On the first floor, plates and silverware clattered as the waitresses prepared for the evening meal.

The back of the hotel faced a patch of woods where snow was packed hard between the trees. Sundance pushed up the window and looked out. If they were waiting, there was no sign of them. Nothing moved but pine branches and snow crystals stirred by the wind. It seemed to have gotten warmer; that could mean more snow. They could track him a lot easier in snow, Sundance realized; but they could track him anyway if they had the right man—and they would.

Buckling on his weapons belt over his thick woolen coat, Sundance pulled on his gloves, figured the drop, and let go the windowsill. He landed lightly in packed snow and ran quickly to the cover of a stack of lumber. No one yelled at him to stop.

He went along behind the hotel, across the mouth of an alley, and kept going until he was in back of the livery stable. An alley ran between the stable and a freight office next door. He went into the alley but stopped before he got to the street. Down the street, on the far side, was the stone bulk of the North West Mounted Police barracks with two Gatling guns drawn up in front of it. There was the crash of heavy boots as the police sentries changed guard.

From the alley, Sundance watched the far side of the street. A lumber yard with a fence around it stood dark and quiet, locked up for the night. No lights showed anywhere in the two-story buildings, and the gate was closed. He backed away quickly when he heard the faint noise of a horse pawing the ground. If the wind had been blowing the other way, he wouldn't have heard it at all.

There it was. They were in there waiting for him to get his horse and come out the front door of the stable. Then they would ride after him. Sundance smiled and hoped they wouldn't get too cold waiting there in the dark and thinking of hot food and the heavily sugared tea Canadians liked so much.

Back behind the stable, he inspected the padlock on the door. It was sturdy and the wood was new, but he figured his hatchet blade would pry it loose. It had to be done quietly, or the livery man would start shooting or yelling for the Mounties. One was as bad as the other.

He put his ear to the door and listened for sounds inside. At first there was nothing, then he heard the sound of snoring. The snoring went on interspersed with a loud snort every so often. This was the best chance he would get, Sundance knew, because it was always possible that the police would decide to look in his room. If they found him, they could toss him in jail until the trouble with Riel was over. That could be months. If it came to a showdown, he knew he wouldn't kill any Mounties.

Working carefully but steadily, he dug his keen-bladed hatchet into the door, stopping occasionally to listen for sounds. Wind hummed in telegraph wires at the front of the stable. Nothing else was heard. He was sweating in spite of the cold when the hasp of the lock began to come free of the wood. It moved some more when he slid the blade of the hatchet under the hasp and used the handle as a lever. Another short pull on the handle was all it took to open the door.

The stable had horse stalls on both sides of a central open area. In a corner a man lay on a cot under a huge pile of blankets, a whiskey bottle on the floor beside him. There was no heat of any kind, and the only light came from a lantern turned down low. The front door was barred from the inside.

Sundance squinted through the crack between the two halves of the door. Across the street, the lumber yard was dark, its gate still closed. Powdered snow blew in the wagon ruts in the hard-frozen mud.

Sundance spoke quitely to the other horses in the stable, soothing the animals while he saddled Eagle. On the cot the stable man muttered in his sleep. Sundance stayed perfectly still in Eagle's stall while the man, with his eyes closed, reached down for the whiskey bottle and took a long drink. "Damn, it's cold," he grumbled.

In moments, he was snoring again.

Sundance closed the back door of the stable and put a board against it to keep it closed. It wouldn't be long before they traced him from the hotel to the stable. Their big advantage was that they knew the country and he didn't, not at all.

There was only one way to get out, and that was to do it head-on. Once he got out of town, he would have to look for Mountie patrols and head for the Red River. From the maps he had looked at, the Red River would take him north to Batoche. If he didn't find Riel there, he would have to keep on looking, that is, if some *metis* sharpshooter didn't knock him out of the saddle at a long distance.

It was rough country up on the Red River: during the winter it was frozen solid for five months. To be caught out there unprepared or injured was to die. The Red River was a land without mercy for the stranger.

Sundance had some supplies but he hadn't loaded up too heavily because that would have attracted suspicion. Few men were going north in the Territories with war about to break out. What he hoped for was to buy food at *métis* farmhouses along the way or to shoot what small game he could find.

Leading Eagle, he went into the woods behind the town and kept going until there were no longer any lights or sounds. Then he found the road and mounted up, heading northwest toward the river. Finding the Red River would be easy. After that, he'd be facing a frozen hell.

Five

An Arctic wind swept into the town of Batoche, sending flurries of snow down the chimney of Louis Riel's thick-walled log cabin. Riel sat by the fire talking to the New York Irishman, Colum Hardesty, who had come so far to strike a blow at the hated English.

Hardesty was in his late thirties, big bones, black haired and blue eyed. Even in a chair, he moved with a sort of swagger. His voice was deep and musical. When he made a point, he had the habit of punching his right fist into the palm of the left.

A big iron pot of stew was bubbling, suspended over the fire by a crane. Outside, the wind strained against the door and rattled the shutters. The two oil lamps flickered as the wind grew stronger.

Hardesty ladled stew into a bowl and cut a chunk of bread from a loaf. "I'm telling you it can be done, Louis," he said. "All through history, men have been doing things other men said couldn't be done. Now is the time to free your people once and for all, but you must act decisively. Show the Canadians that you won't stand for any more of their false promises."

Riel smiled, "I think you are more concerned with the

British than the Canadians. You know this, but I will tell you anyway. Our quarrel is with the Canadians and not the British. As long as the British controlled the North West Territories, they treated us fairly. It was when they handed the Territories over to the Canadians that our troubles began. The British are harsh but fair, while the Canadians are too much like the Americans—and much less honest."

"Action is what your people need, not words," Hardesty said impatiently. "What does it matter who rules you if you're not free to rule yourselves? This can be a time of greatness for you, a chance to create a government of your own without interference from Ottawa or London."

"What about Washington and this talk of annexation? You say you have guarantees from certain people in America. And why would the Americans be any better than the Canadians? The Canadians never treated the Indians as badly as the Americans."

Hardesty said, "The independence of the North West Territories has been guaranteed. This is in appreciation for your help. Annexation is going to take place anyway. It's always been inevitable, so now is the time to strike a blow for freedom."

"For Ireland? Ireland is so far away. I am afraid your country doesn't mean much to me. If it comes to that, many of the Canadians are Irish. The Irish are Catholics, as we are, but they have taken sides against us. I must be honest with you, Colum, I must tell you that my only concern is for the *métis*, my own people. We fight our own fights and always have."

"And you should be honored for it," Hardesty said, "but this isn't fifteen years ago, when you first tried to shake off the Canadians. Now Canada has grown powerful. What you are facing is no longer a series of skirmishes but battles. And guerrilla warfare isn't the answer. You know yourself the country here is too harsh. In British Columbia it would be different. No, Louis, if you are going to fight the Canadians and win against them, you are going to need all the help you can get. That means men and money."

"And annexation?"

"Call it intervention. The United States is a nation of businessmen. What you must do is exchange economic benefits for military and political pressure. *You* will get independence for the North West Territories, and the Americans will make money."

Riel said, "They broke every treaty they made with the Indians. According to the U.S. Constitution, every state had the right to secede. But look what happened to the South when it tried: crushed, ruined, degraded."

Hardesty said, "You have a point. But I don't see how you can win any other way. Anyway, the North West Territories aren't the South. The real reason the North attacked the South was to seize control of its agriculture and its trade. The Americans would scarcely fight that hard to take your Territories. Marching through Georgia isn't like marching up the Red River with the temperature at twenty below."

Riel smiled at the Irishman. "Yes, we have that in our favor. Yet, if men want something badly enough, they will do almost anything."

Hardesty smacked one hand into the other. "That's what I've been telling you. You've made your own point, now let me make another, which is that this is probably the last chance you'll ever get to free your people. Already, the Canadian Pacific has come through. But railroad tracks can be dynamited, bridges blown up, tunnels caved in. That can all be done to prevent the Canadian troop movements that are sure to come. But I'm not just talking about railroads, I'm talking about tens of thousands of people moving into the Territories.

They'll bury your people with their numbers."

Riel stared into the fire as though looking for answers. "You're right, of course," he said. "They will bury us if we—I—let them. I don't want you to be right about some of the things you've said, but you are. But this last thing I must think about. A general Indian uprising could be a terrible thing, more terrible than the war we are planning against the Canadians, much more savage."

Hardesty was stubborn, hard eyed. "It's all part of the same war. The Sioux, the Blackfoot, the Cree, and the Assiniboin all want to strike at the whites."

"All I want is a measure of freedom for my people," Riel said. "There was a time when I would have accepted limited independence. It was never my intention to rebel against the authority of the central government, but they forced me. If only they would let us go, withdraw their mounted police, take their steamboats from our rivers, and leave us in peace."

"You're dreaming when you talk like that," Hardesty said. "In Ireland, all we asked was the same thing. We had our own parliament, were loyal to the king, and then they dissolved it because a few greedy men wanted it that way. Now, eighty-five years later, my country is in poverty."

Louis Riel spooned some stew into a dish and proceeded to eat it without much enthusiasm. "We have talked enough for the moment about ideas and old wrongs. It is time to be practical. These Fenians of yours, will they fight? I know they have the will to fight, but what if they have to fight Canadian regulars?"

Riel's voice was apologetic. "Your Fenians tried to take Canada nearly twenty years ago. When was it? 1867. They were defeated and driven back across the border. 'General' O'Neill did not lead his men very well."

Anger glinted in Hardesty's eyes. "O'Neill was a fool and certainly no general. The men he lead on this comic-opera invasion were mostly hooligans from the slums of New York. Some had served in the Union Army in volunteer regiments. The men I have coming here are all ex-regulars, many of them veterans of the Indian Wars. They are all well trained and will be well paid. Some are Fenians, some are not. I don't care what they are as long as they fight. I will lead them under your command, and we will win. I didn't spend seven years in the British army just for nothing. I joined because I wanted to learn how to fight. There was no chance to become an officer, but I read every book I could find on tactics and military history. I've been preparing for this day a very long time."

Riel said, "It is not good to have so much hate, Colum. You have to learn to fight the enemy without hating him. That makes you better than he is."

Hardesty laughed. "You fight your way, Louis, and I'll fight mine. What would be the good of fighting your enemy if you didn't hate him? After Ireland wins her independence, I'll write a letter to the Queen and tell her what a fine, fat old lady she is. But until then..."

"How will the men get here?" Riel asked.

"Obviously, not all together and not from the same direction. Some will go north from Boston to Montreal and Ottawa and from there all the way west by Canadian Pacific. Others will come in through Minnesota and Montana. I have men from San Francisco who will go north to Vancouver and take the railroad over the mountains from there. None are halfbreeds, so they shouldn't attract much attention."

"And the guns?"

"The guns will be here. Modern military rifles, Gatling guns. Maxim guns if I can get them, but I hardly think so. There are Maxims in some of the eastern arsenals. I will have word from Ottawa. A friend of the movement—yours and mine—is a sergeant of supply. If we had Maxims, we could really turn this war against them."

"You haven't mentioned artillery. The militia is well equipped with artillery. I don't see how we can stand up against it."

Hardesty didn't look so confident. "The only way we can get artillery is to capture it. Rapid-fire guns can be dismantled and moved easily enough. Artillery is too heavy. What we have to aim for is speed and surprise. Do what they don't expect. Don't dig into fortifications unless there is no other way. We have to gain control of the forts and mounted-police barracks. That's where their strength is—and their weakness, too. If we can pin them down, they will run out of food and will be forced to surrender. Your people can last a lot longer without food than they can."

"There must be no massacre, Colum. I don't care what happens. I won't tolerate that, even if we have to lose the war."

"It will be hard to take prisoners, Louis. Where would we keep them? If we turn them loose, especially the Mounties, they will be back breathing fire. My motto is: Show a man mercy and he'll kill you for it. Besides, if we kill them, there will be no way back, not for you, not for me, not for any of us."

"And if we lose?"

"They will hang us by the dozen, send hundreds to prison for the rest of their lives. So there's no way out, even if we don't kill the prisoners. It may sound brutal, but in the end it's very practical. When a man has a chance to surrender, he may or may not take it. When he hasn't, there is nothing to be lost but his life, so he fights on."

"Until he's dead. Until we're all dead? Is that what you're saying without really saying it, Colum? Do you want to die in a blaze of glory. You may not know that's really what you want."

"Now you're talking wild, Louis. That's the last thing I want. What I want is a nice soft job in your administration when you take over. How does that sound?"

Riel said, "That's the last thing you want. You want that no more than I do."

"You're right, Louis. That's not what I want."

"You can't kill the prisoners," Louis Riel said firmly. "If that's what you want to do, then we must part company. There will be enough killing as it is. That is my decision, only one of the many I have to make. Another thing I must tell you so you can tell it to your friends in Washington. If we defeat the Canadians and the Americans follow them, then we will fight them too. That must be understood."

Hardesty looked sullen, at the point of insubordination. "Since you're getting things in order, we'd better talk about Gabriel Dumont."

"Talk about what? You have alread raised the question of Dumont, and I gave my answer. I though it was settled."

"But he isn't qualified to command your army."

"And you are?"

"I'm better qualified than he is."

"Yes, I know you served in the British Army for seven years, in Africa and India. That's not the point. Gabriel Dumont has been part of this movement for more than fifteen years. He's a fighter, and he knows men, especially the *métis*. In a way, fighting and the *métis* are all he knows. He will be a good commander, believe me."

"I wish I could, Louis. I don't mean that disrespectfully, but you are not a soldier."

"Colum," Riel said, "if Gabriel or I don't lead the *métis* in battle, they won't fight. I could lead them, but what good would that do? It has to be Gabriel Dumont."

"My men may not want to serve under him?"

"Why? Because he's a halfbreed?"

"They would rather serve under me. Some of them have known me for a long time; at least the ones from New

York and Boston have. What do you think of the idea?"

"I will have to think about it. Now let me tell you something, and this must be said so there won't be any misunderstandings. You will not play politics with my people. I am not saying that is your intention, but men have a way of changing when the stakes get big enough. If I say Gabriel Dumont commands, that decision is final. Another thing, and I regret to say it, if you want to back out of this, now is the time. There is no ill will in anything I say."

"I didn't think there was, Louis. We were just talking, clearing the air, as they say."

A fist banged on the door and Hardesty jumped up with a Colt .45 in his hand. He motioned Riel away from the line of fire, if it came.

"It's Gabriel Dumont," a rough voice called out. "I think we have a spy. Open the door."

Hardesty unbarred the door and Jim Sundance, half numb with cold, was shoved inside.

Looking at his yellow hair and copper skin, Hardesty said, "Well now, what have we here?"

Six

"Look at the weapons he was carrying," Gabriel Dumont said, putting the Colt .44, throwing hatchet, and Bowie knife on the table. "He has a .44 Winchester and an Indian bow. They're with his horse, a fine stallion. He tried to kill me when I got close to him."

Hardesty, sizing up Sundance, asked, "Where did you find him?"

Dumont said, "Half frozen in the stable of the old Heber farm—down by the river. We were half frozen too. The snow was beginning to let up by then. No, he didn't try to resist. It wouldn't have done any good if he had. He'd better have some food and coffee. Is there any stew left?"

"Enough," Hardesty answered.

"You'd better sit down," he told Sundance, handing him a cup of black coffee. "Now, my lad, you'd better come up with some believable answers, or you'll never see daylight. Who are you and what do you want? Our friend here thinks you're a spy. I think so, too. First, your name?"

"Jim Sundance?"

"From where?"

"All over. I know all over is a big place, but it's true."

"We'll see about that." Hardesty jerked a thumb at Riel. "Naturally, you wouldn't know who this gentleman is?"

"Louis Riel. I know who he is."

"I'll bet you do. And you came all this way to join up with him?"

"I had that idea. Everybody knows what he's trying to do. I belong here more than you do. You're not a halfbreed."

Hardesty smiled. "I'm a green halfbreed. Now, Mr. James Sundance, how did you get all the way up here? You didn't come through Regina."

"That's how I came."

"And the Mounties didn't stop you, a halfbreed armed to the teeth?"

Sundance said, "A police spy followed me around after I arrived in town. I managed to get away from him."

"How?"

After Sundance explained, Hardesty said, "You're tricky all right, too tricky even for the Mounties. My opinion is that you're too tricky to live."

"Did you see anybody else?" Hardesty asked Gabriel Dumont.

It was obvious to Sundance that there was bad blood between the Irishman and the halfbreed. "You are asking plenty of questions, Hardesty. While I was catching this prisoner or spy—I don't know—you were sitting by the fire. But I will answer your question. There was nobody with him. If there had been, my men would have been back by now."

"Next time you can sit by the fire," said Hardesty. "You captured this man. Do you think he's a spy—for the Mounties or the militia? I think he is, but you don't have to agree with me."

"You don't have to tell me that. Yes, I think he's a spy. There is no reason to think he is not. He is not one of our

218

people, and no other American halfbreeds have offered to fight for us. I think he was sent here to do harm to our cause, perhaps to kill our leader. There is only one way to deal with spies." Gabriel Dumont shrugged. "And if it turns out that he is not a spy, what difference will it make?"

"My own sentiments," Hardesty said. "But I'd like to ask our visitor a few more questions."

"Ask away," Sundance said. "You won't believe me anyway."

Hardesty continued. "It doesn't make sense for you to come up here and try to walk in without a name to recommend you. Give us a name, some name that we know. It would be dumb for a man to come up here without a name to pass him through. What about it? Was it Fournier in Fort Garry? McBride in Toronto?"

Sundance said he didn't know the names.

Hardesty said, "And it's no wonder, since there are no such people. "It isn't looking too hopeful for you, Mr. James Sundance. A fanciful name that. Did you make it up yourself?"

"What did you see in Regina?" Hardesty asked. "You'll probably tell us you saw five regiments of militia. Be honest now, tell us what you saw."

Sundance said, "No militia, just mounted police. There are two Gatling guns in front of the barracks."

Hardesty glanced over at Louis Riel, who hadn't said anything. "Well, I suppose you did pass through Regina after all. We know about the two Gatlings. Knew since they were brought there on the train. We know about the militia, too."

Gabriel Dumont was becoming impatient, but he ate his stew in silence. Riel was staring at Sundance with a puzzled look on his face.

Hardesty started again. "You have blond hair. How did you get that?"

219

"My father had yellow hair. I got it from him."

"Frenchmen aren't usually blond."

"My father was English."

"So you're half English, are you. That means I hate you only half as much as a regular Englishman."

Turning to Gabriel Dumont, the Irishman said, "That was a joke."

Hardesty asked, "And what's the other half of you?"

"Cheyenne," Sundance answered.

Dumont said slowly, "You are a long way from your mother's people. It would have been better if you had stayed there."

"I'm beginning to believe that."

"It's a bit late for that," Hardesty said. "We can't let you stay, and we can't let you ride out. So you know what it has to be. We're going to have to kill you. But first there will be more questions. I think you're a goddamned liar. But before you go, you're going to tell the truth. You're going to tell us who really sent you and how many more men there are like you. You're going to tell us about the things you've seen. By the time we get through with you, you'll be begging for death."

Gabriel Dumont put down his fork and took out a skinning knife from a slender sheath. He held it over the chimney of a lamp until it began to glow white hot.

"Wait a minute," Hardesty said, "we'll try the easy, the humane way first. A man talks more sensibly if he isn't in agony. But you will be in a minute if you don't talk. Keep the knife hot, Gabriel."

Hardesty stood over Sundance, "Now, my friend, the name of the man who sent you. Mountie or militia, it doesn't matter. I want his name, because we're going to send a man to kill him. I want his name and the men who work under him. It's time they learned that they can't just send spies in here pretending to be patriots. What's his name?"

"There is no man."

"What's his name? His name and all the others?"

"I can't tell you. There's nothing to tell."

Hardesty pointed to Dumont's thin-bladed knife. "We're just wasting our time. Go to work on Mr. James Sundance, and see how he likes it."

Sundance started to sweat as the glowing blade came close to his face. He could already feel its white hot edge.

"Wait!" Louis Riel shouted, standing up. "I think I know this man."

Seven

Riel came over to where Sundance was standing and said, "You say your name is James Sundance."

"Jim Sundance. People call me Sundance."

"And you are of·the Cheyenne?"

"My mother was."

Gabriel Dumont was still holding the knife. Riel waved it away.

"You know this man, Louis?" Hardesty said, looking doubtful.

"Perhaps," Riel said. "When I first heard the name, it meant nothing to me. Now I am not so sure."

To Sundance he said, "Your name has been in the newspapers in the United States. When I was in Montana I heard your name, something about your fight against the Indian Ring in Washington. Are you the same Jim Sundance?"

Sundance said he was.

"Anybody can use a name," Hardesty said. "You have used many names yourself, Louis. So have I. So has Gabriel."

"Never," Gabriel Dumont growled, waving the knife in the air to let it cool. "My name is my own."

Outside, the wind whipped against the walls of the cabin as if it were trying to kill those inside. Powdered snow sifted in under the bottom of the door. It was quiet except for the wind and the crackling of the fire.

Riel raised his hand in a command for silence, his forehead creased in thought. "What was your father's name?" he asked Sundance.

"Nicholas."

Riel said, "Many years ago, when I was a boy on the Red River, I knew a man of that name. My father had a mill and a man of that name, an Englishman, worked for him. He had a Cheyenne wife and there was a son. Are you that son?"

"I don't know," Sundance said. "If I was, I don't remember. My father worked at many things, at many trades. We were in many places. I know we were in Canada at one time. I think I was about five at that time."

"I am forty," Riel said, "and that would be about right. I was about ten then, and I remember an Englishman, an Indian woman, and a child with yellow hair. I don't know how long they stayed. It was not long. There was a scar on the man's hand. I can't remember which hand."

"A long scar on the palm of the left hand," Sundance said. "A drunken buffalo hunter tried to stab my father, and he blocked the thrust with his hand. He told me about the scar when I asked him. His hand gave him pain all his life."

"You could be who you say you are," Riel said, staring at Sundance as if by doing so he could relive the events of thirty years before. The *métis* leader's face was clouded in thought.

Hardesty cut in with, "A scar on a man's hand! What does that prove? It proves nothing to me. It could all be a plan to hoodwink you. Ask him something else."

"Please, Colum," Riel said mildly, still looking at Sundance with his bright black eyes. "What book did your father always carry in his pocket, the one he read while he was eating?"

"The Bible," Sundance answered. "My father was not a religious man, Mr. Riel, but the Bible was his favorite book. In it, he always said, was enough reading for a man's lifetime. There was enough even if a man lived to be a very old man."

"And the color of the cover? Was it black?"

"No. Dark red."

"Do you want some coffee, Sundance?" Riel asked, turning to get the pot.

"Listen, Louis," Hardesty said. "If the Mounties or the militia sent this man, they would tell him things like that: the scar on the hand, the Bible.

Riel handed a cup to Sundance. "Things that happened thirty years ago? A Bible with a red cover? I hardly think so, my untrusting friend."

The Irishman protested: "All right, maybe he is who he says he is. I'll grant you the scar and the Bible. Does all that prove that he isn't a spy or an assassin? A hired killer sent by the Canadians to murder you? Back in Ireland, I knew of a man who took money to kill his own brothers, two of our organization. He killed one, but we got him before he killed the other. Louis, you're not risking just your own life. You're putting the whole movement in danger. I say kill him now."

Riel said, "You're so ready to kill, my friend. I will remind you that I have not survived fifteen years with a price on my head by being a fool."

"I still say I'm right."

Riel's voice was still unemotional. "If you are right, then we will kill him. Is he right, Sundance?"

"No."

"Do you believe him, Gabriel?"

Dumont said, "I don't know. I trust you, Louis. You are our leader. Say kill him and it will be done."

"That's mighty obliging of you," Hardesty said to Dumont.

"I wasn't talking to you, Irishman."

Riel said, "The war isn't in here, gentleman, and name calling won't help us win it."

Hardesty said, "We don't need this man to win it."

For the first time Riel's dark eyes displayed anger. "We're going to need all the men we can get, and if this man is Jim Sundance, he's worth ten of your paid soldiers. Wars are not won with money but with the heart. Sometimes I think you forget that Colum. For you, I think, war is more important than the winning of it. I have been called many things in my lifetime, but I do not love war. If the Canadians would let us go, there would be no killing. To wage war is what you have to do when all else fails."

Looking at Riel, listening to his formal way of talking, Sundance thought of what Crook had said about the *métis* leader. He had spent nearly two years in an asylum, wanted to start his own church, talked about his divine mission. He was ready to take on a powerful government with a few hundred halfbreeds. A white man might have decided that Riel was mad, but Sundance wasn't so sure. After his own parents had been tortured and killed by renegades. he himself had been close to crazy for a while, drinking heavily, courting death at every opportunity. If George Crook hadn't knocked the craziness out of his dead, he would almost certainly be dead by now. Grief often drove a man crazy. It was clear that Louis Riel was tormented by what had happened to his people—robbed of their land, degraded by the whiskey traders from the States, left without hope.

"You served as a scout for the army?" Riel said to Sundance, pouring more coffee. "As a scout and a hunter?"

"With General Crook, in many campaigns."

"Then you fought against your own people?" Hardesty cut in angrily. "Now you want to fight *for* them, is that it? What made you change your mind, turncoat? Was it because you thought there was money to be made by working for both sides?"

Sundance said, "I have fought for and against the Indians. With Crook it was different. I worked for the General because that was the only way I could help my people."

Hardesty said, "Crook killed plenty of Indians while he was talking out of both sides of his mouth. At least Sheridan was honest when he said he'd like to see them all dead. Now I'll be honest with you, friend. I'd like to see you dead."

Riel lay back in his chair and ran thin fingers through his hair. Lines of worry and sadness furrowed his cheeks; his eyes were very tired. His dark clothes were stained with mud; only his moccasins looked fit for this hard northern country.

"You're wrong about General Crook. When he gave his word, he kept it. Do you know that he once hanged four whiskey traders in the Dakotas for selling poisoned whiskey to the Sioux? Many Indians went blind or died in agony. Crook didn't waste any time. He led the four white men to a tree and they were hanged. The incident almost cost him his career. Do you remember that, Sundance?"

"I was with him when it happened. It was where the town of Deadwood is now. The whiskey traders worked for the Indian Ring in Washington. When they heard about it, they tried everything they could to get him cashiered, but Sheridan backed him up."

"How do you balance four dead whites against I don't know how many thousands of dead Indians?" Hardesty said. "Did Crook do it because his heart was so pure? Or was it because he hated the Indian Ring for political reasons? Nothing is ever what it seems to be, Louis. What does it matter what this man did in the past? We're talking about the here and now, which is all that matters. It's your decision to make, but I'll say it again. Get rid of him. He smells of death."

Riel said calmly, "He certainly looks like a dangerous man. Are you, Sundance?"

"So I've been told. What's it going to be? Do I stay or get a bullet in the back?"

"There will be no bullets in the back. If you give us cause to kill you, then you will be judged and executed by a firing squad. You will have a chance to face your executioners. You want an answer and I can't give you one. Not yet."

Gesturing toward Hardesty and Dumont, Riel said, "These men are my friends, and I must consider what they have said. For the moment you can stay, but you will be watched all the time."

Hardesty grunted with sour satisfaction. "That's better. He'll be watched all right, and I'll do most of the watching."

Dumont nodded silently as he put the thin-bladed skinning knife back in its sheath. Sundance knew he hadn't made an enemy in the scowling halfbreed; Dumont was just a hard-eyed man who would kill him for the good of the cause, if it came to that. Hardesty was different. Sundance thought he knew why the scheming Irishman wanted to kill him. Hardesty figured that somehow he would get between him and Riel. Probably the Irishman figured Dumont could be pushed aside or, failing that, killed and buried in some lonely place. Riel could then be made into a puppet. If he failed to jump when Hardesty pulled the strings, another more easily managed *métis* leader could be found. Here in the North West Territories, there was great wealth; the man who controlled it could live like a king. That would be, Sundance decided, the Irishman's way of thinking, since there was always a faint undercurrent of contempt when he spoke to Riel.

"Do I get to keep my weapons?" Sundance asked Riel, nodding toward the pistol, knife, and hatchet on the table.

"You won't need them for the moment," Riel answered. "If I decide you can stay, you'll get them back. Nothing will be stolen from you here. There will be food and a warm place to sleep. Do not attempt to leave the camp at any time, even to walk over to the village. The sentries will shoot if you do. Their orders are firm. Other than that, you may move freely about the camp"—Riel smiled—"since nothing you see can ever be reported. Now Gabriel will show you where you are to be billeted. I will talk to you again tomorrow."

The snow had stopped by the time Sundance and Dumont left the cabin. Hardesty stayed behind to talk to Riel. Stars were beginning to appear in the deep-black sky; the wind whipped through the pines, knifing through their clothes. Now it was possible to see what the camp looked like. Except that the buildings were all made of rough-hewn logs, it didn't look much different from an army encampment. There were barracks on three sides and a wide space in the center. Several hundred yards away was the beginning of the village of Batoche. It was late, and no lights showed in the windows. A frozen river gleamed in the moonlight; the snow under their feet already had a crust on it. In the village, a dog barked furiously and then was joined by another dog. They both stopped. The only sound was the wind howling down from the Arctic wastes.

"Look where you're going," Dumont yelled above the sound of the wind. "Those are trenches."

Sundance looked and saw the outlines of long rows of trenches, now completely filled with snow. In the barracks on the north side, only one light was burning.

Sundance was still chilled, even after the food and coffee. The thought of rolling up in thick blankets looked better every time he braced himself against a fresh blast of wind.

"Your horse is all right," Dumont said, plodding through deep snow with the patience of a man who has lived with it all his life. "Warm, well looked after—a fine animal."

Nothing else was said until they were close to the barracks. "You will sleep in my cabin," Dumont said. "There is another bunk. You would like something else to eat? There was not much stew."

"I could use it," Sundance said. "Anything—not necessarily something hot."

"You would eat a bear steak raw?"

"Not unless I had to. I've seen it done."

Leading the way to his quarters, Dumont said, "That was a Gatling gun you were looking at back there. Soon we will have others."

Sundance had seen the rapid-fire gun, a hump in the snow wrapped in blankets and covered with tarpaulin covers. He had wondered why nobody was guarding it. A rapid-fire gun was worth an additional thirty men. Then he knew the reason it wasn't guarded. Batoche was two-hundred miles north of Regina; no force of Mounties would travel more than a few miles without being spotted by unseen lookouts.

"We will soon have more Gatling guns and many more men," Dumont said, opening the door of the warm cabin. He banged the door against the wind and barred it, then placed a stack of logs on the fire. The seasoned wood took hold immediately, sending sparks flying up the massive stone chimney. Dumont turned up the wick of the lamp, revealing a long, cluttered, low-ceilinged room. Rifles and bayonets, even sabers and daggers, hung from pegs driven into the walls. A skinny dog stretched lazily in front of the fire. There was a smell of sweat and cooking. In this cabin there were no books; Riel's cabin had been littered with them.

"That is my bunk," Dumont said, pointing to a roughly built platform covered with a buffalo robe. "Yours is there. Put on more blankets if you are cold. But it won't be cold. The *métis* know how to keep out the cold. Do you want a drink of whiskey?"

Sundance said yes.

"I would like to drink whiskey, but I dare not," Dumont said. "Now that I am a leader, I dare not. Whiskey does something to my head. At first for a while I am happy, then a rage takes possession of me. So I dare not drink. But when this war is over, I am going to go far north to a cabin I once built, and there I will be drunk for a month or until the whiskey is gone. Up there I will bother no one, hurt no one, except the bears."

Sundance decided that Dumont looked more like a bear than a man. He was built like a grizzly, was barrel chested, and had a big shaggy head set squarely on a short, thick neck—obviously a man of tremendous strength. A brute, but an intelligent brute.

While two big bear steaks were frying in skillets, Dumont gathered all the weapons from the walls and locked them in a long box that looked like a coffin. "So you will not be tempted," he said, turning the steaks and adding seasoning.

He pointed. "The whiskey and glasses are in the cupboard. Drink as much as you like, but please do not make sounds of enjoyment. It would sadden me if you did."

Sundance got the whiskey and a glass. He uncorked the bottle. The whiskey had a strong smell and no color: moonshine. He poured a glass and drank it carefully. It was easy not to make sounds of enjoyment. What wasn't easy was to get it down.

Dumont speared the bear steaks and served them up smoking hot. The look and smell of the properly seasoned meat made Sundance forget the foul taste of the whiskey, because when bear meat is aged and cooked just right, there is nothing else as good. This steak was tender enought for Sundance to cut it with the side of his fork.

They ate in silence for a while. Now and then, Dumont wiped his mouth with the back of his hand. When he finished, he threw scraps of meat to the dog, then put the plates in a tin basin of soapy water. Later he climbed into his bunk after lighting a long clay pipe. Sundance was already covered up by five blankets, a great weariness creeping over him. It had been one hell of a trip from Regina.

Dumont asked, "Was the whiskey to your liking? And the steak?"

"Everything was fine," Sundance answered, opening his eyes to look at the other man. There was neither friendship nor hostility in the halfbreed's eyes. He just wanted to be sure Sundance had enjoyed his meal.

Maybe my last meal, Sundance thought sleepily. In the morning, Dumont might have to kill him.

Eight

Dumont was brewing strong tea when Sundance woke up in the morning. It was the smell of the tea that woke him more than anything else. The halfbreed had made two pots, one for Sundance, one for himself. The fire had been built up again, and the cabin was warm; the windows were clear of snow.

Sundance pulled on his shirt and pants and watched impassively while Dumont cut slices of black-plug tobacco and dropped them into the already boiled-black tea. He had heard of this custom, which was said to exist among the hermit trappers of the North West and Alaska, but he had always thought it was just another tall tale from remote places.

Sundance's own black tea was ready to drink; he didn't add sugar or milk, as was the custom in the north. He didn't much like any kind of tea, but it was a cold morning and the tea was hot.

"You have never tried this?" Dumont said, putting the metal pot back on the bed of coals at the front of the fire. Immediately, it began to bubble, and the smell was no longer that of tea.

"No," Sundance said, adding that he wasn't ready to try.

"You have to get used to it," Dumont explained, stirring the awful-looking mixture, "and you must have a strong heart. I have known of men with weak hearts who were killed by it." The big halfbreed thumped his barrel-shaped chest. "I have a heart like a bull buffalo. It gives me great energy, but my heart remains steady. Once, when I was badly injured in the woods and couldn't hunt, I lived on it for ten days. In all that time, I never felt hunger. If you drink enough of it, you can go without sleep for days."

Dumont paused. "It can also make a man crazy. One time in the Yukon, I came across an old hunter running naked in the snow. It was a bitter cold day with a strong wind. I grabbed him and dragged him back to his cabin before he froze to death. Beside the fire was a whole bucket of this tea. There was snuff in it, too. I had to tie him to his bunk to keep him from running out again. He kept saying his body was on fire, and the only way to cool off was to run in the snow. It took him two days before he was able to recognize me. An old man like that should never drink it."

"Is there any special name for it?"

"Just tea," Dumont said with no attempt at humor. "I drink it only in the morning or when I am on a long, hard journey and must go without sleep. There is plenty of bear meat left, plus bacon and duck eggs. We may go hungry before this trouble is over, but it hasn't happened yet. What would you like?"

Hardesty came in without knocking. For a moment, his lanky frame was outlined in the cold bright sunshine that came in the doorway. The earflaps of a beaver hat were pulled down over his ears, and his red face was raw from the wind. He clapped his gloved hands together and stomped the snow from his knee-high laced boots.

He was in better humor than he had been the night before. He had probably decided to take a new tack, but

Sundance felt the enmity in the man.

Hardesty sniffed the air in the cabin. "Taking your morning medicine, are you, Gabriel?"

"Shut the door," Dumont growled and drank a full cup of the bad-smelling concoction. Quickly, he drank a second cup. "Did you come here on business?"

"That I did, so let your breakfast wait till later. Louis wants you to come over right away. Bring the prisoner, he says."

"Did Nolin arrive?"

"Nolin's here. Got here early this morning. So did Ouellette, Duman and Isbister. There won't be any backing off now. I tell you, I feel good this morning."

To Sundance the names meant nothing, but to the *métis* they were names from the past, from the days of Riel's first rebellion. Hardesty went out whistling; Dumont looked after him with a sour expression.

"We'd better go," he said.

After they had bundled up and walked over to Riel's cabin, Hardesty had left. Riel, wearing a shaggy fur coat that fell to his ankles, sat by the fire, drinking coffee. Under his eyes there were dark rings that looked like bruises. Sundance wondered if he had slept at all since the night before. Except for two empty egg shells on the table, there was no sign he had eaten.

Dumont looked around. "Where are they? The Irishman said Nolin and the others were here?"

Riel said, "They have gone to the Lindsay schoolhouse south of Prince Charles. It is the best place to hold a meeting. More people than we knew of will be coming. Such a response encourages and yet saddens me. Ah, well, we shall see what happens."

Sundance found Riel staring at him. After a long silence, Riel said, "I have decided. You can stay. Hardesty is still against letting you join us. He does not want you in

234

his ranks, so you will go with Gabriel. Is that all right with you, Gabriel?"

Dumont shrugged. "I don't mind."

Riel said, "I am trusting you, Sundance. I hope there will be no cause to regret it." He smiled. "You would be paid if you served with Hardesty. He has money to pay his men. The rest of us, the halfbreeds"—suddenly they all smiled—"must soldier without pay. We fight for food and freedom. Soon there may not be much of either. Now let us ride and listen to the speeches." Riel looked from Dumont to Sundance. "Gabriel hates speeches."

"What is there to speech about, Louis? We're gathering to fight. So do we fight or make speeches? If we wait too long, we'll still be making speeches when the Mounties and the militia march in on us. Regina is where the Canadians will group their forces, because the railroad from the east comes through there. But don't forget, there are Mountie barracks in Prince Albert, Battleford, and Fort Pitt. There are few men, but they are there."

Riel's escort of one-hundred halfbreeds was drawn up in the wide space between the barracks. A ragtag army, by the standards of any country, just like the Confederates, the worst-disciplined soldiers in the world. As they rode along in front of the ranked horsemen, Sundance realized for the first time how much of a fight the Canadians were in for. In all the faces, young and old, there was the same go-to-hell look of defiance; they sat their horses with careless ease. One and all, they were halfbreeds, and they ranged from almost full-blooded Indians to blue-eyed men like Sundance himself. If they had officers of any kind, it didn't show; nobody wore a uniform or insignia. Nobody saluted anyone else.

When they reached the head of the column, all Dumont did was raise his hand and they moved out to the north. Sundance could see that, unlike the others, Riel was not a very good horseman. He sat the animal properly enough, but there was none of the grace that belonged to Dumont and the others.

Their breath steamed in the morning cold; there had been an ice storm recently, and the trees were still sheathed in ice, some of the branches broken by the weight.

The village of Batoche, mostly cabins, straggled for a mile or two along the river. At the center of the settlement was a ferry, known as Batoche Crossing. Here, a few stores of log and frame hugged the riverbank. From the ferry, a path about a mile long led up to the crest of the river valley. That crest was crowned by the church, with the parish house across from it. Six miles upstream there was another ferry.

"Gabriel owns that ferry," Riel said. "It is even named after him. After that, it isn't too long to ride to the Lindsay schoolhouse. I chose it for two reasons. It is centrally placed, and there are many English halfbreeds in the Prince Albert region. They are fine people in their own way, but like all people they are different. Like us, they want to be left in peace. We are stronger than they are, so they know that if we are defeated, they might as well move beyond the maps. There will be no hope for them. They are inclined to make common cause with us, but they aren't sure they can trust us. They are Protestant and we are Catholic. Religious rivalry has always been the curse of the Territories, as it has in Canada."

Dumont had been listening. Now and then he looked at Sundance. When they were a mile from the second ferry, he sent a party of riders on ahead to look out for the possibility of an ambush.

Riel asked, "Did you know that I want to start a new church in the Territories?" Suddenly he laughed. "I can see by your face that the answer is yes. And when you heard or read about it, you thought I was mad, a mad messiah with not only his own country but his own church. And if I had a crown, I could be king or emperor."

"Well," Sundance said, "both churches you mentioned have been around for a long time. People are sort of attached to them."

"They have been around too long. Religion as we know it has caused the death of more people than all the plagues. Here in the Territories I am going to change that. I am going to try. Religion brings people together or tears them apart. Here in North America, the Catholics and Protestants have been at each other's throats for more than a century. I see no hope for peace until there is one true church. A new church, a new country."

They reached the ferry and crossed the broad river. Sundance was thinking. When you began to know a man, many things you heard about him in the past and didn't understand made sense. There was no way of knowing how this new church idea would work out, but it was a bold stroke. From a political viewpoint, it had some chance of success.

On the other side of the river, they stopped at the snow-covered cabin of an ancient halfbreed with a leathery face and no teeth. Bowing, he invited them to come in, but Dumont said there wasn't time. The old halfbreed hurried into the cabin and came out with cups of bark tea. It was boiling hot and had a pleasant smell in the still air.

The old man stood and waved after them until they were out of sight. Not much more than an hour later the tall, white-painted frame building of the Lindsay schoolhouse was in sight. The road leading to it was well guarded. The schoolhouse stood on a hill. On all sides of it were tethered horses, buckboards, spring wagons, and sleighs. Horses pawed the ground and half-wild dogs ran back and forth, barking with excitement. In the churchlike tower of the schoolhouse, a man with field glasses scanned the countryside. There were hundreds of people there, both inside and outside the school. Before long, the figure would pass a thousand and keep climbing. Still they kept coming, trailing down from the hills, from out of the frozen swamps, by dogsled on the ice-hard river. Among the crowd were Indians and a handful of whites, long settled in the Territories.

Riel was smiling with satisfaction. "Look at them, Sundance," he exulted. "My people are answering the call. This time it won't be what it was in 1869. We were poorly organized then, no money, no friends. The halfbreeds are finally having their day. Don't tell me you are not moved by it!"

Sundance nodded. At the same time, he was thinking that these poor people, brave though they were, didn't have a chance. Among them, there were many who had never seen a train. Most knew little of the outside world, the tricks of politicians, the deviousness of men like Colum Hardesty. They lived in a world where all that mattered was family and honor; where a promise once given had to be kept. Yes, he was moved by their faith. For the moment, that was all he knew.

A loud cheer rang out when the crowd at the schoolhouse saw the column of horsemen coming along the south road. Hundreds of men snatched off their hats and caps and waved them in the air. A small band of musicians with miscellaneous instruments blared on the steps of the school. Riel's bodyguard dropped away, and he rode in, a vulnerable-looking figure in the full-length fur coat. Children threw handmade paper flowers in front of his horse's feet. The bell in the tower began to peal. Sundance looked up; the man with the field glasses had his hands pressed over his ears.

Hardesty stood on the steps with another man, who looked Irish. General Crook had mentioned two other Irishmen, Cunningham and Lane, in his report, but there had been no descriptions. It could be either one. The Fenians were a dangerous bunch all right; their favorite sport was to kill prominent politicians who didn't agree with them. They were mixed up in dirty business from Central America to Hudson Bay. In Mexico, they were giving aid to the rebels because President Diaz was too friendly with the powerful British mining companies. During the Civil War, they had tried to blow up Confederate warships being built in British seaports. Sundance knew the blood of innocent people had no meaning for them.

Riel dismounted awkwardly, hampered by his long coat. One of Dumont's men ran to grab the reins, and the crowd cheered the horse as it was led away. Dumont good naturedly pushed people aside as Riel walked up the steps of the schoolhouse. Now and then, Riel stopped to speak to a child or an old man; there was a cheer every time he did. At the top of the steps, he shook hands with Hardesty and the other Irishman. The two Irishman looked at Sundance with blank faces, and he knew they had been talking about him.

"We can't get any more in," Hardesty said. "The place has been packed for an hour. We'd better go in. Nolin and the others are waiting."

Riel raised his hand. "In a moment, Colum. Some of these people have come a long way, and the day is cold." Turning on the steps, he spoke to the crowd gathered in front and on both sides:

"I am sorry, my people, but there is no more room inside. But I don't want you to return to your homes. I want you to remain here. By doing so, you will give me your support. News of what is going on inside will be given to you. Today, my people, we are going to decide what must be done if we are to be free. All our leaders are present today, all gathered together for the first time. There will be speeches." Riel made a face and the crowd

239

laughed. "But when all the talking is done, the hard decision still has to be made. You know what that is!"

With the applause of the crowd roaring behind him, Riel walked into the schoolhouse, followed by Dumont, Sundance, Hardesty, and the second Irishman. The thin wooden walls that partitioned the various classrooms had been taken out, so now there was one huge room. The desks had been taken out, too. All that remained was a long table supported by iron trestles on a raised platform at the back of the room. In front of the platform was another table for lesser dignitaries. Many of the seats at both tables were already occupied.

None of the faces meant anything to Sundance. He noted that two of the men were priests; neither looked satisfied with the proceedings. The big room was filled to capacity with men and some women; no children were present. Damp clothes steamed in the heat of several hundred bodies packed together. An officious looking elderly man, who might have been a lawyer's clerk if not for his copper skin, made a fuss about opening some of the windows. There were no benches in the room. Some people remained standing, but most had settled down on the muddy floor. Several had brought food, for they had been told it was going to be a long day.

The crowd made way for Riel, and he walked directly to the platform. The men there rose to greet him, some with the warmth of old friendship, some with reserve. Sundance noticed that one of the two priests did not shake hands with Riel. The priest who shook his hand was lean and quick-eyed, in his middle thirties; the other cleric was an old man with a stocky build and a great mane of white hair.

The hand shaking and hugging went on for a while. Sundance wondered where it was all going to lead. If it went far enough, it would lead many people there to death. But, Sundance decided, few if any of the men on the platform would die. That was how it worked. The politicians made rousing speeches and the foot soldiers died.

Among the men on the platform there was an uneasiness. From time to time, their eyes darted to the two empty chairs, then to the door. Sundance, stood with his back to the wall, watching while Hardesty whispered something to Gabriel Dumont. After that, Riel whispered to Dumont. Both times Dumont shook his head.

There was more whispering. Finally, Riel took out a large silver watch, opened the face cover, and put it on the table in front of him. He was about to speak when, suddenly, there was a commotion outside the church. He leaned over to speak to Dumont, who sat beside him, and this time the big halfbreed nodded. Riel smiled, Dumont did not.

Riel raised his voice until it could be heard clearly in every corner of the big room. "Our Indian brothers are here," he said. "As soon as they have been made welcome, this meeting—this convention—will begin."

The crowd remained silent, almost fearful, while two Indians came in the door and walked toward the platform. Both were big men; the older one was handsome and looked intelligent. Sundance recognized them as Crees, tribesmen of great ferocity at one time and, from all reports, becoming increasingly hostile to the whites on both sides of the border. Looking at the two Cree chiefs, Sundance could well understand General Crook's fear of an all-out Indian war in the North West. In the Territories alone, there were twenty-thousand fighting Indians: Plains and Woods Cree, Blackfeet, Assiniboin, Stoney, runaway Sioux from Montana, and others. There had been little of the savage Indian fighting in the Territories that had plagued the States; but as the buffalo died out and food grew scarce, hatred was beginning to simmer. Then there was the matter of manhood. The warlike Sioux, still boasting of their victory over Custer nine years before, taunted the Cree's and the others as "tame" Indians and "old women." That alone would be enough to start trouble.

The two Indians stopped in front of the platform, and Riel reached down to shake hands with them. It was all done with great dignity. Then they sat in the two empty seats and folded their arms across their chests. Sundance looked at their faces and saw nothing but masks. He wondered what they were thinking; there was no way to tell.

Louis Riel stood up and raised both hands above his head. His voice was shaking with emotion when he spoke:

"Let us begin."

Nine

First, Riel introduced the men on the platform. "You know some of them, my people. Everyone knows Gabriel Dumont, good Gabriel of the rough tongue and the good heart. If war with the Canadians must come, Gabriel will lead our men. Does anyone object?"

The crowd thundered its applause. Riel nodded and motioned the people to be quiet. "That is good," he went on. "I am your leader. I returned from exile because you sent for me, but I rule only with your consent. If at any time you are displeased with my leadership, then you must tell me. I will step aside in favor of a better man."

The crowd roared, "No! No!"

Riel was very good, Sundance thought. Maybe he was a little too good. He was playing the crowd like a melodeon, squeezing out the notes and watching them dance. But that's what all politicians, even honest ones, did or tried to do. It was a tricky trade, no matter how you looked at it.

Next, Riel introduced the two priests, though everyone knew who they were. Sundance knew that, in a French-Canadian community, the priests should have come before Dumont. Riel, the politician, was making a point no one there could miss. The priests were in a place of honor at the meeting—only as long as they didn't get in the way.

Riel spoke their names: Father André and Father Grandin. Both men nodded. The old one with the white hair was Father André. Grandin, the priest who was eager to please Riel, smiled nervously and half rose from his chair.

Then the other men were introduced: Charles Nolin— "my cousin"—Riel said to loud applause. Moise Ouellette, Michel Dumas, James Isbister. And there were others.

Riel said, "These men have been with me from the beginning. Through the years, we have been harried by the police and insulted in the newspapers. At one time, an attempt was made on the life of Michel Dumas. They say the Mounties always get their man, but somehow they let this one get away—because, of course, he was known by certain men in the Canadian government. Michel still carries the bullet, a reminder of Canadian democracy in action."

After Riel let the crowd laugh for a while, he protested, "It isn't funny. Michel's only crime was that he talked too freely in the name of freedom. Yes, my people, for more than fifteen years they have been trying to stop us. Petitions, genuine letters of complaint, have been sent and never received—so they say—and always never answered. And when there is some sort of response, it is unfailingly the same: Be patient! Trust the good men in government! Trust in John A. Macdonald, Prime Minister of the glorious Dominion of Canada! Soon, everything will be wonderful! All you have to do is wait!"

Riel raised his fist. "Do you want to wait?"

Looking at the excited faces turned toward the speaker, once again Sundance decided that Louis Riel knew his business. His voice was clear and deep, but it was his hands the crowd watched, fascinated by the way he used them. All Frenchmen used their hands when they talked. Riel had gone far beyond the usual gestures; maybe he had practiced this spellbinding, and maybe it was natural. It didn't matter. The effect on the crowd was the same.

Continuing after the noise died down, Riel said: "For more than fifteen years we have been patient. Is that not long enough? Now the Canadian Pacific Railroad is complete, and the government in Ottawa has plans to bury us under tens of thousands of immigrants. Not just Scots and English and Irish, but Germans, Russians, and Swedes—people who do not know our ways and would despise them if they did. If we wait any longer, it will be like trying to fight a plague of locusts. And like the locusts in the Bible, they will fill the land until they occupy every square inch of it. When that happens, there will no longer be any chance for a *métis* nation. Instead of living as free men and women, you will be crowded off your land.

"For some of you it has already happened. And how will you live then? I will tell you how. The men will work as hired hands, slaving from dawn to dust, on farms across which their ancestors roamed freely. There will be no more joy in life, nothing but these sour-faced Scotchmen with their hellfire hymns. And, men, if you don't work on their farms—*their* farms, mind you—you will be forced to load their wagons, sweep out their stores, or break your backs in their lumber camps and mines. And what about your women and children? I will tell you..."

Beating on the table and raising his eloquent voice as the moment demanded, Louis Riel continued to stir up the crowd. Some of the other men at the table were given a chance to speak, but it was clear that Riel's talk of out-and-out rebellion frightened some of them. It frightened James Isbister, the English halfbreed from Prince Albert,

245

a skinny sallow-faced man with the nervous habit of coughing after every few words. He argued that freedom, or at least partial independence, could be gained without bloodshed. First, he said, they had to show the Canadians how determined they were. On the other hand, they had to move cautiously.

Some man in the crowd who knew Isbister yelled, "You say that because you have more to lose than we have. You are a townsman with a hardware store. What do you know about the land or what it is to be really free?"

Michel Dumas, the man who had been wounded, was even more extreme than Riel. His dark eyes glittered with hatred, his knobby fists clenching and unclenching as he spoke:

"The time has come to wash the Saskatchewan Valley in blood. There is no other way. They call us stupid, dirty, careless. We are half starved now because we wiped out the buffalo in our stupidity. Serves us right, they say, so we should be glad to eat their salt bacon instead of real meat. But what about the railroad? Everyone knows the railroad wiped out the buffalo. The buffalo will not cross a railroad track unless driven over it by fire. So the herds were split into north and south, divided and scattered. They talk of our stupidity! And I will say now what I have often said before: The Canadians don't just want to control us. They want to exterminate us!"

A wild roar went up from the crowd. Sundance noticed that Riel stood up quickly, as if to prevent any more firebrand outbursts from Dumas. He was getting too much attention. No clever politician could let that happen. Sundance knew Riel was going to say something that would startle and infuriate the crowd.

His voice was low and penetrating: "My people, I do not know if they want to exterminate us, as Michel says, but I do know they want to get rid of me. Wait! Wait! Let

246

me continue. Most of you know who D. H. MacDowall is—a powerful man in the Territories, a man who would like to become even more powerful. When I first returned from Montana, word came to me that MacDowall wanted to have a meeting with me. I refused. I know MacDowall and have never had any reason to trust him. I did not think there was anything to discuss. Another messenger came, and again I refused." Riel paused. "Then a third go-between came to me. I will not reveal his name, but he is in this room at this very moment. Wait! I will not reveal his name because I leave what he did—tried to do—to his own conscience. This great friend of our people said MacDowall and his friends—meaning, I suppose, the Canadian government—were willing to pay me one-hundred-thousand dollars in cash on condition that I leave the Territories, never to return. Think about it, my people, one-tenth of a million dollars just to get rid of a poor schoolteacher!"

Riel spoke quickly now. "Do you have any idea how much money that it? I am what they call an educated man, and it is almost beyond my understanding."

Finally, the shouting faded. Riel said: "I have worked as a store clerk and a prairie schoolteacher, and for several years I roamed with the buffalo hunters of Montana and Wyoming. I have never had more than two-hundred dollars at once in my life."

He laughed. "And I thought myself rich when I had that much. But one-hundred-thousand dollars! My God! the figure danced in front of my eyes! And do you think I was tempted?"

The crowd roared, "No!"

Riel smiled slyly, as though taking them into his confidence. "Yes," he said, "I was tempted. You don't want to think your leader is a fool, do you?"

The crowd remained silent.

"For about ten seconds I was tempted," Riel shouted,

"and then I told MacDowall's emissary to go back and tell his master the answer was no. Not for a million and not for ten million!"

Father André stood up shakily. The crowd stopped yelling and stared at him, unsure of what he was about to say. Riel's dark eyes flickered from face to face. It was very quiet in the big room.

"I am the man Louis is talking about," the old priest began. He waited for the yelling to start again, but there was only silence. "MacDowall is not my master. Only God is my master, and I serve Him willingly. When Louis first returned from Montana, I welcomed him because I know how much you have suffered and how much you respect him. Louis is back, I thought, and he is fifteen years older, not so hotheaded as he was. He has been a schoolteacher, is married, with a wife and two daughters in Montana. He is even an American citizen. We talked, and at first I like what he had to say. Then, as weeks and months passed, I saw that he was more hotheaded than ever."

Michel Dumont started to say something. Riel silenced him immediately: "Let the friend of the people speak."

Father André said, "I began to see nothing but bloodshed ahead. I still do. When I heard of MacDowall's plan, I went to him; he did not come to me. I thought it would be best for everybody if Louis went back to Montana. I knew he would talk to me if not to MacDowall. I was empowered to offer him five-thousand dollars if he left the Territories. Louis said he would leave for nothing less than one-hundred thousand."

"Lying priest!" Michel Dumas shouted. "You always take the side of the rich!"

Sundance's eyes narrowed as he looked over at Riel, who was taking it calmly. Father André remained on his feet, badly shaken by the ordeal. Disregarding him completely, Riel stood up, saying, "Hold your tongue,

Michel. He is still a priest. However, in the interest of truth—not to dirty his name but to clear mine—I would like to ask him if it's true that D.H. MacDowall has promised to build him a new church and parish house?"

Father André's voice faltered. "That was months before."

Riel turned quickly and shouted like a prosecuting attorney, "Why would a Scotch Presbyterian want to build a Catholic church for the *métis*? Why would a Scotch Presbyterian want to do *anything* for the *métis*?"

Sundance knew that the crowd was squarely on Riel's side, and he knew the whole thing had been carefully planned.

The old priest held out both hands toward the sullen crowd. "Mr. MacDowall is a good man, a kind man. He came to the Territories as a poor boy from Scotland. He became rich here and wants only good for everyone here. When the Indians left the reservation and were starving, Mr. MacDowall fed them with his own beef. A wagonload of blankets was provided."

Michel Dumas, the priest-hater, was up on his feet again. "We all know that story. You know damn well the only reason MacDowall fed the Indians was to keep them from raiding his herds and his storehouses. He bought your trickery with the promise of a church. What is the cost of a church? I don't know, but a man like MacDowall would carry enough money to build it in his pocket. But your worst lie is when you said MacDowall tried to bribe Louis with a miserable five thousand. Answer me, priest. How much money would you say the North West Territories are worth? How many hundreds of millions of dollars? And you say MacDowall could spare only five thousand!"

Dumas turned to the crowd. "We know the Scotch are tight with their money. But only five thousand for a whole country!"

Riel slammed his hand on the top of the table. He continued to thump the table until there was absolute silence. "That will be enough, Michel. I do not want to hear any more about it. If this disruption could have been prevented, I would not have mentioned it at all."

Suddenly, Riel's voice rose almost to a scream. "I will allow no man, priest or not, to accuse me of treachery to my people. Because, my friends, honor is all we have. The world outside our borders is trying to destroy us, suppress our customs, push us aside as old fashioned and primitive. To hell with the rest of the world is what I say!"

Riel's voice became quiet, almost sad. "I don't want the world to go to hell. I just want it to keep out of the North West Territories." He raised his arms as if trying to hug everyone there. "We are all we have. That is why we must remain faithful to one another in all things. Without honor, there is nothing. In my mind I see a great host of enemies arrayed against us. To prevail over these destroyers, we must be strong as never before in our long history."

Riel made a grasping motion, as if picking up a handful of soil. Everybody watched his hand as he held it out toward them, his fist clenched tightly. "This—this is *our* land," he said quietly. "This is where our fathers have lived since before men can remember. Out there, the bones of our ancestors lie buried. Land, my people, is not just something you use to make a living. If that is all you think of the land, you might as well run a little dry goods store. No, the land is mother to us all. It gives us life, and we water it with our blood, fertilize it. Yes, that is the word—and with our bodies when we die. By the God that made us all, they are not going to take it away from us!"

Riel sat down as calmly as if he hadn't been ranting a moment before. Sundance thought Riel glanced over his way, but he couldn't be sure. On Riel's face there was a half smile. No, not a smile but a strange, twisted expression. His eyes looked at the crowd, but Sundance wasn't sure he saw anything but his inner thoughts.

The crowd was still yelling and stomping their feet when the old priest got up shakily and left the platform. He was infirm and trembling, but no one helped him to step down to the floor. Well, Sundance thought, he really put the boot to you today.

The crowd made a lane for the old priest to pass through. He walked slowly, eyes fixed directly in front of him. Sundance knew nothing about Father André but figured he had served this people most of his life. In the remote settlements, a priest arrived when he was young and remained until he died. How many births and deaths had this old priest presided over? Hundreds? Thousands.

Louis Riel, very calm now, waited until Father André was gone before he spoke again. It was obvious the crowd was uneasy. In the halfbreed settlement, isolated by distance and choice, a priest wasn't just a psalmsinger dressed in black. He was a living bridge between this life and the hereafter.

Yep, Sundance thought, old Louis knows his stuff. He slipped in the knife and turned it without getting even a spot of blood on his hands. Michel Dumont had done all the tough talking, while Riel had remained regretful and forgiving. How much did it have to do with Riel's new church, his "true" religion, as he called it? It probably had a lot to do with it. And what about the two stories—of the five and the hundred-thousand dollars?

In the end, it didn't matter a damn. Sundance had been sent to stop Riel. Thus far, he hadn't even begun to form a plan. All he could do at the moment was look and listen and keep Hardesty and his Irish friends from killing him. He knew they were going to try. It was in their faces every time they looked at him. He would have to tread carefully if he wanted to stay alive. He couldn't make up his mind about Riel. At times, he sounded like the world's most honorable man. But it was all shot through with trickery and deceit. Whatever he was, and he was probably many things, Louis Riel was no ordinary man. It could even be that he was an honorable man who felt he had to act like a trickster to get the things he wanted for his people. Of course, that was the trouble with so many men of destiny. They always thought they and they alone knew what was best for the ordinary man.

Riel was talking again, this time about concessions. "My plan," he said, "is not to tell the Canadians what we will do if they don't grant concessions. My plan is to do certain things—and then ask for concessions. No matter what people say, I am willing to settle for something less than complete independence." His dark eyes were hooded. "I am ready to settle for partial independence, because that will give us more time to prepare. Yes, that would be breaking a promise, I know. But how many promises have the Canadians broken? It would take an abacus to count the number. We will take whatever they give us. We will wait and prepare and arm ourselves secretly. Then we will make more demands. And so on and so on.

"That is how it is done, my friends. It is not the way I would like to do it, but at the moment we are outnumbered, so we must fight might with guile. Every concession we get takes us one more step away from Ottawa. After a while, they will begin to see complete separation as inevitable. That is how it can be achieved. It is slow, perhaps too slow for those of you who are impatient and angry. But it is the road I would like to follow, if such is possible. If not, then we'll fight. That is what I am afraid we will have to do, and you must not think it will be easy."

Now what was Riel trying to do? Sundance wondered. Sure, that was it. He was trying to sound like a man of peace while urging the *métis* toward war. Nothing Riel had said so far proved to Sundance that the man wanted peace. All his words and actions pointed toward war. It showed in his eyes when the wild words began to flow. It showed in the way he used his hands, literally tearing Canada apart in his mind.

Michel Dumas jumped to his feet. "These Canadians will be no match for us. They are a race of storekeepers and chicken farmers. They don't know this country, and we know every inch of it. We will bury them in the muskeg, lead them into the wilderness until they are lost, starving, blinded by snow. If they come into this country, they will stay here forever!"

Riel held up his hand. "That is brave talk, Michel, but we must look at the facts. They may not come at all. Macdonald is a man who finds it hard to make up his mind. I have observed his career for many years. It is possible that he will put off doing anything, then do nothing at all. Or, being the man he is, he may postpone action for a while, thinking that his militia can recapture the Territories any time he feels like that. My God, if he only took that course! Give us a year, even six months, and we'll be strong enough to turn back any force he can send."

Gesturing toward Hardesty and the other Irishman, Riel said, "Not many of you know who these gentlemen are: Mr. Hardesty and Mr. Lane. Mr. Hardesty is going to tell you a few things you will like hearing."

Hardesty got up and moved out in front of the platform. He told them that he was an Irishman, explaining what being a Fenian meant. He said he was a Catholic and a hater of Great Britain, and therefore of the Canadian government, for what was Canada, after all, but a foreign province of Queen Victoria's?

"Men and guns are coming from the United States," said Hardesty. "Some will be here soon, and others are to follow. Given enough time, we can build an army of volunteers from the United States—men, experienced soldiers who have served in the army, veterans. They are well armed, well trained, and they know how to fight. Whereas, as Michel Dumas says, the Canadian militia are nothing but storekeepers and chicken farmers, led by pot-bellied lawyers and business.

"But," Hardesty continued, "even if they don't give us the time we need, the fight against the Canadians can still be won. What we have to do is prove to them that it isn't worth it. War costs money. The longer it goes on, the more it costs. Hit them in the pocketbooks is what we have to do. In the end, that's all they understand. Contest every inch of ground. They may think war is a gentleman's name, but we will show them otherwise. We will make the war so bloody, so costly, they will wish they never heard the name of the *métis*.

"There is this railroad with which they are supposed to destroy us. In the end, it is just wood and steel, tunnels and bridges. All these things can be destroyed. Telegraph wires can be cut, the poles burned. Towns are made of wood and can be burned with a can of coal oil and a single match. Hit them, and keep on hitting. I know this has a brutal sound, but we have to do what General Sherman did in Georgia—wage total war."

Hardesty looked sideways at Riel. "Of course, there will be no killing of prisoners. We will feed them to the best of our ability. This is the chance you waited for those long fifteen years when Louis Riel was in exile. Well, let us repay them for Louis's suffering, his years of wandering without a country. All we need is courage and determination. In years to come, you can tell your grandchildren that you were here, in the Lindsay schoolhouse, when it all began."

Hardesty sat down to polite applause. He looked disappointed. He had expected a better reception. Sundance grinned behind his hand. The *métis*, poor and largely uneducated, had plenty of everyday good sense. For all his blarney and war talk, Hardesty had failed to win them over completely. That would be at least one setback for the Irishman. But it was not to rule him out as a force in the movement.

Louis Riel stood up, still applauding the Irishman. "It's time," he said, "to talk of our friends, the Indians. I know it's been on your minds. It's time we talked about it frankly and openly."

The two Indians didn't move.

Ten

Gabriel Dumont was very silent as he and Sundance rode back to Batoche across the bleak plains that stretched away on both sides of the South Saskatchewan River. The wind blew as it did all year. This was country where it snowed all through the winter; it hardly ever rained, sometimes not for years at a time. Once the snow was gone, the ever-present wind baked the land, drying it to dust. In summer it was a sun-baked hell. They called it the Canadian Desert. You either froze or fried, and there were times when the crops withered and died for lack of water.

Dumont rode without saying a word, a dead cigar stuck in his mouth. Sundance wanted to talk but knew it would be no use. The meeting at the schoolhouse was over, and with it maybe a whole way of life was over for the *métis*. A lot of arguments had been heard and many things decided. Louis Riel had spoken of the great Indian uprising to come. He had called Poundmaker and Little Bear his "brothers and allies." Together, he said, the Indians would sweep the land of the Canadian oppressors. Both Indian chiefs spoke English, but all they did was nod several times while Riel spoke of the glorious victories to come. He said "victory" and not "slaughter." But everyone knew what he meant. The Canadians still had time to come to terms, Riel said. If the war came, would be up to them. First, Riel said, the *métis* would take several towns and hold the whites as hostages. Word would then be sent to the Canadians that if they invaded *métis* territory the hostages and towns would be destroyed.

In his fierce way, Michel Dumas wanted to start the Indian war immediately. Nolin, Riel's cousin, had opposed the war unless there was no other way. To Sundance's surprise, Dumont had opposed setting the Indians against the whites. The two Cree chiefs had showed no emotion while Dumont said:

"Can we control the Indians once they get started? To set the Indians on the warpath will bring down the fury of both the Canadians and the Americans. I am proud of my Indian blood. For generations the *métis* have been a civilized people. We have towns, churchs, schools. We have books and a newspaper, a way of life that is ours. The Indians are our brothers in the sight of God. But will they remain our brothers as the fighting goes on? Poundmaker and Little Bear are men of honor. But what of men like Wandering Spirit, who hates the *métis* as much as he hates the whites? I do not think they can control such men. This is a fight for the *métis*. Let us fight it by ourselves!"

Finally, a vote was taken, and Dumont's objections were overruled. After some words of praise for Dumont, Riel declared he would return to Montana unless the participation of the Indians was approved. Faced with that, Dumont said he would go along with the majority.

Now it was over. Dumont and Sundance were heading back to Batoche. Riel and Hardesty had stayed behind to continue the talks with the other leaders. Riel's bodyguard had stayed, too.

The wind blew hard and they rode without talking. The early winter darkness was coming on fast; soon, the warmth of the watery sun would be gone. Without pausing, Dumont spat out the chewed-up cigar and put another in his mouth.

The second cigar lasted another ten miles. By then, the first ferry was in sight. Up the slope from the riverbank was the cabin where the old man had given them bark tea earlier in the day. The broad, frozen river was slate gray in the light of the setting sun. Sundance thought with longing of the sunwashed southwest: Arizona, New Mexico, Sonora.

Their shoulders were hunched against the cold as they started down the long slope toward the old man's cabin. Sundance had no idea why the cabin was there. Maybe the old man sold things to travelers coming or going from the ferry. They were not much more than a hundred yards from the cabin when two rifles opened fire at the same time. Dumont pitched off his horse without a sound. He hit the ground hard and lay still. His horse spooked and ran toward the river.

Sundance yelled and rolled off his horse. When he came up again, the Winchester was in his hand and he was behind a tree. But the two riflemen kept firing at Dumont instead of at him. A bullet furrowed its way across the top of Dumont's shoulder. Another tore a hole in the brim of his hat.

Pushing the rifle out from behind the tree, Sundance threw lead at the cabin's door and window as fast as he could lever shells. The fire from the cabin slacked off under the rain of bullets. Sundance jumped from cover, and the firing started again as he grabbed Dumont by the heels and dragged him behind a tree. Dumont cursed and groaned as his face skated across the crusted snow. A bullet blew its hot breath in Sundance's face and another sang over his head.

Dumont's face was covered with blood gushing from a head wound. He tried to get up. Sundance pushed him down in the snow and told him to stay down. "I'll get them," he said.

The light was almost gone as he edged away from Dumont. Bullets tore at him from the window and door of the cabin, the muzzle flashes red-white in the enveloping grayness. The bushwhacker in the doorway was more reckless than the other. Sundance could see his outline every time he fired. They were both armed with repeaters. The trees thinned out close to the cabin. He went down on his belly in the snow and crawled forward, waiting for a clear shot.

It came in the moment the shooter in the doorway fired twice. Sundance killed him before he could fire a third shot. The man hung onto the side of the door, moaning with pain, then he fell on his face as a blaze of rifle fire jetted from the window. It stopped. In the silence that followed, Sundance heard the clack of a loading lever.

Lying in the snow, Sundance let time and the silence gnaw on the second ambusher's nerves. Three more flashes of fire came from the window. Sundance didn't shoot back because the bullets hadn't even come close to where he was. He crawled behind a tree before he told the man to come out. The answer was a single bullet ripping into a tree three feet from where he was. After that there was no more shooting.

"Come out or I'll burn you out!" Sundance yelled. "There's only one way out, and I have it covered." Cabins in the wind-blasted northwest didn't have back doors or windows. "You have one minute before you burn."

"You won't kill me?" It was a *métis*, not a Canadian or Indian voice. "Swear to God you won't kill me."

"You haven't much time left," Sundance yelled. "Come out now. I won't kill you. Throw the rifle out the window, plus any other weapons you have."

He waited. The voice said, "I am throwing out my rifle and my knife. I have no pistol. I am throwing them now. Listen to them."

Hardly able to see, Sundance heard the weapons fall in the snow. He yelled: "With your hands stretched in front of you, the fingers laced, come out."

Sundance stood up as the man came out. There wasn't enough light to make out much more than the thick, dark clothing of an ordinary *métis* with a heavy beard and a stiff-brimmed black hat. "Keep those hands stretched out," Sundance warned. "Stretch them out till it hurts. Now, stand where you are and put your legs wide apart."

Holding the rifle at his hip, Sundance went down the slope and stopped when he was six feet away. "Turn to one side," he ordered. "Now tell me your name and who hired you to kill Gabriel Dumont. The truth or I'll blow your hands off!"

"My God!" the man said, "we did not know..."

Sundance could see well enough to blow off his left thumb. The man screamed and tried to unlace his fingers. "Hold still or you lose the other one. I said, what's your name and who hired you?"

The words came out strangled. "Theodore Parie. No one hired me. Gabriel told us to come here and watch the road to the ferry. From the ferry, is what I mean to, prevent the Canadians from surprising the meeting at Batoche. Is—is Gabriel dead? We did not know. It was getting dark. If Gabriel came, we thought it would be with Louis Riel and his bodyguard."

Sundance said, "He's dead all right, you stupid son of a bitch."

The bushwhacker was lying, but this wasn't the place to make him talk. There was no use forcing it now. There would be time enough when they got him back to Batoche. Once there, Gabriel could make good use of his white-hot skinning knife.

The bushwhacker pretended to blubber, being very emotional and French. "What have we done? I swear on my mother's grave. Kill me! I don't care. But I was just following orders."

"Your own people will have to decide," Sundance said. Suddenly, as he spoke, the man's right hand flashed up toward the back of his neck and a knife appeared in his hand. He almost made it before a bullet stopped him. A .44-40 rifle bullet hit him squarely in the face and went out the back of his head. Except for the roar of the rifle and the body falling in the snow, there was no other sound.

Gabriel Dumont was up on his knees when Sundance went back to find him. "My rifle. Let me get my rifle," he kept repeating.

"Go easy," Sundance said, lifting him by his armpits. He was glad the big buffalo hunter was able to stand, however unsteadily. It would be hell to carry a man of his size. The wind and the cold had stiffened the blood on his face and, the bleeding from the head wound had stopped. Blood soaked the back of his coat, but Sundance didn't think the wound was serious.

"Did you—did you?" he said, still dazed.

"Both of them," said Sundance. "Can you make it to the cabin?"

Dumont did his best to stand up straight. The effort was painful, but he made no sound. Sundance got him to the cabin and helped him over the dead body in the doorway. Dumont had enough strength to spit before he went through.

It was dark inside. Sundance had to strike a match before he found the old man's bunk. The old man lay dead beside it. Under his chin was a knife wound without much blood. Dumont didn't want to lie down, but he didn't fight too hard when Sundance pushed him gently. Embers still glowed in the fire. Sundance built up the fire with bark chips, then piled on logs.

There was nothing much in the cabin; a rough table, two chairs, some cooking utensils on the floor by the fire. On the wall above the bunk were two pictures; a colored print of the Virgin Mary and an engraving of Louis Riel cut from a newspaper. Both were very old. In all, not much to show for a man's lifetime.

Sundance dragged the dead man outside and left him in the snow. He was a *métis*, like the other, and somewhat older. After he brought the weapons inside, Sundance barred the door. The wind was getting colder. When a kettle of water was warm enough, he spilled it into a basin, tore up a clean flannel shirt hanging on the wall, and dabbed at the wound in Dumont's head. It wasn't serious. The bullet had split the scalp without damaging the bone. The bleeding stopped after he washed out the wound.

Behind the stack of logs, he found a half-full bottle of whisky. He poured whiskey in the wound and bandaged it tightly with a strip of flannel. Then he got Dumont's coat and shirt off and looked at the wound in his back. It was long but shallow and would be sore for a while. When he finished with the back wound, there was just enough left for two big drinks.

"Don't worry, you won't go wild," he said, holding the bottle to Dumont's lips. "There isn't enough to make you wild, not the way you're feeling. What's left is for me. How are you feeling?"

Dumont's throat worked furiously as the whiskey went down. He drank exactly half the whiskey and handed the bottled back to Sundance. "I'm all right," he said. "A little man with a big drum is beating time in my head."

"I'll bet he is. Can you see all right? Do what I do."

Sundance stretched out his arm, then touched his nose with his index finger.

There was a deep growl of protest. "Damn foolishness!"

"Do it, Gabriel. Later you can complain all you want."

Looking sour, Dumont touched his finger to his nose. "That whiskey is as bad as mine," he said.

Sundance drank what was left in the bottle and didn't think it was any worse than Dumont's. It might even have been a little better. "I guess you'll be all right," he said. "We'll rest here for a while, then start back to Batoche."

"I can start back now."

"In a while, I said."

Dumont raised himself on his elbow, his forehead creased with a massive headache. "Who's in command here?"

Sundance said, "Right now, I am. Those two men I killed, you didn't post them here? They were *métis*."

"Not *métis*. Men dressed as *métis*."

"They were *métis*. And they knew you'd be coming back alone."

"Hardesty!" Dumont's dark eyes were dark with sudden anger.

"That's right," Sundance said. "The meeting was over, and we were getting ready to leave when Hardesty told Riel there were other things, important things, to talk about. Riel told you to go ahead and to take me with you."

"Oh, not Louis. Why would he?"

"I didn't say that. Maybe it was something Hardesty said about me. They had been talking; I couldn't hear them."

"I'll kill him," Dumont said quietly, touching the bandage on his head.

Sundance wasn't about to plead for the Irishman's life, but he didn't want to agree too quickly. "You have no proof it was Hardesty who planned this."

The big buffalo hunter thumped his chest. "In my heart I have proof. In my head—especially in my head—I have proof. I knew it would always come to something like this. To killing. But I thought he would face me like a man."

"One of the men said his name was Theodore Parie. Do you know him?"

"That dog! He is one of the Montana *métis*. We heard he had escaped from prison after having been sent there with others for robbing a bank. When he came here, he swore he had done it to get money for the cause. Another *métis* of the same gang came with him. The other man you killed?"

Sundance described him.

"Elzear Bedard," Dumont said. "They were always together." Dumont smiled viciously. "Now they are together in death. In their pockets I think you will find American money. Thieves, killers, now dead assassins. I never believed their story about the bank robbery." Dumont shrugged. "But we need men and still do."

It was hard for a man like Dumont to express gratitude. "You saved my life, Sundance. They were shooting at me. You could have ridden off and left me."

"Where would I go?"

"Back to the schoolhouse."

"They'd think I killed you."

"That was not the reason. Never will I forget what you did today," Dumont said.

"If you can talk so much, you should be able to travel," Sundance said. "If you fight as good as you talk, you'll have the Canadians whipped in no time."

Dumont grinned in spite of his throbbing skull. "Go to hell, halfbreed."

Sundance grinned back. "Look who's calling me a halfbreed!" he said. "Now you rest easy while I go catch your horse."

He found the animal, quiet now, down by the edge of the river. What sounded like pistol shots came from the middle of the river as the thinner ice broke up. There was a channel of clear water where the ferry crossed. He led Dumont's horse back to the cabin and tied it to a tree.

Then he roped the two dead men after searching their pockets where he found a fifty-dollar bill on each body. Next, he dragged them down to the river and dumped them into the channel. The current took them under the ice. It would be weeks before all the ice broke up, months before they floated downstream to Batoche.

Back again at the cabin, he collected the spent shells and put them in his pocket. Dumont looked at him curiously as he rolled the old man's body under the bunk and pushed it out of sight.

"What are you doing, Sundance?"

"I think you ought to surprise Hardesty when he gets back to Batoche. See! Nobody got killed here. There was no shooting. Hardesty will wonder what happened to you. You sure you can travel?"

Dumont thumped his chest, a thing he did often. "I am as strong as I ever was."

"Good," said Sundance. "Then you'll be able to fix the duck eggs and ham you were bragging about this morning."

Eleven

There were fifty prisoners under heavy guard when they got back to Batoche. Fires blazed in the streets of the village and across the river in the encampment. Sundance and Dumont saw the fires from miles upriver. The old man who took them across on the ferry was shaking with excitement.

"We have captured a whole army of Canadians, a whole army," he said. "They came with horses and wagons and guns. Not a shot was fired. Our men trapped them on the road from the south."

Canadians! Dumont looked at Sundance. It didn't make any sense.

In front of the barracks fifty men sat huddled in the wind, watched by two *métis* behind the Gatling gun. Riflemen guarded them on the other side. The wagons and horses of the captured men were standing some distance away.

Men came running when they saw Dumont, but the cheering stopped when they saw the bloody bandage around his head. Dumont roared at them to be quiet when they started yelling.

Sundance and Dumont dismounted and walked over

to the *métis* in charge of the prisoners. "You, Garneau," said Dumont, "what is all this?"

"Their leader says they came to fight with Hardesty, the Irishman. I do not believe them."

Dumont swore furiously. "More Hardestys," he said. "Which one is the leader?"

"The one standing up with the red hair in the caped greatcoat. He says his name is O'Neal."

"What the hell do you think you're doing?" O'Neal demanded when Garneau brought him over. "Who are you and where the hell is Hardesty? We didn't come a thousand miles, dodging the Mounties, to be treated like this. Senator Niles in New York is going to hear about this."

"He is lying," Garneau whispered.

"Go away!" Dumont roared.

O'Neal was still outraged. "My men are freezing out here. If we are to be prisoners, then treat us like soldiers." The redheaded Irishman looked like an ex-cavalryman to Sundance, probably a good one too. He wore wire-rimmed spectacles that took nothing away from his military bearing. An empty holster was strapped to his broad leather belt.

"Can you prove who you are?" Dumont was not impressed with the other man's anger. "A paper, a letter."

O'Neal said, "I have a safe conduct pass with Hardesty's signature on it. I showed it to your man, but I don't know if he can read."

"He can read French, his own language." Dumont said, unfolding the paper. After he read it, he gave it to Sundance. "It looks like Hardesty's signature. Look at the fancy way he writes his name.

"I see he's made himself a colonel," Sundance said. Colonel Hardesty—the noncom in the British Army had come a long way in a few years. Among the Fenians there were more colonels than in the Mexican army.

Dumont kept the safe conduct pass. "My apologies," he said, not sorry at all, "but you arrived early. Hardesty said the first men wouldn't arrive until the end of the week."

O'Neal said with a sneer, "We should have taken our time, but I thought there was a war to be fought. Next time we won't be so prompt."

His sarcasm was lost on Dumont, who said, "Next time I think you better stay in New York. But you're here, and your men will need food and shelter. Garneau did not make them sit here for nothing." Dumont called Garneau. "See that these men are quartered and fed. Join your men, Mr. O'Neal."

"I am Major O'Neal."

"Be anything you like. Join your men."

To Garneau, Dumont said, "Turn the Gatling gun around and move it back. You had it too close to them. If they had attacked, you would have had no chance to use it. Don't make the same mistake again. Guard them well. There may be trouble with Hardesty."

Dumont told Garneau to go away when he asked about his head. "And put out those damned fires! I don't want Mr. Hardesty to get excited when he rides in. No one has seen me. Do you understand?"

Garneau didn't understand, but he nodded.

"Give them the best food we have," Dumont ordered. "No slop. These men are our *friends*. But don't give them whiskey." Dumont smiled at Sundance. "Irishmen are worse than Indians."

When they got to the cabin, Sundance wanted Dumont to rest. "Then who will cook the ham and duck eggs?" Dumont asked. "You have eaten duck eggs?"

Sundance had to admit not lately. "Well, they're here, the first of them are," he said and stretched out on his bunk, while Dumont greased a skillet. "What do you think?"

"I think duck eggs have to be fried right, or they taste like rubber. About the Irishmen? I don't know what I think. This one called O'Neal looks all right. I don't know about the others, but they brought a Gatling gun. Now we have two."

"The Canadians have more than that."

"I know," Dumont said, turning away.

They were eating when horseman thundered into the encampment. Shouting started and stopped. Dumont swigged down the last of his tea and put his Winchester on the table. Sundance eased the Colt in his oiled holster. The door opened and Riel came in, followed by Hardesty.

"Gabriel! They said you were wounded," Riel said. "Did you see the man—the men—who did it?"

So much for the surprise, Sundance thought, watching Hardesty instead of Riel. Hardesty didn't miss the rifle on the table. He didn't speak because Riel was asking the questions.

"Sundance saw them and killed them, Louis. They were Theodore Parie and Elzear Bedard, two good *métis* from Montana. Each man had fifty American dollars in his pocket. They had no money when they came here from jail, just the ragged clothes on their backs."

Riel passed his hand over his face and sat down. "But this is unthinkable. Two of our own people took money to kill you? Where are they now?"

"In the river," Sundance said, still watching Hardesty.

Hardesty was a quick thinker. "Maybe the Canadians made a deal with them while they were in jail and bribed the jailers to let them escape."

"That won't wash," Sundance said. "Why would they try to kill Gabriel? Louis is the man to kill."

Without looking up, Riel said piously, "I am not the whole movement."

Dumont stood up, almost knocking over the table. "They were paid by someone closer to home I think. I will speak plainly. You could have hired them, Hardesty. I say you *did* hire them."

Hardesty's hand jerked toward his gun, but Sundance knew he wasn't going to draw it. It was the Irishman's way of showing how shocked and angry he was. Dumont's hand was on the rifle. If Hardesty had tried for a draw, Sundance would have killed him before his hand had touched the butt of the gun.

"Please, my friends!" Riel got between them with outstretched hands—the man of peace. "This is what they want, to have us quarrel. There has to be some explanation."

"Hardesty wants to get rid of me, Louis."

"Louis, why would I want to do that? I lead my men, Gabriel leads his."

Dumont said, "I lead all the men. That was the plan."

"That was the plan, Gabriel." Riel seemed to be speaking in the past tense. So it seemed to Sundance.

"Even if you were dead, the *métis* would never follow me," Hardesty argued.

Sundance knew the *métis* would follow anyone Riel told them to.

"But you have no proof, Gabriel," Riel said. "Did the men talk? They didn't accuse anyone?"

"They would have, Louis. If they were alive, they would talk." Dumont touched the haft of the skinning knife. "They would have told everything."

Riel shook his head. "But they aren't alive. The American money you found was just American money."

"And who has the most American money in Batoche?"

"Certainly I don't, Gabriel. Mr. Hardesty has the most American money. Would you condemn a man for having a lot of money? But I have *some* American money. Why don't you accuse me? We argued today in public, so I became angry at your insubordination and paid Parie and Bedard to kill you. Simple, is it not?"

"Bah!" Gabriel Dumont said.

"Of course it's foolish, Gabriel, but I could have done it. You are wounded, and you are angry, and you want to blame Mr. Hardesty because you don't like him."

"I don't give a damn if he likes me or not, Louis. You want to see how much money I have, Dumont? I'll show you." The Irishman took a thick leather-clasped wallet from inside his coat and snapped it open. It was stuffed with money in big bills. "See, Dumont, American money, Canadian money, even English pound notes. You think that's all the proof you need? You know what I think? I think you don't want to admit that two of your own people tried to murder you. Those two men didn't belong to me. They belonged to you. I didn't know them, and I didn't send for them."

Riel shrugged. "What he says is true, Gabriel. They were your men, your responsibility."

The Irishman sensed that he had the advantage now. "I don't give a damn if you believe me or not. We can settle this right now, if that's what you want. Nobody interferes. Just you and me."

Brave, Sundance thought, very brave! Challenging a badly shaken man who ought to be resting in his bunk.

"No! No! This is madness!" Riel said.

"With respect, Louis," Dumont said, "this is between the Irishman and me."

Sundance stood up, his hand not far from his gun. "Maybe not," he said. "It could be just as well be between Hardesty and me. Gabriel is a little tired right now. If that bullet had been an inch or two closer, he'd be dead."

"Who says I'm tired?" Suddenly Dumont was as wild as a bull getting ready to charge.

"With respect, Gabriel," Sundance said. "Shut up! What's it going to be, Hardesty? They shot at me too. I'm almost as mad as Gabriel. How would you like it to be? It can't be pistols. You wouldn't have a chance. It can't be knives because I'd cut you to ribbons. What about fists and feet? You Irishmen are good with your fists and feet."

This time Riel didn't protest. Sundance knew then that the *métis* leader liked to see what his men were made of. There was no need to test Dumont, even if he had been in condition to fight. Riel had known him too long.

"Fine with me," Hardesty said truculently. "Now is fine with me. After you, sir." The Irishman was putting on airs again—the British Army noncom who wanted to be a gentleman. So far, nothing had been said about the fifty Fenians.

They left their weapons on the table in Dumont's cabin and went out into the snow. It was biting cold, one of the coldest days of that March of 1885. Soon they would be sweating.

"Any rules?" Hardesty asked.

"None," was the answer.

Bundled in a long fur coat with his hat pulled down over his ears, Riel came out to watch the fight.

Moving away from the cabin, Sundance and Hardesty stopped when they reached a place where the snow had been beaten down by horses. Pale moonlight filtered through the clouds. The wind was blowing steadily.

Hardesty moved with ease for a big man. He was the veteran of many brawls and knew how good he was with his fists. Sundance decided it wasn't going to be a cinch to knock him down. He was going to do his damnedest, because a man who would pay ambushers to murder a decent man had pain coming to him. 'Colonel' Hardesty would learn that he had come to the wrong place to play tin soldier.

There was a long pause while they sized one another up. Then the Irishman came at Sundance, taking his time, fists weaving, shoulders hunched. Well now, thought Sundance, Hardesty fancies himself a boxer as well as a gentleman. A fist came straight at Sundance's face and he turned it aside. While he was doing it, a left thumped him hard in the ribs. Sundance punched back with his left and missed. He followed with the left again, and this time it landed—not a hard, telling blow, but one that got inside the Irishman's defense. Hardesty moved in, throwing rights and lefts but keeping the punches short so he would not be caught off balance. Sundance had one big advantage. His thick-soled but flexible north-country moccasins gripped the frozen ground, while Hardesty's heavy boots skidded.

A punch that seemed to come from nowhere rocked Sundance's head. If he hadn't jerked it aside, another would have landed in the same place. The Irishman bored in again and grunted with pain when he was stopped by a blow to the heart. Suddenly, Hardesty lowered his left and jabbed at Sundance's belly. Even though he sidestepped some of the force, the Irishman's hard fist made the halfbreed's stomach muscles tense with pain.

Both men backed off and circled one another. The sweat on their shirts was beginning to freeze. So far, there had been no kicking. The Irishman would have to start it first. Sundance knew he would.

The first kick came after Sundance nearly toppled Hardesty with a right to the jaw. He braced his feet against the force of the punch and his arms waved as he tried to regain his balance. Sundance was moving in to deliver another right when Hardesty kicked at his knee. Had the kick landed, the kneecap would have been shattered by a heavy boot powered by a muscular leg.

After dodging around the Irishman kicked again. This time it dug into Sundance's thigh. The whole leg felt as if it had been whacked with an ax handle. Hardesty followed the kick with a mad rush. Down and down he dived at Sundance's belly, trying to knock him down in the snow. Sundance let himself go with the force of the rush, then he reached up and grabbed Hardesty by both arms, and threw himself flat on his back so that his feet came up at the same time. There was a wild shout as the Irishman was thrown ten feet over Sundance's head. He landed with a crash with the wind knocked out of him and was still gasping when Sundance turned, jumped in the air, and landed with all his weight on the small of Hardesty's back. Then, jumping to one side, the halfbreed kicked the Irishman in the side, and then did it again.

Hardesty screamed and tried to get a hold on Sundance's kicking foot. He got a grip but lost it, and then he was kicked again with the other foot. The Irishman tried to roll away, but Sundance followed him with kicks. Finally, he lay on his back, holding up his hands, quivering with pain and anger.

It would have been easy for Sundance to kill him with a right kick to the temple, the weakest part of the skull. The Irishman's hands were still grabbing at nothing when Sundance drew back for that last kick.

"You want more?" Sundance yelled, still thinking of the ambush at the cabin and the old man's knife wound in his throat. "You want more? I'll give you more. But you have to say what you want."

"I've had enough," Hardesty groaned. "No more." He rolled away, and Sundance let him go, though he knew it wasn't finished. No matter what happened, from now on Hardesty would never let it drop.

Hardesty stood up, holding his ribs and trying to smile. He had a smile like a rabid wolf. Dumont watched silently. Also smiling, Riel came forward. "Enough of this stupid brawling," he said. "I want you two men to shake hands and say there is no hard feeling between you. Come on now, that is an order."

Holding out his hand, Sundance said, "I have no hard feelings." He was lying.

They shook hands.

"None here," Hardesty said. He too was lying.

"Good! Good!" Louis Riel declared. "We will attack the day after tomorrow."

Twelve

That same night, in the Parliament Buildings in Ottawa, lights were burning late. All day long, messengers from the telegraph office on the fourth floor had been running up and down the private stairs to the Prime Minister's office. The guards outside the building had been doubled, and no one was allowed to enter or leave without a pass or in some instances, a complete search.

John A. Macdonald, Prime Minister of Canada, sat behind his desk. Passing his hand through a shock of graying hair, his deep-set eyes were pools of worry and fatigue. For days now, he had remained at his massive oak desk, reading reports from the North West, trying to sift the different advice given to him. Some advisors sneered at the Riel threat as being nothing more than the usual *métis* bragging. Others urged him to crush the *métis* without mercy.

Macdonald and his military aide, Colonel Carson, were smoking silently when another telegraph messenger knocked.

Macdonald took the message and said to Carson, "When will they stop coming? I wonder what this one says."

50 MEN BELIEVED FENIANS CROSSED WYO-
MING BORDER FAR WEST REGINA THIS WEEK
DIRECTION NORTH.

CROWDER

Colonel Carson, a lean-faced man in civilian clothes
that did little to hide the fact he was a soldier, picked up a
cup of cold coffee and drank it. He had been pacing, but
now he sat down beside the P.M.'s desk.

"I don't think there's any doubt of the Fenians' coming
in," he said. "Fifty isn't a large number, but there will be
others. And they have what the *métis* don't have: money.
Some of it is their own money, collected from the poor
Irish in the back streets of New York and Boston and
Chicago. The biggest part of it comes from American
politicians, who are determined to annex this country.
You have to act now, Prime Minister. There's no other
way."

The Prime Minister nodded, still staring at the large
wall map behind his desk. "We're a big country, Carson.
That's one of our problems." He picked up a pointer and
traced a line between Ottawa and Regina. He gave Regina
a rap to express his annoyance.

"How," he said, "are we going to get troops from here
to here without a lot of delays? Look at the distance
involved. It frightens me."

"It doesn't have to, Prime Minister," Carson said
calmly. "The troops can move west on the Canadian
Pacific."

"But it isn't finished. You know that. They may never
get it finished north of Lake Superior. Everything—track,
locomotives—sinks in the muskeg. It's like trying to lay
tract in quicksand. Van Horne has tried everything to
beat that stretch and he still hasn't succeeded. That
muskeg must be a thousand feet deep. Anyway, there are
other unfinished stretches, too."

Carson said, "I took the liberty of asking Mr. Van Horne to come here tonight, sir."

"Why tonight?"

Carson smiled. "You have a way of making decisions on the third night, Prime Minister."

"Don't think you ever know me too well," John A. Macdonald cautioned. "But you're right. I had just about made up my mind to telegraph Middleton when Crowder's message came. The Fenians! If they want to fight England, they why the hell don't they go to England? You say Van Horne is coming?"

Carson looked at his watch. "He's been in the building for fifteen minutes. I was about to tell you."

"Then fetch him here, man. At once. Still, I have my doubts about sending a whole army by train. I don't think even the Americans have done that. By God, it would be something if we could do it!"

Colonel Carson went downstairs and came back in a few minutes with a barrel-shaped man in a hopsack suit and the look of one who hates to sit still for long. The Prime Minister came from behind his desk to greet him, for here was the greatest railroad builder in Canada, the United States, or anywhere else. Son of an old New York Dutch family, Van Horne believed there was nothing that couldn't be done if you tried hard enough. Van Horne was Canada's favorite American.

"Cigar?"

"Indeed, yes," Van Horne said, settling back in his chair.

"Whiskey?"

"Nothing goes better with a cigar."

They all had scotch whiskey.

"You are aware of what's happening in the North West, Mr. Van Horne?" the Prime Minister said. "Of course, you know some of it."

"Carson here has been filling me in," Van Horne said.

"And I get information from my own people in Saskatchewan. It has occurred to me that they may try to dynamite the tracks and cut the telegraph lines. I have had men patrolling the track for two weeks."

Macdonald said, "Then you do know how serious it is?"

"Not entirely, Prime Minister. But I know that any internal war, any civil war, must have terrible consequences. Look what happened to my own country. The effects will last for a long time. I would hate to see the same thing to take place here."

Macdonald said, "I'm told your motto is: 'If you want something done, name the day when it must be finished.'"

"Yes, I believe that." Van Horne smiled. "Give or take a day or two."

"Can you move five-thousand soldiers to Saskatchewan in a week? A week and a half at the latest?"

Van Horne regarded his smoldering cigar. "Yes, Prime Minister, I think a week to ten days would be all right. If we had a clear track, I could have them there in three days. But I'm not making excuses for the track. It will be finished before long."

"Are you sure, Mr. Van Horne?"

"As sure as I can be, Prime Minister. This isn't a snap judgment. I've been going over it since Colonel Carson first talked to me, and I have decided what can be done about the unfinished stretches of track. What's the final destination?"

"Fort Qu'Appelle."

Van Horne said, "It can be done, but it's going to be hell for the men. The worst part is the 105 miles of scattered gaps north of Lake Superior. You know that. Where I can, I will lay track on ice or snow and trust it to hold. There will be many places where that isn't possible. Some of the men will then travel by sleigh, but most will have to walk. We will have to leave trains behind when the tracks end. It will be easy for the men until we reach Lake Superior. Until that point, they can ride in regular passenger cars. On the far side of the lake, past the 105 miles of gaps, there are no passenger cars, just construction flatcards, with no sides, no roof, and no heat. But I can have my men working on those flatcars by morning, nailing up thick walls and looking for all the stoves they can find. Some of the men will travel comfortably enough; the others will be mighty cold. Some may die of it."

"It can't be helped."

Colonel Carson asked, "What about the artillery?"

"That's going to be the worst problem of all. If you didn't need it, I would say leave it behind. Yes, I know it has to go. But it's going to have to be loaded and unloaded a dozen times. There is nothing like trying to get a field piece on or off a flatcar when the temperature is fifty below. It gets that cold on the lake this time of year."

Macdonald didn't want to hear any more about hardship. "Do what has to be done, Mr. Van Horne. I will write you a letter of authorization right now. Colonel Carson will be your liaison between my office and the military. If anyone, and I don't care who he is or of what rank, refuses to cooperate or otherwise shows a disinclination to help, I will deal with him immediately."

Macdonald wrote as he talked, making broad angry strokes of the pen. He signed with a flourish and pressed a rubber stamp to the lower right-hand corner of the letter. "There," he said, passing the document across the desk.

Van Horne read it and said, "This makes me dictator of Canada for ten days!" He put the letter in his pocket and stood up. "I just want to ask you one thing more, Prime Minister. I anticipate trouble along the line when we get to Saskatchewan and have already taken precautions. But what about here?"

Macdonald said, "Most of our French-Canadian

citizens are loyal. There is talk of support for Riel and the *métis*, but," said Macdonald, smiling without much humor, "if you can deliver the troops to Fort Qu'Appelle on time, the talk around here will remain just talk."

Thirteen

The cold northern dawn was breaking when Sundance, Dumont, and fifty mounted *métis*, all seasoned frontiersman, saw Duck Lake up ahead through the whirling snow. The wind whipped through the pines, penetrating their thick wool clothing and fur-lined boots. Men and horses were blinded by snow as they plowed through the deepening drifts. Halfway between Batoche and Fort Carlton, the lake shone like silver in the weak half-light of the morning sun. Willows and poplars fringed the lake on all sides. On the far side of the lake were the log houses that contained the food, rifles, ammunition, and other supplies stored for use by the Mounties and the militia.

Wiping snow from his eyes, Dumont said, "It looks like we got here first, but we'd better make sure. One of my men in Fort Carlton said Superintendent Crozier was getting ready to seize the stores some time today."

"Makes sense," Sundance said. Dumont had just sent two men ahead to check for an ambush, and Sundance watched while their outlines became lost in the falling snow. Once they raided the supply camp, the *métis* would be in open rebellion against the government of Canada, as he would himself, Sundance knew. Before it was over, he might hang for it. So far, he hadn't come up with a plan that seemed to have any chance of working.

The two scouts rode back and reported that the camp was deserted. Dumont nodded. "So we win the first fight of this war. This is where it begins." The big *métis* shrugged. "Or where it ends."

They rode around the edge of the lake that was now beginning to thaw in the center. There were two log houses there, shuttered against the ice and wind. Both doors were secured with heavy padlocks. Dumont broke both locks with a hatchet, and they went in out of the cold. Rifles and boxes of ammunition took up most of the space in the first house; in the other, canned goods were stacked on shelves from floor to ceiling, with smoke-cured ham and frozen sides of beef hung from hooks. A rough table was piled high with blankets.

"We won't go hungry or cold, not for a while," Dumont said. "Those Lee-Metford bolt actions will make the Canadians wish they had let us go in peace."

Sundance picked up one of the fast-firing British-made military rifles. He tested the action; the short-pull bolt slid back and forth smoothly. "A fine gun," he agreed.

Dumont told his men to start loading the sleighs. "Don't overload. Take what you can, then throw the rest in the lake. We'll burn the houses before we move out."

The sleighs were about half loaded when a young *métis* on a winded horse came galloping from the other side of the lake. He jumped down, yelling, "Crozier and a big party of Mounties and militia are coming up fast. They have a seven-pound gun."

"How fast?" Dumont asked.

"Not much more than an hour, Gabriel. What are you going to do?"

"Ambush them," Dumont said calmly. "Have they spare horses?"

"All they need to catch up to us."

Dumont said, "Then we can't run, even if we wanted to. We can't trap them here, because Crozier might guess that's what we'll do. Let's ride out to greet the Canadians."

About a mile and a half from Duck Lake, Dumont found the position he wanted: a low hill intersecting the road, with ravines running forward on either side toward the police and militia and clumps of brush and willows to provide natural cover. He posted most of his men here while a smaller party occupied an abandoned cabin to the right of Superintendent Crozier's advance.

It was a perfect place for an ambush. Unaware of what lay in store for them, the police and militiamen trudged on through the falling snow. As the snow grew heavier, everything melded into the enveloping grayness. Crozier's men crossed the first ridge and started down into the valley. Then, half frozen, they climbed the next hill. Nothing moved yet in the snow-blotted distance. They were still climbing the icy slope when Crozier saw a line of *métis* riflemen in motion, snaking around his left flank.

As Crozier ordered his bewildered men to open fire, a deadly hail of bullets crackled from the *métis* line, ripping through the Canadian force with terrible effect. The *métis* were in deep cover while Crozier's men were out in the open, with not a rock or tree in sight. When the militia tried to expand their line, they came under intense fire from the abandoned cabin. Crozier ordered up the seven-pounder, but by then the militia had advanced too far and were in the line of fire.

Yelling like a madman, Crozier ordered the militia to fall back. The seven-pounder opened fire. After only three shots, an inexperienced gunner rammed in a shell before the powder, and the gun was put out of action. Rallied by Crozier, the militia made a direct assault on the cabin; however, they were driven back with heavy losses.

Mounting his horse, Gabriel Dumont ordered the

métis to counterattack. An instant later, his horse was shot out from under him and he fell heavily in the snow. The wound in his head opened again and he began to bleed. Sundance rushed to him and dragged him to his feet.

"Enough, Gabriel," he yelled above the crackle of rifle fire. "You've beaten them. Don't make it a slaughter. Let them retreat."

For a moment, Dumont fought to break Sundance's hold on him. Blood dripped from his head, staining his dark blue coat. The fury died in his eyes and he started to sag. Down the slope, the *métis* were driving the Canadians force back into the blinding snow. Dead Mounties and militiamen lay everywhere. Then, after a few more outbursts of firing, the fight was over. It had been a decisive victory for the *métis*; they had even captured the seven-pound cannon.

"The funny thing is, I don't hate them," Dumont said, watching while the *métis* collected weapons from the dead Mounties. "They are hard men, but they have always been fair according to their rules, their law. They are nothing like your United States cavalry. But the militia are volunteers, and they would like to destroy us, drive us from our land and far into the icy regions. Before they do that, we will give them a fight to remember."

Sundance said, "Then you don't think you're going to win?"

Dumont rubbed his snow-crusted beard and looked very tired. He raised his rifle when he saw one of his men going through a dead policeman's pocket. He fired one shot and the looter jumped back in terror.

"Only the guns, Henri," he roared. "Take anything else, and I'll shoot your eyes out."

Turning back to Sundance, he said quietly, "You ask are we going to win. You have served with the Americans, and you know that the white men are like locusts. Kill a

285

hundred, and soon you are faced with a thousand more. Do *you* think we're going to win?"

Sundance liked the big, life-hardened buffalo hunter. He spoke the truth. "No, my friend, but maybe you can make it so costly for them that they'll come to some kind of terms. I think that's the best you can hope for. You can't win big battles against them. Let them see what you can do, then give them a chance to think about it. My advice is: Don't push them to the point where they can't back off."

"I think that is good advice," Dumont agreed, looking at Sundance with narrowed eyes. "We will strike at the other towns and forts along the Saskatchewan and we will take them. Then, when we are in a position of strength, a good place to bargain from, we will send them our terms. If they refuse to bargain, we will fight on until we are all dead. But killing us all will not be easy. Before they have done it, we will make the name of Canada stink in the nostrils of the world."

Dumont waved his hand toward the bleak landscape, made even more bleak by the corpses dotting the slope. "This is our land, this wilderness that nobody wanted until they smelled the money to be made here. Our ancestors are buried here in the frozen earth. We were here before there were maps, and we will die here if we have to."

There was nothing to be said, Sundance knew, because in his bones he felt the love these brave people had for their windswept land. He knew the bitterness they felt at being cornered, fenced off by laws that meant nothing to them. The law—white man's law—had no meaning for the halfbreed or the Indian. The land itself was all that mattered. In their way, the whites loved the land, too, but to them it was always property, something to be coveted and fought over, not something to be felt in the blood and bones.

Turning his horse away from the battlefield, Dumont said, "I owe you my life, Sundance, so I will say this now—it is not too late for you to get out."

"No," Sundance answered. "I'm here, and here I stay."

Fourteen

On the night of March 28, 1885, Sundance, Dumont, and Riel, accompanied by a large force of well-armed *métis*, watched the evacuation of Fort Carlton by the Mounties and militia. From a long, sloping ridge they listened to the shouts of command as the Canadians moved out, led by Commissioner Irvine.

The day before, after learning of the defeat at Duck Lake, Irvine had decided there was no choice but to abandon the fort. The old fur trader's post had not been built for defense. It was on the river's edge, and the three-hundred foot hill behind it commanded the fort square from all sides. In addition, the militiamen, all drawn from Fort Albert, wanted to get back to their families, now undefended.

"We could strike now," Dumont said. "They are already in a rout."

Riel said, "No. We will save our strength for the bigger battles ahead. The Indians will soon be joining us. Already I have sent news of Duck Lake. All they need is a little more persuasion. Soon, all the towns on the Saskatchewan will be in our hands. But listen to me, Gabriel. The Irishman is growing impatient. He wanted to be with us tonight. Hardesty and his Irishmen have come a long way to fight on our side."

Dumont said, "Let him stay in Batoche and wait for the rest of his men to come from the States. We will use them when the time comes. There will be plenty of fighting for Hardesty before this war is over."

Riel said, "I think you would like to win this war without his help. Speak plainly, old friend. Is that what you're thinking?"

"It would be better if we could. If we can't, well, so be it."

Turning to Sundance, Riel said, "You have become Gabriel's friend. He trusts your judgment. What is your opinion?"

Sundance said, "So far, the fight has been between you and the Canadians. Turning foreigners, paid mercenaries, against them will make them angrier than they are now. No country likes to be invaded by foreigners. Even the French-Canadians in the east may turn against you. I would say keep the Irish out of the fighting if you don't need them."

Riel sighed. "You are probably right, but it's so hard to decide. Everything keeps changing from day to day. What I don't understand, Gabriel, is why you have changed your mind. Two weeks ago you were ready to welcome the Irishman."

"Two weeks ago I hadn't met Hardesty. There is something about the man I don't like and don't trust. I have been thinking that, if we win this war, Hardesty and his band of trained soldiers won't be so easy to get rid of. Hardesty talks of bringing in a thousand men, maybe more. Most of these men have no families to care about, and I think many are criminals and killers."

Riel said, "Say what you have to say, Gabriel. There is more."

"Already there is bad feeling between these Irishmen

and our men. Our women..." Dumont spat in the snow. "Hardesty is too eager to set the Indians against the whites. He would bathe the country in blood from here to the Rockies. Who can say what mad plan he has? To seize the whole North West and hold it with American support."

"This is incredible," Riel said. "Hardesty has accepted my leadership without question."

Sundance said, "Not so incredible. Other bold men have tried to build their own empires. Walker tried it in Nicaragua and nearly succeeded. He ended up in front of a firing squad, but he gave it a fair try."

Riel's voice faltered a little. "I would not permit such a thing. I have given my word to my people."

Dumont spat again. Sundance didn't say anything.

"They're moving out," Dumont said. "The fort is on fire."

Flames streaked the night sky as the last of the garrison disappeared into the darkness, taking the road along the edge of the river. Horsemen led the way, followed by sleighs, while more mounted men brought up the rear. Then the last sounds died away and there was nothing but the fretting of the horses and the ever-present wind blowing from the north.

"I wish they'd all go as quietly as that," Riel said, clapping his mittened hands together. The *métis* leader was a man of constantly changing moods. Now he was cheerful again, all talk of Hardesty forgotten. "Maybe they will, my friends. They are just men, like us, and do not wish to die. We can live in peace with the Canadians, the English Canadians. If only they could realize that we are not a subject people. Come on now. Let us look at what is left of Fort Carlton."

There wasn't much left by the time they reached the burning buildings. The Canadians had left nothing that could be salvaged. The flag had been lowered and taken away; the flagpole stood gaunt against the glare of the flames.

"Chop it down," Dumont ordered. "Chop it down and burn it."

The *métis* cheered as the flagpole toppled to the ground. Scouts were sent out to watch for a counterattack by Irvine's forces, while cook fires were started and the pungent smell of thick pea soup with chunks of ham rose into the frosty night air. It stopped snowing and the wind died down. Around the fire, they ate with the appetites of men who had been long on the trail. The buildings of the fort were all but gone.

Hunkered down beside the fire, Dumont sniffed the air. "The spring will be here earlier than we thought. I can smell the thaw coming. We must move on Fort Battleford without delay. Winter is our friend and we must make use of it while we can. Already the people from the town have moved into the fort. It is well fortified, and taking it will not be like Duck Lake or this place here. They know we are coming and will be waiting. Our men will die in the taking of the fort, but there isn't time to starve them out."

"What about Fort Pitt?" Riel asked. "There is a garrison there."

"It is not so important as Battleford, Louis. After taking Battleford, we can pass it by, then attack Fort Albert. Pitt will be caught in the middle, with our forces to the north and south of it. Are you sure the Indians will be at war by the time we reach Battleford?"

"I am sure, Gabriel. Dumas has gone ahead to the reservation. If any man can rouse the Indians, Dumas can. He says Little Bear and Poundmaker can throw nine-hundred braves against the Canadians, more than that if other tribes join the war. For years, Poundmaker's people have starved on the Battleford reservation—bad food, what there is of it, not enough blankets to keep the women and children from freezing. Yes, Gabriel,

Poundmaker and his people have had enough of Canadian promises. They will fight."

Sundance asked, "But can they be stopped once the killing starts?"

Riel's deep voice was still full of confidence. "Any man is only as good as he is treated. Give the Crees and the Stoneys food and blankets, give them back their pride as men, and they will see us only as friends. They will stop because I tell them to stop."

Dumont had no comment to make, and it wasn't because of the chunk of steaming ham he had just put in his mouth. He looked from Riel to Sundance, then began to scrape out his plate. He stood up and wiped snow from the barrel of his Lee-Medford repeater.

"It is time to go," he said, "if we want to get there by first light."

It snowed lightly during the night, but the sun was trying to break through by the time they reached the outskirts of Battleford. Long before they got there they heard the sound of rifle fire. At first it was uneven, but it grew more concentrated as the sun broke through the watery sky. They topped a ridge, and from the summit they could see down into the valley containing the town and the fort.

Dumont took a short brass telescope from his pocket and opened it and grunted with satisfaction at what he saw. Riel took the telescope and scanned the valley.

"It looks like Dumas did his work all right," Dumont said. "The town is deserted except for Dumas and the Indians. Everybody else is in the fort."

Riel handed the telescope to Sundance. He moved it from the town to the fort, some distance away, and back again. Most of the firing was being done by the Indians, now under cover of the houses closest to the stockade. The Indians were all in war paint. While Sundance watched, a group of them tried to rush the main gate, only to be driven back with the loss of half their number.

Dumont cursed. "What does Dumas think he's doing? His orders were to pin them down in the fort, not to get half the Indians killed."

"You should have taken the Gatling gun from Batoche," Riel said. "It would make all the difference now."

"No, Louis, Batoche is the center of our country, our capital. It must be defended by every means. If Batoche fell, it would take the heart out of our people."

The fort was on a hillside some distance from the town. The Indians had already ridden up to parley. By that time, they had plundered the stores and buildings of the town. Inside the fort there were six-hundred settlers and townspeople, three hundred of them women and children. They watched fearfully through rifle slits while the Indians dressed themselves in silk party gowns and bonnets, screaming like maniacs while they guzzled whiskey and hacked pianos to bits with their tomahawks.

When the attempt at holding a parlay failed, the Indians fell back before they attacked. Driven back by rifle fire from the stockade, they waved a flag of truce before encircling the fort, waiting for it to surrender. Now they were attacking again.

Followed by Sundance and Riel, Dumont galloped down the slope toward the town, yelling at the Indians to fall back. He jumped off his horse and grabbed one of the *métis* who was with the Indians.

"Where is Dumas?" he roared, trying to make himself heard above the war crys of the Indians.

"Dead! Shot!" the man yelled back. "The Indians will no longer obey their leaders."

"They will obey me," Dumont roared. Taking no heed of the bullets from the fort, he rode his horse straight into a bunch of Indians who were fighting over a bottle of whiskey. One Indian swung a tomahawk at Dumont.

Dumont upended his rifle and struck the brave between the eyes with the brass-shod butt. The Indian grunted and went down. Another whiskey-crazed brave jumped at Dumont with a knife. Dumont jerked his foot from the stirrup and kicked him squarely in the face. Then Dumont rounded his horse and knocked the others sprawling in the snow.

"Get back!" Dumont yelled. "Get back under cover."

"What do you think?" Sundance asked Dumont when they were crouched down inside the broken window of a thick-walled cabin. Now that the Indians had pulled back, the fire from the fort had slackened. Riel had gone to talk to the Indian chiefs, followed by the *métis* Dumont had appointed in Dumas's place.

"Do you think that seven-inch cannon can be put in working order?" Dumont asked. "If it can't, I have been thinking about fire arrows."

"There are hundreds of women and children in there. You want to burn them out?"

"I want to capture that fort. We can't leave a garrison behind us. What about the cannon?"

"The shell can be pried out," Sundance answered. "It will take time, but it can be done. We only have two shells and just enough powder to fire them. The militia managed to save the rest when they retreated at Duck Lake. But for all they know in the fort, we could have all the shot and powder we need."

Dumont asked, "Can you do it, get the gun back in working order?"

"I've seen it done. You heat the barrel very fast over a fire. The shell isn't explosive, it's just a ball propelled by powder. If there is no powder in the barrel, there's no danger of an explosion. The barrel heats faster than the ball and expands faster. Then you hoist the gun with ropes, muzzle pointing straight down, and hit the breech hard with a sledgehammer or something else. With luck, and if it isn't too badly jammed, the ball will fall out. Then you let the barrel cool slowly so there won't be any distortion."

Dumont ordered his men to bring the cannon up from the rear of his column. Sundance found the town's one blacksmith shop and ordered the seven-pounder brought there. He pumped the bellows and got the fire in the forge white hot again. "Get the chains on the gun," he ordered. "Don't bring it down too close to the fire. I'll tell you how close. Once it starts to get hot, keep the barrel turning. Do it at a steady pace. It has to heat evenly. Once it's hot, don't let it drop or bang into something. If the barrel gets bent, there is no way we can straighten it. All right now, start lowering it toward the fire. Easy, not so fast. I'll tell you when it's hot enough, then point the muzzle toward the ground and make sure it doesn't swing when I start hitting it with the sledge."

Dumont and Sundance watched closely while the barrel of the cannon was rotated above the flame. Soon it began to glow a dull red; before long the red turned to white.

"Quickly now," Sundance said. "Point the muzzle downward and hold it firm. Move before the ball expands as much as the barrel."

Sundance had pulled a keg close to the forge. Now he climbed up on it, measuring for the first swing of the sledge. If it took more than two or three blows, it wouldn't work. He wanted it to work; he wanted the garrison in the fort to surrender.

Lifting the heavy sledge-hammer and sweating in the fierce glow of the fire, he struck the back of the cannon. The three *métis* held it firmly under the impact of the blow. Sundance raised the sledge-hammer again and struck the gun in the same place. Inside the gun there seemed to be a small shifting movement. Without waiting, Sundance put all his weight behind the third blow. With it, the *métis* yelled as the ball rattled out of the barrel and fell on the floor.

"Let the cannon hang the way it is, muzzle straight down," Sundance said. "And keep that door closed so it won't cool too fast."

They waited for the barrel of the seven-pounder to cool. Doing it carefully took more than half an hour. Sundance ordered the *métis* to put the gun back on its carriage and he ran his hand over the still-warm barrel. "It looks all right. We'll know for sure as soon as I fire it."

Dumont grinned. "You mean it will blow up if it isn't all right?"

"I'd say so."

"Then I'll fire it."

"No, I fixed it—at least, I hope I did—so I'll touch it off. But first I'd like you to get Louis and have him talk to the commander of the garrison. They may be willing to surrender to you but not to the Indians. If they're afraid enough of the Indians, especially the Crees, they would rather die fighting than be scalped and tortured. Louis has to give his word that the Indians won't harm them, that they are free to march into Alberta with a safe conduct all the way. If Louis allows the Indians to massacre them, it could well be the end of your cause. There would be no bargaining with the Canadians if that happened."

Dumont nodded. "I will go and find him. Where will you be when I am doing that?"

"Pointing the seven-pounder straight at the gate of the fort. It may take one shell to get them to parlay. But in the end, it's up to Louis and how convincing he can be. I'd hate to see them make a real fight of it."

Sundance positioned the cannon between two log houses after pushing a wagon out in front of the gun. Under cover of the wagon, he primed the gun, then rammed in the ball. He lined up the muzzle with the gate, then adjusted it for the drop of the shell. If he hadn't misjudged, the shell would strike the log gate about halfway to the top, just where the crossbar would be on the inside. One shell might not smash open the gate; maybe even two wouldn't be enough. What was going to happen next depended on so many things.

Dumont came back with Riel, who was carrying a flag of truce, a white tablecloth tied to a broomstick. Poundmaker, chief of the Crees, was with them. At first, Riel wanted to walk right out in the open waving his peace flag. Dumont and Sundance had to hold him back.

Riel didn't seem to understand, "But they wouldn't shoot me. I am not armed. I carry a flag of truce."

"Wait," Sundance warned him. "Somebody might shoot you. It doesn't have to be a Mountie, but one of the militiamen might take a crack at you."

"Then what do you propose to do, Sundance?" Riel gripped his broomstick with fierce determination.

"Fire a shot at the gate. One shot to show them what we can do if they refuse to surrender. They have no way of knowing that we only have two shells. After that, you can talk. They will want to be very sure about the Indians. Otherwise, we're in for a long fight."

"Cover me," Sundance said to Dumont. "Tell the *métis* to fire over the heads of the men on the stockade."

Dumont rapped out the order. Immediately, a hail of lead was thrown at the fort, the *métis* firing the ten-round Lee-Metfords as fast as they could work the bolts.

Sundance and Dumont manhandled the cannon around the side of the wagon. "Get back now," Sundance warned Dumont. "Your people need you more than they need me." He adjusted the range and elevation again. It looked all right, as good as he could make it. A lot of lives were riding on those two shells.

"Now!"

He touched a lighted fuse to the cannon. It dug back on its wooden carriage as the shell screamed straight at the gate of the fort, going slightly higher than he had figured. There was a splintering crash as some of the thick verticals in the gate gave way. White smoke boiled up from the muzzle of the cannon, and from the *métis* ranks a wild cheer went up.

Sundance took the peace flag from Riel's hand and waved it from behind the wagon. A flurry of shots came its way. He yelled and waved the flag again. This time there was only one shot, then a man's voice on the stockade yelling for the defenders to cease firing.

"What do you want out there?" the same voice called out.

"To talk," Sundance answered. "We demand your surrender and will guarantee safe passage to Alberta. Louis Riel is here and wants to talk to you. He will walk out under a flag of truce. If anybody shoots at him, you will all be killed. No one will be spared. Do I have your word?"

"Who are you?"

"My name is Jim Sundance. And yours?"

"Inspector Kennedy, Royal North West Mounted Police. You have my word. Riel will not be shot. I am coming out now with one of my men. You will walk with Riel?"

Sundance said he would. He took the flag of truce from Riel and began to walk toward the gate. Dumont and the *métis* watched from cover, their fingers twitching on the triggers of their rifles.

Riel and Sundance walked without hurry, the crunching of their boots in the muddy snow being the only sound heard on the slope that went up to the gate. Then the gate opened and a tall Mountie officer with bushy red hair came out followed by a noncommissioned police-man. Both men had left their sidearms behind. The gate closed. They met about twenty-five yards from the gate.

Kennedy, the officer, looked from Riel to Sundance

with frosty blue eyes. He was about thirty and stood very straight. His fair skin was reddened by the cold. "Do you have any idea of what you're doing?" he rasped in a British military voice. It was a voice well accustomed to being obeyed instantly. He was speaking to Riel. "You are in armed rebellion against the Dominion of Canada. Do you know what that means? Do you realize what you're facing? I advise you to put down your arms immediately. Of course, you realize I can promise you nothing but a fair trial. Well, what do you have to say for yourselves?"

Sundance couldn't help grinning at the arrogant Britisher. "I can promise you something better than that," he said. "Unless you surrender and march out of here, we will blow the fort to bits, then burn it."

Fifteen

Major General Frederick Middleton's beefy face was almost as red as the tunic he wore. Usually, it was red from many years of drinking brandy and soda in the far corners of the British Empire. A veteran of the Indian Mutiny and the savage Maori Wars of New Zealand, General Middleton was an Englishman and never let anyone forget it for a minute, especially the Canadians he was now forced to command.

On this bright morning in April 1885, the General's face was red as with rage, not brandy. After a lifetime of service to the Empire, the bad-tempered old soldier had been sent from England to take command of all the Canadian militia, in all the provinces and territories. It was not a job that appealed to him, but it was either that or face compulsory retirement. The old warhorse had been put out to pasture in Canada in a post that was supposed to be a sinecure. By the time he had arrived in the Dominion, he had become paunchy, stodgy, opinionated, and openly contemptuous of the fighting abilities of the Canadian militia. Now he had a rebellion on his hands.

Waving the telegraph message he had just received

from Prime Minister John Macdonald, the General sputtered with anger while his aide, Captain Winfield, another Englishman, listened in sympathy. General Middleton trusted no one but the British officers or former British officers on his staff.

"Damn these colonials!" Middleton was raging. "Who the blazes is this fellow Riel? I never heard of him before this week. Who in hell is he, and what does he want?"

"Riel is leader of the *métis*, sir. That's what the halfbreeds are called. Riel wants to establish a separate country."

"Yes! Yes! I've been told all that. They tell me he's even tried it before. Why didn't they hang him the first time, when they had the chance? A length of strong hemp would have settled the whole blasted problem. Now I'm supposed to go up there and clean up this mess. And what have I got to do it with? A thousand ragtag militiamen who hardly know one end of a rifle from the other. Probably half of them are in sympathy with this mongrel Riel. Ah, Winfield, if only I had two-hundred British regulars, I'd march up the Saskatchewan, burn their towns and hand the ringleaders. I'd give them a trial all right, about thirty seconds of a trial, then..."

General Middleton twisted his thick neck to one side and made a strangling sound. "By God, I gave those buggers what for in India. I'd like to do the same here. Burn them out. That's all these savages understand. Burn them out and hang a few dozen for good measure."

Captain Winfield said without irony, "So far, sir, the *métis* have been doing most of the burning. Fort Carlton and Fort Battleford have already been burned to the ground. However, except for the battle at Duck Lake, there has been remarkably little bloodshed. Even the Indians seem to be under some kind of control."

General Middleton scowled as he hacked at his breakfast of bacon, liver sausage, and eggs. "If I had my regulars, I'd put them under control all right. I can't say I have much respect for the Americans, but they do seem to know how to deal with savages. Treat them kindly and they think you're stupid. The iron fist, hot lead, cold steel—that's what they respect. They look up to the man who can flog them back into place."

"Do you have a plan of battle, sir?" Winfield drank the tea the General had graciously poured for him.

Behind the General, there was a map of the North West Territories on the wall. He picked up a ruler from the table and tapped Fort Qu'Appelle. "That's where we are, and up there is Batoche. That is where we will strike, at the heart of this miserable rebellion. That is where their women and children are concentrated. Once we take Batoche, the back of this rebellion will be broken."

Wingate asked, "When you say strike, did you mean cavalry, sir?"

"I do not! This isn't country for cavalry. No, Winfield, we will do it the way the British army has always done in its wars. The old foot-slogging infantryman may not have the dash of the cavalry, but he gets the job done. Let these halfbreeds gallop about on their ponies as much as they like. While they are doing it, we will march into the heart of their country. Of course, we will use the militia cavalry, but only to guard our communications. Always watch your communications, Winfield, because if you don't, some fine day you'll find yourself cut off, isolated. A lifetime of campaigning has taught me that."

"What about the two other forces, sir? General Strange's and Colonel Otter's. General Strange is on his way to Edmonton with six-hundred men. Colonel Otter is moving north with another six hundred. Here in Fort Qu'Appelle we have eight-hundred men, including the Winnipeg and Ontario cavalry. Colonel Dennison thinks we should send a strong force of cavalry to drive the *métis* out of the towns they have taken. By the time they can regroup, our main force will command the whole Saskatchewan Valley."

At the mention of Dennison's name, the General's face grew even redder. "Dennison would like to make a name for himself, become the General Custer of the North West. Well, sir, we all know what happened to him. The Winnipeg and Ontario cavalry will guard our supply depots. There isn't much glory in that, but the Colonel will have to make the best of it."

"The Prime Minister requests an answer to his message, sir," Winfield said as diplomatically as he could. "His suggestion was that you move at once. What do you want me to say, sir?"

"Tell that gibbering Scottish idiot to go to the hottest part of hell. And while you're at it, ask him how many wars he fought in. Ask him if he ever did anything in his life besides sucking around for votes."

Winfield waited patiently.

General Middleton raged on. Finally, he said, "Tell Macdonald I'll move as soon as I'm ready. If that doesn't suit him, tell him to take it up with Her Majesty's government. No, don't say that. Just say I'll move when ready. But do tell them this. Request that the five-hundred British regulars now stationed in Nova Scotia be sent here immediately."

Winfield finished writing the message. "Mr. Macdonald may not like that, sir. He's already told the newspapers that he is determined to keep the Dominion intact at all costs. He speaks of an all-Canadian army. I think he sees himself as another Abraham Lincoln."

Middleton stabbed at an egg and let the yolk run out. "Macdonald's a bloody fool, but I still request transfer of the British regulars. I don't care how many Canadian militiamen are being sent from the east. I want those regulars if I can get them. Then you'll see those half-castes run. I don't think Macdonald will grant my request. What

I want is to get it down in writing."

General Middleton finished his tea and sat back in his chair. Winfield hurried to light his cigar. "Thanks, my boy," the General said, his anger fading away as he thought of the campaign ahead. "In a way, it's going to be good to get out from behind a desk and into the field. It isn't much of a war, but it's the only one we've got, I suppose. But what a country to fight it in! These half-caste blighters—what did you say they're called?"

"They call themselves the *métis*. I think it means, the people."

"The people, eh! Peculiar thing to call themselves. I wonder. Can they fight, do you think? Not just burn a few isolated posts, but really fight. The Maoris in New Zealand fought like tigers. And during the Mutiny, the sepoys were a pretty game lot. But these half-castes are quite new, quite strange to me. I suppose they're strange to everyone."

Winfield's voice was quiet. "From what I've been told, they fight very well. They believe they have nothing much to lose."

"Their lives, of course. Oh, I see what you mean. Well, that's going to make this campaign all the more interesting. Isn't it?"

"A campaign to be remembered, sir," Captain Winfield said.

After Inspector Kennedy had surrendered the fort and marched away with his people, Gabriel Dumont ordered the stockade burned. "But do not burn the town," he warned his men. "If the people who lived there want to return when the war is over, they are free to do so. Everything must be left as it is. We will have no use for the fort."

Riel was sitting on a waterproof blanket in the snow. He looked at the burning fort and sighed with satisfaction. "These have been fine victories, my friends. It seems as if God is with us. They run from us like sheep, even the Mounties. Do you remember, Gabriel, when the Mounties were first established? Ten or twelve years ago it was. One Mountie was worth a hundred men, white or red or halfbreed. Kill a Mountie, they said, and you would be hunted to the ends of the earth."

Sundance looked up from his food as Riel laughed harshly. There was no way to know how to take this man. One moment he was the commonsense and gentle leader of his downtrodden people; the next he was gloating over the number of men they had killed.

"We have killed many Mounties," Riel said, "and we are not hunted. Instead, we are the hunters. The Mounties died by the dozen at Duck Lake, and they slunk away from Fort Carlton and Fort Pitt like whipped dogs. And they talk of the power of that pudgy old woman they call the Great White Mother. The Great White Mother will take care of you, they told the Indians."

Riel laughed again. "The Great White Mother cannot even take care of them."

"They would have fought if the women and children hadn't been there," Dumont said. "Do not count on them always running."

"I did not know you admired the Redcoats so much, Gabriel."

"I admire all brave men, Louis. It is best to know the kind of men we face. When the women and children of the settlers and militia have been cleared from the Saskatchewan Valley, there will be fighting. It won't be like the fighting that has been going on. I think, when we have taken Fort Pitt, we should offer to make peace on our terms."

Staring into the fire, Riel said, "Is that what you think, Gabriel? You think they will want to make peace? But there is another question, one even more important, and that is: Do we want to make peace so soon? Is it not possible that *we* do not have to come to terms? What if our terms are simply get your forces out of Saskatchewan and do not return?"

Sundance knew it wasn't his place to interfere in this discussion. He knew, too, that arguing with Riel when he was in a certain mood was a waste of time.

"You are so silent, Gabriel," Riel said. "Why is that?"

"Because I am thinking what it would be like to have peace again along the Saskatchewan. Very soon there will be spring flowers on the prairie and along the banks of the river. The sun will be warm and the days long and the wind from the north not so cold. I would like to see peace before the end of spring."

Riel said, "It may not come by next spring. Who can say when it will come? Perhaps it will never come for the *métis*. We must accept the inevitable."

"Nothing is inevitable, Louis."

"For some men it is, my friend. It may be that way for me. Often, late at night when I can't sleep, I think it is. Some things can't be changed."

"Nothing is inevitable," Dumont said.

"Perhaps not for you. You are a good man, but there are some things you don't understand."

"I understand that I am going to blow the railroad bridges on the Canadian Pacific. More than five-thousand men are on their way from the east by rail. I don't know where they are now, but I would think more than half way. That is why some of us have to ride south and do what we can to tear up the tracks. But the bridges and tunnels are more important than the tracks."

"But you are needed here, Gabriel. I am no general."

Dumont said, "I will send Boudreau and Roberge. They will take twenty men. I know the tunnels and bridges will be heavily guarded, but we have to hope. If we can stop the main force long enough, we can deal with the others. They are not so many, and the old Englishman

306

who leads them, Middleton, is slow and cautious."

While they were talking, a rider came into camp at full gallop. "It's one of the relay men," Dumont said. They all stood up. Sundance had already guessed what it was.

"They're on the move," the relay rider said. "Middleton and a thousand men left Fort Qu'Appelle the day before yesterday. They have a big supply train guarded by cavalry, with Gatling guns and cannon."

Dumont looked puzzled. "The cavalry is guarding the rear? I do not understand. Are you sure of what you're saying? Have any cavalry units been sent forward of the column?"

"No. Our scouts have been watching them ever since they left the fort."

"What about scouts?"

"There are some scouts." The relay rider smiled. "But they do not scout so well. Or maybe they are acting under stupid orders. The whole column is moving very slowly."

"Good! The slower they move, the more time we have to get ready for them. Any news from the east and west? They will come at us from three sides. Anything from the north?"

"Not yet, Gabriel."

"All right, get something to eat, then ride back. Tell Campeau to send extra men to watch east and west. General Strange commands in Alberta, and he will come from there. But the man we have to worry about is General Otter from the east."

"Why Otter?" Sundance asked after the relay rider left.

"A Canadian," Dumont answered. "His is a rich lawyer who has written books on war. Twenty years ago, as a very young man, he served with your General Sheridan's cavalry. Ever since then he has been arguing, in Parliament and out, that cavalry is the driving force of a modern army. Of course, he is right, though the old men in Ottawa don't agree with him. I would say that, right now, General Otter is delighted to have this opportunity to prove how right his arguments are. That is why I think we have more to fear from him than from Middleton's main force. True, Otter is a militia officer and not a regular. It makes no difference. As a soldier, he is worth more than ten stupid Englishmen."

Sundance said, "If he rode with Sheridan, then he believes in the fire and the sword. Does he?"

"I have been thinking about that," Dumont answered. "If he starts to kill our people and burn our farms, we will answer him in kind. I pray he does not. But if he does, then we will show them what the word 'savage' means."

Dumont smiled bitterly. "They call us savages. I hope they don't make us prove it. We have spared many lives since this fight began. If they start killing, we will spare no more. One thing you can be sure of with Otter, and that is he won't worry much about supply lines. He'll carry all the supplies he can and forage for the rest. He once wrote that every cavalry unit ought to take along extra horses, not to be ridden but to be eaten when the food ran out."

"Sounds like a smart soldier," was Sundance's only comment.

Later, after Riel had wrapped himself in a buffalo robe and was sleeping close to the fire, Sundance and Dumont talked.

"He is marching on Batoche. Of that I am sure," Dumont said. "That is what I would do. I cannot let him take it. We could retreat to the north and draw his force in after us, then strike him in a number of suprise attacks." Dumont shook his head. "That would be the military way to do it, but I can't. Batoche must not fall."

"Then maybe now is the time to try to come to terms. It looks like this general, Middleton, isn't that eager to fight."

"I don't think he will come to terms, not yet. We must show him what it's going to mean to Canada if the fighting

308

goes on. Anyway, Middleton has no authority to make a bargain with us. That will be up to Macdonald. It would be easier if some other man ruled in Ottawa."

"Why? Does Macdonald hate the *métis*?"

Dumont lowered his voice. "Not the *métis*. Louis Riel. He could have hanged Louis after the first rebellion, but he let him go to Montana instead. Maybe some of it was mercy. Most of it, I think, was politics. To have hanged Louis would have turned the French-Canadians against Macdonald's government. But no matter, Macdonald let Louis go free and suffered much abuse because of it. Ontario turned against him, wanted to kick him out. There was an unspoken agreement between Macdonald and Louis: his life in exchange for permanent exile in the United States. From where Macdonald sits, Louis broke his word. I suppose he did."

Sundance said, "Then it won't be easy no matter what happens."

"That's right. Macdonald can't back down again, even if he wants to. It would make him look like a fool, and no man wants to look like a fool. But Louis is our leader. He has kept our cause alive all these years, and we must follow him wherever it takes us. Now I think we'd better get some sleep. Dawn comes quickly, and there is much to be done. Soon we will discover what it is like to fight a real English general."

"You don't like the English, do you?"

"Not much."

"My father was an Englishman."

"I think he was a different kind of Englishman."

They both laughed.

Sixteen

Every step of Middleton's advance was being watched by *métis* scouts. There was even a *métis* spy working as a freighthandler in Middleton's wagon train. The column moved as ponderously as the mind of its commander. To the rear, the cavalry officers cursed the inactivity, the slow pace, the futility of not being able to take action. It began to snow again, though it wasn't as cold as it had been. Under a slate-colored sky, the combined force plodded on.

General Middleton, it seemed, was in no hurry to engage the enemy. His tent was elaborate and had a wooden floor made in sections, a folding bed piled with blankets, and buffalo robes. He had even brought along books and a chess set. At night, a small brazier of charcoal heated his quilted tent. He ate well, drank well, and slept well. There were many meetings with the staff of English officers. When it became necessary to have some of the Canadian militia officers present, he invariably disregarded their suggestions with a grunt or a growl.

The General liked to look at maps. The more maps the better. He used his ruler to measure distances, not knowing that, often, the shortest distance between two points was right through the middle of a swamp. Captain Winfield, the ambitious young career officer, was still his favorite audience. Middleton's meals were as elaborate as the rest of his equipment. Winfield was always glad to dine with the General because the food was so good: steak, glazed ham, fresh bread, baked potatoes. And always brandy and fine cigars.

General Middleton would say, "War is a science if nothing else. Strategy is what counts. Consider the situation carefully, then act on it. But always be sure of what you're doing. I have been a soldier more years than you are old, my boy, and I always know exactly how to proceed. Only fools rush in. Always remember that. I don't want to sound boastful, but I didn't get to be a major general in the best army in the world for nothing."

The General paused and Winfield came in quickly with, "You've had a most distinguished career, sir. Would you like to continue dictating your memoirs tonight?"

While the *métis* scouts watched silent and unseen, General Middleton, mellow with good food and aged brandy, would lie on his comfortable bed, with the charcoal brazier throwing off steady heat, and talk on and on about the campaigns of thirty years before.

"During the Indian mutiny, a regrettable episode in our history, we were forced to take stern measures against the ringleaders. One particularly severe form of execution was to tie a man across the mouth of a cannon."

Middleton's scouts reported back that there was no sign of the enemy. But the moment the scouts had ridden past, the *métis* would emerge from their hiding places. The snow stopped and the weather was bright and clear for a while. The column, slow as it was, was getting closer to Batoche. Soon it was only twenty-two miles away.

"If he doesn't drink too much, then it must be old age," Gabriel Dumont remarked to Sundance. Our man in the column reports that he sits up half the night in his tent, reading and playing chess. His breakfast takes an hour. There have been times when my scouts were close enough to shoot him through the head. When I heard that one of them almost did, I sent word that not a hair on his thick head must be touched."

Dumont began to laugh and Sundance had to grin. "Middleton is our friend. I love him like a brother," Dumont said. "Oh, please God, let him continue the way he is going. I know! I know! Sometimes wars are won by fools. It is time to stop him *now*!"

Middleton's right column of about five-hundred men was in camp about twenty miles south of Batoche. His left column, with the same number of men, was on the other side of the river.

Seventeen miles south of Batoche, on the east side of the South Satkatchewan River, Fish Creek emptied into the broad river and cut a forty-foot-deep ravine across the prairie. It was on all the maps, but General Middleton didn't seem to have given it any thought.

"This is where we will surprise them," Gabriel Dumont decided. There, part way down the slope nearest the Canadian advance, he posted one-hundred and fifty of his men. He led another fifty mounted *métis* further south to hide them in a coulee so that they could swoop down on the Canadian rear and herd them into the trap.

"It should work," Sundance agreed.

Early on April 24th, Middleton broke camp and moved forward, his scouts out in front. Then, for the first time, the scouts earned their keep. Riding back fast, they reported finding horse tracks on the road. The alarm was sounded, and Dumont's fifty horseman had to make a hasty retreat to the deep ravine. For once, Dumont's cunning had failed—and the fight was on.

In the ravine, the *métis* had dug rifle pits. If Middleton were a more intelligent commander, he would not have sent his force directly against the ravine. But that was what he did. On and on the Canadians came. When they reached the edge of the ravine, the *métis* opened fire, driving them back with heavy losses.

Middleton ordered his two cannons to open fire, but no damage was done to the concealed *métis*. Desperate now, he sent a message to his column on the other side of the river for them to cross as soon as possible. But the river was deep at that point. The water was filled with melting ice and cold enough to kill a man in five minutes. All the second column could use to cross was one leaky scow; on top of that, it began to rain.

Around noon, Middleton's forces failed in another attack, which even the support of the two Gatling guns didn't help. The cold April rain beat down harder than ever. For a while, the fight settled down to an exchange of rifle fire, broken here and there by futile charges by the Canadians. The militia fought well, but they were facing an enemy they couldn't see. They died in waves in the freezing mud. One of the Gatling guns went out of action and couldn't be fixed.

During the afternoon, the rain stopped and a watery sun appeared, giving no warmth. By now, some of the other column had managed to cross the river, but their crossing was slow and dangerous. Hardest of all was getting the horses across; and all the while, it was getting dark, with rain coming down again in great gray sheets.

By the time most of the second column had crossed the river, there was still enough light for a determined attack. Some of the Canadian officers argued, but Middleton refused to listen. He also refused to admit that he had been beaten. They were going to make a tactical retreat, he said. He became even more adamant when he saw a large column of mounted *métis* coming from Batoche to join the men in the ravine.

"We are going to pull back to Fish Creek," Middleton told his aide. "That is the order to be relayed to my Canadian subordinates. There will be no further discussion of the matter. We have a lot of wounded men, and they cannot be treated here, thanks to the wretched medical services provided by the Canadians. We had the men to take that ravine, but they didn't know how to do it. I doubt that the reinforcements coming from the east will do any better."

The British general laughed bitterly. "Ah, Winfield, if I only had some regulars—or a few *métis*. Say what you like about the half-castes, they know how to fight." His bitterness turned to sarcasm. "And do any of our Canadian friends know what has happened to the *Northcote*? We could turn that paddlewheeler into a gunboat—that is, if it ever arrives."

To convert the riverboat into a gunboat had been one of Middleton's first ideas when the campaign began. Built in 1874, the shallow-draught paddlewheeler had plied the South Saskatchewan in times of peace. It had two decks, with an exposed engine and boiler on the lower one, and a cabin and pilothouse above. On it, Middleton had placed thirty-five militiamen, a cannon, and a Gatling gun. The lower deck was fortified with a double wall of two-inch planks; the upper was protected by piled-up sacks of sand and grain.

Middleton's plan was to attack Batoche by land and by water. It was still a workable plan. But where was the *Northcote*? "I ask you, where is it?" Middleton grumbled. "What in blazes is causing the delay?"

Winfield did his best to explain. "The river is full of floating trees and sand bars. Even at full steam, the *Northcote* is slow. It's coming, sir."

"When? Next spring? Winfield, I want you to draft an order above my signature, using the strongest possible terms. I order the captain of the *Northcote* to proceed here with all dispatch. Never mind the snags and sand bars. I don't give a damn if he blows up the boilers. I want that infernal craft *here*! Send a rider downriver at once.

Now we will pull back to Fish Creek and wait."

"Looks like they're pulling out," Sundance reported to Dumont, handing him the telescope. Both men were concealed by heavy brush at the edge of the deep ravine. All along the ravine, the *métis* were spread out, waiting for the order to counterattack. Those closest to Dumont kept their eyes on their commander. It was raining again, a cold April rain. All day there had been nothing to eat but stringy jerked beef, with canteens of cold tea to wash it down. The *métis* fighters were cold and hungry. But the killing mood was still on them. A word from Dumont would send them swarming out after the retreating Canadians.

"If you go after them now," Sundance said, "You'll be fighting on the same ground they are."

"I know," Dumont agreed. "We could lose what we have gained. We will fall back and make ready to defend Batoche. They will not take Batoche, not even with that stupid steamboat they are bringing up the river. We will stop them at Batoche. It is then that I will ask Louis to offer his terms. It began at Duck Lake, but Batoche will be the place of decision. Our friend Hardesty will at last see some fighting."

After a forward party had been left behind in the ravine, the orderly retreat to Batoche began. The dead and wounded were brought home on sleighs. Compared to the Canadian losses, the *métis* losses were light; even so, many brave men had died defending the raw slash of earth that ran down to the river and continued on the other side. It was a somber procession that made its way back to Batoche.

Sundance and Dumont were among the last to leave the ravine. Looking back at it, Dumont remarked quietly, "This is called Fish Creek, but it is just a ravine. Yet so many men on both sides died here."

315

Some of the *métis* began to sing. "Listen to them," Dumont said wearily. "Most of them have lived along this river all their lives. They have stopped the great British general, and so they are happy and proud. They have reason to be. None has ever served in an army, none know of tactics. Farmers, trappers, fishermen, hunters—never soldiers—they have done what people said could not be done. Middleton's stupidity or caution helped, of course, but that is only part of it. They would have fought as well against a better general. But Middleton will come and continue to come, to advance like a great dead weight, a glacier. I hope my people will be able to go on singing. I do not sing myself, but I like to hear others."

That night, after Sundance and Dumont ate fried deer meat and oaten bread in the cabin, they went to the new meeting house to listen to Riel and the others. Hardesty and his Fenian subordinates were there, trim and warlike in contrast to the bearded, careless dressed *métis* commanders. The inside of the meeting house smelled strongly of raw pine and turpentine and tobacco smoke. Hardesty was holding forth when they came in. Hardesty nodded stiffly at Dumont and went on speaking, directing his arguments at Riel, who sat by the red-hot stove with a mug of steaming tea in front of him.

Hardesty was saying, "Louis, my friend, when I came here I thought it was to fight an all-out war. Instead, my men and I have forced to stand aside and listen to news of a lot of skirmishes, half-won battles. You beat them at Duck Lake, but instead of finishing them off, you chose to let them go. In the name of God, why? Where was the sense? Do you think they would have been as merciful? I think not. They would have hunted you down in the snow and killed every last man. You had them at Fort Carlton and Battleford. Once again, they were allowed to march away. Today, especially today, my men were held back again. For what reason? To defend Batoche was the reason given."

Hardesty paused to make his point. "I am ready to call it quits. I have had enough. With your permission, we will leave here as soon as we are ready. I have no more to say."

Riel answered him without standing up. "Don't be so hasty, my friend. Middleton and his forces are facing Batoche. Now is your time to fight."

"But why is Middleton facing Batoche, Louis? You said yourself he was defeated today. Why was your victory not followed up? Why are Middleton's forces still intact? Why aren't they scattered and broken, his men dead? If my men had been allowed to fight, there would not be a Canadian left alive. Instead, you are now forced to defend your most important town."

Riel looked at Dumont. "Do you want to answer him, Gabriel?"

Dumont nodded. "I know that some of my own people are turning against me because of the way I have been fighting this war."

From a number of *métis* commanders there was an angry murmur, and some of the faces that looked at Dumont were set in anger.

"Maybe they are right," Dumont continued. "For right or wrong, I was chosen as your general. From the beginning I never believed that we could win an all-out war against the Canadians. I still don't think it is possible."

A *métis* commander, named Thibault, a tall man with an eyepatch and a scarred face, shouted, "Then make way for a man with more courage. I have followed you faithfully, and so have my men, because we thought you knew how to command. But always, when victory was ours, you hung back at the last moment. What the Irishman says is true."

"Let him finish," Riel ordered without raising his voice.

Dumont said, "True. Everything Hardesty says is true. We could have slaughtered the Canadians at Duck Lake

317

and Fort Carlton. We could have killed every last man, cut the throats of the wounded. At Battleford we could have let the Indians scalp and torture and massacre the entire garrison—women and children, too."

"Mercy has no place in war," Hardesty said deliberately.

"Mercy didn't have much to do with it," Dumont went on. "If I thought a slaughter would guarantee freedom for our people, then I would soak this land in blood. I would spare no one, God forgive me, not the smallest Canadian child. I could go to my grave with that on my conscience if I had to. I didn't do it because I didn't think it would work. It has always been my plan to leave some opening, some middle ground where a bargain can be made."

Thibault's voice was heavy with sarcasm. "This is a fine time you have picked, with the British general only a day's march away. Is it part of your plan to let him take Batoche?"

Dumont said quietly, "My plan is to fight him at Batoche as we have never fought him before. Batoche has always been his objective. Batoche and nowhere else. If he fails to take Batoche, then he will know that his campaign has failed. That is why, if I am to remain your leader, we will stop him here. Stop him completely, fight him to a standstill. And when that is done, when he can fight no more, we will offer our terms to the Canadian government."

Hardesty stood up looking startled. He spoke to Riel. "I protest against this. Nothing was said to me about coming to terms. All along you talked of nothing short of complete independence. That was our understanding, and you gave your word on it. Do you think I have brought my men, some of them thousands of miles, to fight for half a cause? If all you wanted to do was discuss limited freedom, why didn't you get some of your French-Canadian friends to do it in Parliament?"

Riel refused to be baited. "You sound as if you would prefer war to any kind of peace."

"To the kind of peace Dumont seems to be talking about—peace without honor."

For a moment it seemed as if the debate would end in a killing. Gabriel Dumont's hand dropped to the hunting knife at his belt; his bearded face was twisted in sudden anger. "Are you saying I am without honor?"

Hardesty's thumb was ready to flip up the leather cover of his army holster. The other Irishmen were waiting to see how it went. "Your words speak for themself," Hardesty said, knowing that he had support from some of the *métis* leaders.

Riel got between the two men and ordered them to stop. "It would please Middleton and the Canadians if they could see you now. We are all men of honor. You, Hardesty, are so blinded by your hatred for the British that you can't see anything else. Maybe it will turn out that you have been right all along."

Hardesty said, "I know I'm right. They may accept your peace offer, but can you trust them? Once you lay down your arms, you will have nothing left to fight with, while they will still have their armies and their machine-guns. A peace made with a halfbreed rabble! Do you think they will honor such a peace? Yes, Louis, a halfbreed rabble! That's how they think of your people. I know, because that's how they think of *my* people—and they are the same color and live in the same islands. If my people are dirt to them, dirty, drunken, illiterate peasants, then what are yours?"

"I don't know," Riel said calmly. "Worse, I suppose. What would you do?"

Hardesty was no longer excited. His eyes narrowed and he spoke quietly, though his voice carried to every corner of the big room. "What would I do?" he repeated. "If I had been your commander from the beginning, I would have waged total war against the Canadians. There would have been no indecision. None! I would have made them feel the armed might of the *métis*. There would have been no talk of peace, not even a hint. Peace would come only when they had left our borders, when every one of their soldiers and surveyors and land speculators had gone. Armed might is all they understand. Make no mistake about it. How do you think the British—and the men who control Canada are British—built their Empire? By force. And by force it shall be torn down—not by peace offers or debates in Parliament."

Riel shook his head in wonder. "You would destroy the British Empire?"

"That will come, Louis, in a dozen small countries such as yours. Not now, but some day."

"But what about now, Hardesty?"

"It is still not too late to show them what you—we—are made of. Don't just fight Middleton to a standstill. Destroy him! Rouse up every *métis*, every Indian, who is not with you now. Let the English halfbreeds in Saskatchewan know that they must join our cause or be driven out. I would be ruthless toward our enemies and those who are waiting to see which side wins. After I destroy Middleton, I would turn the combined tribes against Prince Albert, the biggest Canadian stronghold in Saskatchewan, and burn it to the ground. With Prince Albert obliterated, its garrison wiped out, we would then control all of Saskatchewan except the towns in the south."

Dumont yelled, "The Canadians would still come!"

Hardesty nodded and continued to speak quietly. "They would. But I would make sure that, south of Batoche, they came into a country where nothing lived, where not a house or village stood. I would clear the land of livestock, burn every homestead, dynamite every bridge. South of Batoche, they would not find one scrawny chicken to make a pot of soup. Summer here lasts only weeks and winter comes quickly. By the time the first snow came, they would have had enough."

Some of the *métis* leaders murmured approval; others stared at the floor. Riel held up his hand. He spoke to Hardesty. "What you propose turns my blood cold, my friend. And yet...and yet. It may come to that if they refuse to meet our terms, or to offer terms of their own that we can accept."

Hardesty turned away but didn't leave. "Then all I've said hasn't meant anything. You're still ready to trust them after all I've said?"

"I'm ready to talk," Riel said. "I am ready to give Gabriel's plan a chance to work. And now, Gabriel, I am going to ask you a question, so there will be no misunderstanding later. What if they refuse to bargain?"

Gabriel Dumont's eyes were sad. "Then we will fight the Irishman's way." He looked directly at Riel. "Am I to continue as leader of the *métis*? If not, Thibault is a good fighter. And there is always the Irishman."

Dumont was so tall that Riel had to reach up to slap him on the shoulder. "You are still our general, Gabriel. So far you have led us well."

"I don't mind if you change your mind after I have left here. If there is any change, you will find me with my men."

Riel protested a little too strongly, Sundance thought, not at all sure that Riel wanted peace, no matter how much of it he talked. He was even less sure that Riel was determined enough to stand up to firebrands like Thibault.

There was silence as Dumont and Sundance left the room. The door had hardly closed behind them when voices were raised in loud argument.

The two men walked away, their shoulders hunched against the wind. "Listen to them" Dumont said without bitterness. "A few small victories and everyone wants to become the new general."

"What do you think?" Sundance asked.

"About what?"

"About Louis Riel? Will he turn against you?"

"Louis is my friend. I do not want to talk about it."

"All right, we won't talk about it," Sundance said. "I shouldn't have asked you."

Dumont said gruffly, "That's right. You shouldn't have asked me."

They walked in silence toward the barracks. The wind was very cold. Dumont stopped suddenly and looked at Sundance. "I don't know what to think about Louis," he said. "He is a good man, but . . . Hardesty knows where his weakness lies."

"It's still not too late to do something about Hardesty," Sundance said.

Seventeen

In the morning, the strengthening of Batoche's defenses began once it was light enough to see. Men wolfed down big breakfasts of fried meat and potatoes and mugs of scalding hot tea. For a while, it was quiet along the fog-shrouded river. Acrid wood smoke from cook fires mixing with the fog, as ice crackled in the river. Relieved after the long night's watch, stiff-legged sentries hurried to get a few hour's sleep before the work began again.

Dumont had worked during the night with a pencil on a rough map of the town and its approaches. Now it was morning, and he rubbed his eyes wearily while he speared chunks of hot ham swimming in raisin gravy and drank his third mug tot of tea. "We will dig more rifle pits and trenches," he said, "but not one behind the other the way it is usually done. The first line of trenches will be very shallow. If the Canadians capture them, there will not be much cover."

Dumont smiled grimly. "But before they capture anything they will have to get through the barbed wire—their own barbed wire. They left a lot of it behind when they surrendered Battleford. It was to be used to

323

fence off the land the surveyors decided did not rightfully belong to the *métis*. Have you ever seen it used in a war, Sundance?"

"Only in range wars. Usually, it was the wire that started them. No, I've never seen it used in a war. It hadn't come in yet while we were fighting the Confederates. It's one thing the Canadians won't be expecting. How do you figure to string it?"

"Not string it, Sundance. I though about that during the night. There is enough to roll it, using X-shaped supports. It will be rolled loosely but thickly. When it's rolled, it can't be cut, can't even be moved. The deeper a man gets into it, the more tangled and helpless he becomes. A brutal way to fight? It is. And there will be more surprises for the Canadians, especially for those on the steamboat."

Late the night before, they had discussed how the gunboat could be put out of action. It looked as if the plan would work. Dumont said it had to work, or the *Northcote*, sailing into the heart of Batoche, would play hell with its well-protected cannon.

Sundance was now thinking about the barbed wire. "They'll hang you for that, Gabriel," he said. "If they capture you, they will."

"Because it's against the rules of war? Do these rules really exist?"

"They claim they do. Both sides break them, but they're written down somewhere. They dust them off when it suits their purpose."

"There's a rope waiting for my anyway. It's been waiting since the first shot was fired at Duck Lake. I am not the brave man my people think I am. I think about that rope."

The work went on all through the day. Ax blades bit into tree trunks, and far into the night the circular saw in the steamdriven sawmill whined and snarled. Wagonloads of barbed wire were driven out past the first line of trenches and dumped in the mud; past there, the trees were cleared for three hundred yards. Whips cracked, and men cursed as the felled trees were dragged by teams of horses and piled one on top of the other in an impenetrable wall of defense that stretched from the high ground down to the edge of the river. On a knobby hill that dominated the road, more trenches and rifle pits were dug. One of the two Gatling guns was hauled up there by ten sweating *métis*.

"Don't drop that gun, you donkeys," Dumont roared, matching anxiously as the heavy rapid-fire gun was dragged up the steep slope. Five of Hardesty's Irishmen went up after it, carrying boxes of ammunition. During the day, another hundred Irishmen, looking hunted and tired, had arrived from the west, after having managed to evade the military patrols in Alberta. They had sailed from San Francisco to Seattle, then crossed the border into Canada from Washington state. They had hoped to follow the Canadian Pacific tracks into Saskatchewan but were forced to abandon the idea because military traffic was so heavy on the line. Instead, they had struck north into Alberta and headed due east toward Batoche. All Alberta, they reported, was up in arms.

"How do you like that?" Hardesty sneered at Dumont while the leaders were gathered around a fire for a late afternoon meal. "Does that sound as if they're getting ready to make peace."

Instead of answering, Dumont took his plate of food and walked away from the fire to sit on a tree stump some distance away. Sundance joined him, deciding he would never get used to drinking tea, no matter how strong it was brewed.

"What are you looking so gloomy for?" he asked Dumont. "The work here is going well. Even if they attack now, you are prepared. I can't say I ever saw a town as well defended as this."

Dumont chewed his meat without enjoyment. "I am

325

not worried about the town," he said. "I think Middleton can be stopped. I think they will fight harder this time. But that isn't what is on my mind."

"Then what?"

"I don't know. I have a bad feeling. I don't like the way Hardesty keeps talking to Louis. Every time I look, he is telling him something else. You are my friend, so I can speak plainly to you. This war seems to be affecting Louis more than I thought it would. I talk to him of one thing and he talks of another. One of the things he keeps coming back to is this church of his, this new Universal Church of North America. We are preparing for battle and he talks of a church. I talk to him of drafting a list of peace terms, but his concern is who shall be the pope of his church. He asked me if I thought Bishop LaFarge of Montreal might not be a good choice. Sundance, I don't even know who Bishop LaFarge is."

Sundance didn't know what to say.

"I am far from sure that the Canadians will even talk terms," Dumont continued. "It may well come down to the kind of war the Irishman wants so much. But Louis's mind seems to have gone beyond even that. You know what he asked me today? I was working with the men on the barbed wire and Louis walked all the way out there and called me aside. His face was pale and strained, and I though it was something important. Do you know what he wanted to talk about? He wanted to know what he should call himself when Saskatchewan becomes independent."

"What did you say?"

"If it hadn't been Louis, I would have thought he was joking. I was so surprised at first I didn't know what to say. 'I suppose president,' I said. We hope to be a free people with no allegiance to kings or queens, so I said president for want of a better word. Louis admires the French; they have a president. I thought that would

326

satisfy him. But he shook his head and said that wouldn't do. All this time the men are waiting for me to get back to the wire. Louis then said perhaps 'protector' was a better title. He had other names written on a piece of paper; he didn't tell me what they were. He just walked away, still looking at the names on the paper. Later, I saw him talking to Hardesty; they were both looking at the list of names he had picked out for himself. Hardesty looked most interested, and they talked for a long time. It is possible that Hardesty added some grand-sounding titles to the list."

Sundance agreed that the Irishman was crafty enough to do just that—anything to get closer to the erratic man who held the fate of the *métis* in his hands. "But what does it matter what he calls himself?" he asked, knowing full well what Dumont was driving at but not wanting to put it into words. He knew the doubts that were going through the other man's mind. On the other hand, Dumont and Riel had been together for a very long time.

"If Louis's ideas become too grand, he won't be able to settle for a limited freedom," Dumont said. "Freedom within Canada won't be enough for him. My greatest hope is that the Canadians will agree to let him rule as governor of the *métis* province of Saskatchewan, our independence and land claims to be guaranteed by Ottawa as the rights of the other provinces are guaranteed."

"It sounds reasonable," Sundance said. "I can see the Canadians agreeing to that, even Macdonald, for all that he hates Louis Riel."

"Yes," Dumont said, "but will Louis agree even if Macdonald agrees?" He scraped out his plate without having finished all the food on it.

"You're not telling me everything, Gabriel."

Dumont looked at Sundance, then far out over the river, a grim gray in the gathering dusk. His dark eyes were as bleak as the icy river and the bare hills beyond.

"I think Louis is going to try to make it hard for the Canadians to talk peace."

"He's the leader; he doesn't have to talk at all."

"One side of him knows he has to talk, wants to talk. He would be going against everything he has ever said if he refuses to make the offer. Always, he has said that the Canadians forced this war on the *métis*. He is the peacemaker; *they* the warlike ones. Besides, our people do not want this war to continue. What do they care of governments or titles? As long as they can live freely in the old ways, they do not care who rules. They are simple people, but they are not stupid. No matter what Louis says, and they love him no less for his wild dreams, they know there will always be somebody in a frock coat who claims to rule them. The priest rules the village, and so on up the ladder to Ottawa. All my people ask is that their ruler's hand be light.

"But I think Louis wars against himself. Now, instead of drafting reasonable proposals, he is drawing up a list of personal grievances. That's right, Sundance, *personal* grievances. He has not talked to me of this, but I have been told that is what he is doing. He says the wrongs done him, including the years in exile, must be paid for with money. The sum in huge. The Canadians will certainly not accept that. That is why I think he does not want to talk."

"Then the war can only get worse."

"I know, and that is what worries me. It sickens me. It means that all this," Dumont waved his hand, "will come to nothing but more bloodshed. We have food now, but how long will it last? Hardesty talks of total war. Even if that fails, he can sneak back across the border and work his mischief somewhere else. Fools and rogues will always thrust more money upon him. Oh yes, Hardesty and his kind always manage to survive. But what of the *métis*?

Where can they run to?"

Suddenly, Dumont's face grew dark with fury. "I'll be damned to hell before I let my people die for nothing. I don't care if I have to . . ." He left the sentence unfinished and walked away.

Soon it was dark. Sundance went to Dumont's cabin; after lying on his bunk for an hour, he got up and cooked a solitary meal of steak and potatoes. There was some stale coffee, and he cooked that in one of the tea cannisters until it was as black as he could get it. The steak was thick and juicy; he didn't have to do much except singe it on both sides. It was warm in the cabin, and it was good to be in there with the wind buffeting the doors and windows. He ate slowly. It was an hour before he finished the last of the coffee, and still Dumont hadn't showed up. Sundance washed up and went back to his bunk.

Lying there with his hands clasped behind his head, he thought of all that had happened since he had left Chicago. So far he had accomplished nothing except to earn the friendship and trust of Gabriel Dumont. He realized there was nothing he could have done to prevent this war. Killing Louis Riel had never been an answer, even if he could have brought himself to kill the *métis* leader. There was something about the man that compelled respect, even when you knew he was more than a little crazy. All men that others followed blindly were like that. It had been a small war thus far, hardly a real war at all; there was still a chance it could be settled peacefully if Riel could be made to see reason. But as Dumont had pointed out, that wasn't going to be easy to do. When the time came, Sundance knew, there would be a split between those who wanted peace and those whose blood was hot for war.

Hardesty, of course, would be on the other side, and the Irishmen would follow where he led. Thibault would side with Hardesty. How many others? The ordinary *métis* soliders, the ones who dug the ditches and did the fighting and the dying, all looked up to Gabriel Dumont. Even so, there was Riel to be reckoned with. Even from an exile in Montana, he had maintained powerful grip on his people. The fact that he had been able to defy their priests, the center of their lives, and still maintain his popularity was proof of this. If it came to a showdown between Riel and Dumont, which man would the *métis* follow? It was hard to say. Riel appealed to their wild imaginations, but Dumont spoke in practical terms.

Sundance liked and admired Gabriel Dumont almost as much as he did General Crook. The two men were so different on the surface, but they had the same rough honesty, the same contempt for fancy phrases. Dumont and Crook were natural leaders, born fighters with no love of fighting. True, Dumont was a rebel, but so was Robert E. Lee, and there were few men with more honors than the old Confederate.

In the days to come, Sundance decided, Dumont was going to need all the help he could get. Hardesty was the man who was going to force the split in the *métis* ranks. As yet, there was no talk of the American expansionists coming into the war. They wouldn't try to grab Canada until the war got out of control. No doubt Hardesty was counting on that. There would be big rewards for the man who delivered such a rich prize into their hands.

The door banged open and Dumont came in, angry and tired. Sundance had a big steak waiting on the skillet; he put it on a bed of raked coal without saying a word. Dumont had a quart bottle of whiskey in his hand. He found two mugs and set the bottle down on the table. He filled both mugs and pushed one across the table to Sundance.

"Your steak'll be ready in a minute," Sundance said, tasting his whiskey.

"The hell with the steak," Dumont growled. He didn't

take the mug away from his mouth until it was empty. More whiskey splashed into the mug. It was gone in two swallows. "The hell with everything, my friend."

It wasn't the time to be talking temperance, Sundance knew, but he wondered where this drinking was going to lead. By his own word, Dumont was wild and dangerous when drunk.

"What happened?" Sundance asked.

Already Dumont had a wild look in his eyes. "Nothing much," he said, going at the whiskey again. "They were all there: Louis, Hardesty, Thibault, the others. I had to force Louis to agree to offer peace to the Canadians. You would have thought I wasn't there, the way they exchanged looks. When Louis saw how angry I was, he said, 'All right, my dear friend, Gabriel, my old comrade, we will try to make peace with them. We will do our best.' But he didn't hold out much hope. That's what Louis said."

Sundance didn't think it would do much good, but he dished up the steak and put it on the table. Dumont didn't even look at it. "I am tired," he said. "I have done my best for the *métis*, and for thanks I get strange looks." More whiskey slopped into the mug. "You know what I think I will do, my friend? I think I will take my rifle and my traps and ride far into the north. In my time, I have been in places few men have ever seen. I think I will go far into the Yukon, maybe to the mountains of Alaska. I can live out my life there."

"You can't do it, Gabriel. Everything will go to hell if you desert the *métis*."

Dumont yanked the hunting knife from his belt and stuck it in the table. "Desert! You call me a deserter? You are asking for your death, my friend." He finished another mug of raw whiskey. By now, the bottle was nearly empty. Dumont's eyes, red-rimmed from lack of sleep, glared across the table at Sundance, as if he didn't quite know who he was. "Who are you to talk to me like that? I don't know you. Who are you?"

Dumont didn't want an answer. He finished the bottle and smashed it against the wall. His hand was close to the knife. "I don't like your face, you goddamned foreigner! You sit here drinking my whiskey, eating my food, and I see nothing but lies in your face."

Sundance's eyes were on the knife. "It's me, Sundance," he said, not wanting to fight the big man he liked so much. "I eat your food because I like your cooking. You fix the best ham and duck eggs in the North West."

"Duck eggs?" Dumont was puzzled, his eyelids getting heavy. "Duck eggs? You are talking like a fool. Or do you think I am a fool?"

"Never a fool, Gabriel."

"You're Sundance?"

"That's who I am."

"You saved my life."

"It was worth saving. Why don't you eat the steak? It's a good steak."

It was the wrong thing to say, and it made Dumont angry again. He picked up the steak and threw it in the fire. "I will eat when I have killed Hardesty and Thibault. No, I will drink."

Dumont lurched to his feet and picked up his rifle. He bolted a round into the chamber of the Lee-Medford and pointed the rifle at Sundance. "Get out of my way or I'll kill you," he threatened, swaying on his feet.

"You need another drink. I have a bottle in my warbag," Sundance said. "Over there."

When Dumont turned, Sundance drew his Colt and hit the big man across the back of the neck and caught him before he fell. The rifle clattered to the floor.

"You need some rest," Sundance said.

Eighteen

Gabriel Dumont groaned and opened his eyes as the good smell of strong tea and frying steak filled the cabin early the next morning. He closed his eyes and felt his head. Stooped in front of the fire, Sundance turned the steak with a fork. He filled a mug with bubbling hot tea, added brown sugar, and brought it over to Dumont's bunk.

Dumont took the mug and shouldered himself up on the pillows. "Thanks," he said, not wanting to look at Sundance. "My head...."

Sundance grinned at Dumont, who looked, for all the world, like a sick bear. "Drink your tea. The steak'll be cooked in a minute. If you don't want steak, I can fix ham and duck eggs."

Dumont drank the hot tea noisily. "I remember something about duck eggs."

"You wanted whiskey more than duck egges. That hurt my feelings, you hairy drunk."

Feeling the back of his neck, Dumont winced, then grinned with embarrassment. "You hit me, halfbreed. Thanks for hitting me."

"Don't mention it, friend," Sundance said, still

grinning. "Always glad to do a favor. You were mad and getting madder by the minute. In case you don't recall our little party last night, you were all set to kill Hardesty and Thibault. Can't say that I blame you. Still, I couldn't let you do it You were drunk, and they might have killed you. You still planning to head for the Alaska mountains? You were fixing to become a hermit the last time we talked."

"Hurry up with that steak," Dumont complained. "One won't be enough."

When the first steak was half gone and the second one was frying, Dumont held out his mug and Sundance filled it with tea again. "I'd still like to kill the sons of bitches," he said. "I don't trust them, no matter what they say. How does it look out there?"

"Quiet. I was out at first light."

"I wish Middleton would attack. I'd like to get it over with." Reading Sundance's thoughts, Dumont said quickly, "I won't do any more drinking. Last night I though I'd go crazy if I didn't have a drink. I had my drink—my bottle—and I'm all right now. Did I... did I threaten to harm you?"

Instead of answering, Sundance took the second steak off the fire. "I don't see how any man can eat so much. You sure this will hold you for a while?"

"I'm a savage," Dumont said quietly, his eyes full of hurt. "To threaten a friend!"

"That's all right," Sundance said. "I'm a savage, too. When I drink I am."

"That doesn't make me feel any better."

"Eat the goddamned steak before it gets cold."

"I still don't know what to say."

"They don't say it. You know, Gabriel, you could get on my nerves if you tried a little harder. And by the way, general, you aren't fixing to stay in bed all day, are you?"

"Have some respect for a great leader," Dumont said, and they both laughed.

When they went outside, a group of men waved at them. Dumont yelled at them to come forward. One of them was scout from downriver. "The riverboat has arrived at Fish Creek," he said. "It got there this morning after sailing all night. Bugles are sounding everywhere."

"At last," Dumont said calmly. He called his leaders and told them what was happening. "The attack may come today. None of Middleton's men are on the move yet, but they will be moving soon. If they don't get here until late today, they won't attack until early tomorrow. That is my guess, but we won't count on it. They may hope to surprise us with a night attack. Double the scouts and strengthen the advance parties. All we can do now is wait."

Dumont and Sundance walked along the outermost line of defense. "Middleton has a thousand men," Dumont said. "We are half that number. This will be the first head-on battle we have fought. The next few days will decide how well courage and determination stands up against numbers and supplies. If we win, that will be just the start of our troubles."

Spirits were high in Middleton's camp. Well rested and well fed, the Canadian forces were eager to do battle with the *métis*. They had learned by their mistakes and had taken a measure of the enemy. Batoche, they swore, was not going to be like the other battles they had been through.

Encouraged, prodded by his aide, General Middleton was in a fighting mood. Winfield, young and ambitious, had hooked his wagon to the General's train. It would not do his career any good if they were defeated at Batoche.

He flattered the old man while hinting that a decisive victory was necessary for the sake of the General's reputation. For several years, Middleton had been talking vaguely of retirement, not to England but to the rich farmlands he owned in Ontario.

"A fitting conclusion to a great military career, sir," Winfield had said the night before. "You will be remembered in Canadian—Empire—history as the man who saved Saskatchewan, perhaps the entire North West, from savagery. You will be the man who wrote finis to Riel's monstrous career. After you have taken Batoche, sir...."

Middleton recognized the hint, the indirect threat conveyed by his aide. "Of course, Winfield, we will take Batoche. All that has gone before was merely preparation for the big battle ahead. Now we will strike quickly and decisively—supported by the *Northcote*. That's our trump card! We will batter down their defenses and take the town."

"I can see many rewards from a grateful government, sir," Winfield said blandly. "I can easily envisage a fine house built by popular subscription. The hero of Batoche! I can't see them doing less."

"Is that a fact, Winfield? Well, damn, why not? Lesser men have been rewarded for a lot less. And there will be a promotion and a decoration for you, my boy."

"Boldness, sir."

"Yes! Yes! Winfield. That's it, boldness!"

Early in the morning, Middleton's forces moved from Fish Creek toward Batoche. When the teamsters and scouts were included, his small army came to just over eleven-hundred men, supported by Gatling guns and cannon. There were six-hundred horses and thirty supply wagons. Signs of spring were everywhere; it was a beautiful day, sunny and fairly warm. The first spring crocuses were out, purple and yellow on the prairie.

The steamer *Northcote* moved north at the same time as the troops. Six miles from Fish Creek it tied up to complete its fortifications. Bags were filled with river sand and added to the upper deck of the makeshift gunboat. Extra ammunition and shells were loaded aboard for the Gatling gun and the cannon, as well as cordwood for the boiler. The Canadian force moved north again through thick brush, willows willows, and poplars. The trail followed by Middleton's force was hilly all the way from Fish Creek. As it neared Batoche it flattened out. There, Dumont added a line of rifle pits to the town's defenses that ran down to the bank of the river. They stretched south of the town for nearly a mile. Behind them was the main position, along the range of hills parallel to the valley. The slopes of the hills were thickly wooded and slashed by ravines. The rifle pits were four feet deep with breastworks of clay and logs. In the forward pits, two-hundred *métis* were positioned. Supporting them closer to the town were other *métis* and Hardesty's Irishforces. Hardesty had split his force; some were in the ravines, while others remained in the town.

All day long the *métis* knew exactly how far Middleton's force had progressed. Scouts reported back the General's every move. But they would have known even without the scouts, for the Canadian force was making no pretense of a surprise attack. Besides, it would have been futile to try to conceal eleven-hundred men and six-hundred horses, wagons, cannons, and machine-guns.

Just as Dumont had predicted, Middleton's army reached the outskirts of Batoche late in the day. The light was thickening fast, too late for an attack. The Canadian force camped for the night, out of range of the *métis* rifles, but the sound of bugles carried all the way into the center of the town. Both sides passed an uneasy night as they waited for the dark hours to drag on toward dawn.

In his tent, General Middleton turned a glass of brandy

and soda in his freckled hand and wondered what they would say about him in the London newspapers. The Atlantic cable had already flashed news of the rebellion to all parts of Europe. The French newspapers would attack him, of course, because the French could never forgive the British for having taken Canada. Damn the French! General Middleton decided. A bunch of jabbering, excitable foreigners who couldn't talk without waving their hands.

Louis Riel bent over a table in his cabin in Batoche; he was writing in his diary, the record of his life that he had kept for many years. "I have decided that I shall be known as Protector of my country after victory is assured and a government has been established. Government is not the correct word, for I shall be the sole ruler, and it is not fitting that I should preside over a quarrelsome assembly of men with differing opinions. I shall begin my rule by. . . ."

Hardesty, oiling and cleaning his revolver, stopped now and then to take a sip of whiskey. It was after midnight and he would go to bed soon. There was a slow drip of light spring rain outside his cabin. Soon, Hardesty thought, soon it will all begin to fall into place. He had left Ireland so many years before, had been all over the world, and had enjoyed small successes and endured small defeats. Now, for the first time, greatness, fame, and power were within his grasp. He loaded the revolver and spun the chamber. He would kill to keep from losing it.

"Indeed I would," Hardesty told himself quietly.

Sundance and Dumont were still talking; the supper dishes had long been cleared away. They lay in their bunks, the fire banked high. Dumont was smoking his short, cracked pipe.

"You know what you have to do, don't you, Gabriel?" Sundance said.

"About the peace offer?"

"If Hardesty and Thibault get in your way, you have to move them. If the talks don't get started with Middleton, they won't get started at all. If they do get started later, the only terms you'll get from the Canadians will be to surrender or be wiped out."

Dumont said, "I have been thinking about it. Louis has agreed to talk to Middleton."

"Middleton may have orders not to talk to Louis—about anything. If Macdonald is as angry as you say he is, somebody else will have to approach Middleton."

"But Louis is our leader. If there is a *métis* nation, Louis is its leader. No one else can talk to the Englishman—to the Canadians through the Englishman."

"And if they refuse to talk to him?"

"Then that finishes it. It would be an insult to the *métis* if they refuse."

"No," Sundance said. "You could talk for the *métis*."

Dumont stared at the ceiling, at the smoke curling up from his pipe. "That is foolish talk, Sundance. All my life I have been a buffalo hunter."

"For a buffalo hunter, you're a pretty good general. You could speak for the *métis*, as well as anybody else—better than anybody else. The *métis* look up to you."

"If the Canadians won't accept Louis, why should they accept me?" Dumont said. "I think they would rather hang me than talk to me. They won't forget Duck Lake or the other battles. Why would they deal with me?"

"I'm not saying they will, but it's more likely than they'll deal with Riel. You are the general in this war. You give the orders. You could have slaughtered the Canadians at Duck Lake, Fort Carlton, Battleford. Instead, you showed mercy and let them march away to safety. You held back the Indians at Battleford when they were ready to butcher every man, woman, and child. How can the Canadians not recognize those facts?"

Dumont sounded irritable. "All right! All right! I know what you're saying. You preach more than a priest. What I'm trying to tell you is that Louis must make the peace offer."

"And if he can't or won't or drags his feet? What then?"

"How the hell do I know? I already told you: no Louis, no peace offer."

"That's no answer, Gabriel. You have to take over, if necessary. I don't mean push Louis out. I know he's your friend and you love him. But this is one time you can't allow loyalty to get in the way."

"If Louis asks me to speak in his place, I will do it. Nothing else. I won't go behind his back."

Sundance said, "That's just fine. But what happens to the *métis*? You know Louis won't ask you to speak for him. You have to do it yourself—when and if the time comes. Look, I know how you feel, but there's no way out of it, unless you want Thibault or Hardesty to do the talking."

"Those dogs!"

"I know. You'd like to kill them. Fine! Kill them later, and I'll help you. This is one time when guns and knives won't help. Face it, Gabriel!"

"Face what?"

"Your responsibility to your people. The other night you were saying that men like Hardesty always manage to survive. That's true, and it's also true of you. Right now, you could go to the States and do just fine. Whatever you want to do: army scout, hunter, a guide for sportsmen. The rest of the *métis* aren't that lucky. If this war goes wrong for them, they could end up starving like the Indians. I'm talking about the *métis* who are left alive."

Dumont turned over on his side and stared at the wall. "I am sick of all this talk. No matter what I say, you keep at it. All these arguments, I am sick to death of them."

"If you don't want to listen, why don't you get drunk? You're good at getting drunk. I ought to know. I had to look at your drunken face and listen to your stupid talk. You can find a bottle if you put your mind to it. Ask one of the Irishmen."

Dumont swung his legs off the bed and stood up, his scarred fists swinging by his side. "I'm going to break your face," he said. "I'm going to break your face and then throw you out."

"Try it, buffalo hunter," Sundance said, getting up and bracing himself. He wasn't sure he could beat Dumont. The man had three inches and thirty pounds on him, but there was more to it than that. Dumont was a wild man, drunk or sober, when he was roused.

Suddenly Dumont began to laugh, a deep, heaving rumble that came from far down in his chest. His huge body shook convulsively and the laughing went on. He bent over to slap his thigh, fighting for breath.

"What the hell is so funny?" Sundance said sourly, though a grin was beginning to twist the corners of his mouth. "Suppose you tell me what's so goddamned funny."

"I don't know. I was ready to break your face when I suddenly thought of duck eggs."

"That's a hell of a thing to laugh at."

"You don't think it's funny? I do. For the rest of my life every time I think of you, I'm going to think of duck eggs."

Grinning now, Sundance said, "That's a hell of a way to be remembered. But I do admit I'm fond of ham and duck eggs."

Dumont went into another fit of laughter. When it passed, he looked at Sundance. "All right," he said. "I got mad at you because I knew you were right and I didn't want to face it. What do you think I should do?"

Sundance said, "If the Canadians—Middleton—

refuse to talk terms with Louis, then you have to take charge. That's What you have to do, even if Louis objects to it. You already know that Hardesty and Thibault will oppose you. They can be handled. But first you must talk to the *métis* you can trust. Be very sure of them before you do anything. If word gets out, Hardesty and Thibault may try to move first."

"It could come to killing."

"It could. Chances are it won't if you catch them surprise. Anyway, it has to be done. If and when you do talk to the Canadians, forget about Louis's list of proposals. You want peace with honor, a pardon for all the *métis*, a guarantee of your rights as free men. Other demands can be worked out later. What is important is to get them talking. But what comes first is a cease-fire, a truce, an armed truce. The *métis* will keep their arms until binding guarantees are given by the Ottawa government."

"God!" Dumont said. "Gabriel Dumont making demands on the Ottawa government! I'd be a lot happier if I had stayed with the buffalo. You think I ought to trim my beard and cut my hair?"

"No," Sundance said. "You wouldn't be the same."

"Maybe Louis will listen to reason," Dumont said. "In his way, he wants only the best for the *métis*. I would hate it if he thought I had turned against him."

"He'll thank you if real peace comes," Sundance said, not altogether believing it himself. "Anyway, the *métis* will be grateful."

"You'll stick with me through this, Sundance? I don't know if I could get through it without a friend. God! I hope a truce comes quickly."

Sundance said, "That's only a beginning. Then we have to make sure that nobody breaks it."

Nineteen

The attack began at 5:30 the next morning. This time, Middleton didn't come directly at the town. The river road was heavily defended with trenches and rifle pits. Middelton sent a small force by the road but took most of his men in a wide circuit out onto the prairie to come in against Batoche from the east.

Watching the movements of the Canadian troops through his telescope, Gabriel Dumont remarked, "So he's trying to play fox at last. It won't do him much good. It's a good thing the high ground to the east is defended. The Gatling gun on the knob will catch them when they start to come down the slopes. If we make it hot enough for him up there, maybe he'll fall back to the road."

It was a lovely spring day, with green grass sprouting and the willows and poplars budding into foliage. The sun was coming up bright and warm, and even the birds were singing. In the river, the last of the ice was being borne away on the current. There had been no contact between the two forces yet. Middleton's soldiers were still out of range, and the *métis* were under strict orders not to do any random shooting. For the moment, there was enough ammunition, but unlike the Canadians, the *métis* had no supply wagon to bring up more boxes of bullets from the rear.

Middleton's men spent the best part of an hour taking up their positions for the attack. At seven o'clock, the *Northcote*, armed to the teeth, began to sail upriver, tooting its steam whistle, the signal that the combined land and water assault was about to begin. As the *Northcote* steamed into range, a hail of lead was thrown at it from the trenches and rifle pits along the bank of the river; but the boiler and the guns were protected by the double wall of planks and sacks of grain and sand. The *métis* riflemen kept firing, but the *Northcote* sailed on as if nothing were happening.

Bugles sounded from the river road and from the high ground to the east. Immediately, the artillery opened fire, sending shells screaming into the barracks. For the moment, the town itself, which was mostly on the west bank of the river, was out of range. The Canadians attacking by the river road ran into furious fire and were driven back almost at once, while the troops charging down from the high ground were met by concentrated fire from the Gatling gun manned by Hardesty's Irishmen.

Peppered by rifle fire, the *Northcote* steamed forward until it reached the center of the town. The cannon and the Gatling gun on the upper deck opened fire at the same time. A shell tore away the side of a house and it began to burn, sending long streamers of oil smoke out over the river. Another shell blew a wagon and a team of horses to bits, while the Gatling gun, firing one thousand .58-caliber bullets a minute, raked the waterfront, chopping up everything in sight. The cannon continued to fire as fast as the gunners could drop in the shells. If the *Northcote* wasn't put out of action, Batoche would be burning in a very short time. The Gatling and the cannon kept on firing until the riverboat had sailed past the limits of the town.

Now the *Northcote* was turning to wreak more destruction as it steamed back through the town. The river was wide there, and the turn was effected quickly. Suddenly, a roar went up from the *métis* as the enormous steel cable of the ferry was raised aft of the boat. The Gatling gun opened fire at once on the wooden shack from which the winches were operated. The shack disintegrated under the rain of heavy caliber bullets, but the cable was up and the winch was locked in place.

A short distance downriver, the second cable was coming up out of the water. In the second shack, the men turning the winch were killed when the Gatling opened fire. The cable began to rattle back into the water and would have sunk to the bottom if three *métis* hadn't rushed forward. One was killed before reaching the shack; the other ran inside and worked the winch.

Every rifle along the river bank was concentrated at the Gatling gun. It was well protected, but the furious fire drove the gunner and his helper into cover. The Gatling started firing again, but the cable in the river was almost taut. Sounding its steam whistle furiously, the *Northcote* headed straight for the cable, hoping to break it. The boat struck the cable held firm and the upper deck, the guns, the two smoke stacks, and the mast were torn away and fell into the river. Screams rang out from the middle of the river as men were cut by the cable or crushed under falling timber. The *Northcote* had shown no mercy to the town of Batoche, and the *métis* riflemen along the shore were ruthless in their attack on the crippled steamboat spinning in the grip of the current. Soon it was past the town, still turning crazily. The *Northcote's* short career as a gunboat was over.

All the *métis* who had manned the trenches and rifle pits along the river were moved back to meet the main attack from the high ground to the east. Up on the knob, the Gatling gun, manned by the Irishmen, was firing furiously. The attack from the road had failed, and Dumont called back half the men from behind the second line of defenses; when the Canadians regrouped and attacked again from the high ground, they were met by deadly, concentrated fire. They fought fiercely, but were slowly driven back.

"It's not going to be so easy," Dumont said to Sundance while they were sharing a canteen of water in a forward rifle pit. The Canadians had been driven back to the high ground, from where they kept up a steady round of sniping. "Middleton seems to be using his head at last—or somebody else's head. We're going to have to move the barbed wire as soon as it gets dark. If they come down that slope often enough, they're bound to break through just by numbers. They're fighting damned well today."

The day dragged on. Several hours passed. The only action was heavy sniping from the high ground. Then, at two o'clock, another attack was launched from the river by men brought down from the slopes. At the same time, there was another fierce attack from the high ground to the east. The Canadians came charging down the slope, firing as they came. Like the *métis*, they were armed with Lee-Medfords. The fire from the bolt-action British rifles was fast and steady. For the first time, they had fixed bayonets attached to their rifles, and the bright steel flashed in the rays of the sinking sun. It took everything the *métis* had to beat them back. When the retreat was over, the slope was dotted with corpses. Just before the sun went down, a Canadian officer came out with a flag of truce and asked to be allowed to remove the wounded.

Watching the stretcher bearers working on the slope, Gabriel Dumont said to Sundance, "I think these militiamen are turning into soldiers. Only a few weeks ago they were farmers and storekeepers, drilling once a week so they could smoke and spit and tell stories away from their wives. Now they are getting the feel of it. Some are even getting to like it. I am thinking there may be a night attack. They will break through if we don't move the wire."

It got dark very fast. Winter was just over; the nights were still long and cold. A wind came off the river. Far up on the slope, the campfires of the Canadians could be seen. Down in the *métis* camp, great iron pots of pea soup were bubbling. The *métis* campfires were protected by trimmed tree trunks buried upright in the ground, that prevented the men from being sniped at from above while they ate. After the men ate, they melted back into the darkness to listen for sounds of the enemy, to watch for an attack.

"What time do you figure to start on the wire?" Sundance asked. The ham he was eating was hot and well peppered. He decided he was getting tired of thick pea soup, the favorite food of the *métis*.

"Not long after the men have eaten," Dumont said. "The Canadians, too. The Canadians are tired after the long day. Maybe even their officers are tired and not so eager for night fighting. We will move the wire into the new position and hope we don't make too much noise."

"They have flares."

"I was thinking about the flares. It can't be helped. The wire must be moved. I don't think there will be any more attacks from the road, so we will move even more men from the positions there. It's taking a chance, I know. I don't think there is anything else we can do. If they overrun the defenses, they have the numbers to finish us."

At eight o'clock, Dumont and Sundance led a party of fifteen men out to the first line of defense on the river road. Another fifteen followed. The first party was to lift the X-shaped wooden supports, the second was to drag the coiled up wire. They all wore leather gloves as protection against the long, glittering barbs.

"There is no way to do it quickly," Dumont warned them. "The wire will dig into the ground, so we must take our time. Don't get nervous if flares go off overhead, because our support will open fire immediately. So will the Gatling gun on the knob. I hope they will not hear us, but I know they will. If they open fire and some of you are hit, the others are to keep going. This whole fight is changing. We can no longer be sure of beating the Canadians. All right now, we begin."

Like a long steel centipede, the line of barbed wire began to move in the semi-darkness. Here and there it twanged as the barbs caught on something, a tree stump or a clump of brush. Dumont urged them to be more cautious. "If we can get it into position without the Canadians knowing, they will destroy themselves on it when they attack. If a flare goes off, get down as fast as you can and don't move. From so far up, they may not see the wire. Move!"

It took a full thirty minutes to get the wire away from where it had been. Up where the Canadians were camped, it was quiet. *Métis* riflemen with bullets already in the chambers of their rifles watched the dark slope while Dumont, Sundance, and the thirty men slowly moved the wire. The men cursed softly as the barbs cut through their leather gloves. They stopped to rest, watching for flares, and then went on.

Soon, the long line of wire had been brought parallel to the bottom of the slope. Then it was stretched across the wide opening on the slope, through which the Canadians would have to attack, since the rest of the slope was slashed with fissures and jumbled with rocks.

Dumont whispered, "I would like to anchor it more securely with stakes, but it's all right. It's not something you can break through or jump over. Get down!"

A flare arced up into the night sky and exploded with a soft popping sound, bathing the slope in garish light.

Sundance and the others threw themselves down behind the wire while the *métis* opened fire. The flare hung suspended in the sky while the brief exchange of rifle fire went on. A second flare went up, and the shooting continued until it went out.

"I don't think they saw the wire," Dumont said. "Nobody was shooting at us. I don't think there's much else we can do now. If they want some night fighting, then let them come."

They were back in camp, behind one of the walls of logs that protected the fires. It was about ten o'clock, with many long hours to go until dawn. "You're right about the Canadians," Sundance said. "They are fighting better. It's all a matter of getting used to it. That's how it was in the Civil War. The Confederates sneered that the Union volunteers from the northern cities couldn't fight. They said they'd wet their pants at the sound of the first shot, and so on. And they were right at first. But a little later in the war, those city men showed them how wrong they were. How long do you think this will go on?"

"They're not beaten yet. There's no use trying to talk to them till they're good and tired. They'll think about talking when there are so many dead they'll have trouble getting them all buried. If they get mad enough, they may not talk at all. If that happens, if they decide to sit it out and wait for reinforcements to arrive from the south, we'll probably have to abandon the town. We don't have the strength to counterattack and destroy them. Now we better get some sleep."

Wrapped in blankets, Sundance and Dumont slept by the fire. It rained along about midnight, but the fire dried them quickly. At one o'clock, they walked the lines of defense where the sentries reported nothing unusual. One old *métis* with a sour sense of humor said, "All I can tell you for sure, Gabriel, is they're still up there. If you don't believe me, you can climb up there and look for yourself."

Dumont said he would take the old man's word for it. "You know how old that man is?" he asked Sundance while they continued their tour of inspection. "He admits to being sixty-five, but I know he's at least seventy. I hope I can let him die in his bed with his grandchildren gathered around him."

Then it was three o'clock, and it was still quiet. Dumont threw a twig in the fire. "I'm thinking there won't be any night attack after all, but I have a feeling—a feeling and nothing more—that they will come a little earlier than usual. Before it is completely light."

"Why do you think that?" Sundance asked, knowing that Dumont trusted his feelings as much as he did. They were both half Indian; there was no need to explain. If you examined your feelings too deeply, the meaning was lost.

Dumont smiled. "Two reasons. I feel it, and that's the most important. The second reason is this: Middelton attacked at five-thirty yesterday morning. Exactly first light, very exact. Now Middleton will want to do something different, something to surprise us. Of course, it's all stupid. He can't very well attack after first light, so he will attack before. In the end, it makes no difference. We'll be waiting for him. The camp will be very quiet when he comes, with all the lazy good-for-nothing *métis* snoring in their blankets."

At four o'clock, Dumont quietly roused every man in camp and issued whispered instructions. The fires had been allowed to die down a little. It was quiet up on the ridge, in the Canadian position.

"If I'm wrong, there is nothing lost," Dumont whispered to Sundance. "Ah, but if I'm right...."

At four-thirty, it was still dark, with just a tinge of gray light appearing in the eastern sky. Gripping their rifles, the lines of *métis* waited. It began two minutes after four-thirty. Three flares exploded over the camp, washing it in blinding white light. They were followed by a wild

350

roar from hundreds of men as the Canadians began their charge from the top of the slope. They had moved one of their Gatling guns to a forward position. Its six rotating barrels began to spit out bullets at the rate of a thousand a minute. Down the long slope they came, firing fast. A boy carrying the Canadian flag faltered and died as a bullet struck him in the stomach. Another soldier was killed before he could pick up the fallen flag.

The bugler was blowing the charge, and the attackers came on bravely, straight into the concentrated *métis* fire. From the knob, the Irishmen kept the Gatling in constant action, firing as fast as bullets could be loaded into the hopper. Still the Canadians kept coming, stumbling over their dead and wounded as they swept down the slope. They didn't falter until they saw the wire. If they had been attacking by daylight, they would have seen it long before. The wire stopped them at last. The first wave of men ran right into it and were immediately entangled in its coils, fighting madly to break loose. All the time the *métis* kept up a steady fire. More flares went up, making it easy for them to kill the helpless Canadians. Now there was even time to aim, to shoot carefully.

The retreat was sounded and the Canadians began to fall back, all except those in the wire. The last of the flares sank to earth, trailing a yellow tail of fire. The light in the sky was getting better. Up on the forward slope, the Canadian Gatling covered the retreat as well as it could. For a while the Gatling on the knob and the Gatling on the slope fought a fierce duel. It ended when the Irish machine-gunner blew the crank and the receiver from the Canadian gun. Then he turned the barrel of the heavy gun and swept the slope from one side to the other, blasting everything that moved. Wounded men held up their hands, but he shot them to pieces with .58-caliber bullets. Men were still struggling in the barbed wire. He depressed the muzzle of the Gatling and chopped them to bits.

"My God!" Dumont cried, waving his arms at the Irishmen on the knob. "Cease firing! Cease firing!"

The Irish gunner didn't obey immediately. On the slope, a wounded man was helping another man even more badly wounded. They were hardly able to walk; both had lost their rifles. A burst from the Gatling on the knob nearly cut them in two. Then, finally, the Gatling was silent.

Dumont and Sundance walked back to the fire. "They won't attack again today," Dumont said. "I don't think they'll attack at all. My God! I am sick of this killing. It has to stop. You know, I didn't really feel it until they machine-gunned those men in the wire. They were like animals in a trap. No chance of escape, just waiting to be slaughtered. I hate the sound of those damned machine-guns. They turn the men behind them into machines."

It was dawn, with a thin rain beginning to fall. On the slope, blood and mud were mixed. The dead crumpled bodies had fallen in awkward positions. Smokeless powder still stank on the fresh morning breeze. Now that it was quiet again, birds began to sing in the trees. The bugle sounded from the top of the slope.

"They'll be wanting to fetch the dead and wounded," Dumont said. "They lost so many this morning. Let them come. While they're doing that, I want them to see what we're doing."

He yelled for one of his commanders, a burly young *métis* named Verrier. "Take a hundred men and move south on the river road. There is a small Canadian force still there, so watch for an ambush. Fight your way through if you have to. I want Middleton to know that there will be *métis* south of him."

Riel walked over to Dumont, followed by Hardesty. Rubbing his hands together, Riel looked very pleased. "Ah, what we have done here today, Gabriel! They are destroyed! They are destroyed! That wire—brilliant! Now they know the armed might of the *métis*. They will be finished when Verrier's men cut them off from the south. Look at them up there on the hill, dragging away their dead. They will all be dead if they attack again."

Dumont said quietly, "Some of our men are dead, too. Many are dead."

"They will be remembered, Gabriel. As long as the *métis* are a people, they will be remembered, these brave men."

"Too bad we can't just wipe them all out," said Hardesty, staring up at the Canadian stretcher bearers. "Did you see the way my boys got that bunch in the wire? Fish in a barrel! Yes, sir, it was a sight to behold. Damn! I'd like to take a crack at the sons of bitches."

Dumont jerked his head to one side. "There's the hill, Hardesty. Why don't you take your Irishmen and climb it? They still have one machine-gun in operation."

The Irishman laughed. "You can't make me mad today, Gabriel. They sent a British general and more than a thousand men against us, and we stopped them cold. Middleton and his goddamned gunboat! Look, my friend, we've had our differences, but that's all in the past. We're on the same side, remember? Our next job is to finish what they started. Wipe them out, every last man—including Middleton."

"You aren't forgetting anything, Hardesty?"

The Irishman put a puzzled look on his face. "I thought I included everything. Was there something else?"

"The peace offer. Louis said...."

"Oh, well now, Gabriel," Hardesty said quickly. "What was said the other night doesn't have much bearing on things as they are now. They're whipped, so there's no longer any need to talk. That's how it is in a war. The situation changes from day to day, sometimes from hour to hour."

Ignoring Hardesty, Dumont turned to Riel. "You gave

your word, Louis. Tell me to my face that you don't intend to keep it. Come on, Louis, I want to hear it from you."

"You don't understand these matters," Riel said. "The other night you were angry and talked of leaving the cause. I—we—could not afford to lose you. That is why I gave my word, to persuade you to stay. It was not a lie, Gabriel. I gave my word because it was in the best interests of the *métis*. You would want that too. Listen to me, old friend. If we show weakness now, our cause will fail. The Canadians respect only strength. We have shown them that we are strong. Let us go on from here to build a nation."

"Then there won't be any peace offer?" Dumont's voice was drained of emotion. "You gave your word. But it doesn't mean as much as a pile of dog dirt!"

"You are angry, Gabriel. You will understand later."

"I'm not angry, Louis. I'm sad over all the fine ideas gone bad. In the end, you're just another politician. How can you say that you're better than Macdonald?"

Riel remained calm, smiling. "I am not offended. What I do I do for my people. There will be no peace offer. When they have had enough they will come to *us*! I don't want to talk any more about it."

Turning away, Riel was stopped by the hard flat tone in Dumont's voice.

"Then I will make the peace offer," Dumont said. "I have no choice but to do it without you. Too many *métis* have died already, and many more will die useless deaths if this war goes on."

Riel said, "You don't know what you're saying, Gabriel. I am the leader of the *métis*. There can be no talks without me. And I say no! After all these years, are you now going against the will of your own people?"

"Only against your will, Louis, or what you think is

your will. What about you, Hardesty? What about your will?"

Hardesty's hand wasn't far from his gun. The Irishmen who weren't in the trenches and rifle pits crowded in close to him. So did Thibault and some of his dissident *métis*.

"We can't let you do it, Dumont," Hardesty said. "It's been decided that there won't be any peace talk. That settles it. You have to accept that fact—or get out now. You threatened to do it the other night. You can still do it. Good as you are, you're just one man. What's it going to be? You can't fight everybody."

Dumont raised his rifle until it was pointed at the Irishman's face. You're wrong, Irishman. There's a round in the chamber," he said. "All I have to do is squeeze the trigger. I don't have to fight everybody. Sundance!"

Sundance drew his long-barreled Colt in an easy motion. At the same time, the *métis* who supported Dumont took a firm grip on their guns. Dumont looked around. "You may have more supporters than I have, Hardesty, but I'm ready to take a chance. When the shooting stops, the Canadians can come down and kill the survivors."

Seconds ticked by. The only sound in the camp was the crackle of the fires and the wind. Hardesty looked sideways at Thibault, who was ready to start killing, no matter what the odds.

"You'll be first, Hardesty," Dumont warned.

Sundance cut in with: "And Thibault will be second. Who'd like to be third?"

No one moved. Then Riel walked away without a word. Hardesty stared at Dumont. "Go ahead, have your peace talk. My guess is they'll spit in your face. I'll tell you one thing for sure, Dumont. You'll be sorry for this."

"Let's go, Sundance," Dumont said.

Twenty

While the *métis* and the Irishmen watched, Dumont and Sundance placed wide planks on the barbed wire and crossed over to the other side. At the top of the slope, a Canadian officer waved them to come up. Sundance carried the white flag; both men were unarmed. The stretcher bearers, not yet finished with their grisly work, stopped to look at them as they climbed the hill. Two hours had passed since the attack, but the sweetish smell of death was still heavy on the morning air. The sun was warm in their faces as they went up the hill. It was a long climb. The only sound was the Gatling gun turning in its swivel. It made a quiet, racketing sound.

"I wish Hardesty would try to take this hill," Dumont said.

"Up or down it's bad," Sundance agreed. "Can your people hold them while we're up here?"

Dumont nodded. "I picked the best men. They will keep Hardesty and Thibault under control, but it won't be easy. I'll bet Hardesty is already spreading stories that I am trying to seize control of the movement from Louis. More and more, I know that Hardesty will have to be killed before he kills me. Somehow I always knew it would come to that. I knew it the first time I saw the man. Has that ever happened to you with a man you met for the first time?"

"A few times," Sundance answered. "The first feeling was the right one."

"Hardesty will gloat if Middleton sends us away," Dumont said. "I guess we can count on not being hanged this morning. These British make such a fuss about honor."

"I hope Middleton isn't any different. You know what you're going to say?"

"No, I don't."

"Just as well. It'll come to you."

A man's arm was lying on the slope, torn from his body by Gatling gunfire. The body had been taken away; the arm had fallen off the stretcher. They both looked at it and continued to climb. If it hadn't been for the stink of death and the six barrels of the Gatling watching them from the summit, it would have been a very nice day.

"I feel bad about Louis," Dumont said. "I know I am doing the right thing, the only thing, and I still feel bad. The look on his face when he walked away. I don't think I'll ever forget that look."

Sundance, not certain that some nervous militiaman might not open fire at any moment, wasn't too concerned about Louis Riel's hurt feelings. He felt naked without his weapons, but there was no other way. If the Canadians found even a knife in his boot, they would hang him from the nearest tree. That would be a hell of a way to end up after all he'd been through.

They were more than halfway to the top. Up above, the Canadian officer waved his sword until it glittered in the bright sunlight. "Keep coming and don't try anything," said the officer, who was very young, in a too-loud voice.

Dumont spat in the mud, "Damn puppy. Why in hell is he carrying a sword? Not a saber, a sword!"

"Be patient, Gabriel. If it works, you'll be the hero of your people—the one and only Gabriel Dumont."

"You can go to hell, too, Sundance. But you're right. I'd like to see the look on Hardesty's face. How long do you think it will be before we get an answer, supposing they agree to even discuss it?"

Sundance did some quick figuring. "All the telegraph lines to the towns north of here are down. The Indians cut the wire to Fort Albert. Middleton will have to send riders south to Regina or Fort Qu'Appelle or to some station on the railroad. The answer will come back over the wires as fast as they decide to send it. An hour, a day, a week. It all depends on Macdonald. At least the message won't be coming to him from Riel."

Dumont looked surprised. "Oh, but it will."

"No, Gabriel. The message will be sent to Macdonald from *you*. You are not a messenger. You are the man in charge. That has to be made clear. As far as Middleton and Macdonald are concerned, you are the new leader of the *métis*. That's how it has to be. I know you don't like it, but there is no other way. What you say has to come from no one but you. Anything you promise, you will back up. So don't promise too much. Middleton and Macdonald will not listen too closely if they think you have to run to Louis Riel to confirm every detail."

"Then I will be a traitor."

"Not a traitor, Gabriel. Middleton and Macdonald must *know* that they have to deal with no one but you. Sundance's voice became soft. "You have been the leader since the beginning."

The Canadian officer stepped forward after sheathing his sword. "If you have any weapons, you must give them up now. Do you have any weapons? All right, follow me. You can throw away that flag. It won't be needed."

The crew behind the Gatling gun stared at them with open hostility as they followed the young officer over the crest of the hill. The riflemen guarding the downslope all turned their heads. A few of them spat.

It looked as if more of Middleton's force was assembled at the top of the hill that stretched back to open prairie. Wagons and horses were drawn up. The dead were in three piles some distance from the three large army tents, where doctors were working furiously to save the wounded. There were pools of blood in front of the tents. An amputation saw rasped on bone as they went past the last tent. Far back from the top of the hill, men were gathered around a line of camp fires, looking cold and tired in spite of the warming spring sun.

"This way," the officer said, pointing to Middleton's elaborate tent, big as a cabin. "Take off your hats. Hats off, I said."

Sundance said, "It doesn't matter."

Dumont took off his battered wool hat and crushed it in one hand. Sundance was forced to grin. As a diplomat, Gabriel Dumont was a good buffalo hunter. "Step lively now," the Canadian officer said.

Inside, General Middleton, his aide Winfield, and two senior Canadian militia officers were waiting. It wasn't a cold day, but the charcoal brazier was burning. Middleton's port-wine face had blotches of white in it; the plate of food in front of him hadn't been touched.

Winfield bent over and whispered to the General, who looked up quickly. "Why isn't Riel here?"

Dumont said slowly, almost painfully, "I am the leader of the *métis* now. I am Gabriel Dumont."

All eyes were focused on the big buffalo hunter, his rough clothing, his scarred hands, the battered hat being turned nervously between them.

"So you are Dumont," Middleton said, not wanting to believe it. "You have caused us a considerable amount of trouble. I ask you again: Where is Riel?"

"Louis Riel is in camp. I have fought this war, and I will talk of peace."

Middleton tried for irony. "Peace! Is that what you

want? You haven't been behaving very peacefully, have you! What makes you think that we are prepared to listen to you. You are nothing but a scoundrel and a rebel. Are you aware that I could have you hanged right now? I don't mean later. I mean this instant!"

To press his point, Middleton banged his fist on the table.

"You could do that," Dumont said. "We are unarmed. We came unarmed under a flag of truce, and you can do anything you wish. As a British officer...."

The Englishman bristled. "So you want to be treated as an equal, is that it! Well, I'll be damned if I do that. You are not a soldier but a skulking rebel. Why should you be treated as a soldier?"

Sundance had remained silent all the time. Middleton turned his bluster toward him. "And who are you? You don't look like one of these people. I don't know *what* you look like, but you don't look like a *metis*."

Sundance gave his name. It didn't mean anything to any of them.

"He is my second in command," Dumont said.

Middleton sneered. "The cheek of these people. Second in command, indeed! Next this fellow will be calling himself general."

Middleton's aide whispered to him again. "All right! All right, Captain, I was about to come to that."

To Dumont he said, "Well, you're here, so I might as well listen to what you have to say—not that I'm going to give it much heed, mind you. Come on, out with it. Before you start, I might as well tell you that the only peace I'll consider is complete surrender."

"Then there is nothing to say," Dumont said. "We will not surrender, not if all your five-thousand reinforcements from the east were to arrive here today."

"Pretty well informed, aren't you?" Middleton said. "Very well, you won't surrender. You don't expect *us* to surrender, do you? From the look of you, you're mad enough to demand anything. Oh, go away. We'll overrun your town in due time."

"Like you did this morning, General?" Dumont's voice was quiet; there was no sarcasm in it.

Middleton's red face grew a darker red. "You dare speak to me like that? All right, never mind. You did put on a good show, but you can't win. Don't you see that? Of course, you don't."

"But I do. I have always know that, even before this war began. A man does not have to be very smart to realize that one small people cannot win against vast forces."

"Then what the blazes are you trying to do? Get everybody killed? Do what I tell you, man. Surrender! If you know you can't win, what else can you do?"

Dumont took a deep breath and released it. "We will fight on until we are all dead, every man, woman, and child. Before we let our woman and children starve, we will kill them ourselves. We will kill them because we love them. But the men will fight on. We will become like wolves gone mad with desperation. There is nothing we will not do. You may take our lands, brand us as traitors, and then you may think it is safe to bring in your settlers and build new towns. But we will be there, deep in the woods, where even your Mounties won't find us. And we will strike at you without warning, in the dead of night, when you least expect."

Middleton's voice was a whisper. "You're a madman."

Dumont shook his head. "Maybe I am, but what I am saying is true. Before we're finished, we will turn Saskatchewan into a place of terror. You can send all the soldiers you like. You can hang and burn and flog. It won't stop us. In time, death will stop us. But death is a long time coming. I ask you this question, General Middleton: Is it worth it?"

"I'll be damned," the General said. "I've never heard such talk in my life, not even in Ireland. "Frankly, I don't know what to say. Tell me, man, are you really serious about all this fighting and killing?"

One of the Canadian officers answered instead. "He's serious, General. You can count on that as on nothing else in this world." .

Middleton was still reluctant. "But I can't make deals with these people," he said to no one. "Anyway, it isn't up to me. I can't imagine what the Prime Minister will say if I forward such a message. 'Dear Prime Minister Macdonald, the *métis* government has offered to make peace with yours.' It's ludicrous. It's a political matter, and I want no part of it."

"Perhaps I'd better explain your position, General," Dumont went on, as if Middleton hadn't spoken. "Your men have fought bravely, but I think they have had enough of it. I know my people have. You still outnumber us, but soon you will be cut off from the south. A force of *métis* has already moved out. If the fighting continues, you will only lose more good men. Let me remind you, sir, that your men are not regular soldiers but volunteers, citizen soldiers, every man with a vote. Fathers, brothers, relatives with votes. The same is true of the men coming from the east."

"They will obey their officers."

"As long as it pleases them. If they find themselves bogged down in a hopeless war, you'll see how long they obey their officers. The French-Canadians don't want to fight at all. And then," Dumont's rough voice became soft, "you always have to consider the Indians, General. There are twenty-thousand Indians in the North West. The Crees and the Stoneys are already with us. So far, I have kept them under control. If they break loose, they will raid and burn from here to the Rocky Mountains."

"But that's unthinkable, man. What I mean is, you are

362

part white, aren't you? You couldn't turn loose the Indians."

"I can guarantee to control the Indians," Dumont stated. "I give you my word on that. If I cannot keep my word, I will give myself up to be hanged. Now, General Middleton, we have talked of many things but not of peace. I would like to talk of it now."

Middleton whispered to Winfield, who nodded and spoke to the young Canadian officer who had brought Dumont and Sundance to the tent. He nodded, too, pleased to be so close to the General.

"Come outside with me," he said briskly to Dumont and Sundance. They waited in the sunshine for about ten minutes. Then Winfield pushed the flap aside and put his head out.

"Bring them in, Parsons," he said, "then wait until you are called."

The young officer looked disappointed. "Very good, sir," he said.

General Middleton looked a little more confident when they reentered the tent. He was holding his large liver-spotted hands over the charcoal brazier and looked up. "I still don't know what the Prime Minister is going to make of all this," he began.

Winfield said smoothly, "I feel confident that he will see it as a wise decision on your part, sir. I'm sure the P.M. has no desire to become bogged down in a profitless and politically harmful war. But you were saying, sir...."

General Middleton was almost genial; he saw a new role for himself as a soldier-diplomat. "Now you must tell me what you want, Dumont. After you tell me, I'll try to sort it all out. If some of your demands are too outlandish, I simply won't relay them to Mr. Macdonald. I won't be made a fool of. Suppose you begin. Captain Winfield will make a list. You might as well know that he has already made a list of those frightful threats you made earlier. I don't know how the Prime Minister is going to react to all that. Before you start, however, I must ask you if you are empowered to speak for the *métis*. I have it on good authority that Mr. Macdonald will have no dealings with Riel. If Riel is speaking through you, it's all a waste of time."

Dumont said, "I am my own man, General."

"Proceed."

Dumont's list was not very long. He used words sparingly and Captain Winfield was able to finish writing as soon as he finished a sentence.

"The rights of the *métis* to their ancestral lands, to be guaranteed by act of Parliament," Dumont said. "That lands taken from the *métis* be returned to them. That no new surveys of *métis* land be undertaken for any reason."

Dumont spoke for no more than twenty minutes. He could have finished sooner if he hadn't been so deliberate, so careful to make everything clear. When he said that was all, Middleton looked at him, as if seeing him for the first time.

"I am going to recommend that the Prime Minister . . . well, I'll be glad to see this damned war over with. As of now, a truce exists between our two forces. We won't be the ones to break it. See that your people don't. If they do, you can kiss your hopes goodbye. It'll be all over for you. Just one more thing. I am going to move my men back down to the river road. You'd better go ahead and give your people the lay of the land."

As Dumont and Sundance walked away with the young Canadian leading the way, the *métis* leader said, "It will be at least three days before we know. If we can only keep the peace until then. Think about it, Sundance. In three days, our people may be on their way back to their families, their farms. It's so close to the finish."

Walking silently, Sundance just nodded.

DOUBLE EDITION
They left him for dead, he'll see them in hell!
Jake McMasters

Hangman's Knot. Taggart is strung up and left out to die
by a posse headed by the richest man in the territory. Choking
and kicking, he is seconds away from death when he is cut
down by a ragtag band of Apaches, not much better off than
himself. Before long, the white desperado and the desperate
Apaches have formed an unholy alliance that will turn the
Arizona desert red with blood.

And in the same action-packed volume....

Warpath. Twelve S.O.B.s left him swinging from a rope,
as good as dead. But it isn't Taggart's time to die. Together
with his desperate renegade warriors he will hunt the
yellowbellies down. One by one, he'll make them wish they'd
never drawn a breath. One by one he'll leave their guts and
bones scorching under the brutal desert sun.

_4185-5 $4.99 US/$5.99 CAN

CHEYENNE

RENEGADE NATION
ORPHAN TRAIN
JUDD COLE

Renegade Nation. Born the son of a great chief, raised by frontier settlers, Touch the Sky will never forsake his pioneer friends in their time of need. Then Touch the Sky's enemies join forces against all his people—both Indian and white. If the fearless brave's magic is not strong enough, he will be powerless to stop the annihilation of the two worlds he loves.

And in the same action-packed volume . . .

Orphan Train. When his enemies kidnap a train full of orphans heading west, the young shaman finds himself torn between the white men and the Indians. To save the children, the mighty warrior will have to risk his life, his home, and his dreams of leading his tribe to glory.

___4511-7 $4.99 US/$5.99 CAN